2
2790

I BEEN THERE BEFORE

Also by David Carkeet

Double Negative
The Greatest Slump of All Time

I
BEEN
THERE
BEFORE

A NOVEL BY

David Carkeet

1817

HARPER & ROW, PUBLISHERS, New York

Cambridge, Philadelphia, San Francisco, London
Mexico City, São Paulo, Singapore, Sydney

FIRST EDITION

Designer: Sidney Feinberg

Library of Congress Cataloging in Publication Data

Carkeet, David.

 I been there before.

 1. Twain, Mark, 1835–1910, in fiction, drama, poetry, etc. I. Title.

PS3553.A688I2   1985   813'.54   84-48584

ISBN 0-06-015426-8

85 86 87 88 89 HC 10 9 8 7 6 5 4 3 2 1

To My Mother
and
To the Memory of My Father

I would like to thank the following people for the assistance they gave me in my research for this novel: Robert D. Jerome, Elmira, New York; Herbert A. Wisbey, Jr., of Elmira College and the Center for Mark Twain Studies at Quarry Farm; Leonard T. Grant, President of Elmira College; Henry H. Sweets III, Curator of the Mark Twain Home and Museum in Hannibal, Missouri; and, especially, Robert H. Hirst, General Editor of the Mark Twain Project at the Bancroft Library of the University of California, Berkeley.

Work on this novel was supported by a National Endowment for the Arts Fellowship and by a Fellowship from the University of Missouri Weldon Spring Fund.

Contents

III   I BEEN THERE BEFORE: THE EAST

APPENDIXES

Preface

"A miracle is by far the most wonderful and impressive and awe-inspiring thing we can conceive of, except the credulity that can take it at par." Thus wrote Samuel Clemens in his notebook in 1905. His maxim inspires me to address the reader somewhat more personally here than would be proper in one of our regular editions of Mark Twain's works. One does not become General Editor of the Mark Twain Papers without sharing at the outset an affinity for Clemens' world view—an affinity that can only increase over the years. No man was a greater enemy of humbuggery than Samuel Clemens, and I number myself among his disciples in that regard. Hence no man or woman could have approached the bewildering question of what happened on this earth between 27 November 1985 and 11 April 1986 with skepticism greater than mine. Yet the evidence that a miracle indeed occurred is so overwhelming that no sooner does one dip into it than the question "Did he *really* come back?" quickly gives way to questions like "When did he go up in the Transamerica Pyramid?" and "Did he fly to New Orleans first-class or coach?"

The present volume is an edition of Mark Twain's work, albeit one that was certainly not foreseen when the Mark Twain Papers was established. In addition, it brings together for the first time the bulk of the evidence bearing on Clemens' "sudden and more strange return": reports of one of our editors out in the field, accounts by people whose paths crossed Clemens', summaries of findings by forensic experts, and the like. Our efforts to track Clemens down have played a key role in determining that *I Been There Before* is an authentic work by Mark Twain, and so this story is also given in some detail.

My list of acknowledgments is so brief that a separate section, so titled, would only draw attention to the almost total isolation in which the editors at the Mark Twain Papers have worked in the preparation of this volume. Thanks, then, go to our own crew: Ricky Olivieri, who was willing to make the ultimate sacrifice; Arthur Goldman; Pam Higgins; Jeff

Langford; Ned Scully; and Gloria Wilson. Thanks, too, to a writer we shall call "Cocoa," for that was the name Clemens preferred. And extremely grudging thanks to the National Endowment for the Humanities, which failed to make good on its highly publicized threatened termination of future support if a penny of its moneys were spent on this volume.

—FREDERICK DIXON

The Mark Twain Papers
The Bancroft Library, #480
University of California
Berkeley, California
December 12, 1987

I BEEN THERE BEFORE

Introduction

For us at the Mark Twain Papers, it began with a telephone call on 18 February 1986, nearly three months after Clemens touched down and less than two months before he left. On the morning of that day, Charles Asquith, a rare books and manuscripts dealer in San Francisco, called to inform me that he had in his temporary possession sixty-four pages of notes, evidently in Samuel Clemens' handwriting. He asked if I would like to see them to judge their authenticity. Normally, I would have been skeptical. We had had two forgeries presented to us in the preceding six months, one of them very polished. But the sheer volume of the manuscript in Asquith's possession argued against a forgery; also, Asquith knew Clemens' hand well, and the passages he read to me were tantalizing. Consequently, within a few minutes I found myself setting out for his shop across the Bay.

On an impulse, I asked a "guest" at the Papers if he would like to accompany me: William Winthrop, a writer for *The Atlantic Monthly*, who had been spending some time in our files doing research for an article on Clemens' long association with that magazine. That impulse, which I would very soon regret, meant that Winthrop was able to monitor our crisis from its earliest moments on, and, writing with dispatch that would have impressed even Samuel Clemens, he then reported on it to the world at large. For the way it captures the flavor of those times, below I shall draw here and there from Winthrop's essay, which appeared in the April *Atlantic*. It is titled, "Who Wrote *Huckleberry Finn?*"

Samuel Clemens habitually kept a notebook, into which he wrote both literary material and more mundane personal memoranda. Forty-nine such notebooks are extant, dating from 1855 to 1910 and covering almost all of his adult life. Of the gaps in our "calendar" of his notebooks, the most significant is the three-and-a-half-year period from mid-1861, when Clemens journeyed with his brother by overland stagecoach from Missouri to the Nevada Territory, until December 1864, when, after six months in San Francisco, he left that city for a brief sojourn in the Sierra

Nevada foothills near Angels Camp. The passages Asquith had read to me over the phone concerned mines in Virginia City, Nevada—precisely the kind of material one would expect from Clemens' notebook for this period. In Asquith's shop, I read the first several pages of the notebook—descriptions of the Nebraska Territory, then of Salt Lake City, and then of the Nevada wastes—with my guard up, looking for something wrong. After a while, a curious thing happened. I found myself *enjoying* the notes. I began interpreting them. I began to edit them in my head. When I realized what I was doing, I turned to Winthrop and said, "It's the real thing." He, in turn, took out *his* notebook, and he began to write.

It wasn't until I was far into the manuscript that I discovered what a disaster it was. I refer, of course, to the strong evidence in the notebook that Samuel Clemens' elder brother, Orion, was the true author of *Adventures of Huckleberry Finn,* which he seemed to have written in 1863 while serving as Secretary of the Territory of Nevada in Carson City. The evidence consisted of three brief notebook entries. The first, dated by Clemens "Feb. 1/63," stated, "Up all night with Orion, who is just *full* of his river book." I gave this little thought on first reading. I knew Orion as a failed author, and, since he was raised on the Mississippi like his brother, one of his failures might well have been some long-lost work about the river.

But what sort of work, exactly? The second relevant entry, whose location in the notebook placed it late in 1863, gave me pause:

> Questions for Orion—
> Why would a slave run *south?* Why don't he flee through Illinois, then no., to Canada?
> Isn't Buck *too* gloomy?
> Does he plan to end it with Buck & Jim's escape from the Wilkses? Not a true ending—no snap to it.

This looked disturbingly familiar. But unfamiliar as well: "Buck"? The last entry about the book apparently dated from 1864, when Clemens was in San Francisco:

> Buck is such a *good* boy—why does he always say of himself that he is "low-down & ornery"?
> How to end it—
> Buck & Jim light out for the Territory—new adventures among the Injuns.
> They join up with a circus.

They go to South America—strike it rich in coca trade; live in high style. Jim becomes a king of the savages.

Send these with MS back to O.

On the face of it—and, for that matter, deep down as well—Orion Clemens seemed to be the author of a "river book" that featured a slave fleeing south in the company of a boy; this is the major plot element of *Huckleberry Finn*. The boy suffered from low self-esteem (one of Huck's most endearing qualities), which evidently perplexed rather than pleased brother Samuel. To quote Winthrop's article, quoting my plaintive lament, "Not only did Sam Clemens apparently not write the novel—he didn't even fully *understand* it." The boy's name was Buck. We hoped we could at least credit Sam with coming up with the name "Huckleberry." It was a small consolation in those hard times.

Of course, it was possible that Orion had written a mere outline, which brother Sam fleshed out later, therefore rightly claiming the work as his own when he published it in 1885. Possible, but doubtful. In the notebook, Clemens wrote of "Buck's" gloominess and moral nature as if he had read a *rendered* representation of them, not just a bald outline, and he called the work an "MS" (that is, a manuscript), which suggested something fleshed out already. Interestingly, the last line—"Send these with MS back to O."—was crossed out.

During the protracted head-scratching sessions at the Mark Twain Papers, two questions arose over and over: first, if Orion wrote the novel, why on earth did he allow his brother to publish it under false pretenses; second and more important, was Samuel Clemens morally capable of such chicanery? Not long after our first reading of the notebook, one of our editors—Ned Scully—tracked down a formerly innocuous sentence in a 15 December 1877 letter from Orion that effectively answered the first question. The letter concerns an adventure-filled yarn by Orion about a journey to the center of the earth. He wrote:

> Sam, I've been seized with an idea. Can't you take my "Kingdom of Sir John Franklin," use it as a skeleton or as memoranda, expand it (with stories told by the imprisoned crew? &c) into a book, send it out in your name and mine (with some nom de plume, if that is best) (or all in your own name, if you prefer that) give me such part of the profits as you please, and enable me to pay you and the government and my other creditors, and leave me something over?

No record of Sam's response to this suggestion exists, but it seemed entirely possible to us that he took it to heart and applied it to a different, far superior work: Orion's long-shelved "river book."

The second question truly haunted us. As another one of our editors, Pam Higgins, put it, "If the notebook is real, it's so long, Sam—I'm off to the James Fenimore Cooper Papers." Prior to the discovery of the notebook, while we would have readily acknowledged Clemens' failings, we would have vehemently denied he was capable of claiming authorship of a work not truly his own. But after its discovery, and after two independently commissioned analyses of its handwriting confirmed the judgments of the staff at the Papers that the hand was Clemens' from beginning to end, and after tests of the notebook's paper, binding, and adhesive yielded nothing to contradict a mid-nineteenth-century date of manufacture, we concluded that he *must* have been capable of doing such a thing, because, after all, evidently *he had done it.* We feared that maybe we hadn't understood him as well as we thought we had.

A word or two about Orion (pronounced *O*rion by his family) is in order here. In those halcyon days before we knew of the notebook, Orion was little more than a running gag at the Papers. He was, by turns, a printer, a lecturer on religion (with the creed varying unpredictably), a lawyer, a writer, an inventor, and a chicken rancher—and a striking failure at each and every one. Here is the way brother Sam described him in his autobiography:

> One of his characteristics was eagerness. He woke with an eagerness about some matter or other every morning; it consumed him all day; it perished in the night and he was on fire with a fresh new interest next morning before he could get his clothes on. He exploited in this way three hundred and sixty-five red-hot new eagernesses every year of his life—until he died sitting at a table with a pen in his hand, in the early morning, jotting down the conflagration for that day and preparing to enjoy the fire and smoke of it until night should extinguish it. He was then seventy-two years old. But I am forgetting another characteristic, a very pronounced one. That was his deep glooms, his despondencies, his despairs; these had their place in each and every day along with the eagernesses. Thus his day was divided—no, not divided, mottled—from sunrise to midnight with alternating brilliant sunshine and black cloud. (*MTA*, 2:269)*

If we alter the occupational history slightly—to printer, steamboat pilot, miner, lecturer, writer, publisher, and inventor—and if we contract

---

See Appendix C, page 313, for list of abbreviations.

the mood swings described above, we have a portrait of Samuel Clemens. In a curious way, Orion was a grotesque alter ego of his more famous brother. Thus the authorship implied in the newly discovered notebook could not be dismissed as preposterous. In a rare, brief flicker of genius, Orion just might have been inspired to write something as good as a prototype of *Huckleberry Finn,* or even something close to the novel as we know it. It would be an anomaly in his career, but there are many who have maintained that *Huckleberry Finn* is such a wondrous miracle of fiction that it is an anomaly even in *Samuel* Clemens' career.

For an account of the discovery of the notebook, we turn to Winthrop's *Atlantic* article:

> The cause of this shock to the world of Twain scholarship is one Arthur Laufbahn—a native of Munich, a bird-watcher, and a shy, reclusive man who declined to be interviewed, exhibiting the fiercest blush this writer has ever observed. On January twenty-second of this year, Laufbahn was on the trail of the tricolored blackbird in the countryside near Angels Camp, California—the small Gold Rush town where Mark Twain first heard the famous jumping frog story. Laufbahn swerved his car to avoid a deer in the road, ran off the shoulder, and plunged down a steep bank into the Stanislaus River. In spite of a broken arm, he managed, along with a traveling companion, to extricate himself from the car and swim to shore. While waiting for help to arrive, Laufbahn spied a metal trunk half buried in the dirt at the water's edge. He pulled it out, opened it, and decided to keep it. Several days later he would learn that what he had found was far more important than the addition of a tricolored blackbird to his life list.
>
> "The trunk," says Dixon [i.e., this editor], "is a typical heavy-duty miner's trunk, for ore samples. There were some blankets in it, an old shirt, a knife, a toothbrush, and a meerschaum pipe. Now, listen to this." Dixon seizes a large volume from the bookcase behind his desk (a volume he knows well: he co-edited it ten years ago), searches, and quickly finds the passage. He reads aloud: " 'Have lost my pipe, and can't get another in this hellfired town. Left my knife, meerschaum, and toothbrush at Angels.' " He holds the book up—*Mark Twain's Notebooks and Journals, Volume I*—stabbing the air with it as he says, "Clemens wrote that after leaving Angels Camp in February of 1865. He wrote it in the first extant notebook after the big gap of 1861–1864. Don't you see? He lost more than a knife, a toothbrush, and a pipe in Angels Camp. Maybe he didn't know it at the time, but he lost his latest notebook, too. It was all in that trunk."

The notebook was not perceived as a complete disaster for Mark Twain scholars and enthusiasts, of course. Winthrop's article touches on some of these other matters, and since they will come into play later in this volume, I shall here quote from his account of them:

> Among its more welcome features is the glimpse the notebook gives us of Clemens' evolving sense of himself. The early entries contain much description, some of it quite florid, of the plains and mountains on the overland route, as if Clemens was toying with the notion of travel writing. Then, after his arrival in Nevada, the notebook is cluttered with pedestrian details from his career as a silver miner—so much for the literary life. But later, his mines having proved unproductive, Clemens joined the staff of the Virginia City (Nevada) *Territorial Enterprise* for a two-year stint as a reporter, and the inscriptions show his literary side once again. The notes enable us to watch the young adventurer, in the midst of his *Wanderjahre*, struggling with his fate to become a writer and finally accepting it.
>
> One particular entry is a historical hallmark. It is a list of the pseudonyms Clemens had used up to that point in his career: "Josh," "Grumbler," "Soleather," "Sergeant Fathom," "John Snooks," "Thomas Jefferson Snodgrass," and "W. Epaminondas Adrastus Blab." This cacophonous assembly ends with a name that seems so right, so *necessary*, that we have to remind ourselves it was arrived at through a process of elimination and hard thinking: "Mark Twain." It is written twice and heavily underscored the second time.
>
> Even the layman can recognize hints of the vintage Twain style in the notebook. Here is the author on Brigham Young, whom he met en route in Salt Lake City: "B.Y. & 44 children. Calls them by number— No. 11, No. 17. Gives one a toy & all must have same toy or die." (This idea made it into *Roughing It*, his later book about his western experiences.) Here is Clemens on Mono Lake: "Tasted water. Didn't *swallow* —just smacked. Taste lingered in my mouth the rest of the day, as nagging as a Presbyterian's conscience." And here is Clemens on his horse, in both senses:
>
>> My beast is overfed & sluggish, but with a wilfulness that makes him boss. I kick & steer, but only for show. He eyes me over his shoulder, with scorn, as if to say, "Enough of that now. *I'm* in charge here. You don't want me to *really* embarrass you." If we ever get to Unionville I shall feed him handsomely & brush him & pet him & put him to bed with a mother's care. Then I shall kill him.

The extreme unsteadiness of the hand here suggests Clemens made the entry in the heat of the moment—while astride the beast so unflatteringly described.

The new notebook also contains references to a rare subject for Mark Twain—sexuality. Some biographers have claimed that given the roughness and sexual license of the frontier environment, and given Clemens' documented excesses of swearing and drinking, it is a natural assumption that he was one of the boys in *all* respects and lost his virginity during those western years. Other biographers believe he made it to the altar every bit as chaste as his extremely chaste bride, Olivia Langdon of Elmira, New York. The notebook approaches this question in an almost teasing fashion. One entry reads, "Miner dreads syphilis so much he can't bear it any longer—checks himself into a brothel for a week-long debauch, sampling *all* the wares. Writes home that he was off in the wilderness wrestling with his soul."

Dixon calls this "a marvelous note." He says, "It draws directly from Clemens' life—but not in the way you think. As a boy, during a measles epidemic in Hannibal, he did just such a thing—crawled into bed with a measles-afflicted chum because he couldn't stand the suspense. He got it and it nearly killed him. But as evidence of anything, the note is worthless. It's just an idea for a story."

The same applies to another somewhat tasteless inscription. It is labeled "D Street"—the red-light district of Virginia City—and contains names and ratings: "Sally—good, d——d good, J.B.—tol'able, Ophelia —original, but high-strung, & a foul-mouthed b——h, Juanita—bouncy, like riding an earthquake, Belle—salacious, always pining, always being disappointed." Says Dixon, "Notice the quotation marks around 'D Street.' They suggest it's a title. So it's another story idea, and it doesn't necessarily reflect on Clemens' activities." Dixon concludes, "As a friend of mine once put it, we still don't know whether Clemens entered marriage as a virgin or as a virtuoso."

Winthrop's article concludes on a melancholy note appropriate for that time:

Editors at the Mark Twain Papers are reluctantly preparing the new notebook for inclusion in the fifth and last volume of *Mark Twain's Notebooks and Journals*—part of its ongoing series of Mark Twain's unpublished works, which, along with definitive editions of previously published works, will total some seventy volumes. The last of these will appear "well after the year 2000," Dixon says with the aplomb of a man accustomed to taking the long view. They are also looking closely at Orion Clemens' life and literary output, meager though it is. And they are still desperately searching, searching. But thus far they have found nothing to contradict Samuel Clemens' apparently heavy and unacknowledged debt to his brother.

At the same time, Mark Twain scholars all over the country who have examined the notebook are puzzling over the implications of their new knowledge. Did Clemens steal the whole book or just part of it? Can *Tom Sawyer* be viewed in the same light as before? After all, *Huck Finn* purports to be a sequel to *Tom Sawyer.* Which work, in actuality, is a sequel to the other? And just why *did* Clemens find it so hard to recapture the magic of Huck's narrative voice in later works, such as *Tom Sawyer Abroad?*

In an attempt to answer these questions, Twain scholars have scheduled a symposium for April ninth and tenth in New York. As of this writing, it seems unlikely that any new evidence will emerge before then to counter what appears to be the sad truth about the authorship of *Huckleberry Finn.*

Thus Winthrop. Thus the Mark Twain Papers. And thus *all* admirers of Mark Twain: confused, saddened, and angry.

Fortunately, there was a new development. On 12 March 1986, just a few days after Winthrop's article shook the world, a foundling of sorts appeared at our doorstep. The doorbell to Room 480 rang; one of our editors answered it and found a package lying at his feet. The editor, Arthur Goldman, remembers hearing retreating footsteps down the hall, out of sight around a corner. Goldman read the label and delivered the package to me, somewhat shakily. The address—"To Fred. Dixon, Esq., Mark Twain Sweat-shop, Berkeley, California"—was written in that hand that is as familiar to me as my own. Inside, also in that neat hand, were nine titled pieces of a travel book, working notes to a tenth piece, eight letters to Clemens' wife, Livy, and one letter to his friend William Dean Howells. (They are all contained in this volume, in Parts I and II; Part III would find its way to me a month later.) The travel sketches and letters, unlike the 1861–64 notebook, made no pretense of dating from Clemens' known lifetime: the travel sketches clearly described the world of 1985–86, and the letters bore dates from 30 November 1985 to 10 March 1986. A brief cover letter accompanied the material:

Dear Mr. Dixon—

I am agonizingly sorry to have gone & troubled you with that other misfire. I mean to make it up to you—dollar for dollar. Please accept this pile of MS as partial payment. At the moment, it is the best I can do for you.

Yours truly,
Poor Mark Twain

The arrival of this package was an incalculable boon to us at the Papers, even as it plunged us into new depths of befuddlement. It showed that there was someone out there who wanted us to believe he was Mark Twain, and who could imitate Clemens' handwriting *perfectly*. It allowed us to view the notebook as a probable fraud. In this new light, the notebook's paper, binding, and adhesive were trivial matters: a clever forger could easily pilfer a half-completed notebook or ledger book from some museum or museum basement, cut out the blank pages, and then rebind them with another cover, also perhaps stolen.

I am certain that at that time not a soul at the Papers suspected for an instant that Clemens had returned to life. In fact, as we examined the travel sketches and letters, while we grudgingly acknowledged that some imagination had gone into them, we were able to find small faults that "proved" them to be mere imitations of Clemens' style. We fell victim to the principle governing the reading of parodies: knowledge that a text is a parody immediately gives the text the ring of falsehood. It would be some time before we would recognize the texts for what they were.

The challenge that then confronted us was to find this "impostor." It might of course turn out that he would claim no connection with the 1861–64 notebook, but this was unlikely, given his apology for "that other misfire." After a quick, breathless reading of the manuscript, I photocopied it for distribution to the staff, and we discussed it late into the night. We decided to keep the news of the material "in house" until we fully understood its origin. I dispatched one of our editors, Ricky Olivieri, to the site that, on the basis of the new manuscript, seemed to me the logical starting point—Carson City, Nevada—with the charge that he should exercise all of his imagination to find evidence of the impostor's sojourn there, to learn his real name, to find his trail—in sum, to learn anything he could that would lead us to the body attached to those retreating footsteps.

The organization of this volume, then, is as follows. It is divided into three parts, each devoted to a geographical area where Clemens was active in 1985–86. Each part contains, first, the travel sketches written by Clemens, then his letters to Livy and others. This sequence has been followed because the manuscript laid at our doorstep was so arranged, and it has always been our editorial policy to respect Clemens' intentions in both the wording and organization of his work. A section of discursive explanatory notes follows each of the three sections of Clemens material, elucidating as they occur any potentially obscure autobiographical references and points of possible confusion regarding Clemens' activities in 1985–86. We recommend that the reader consult the notes on a given sketch or letter after having read the piece in its entirety and before reading the next piece. Following the travel sketches, letters, and notes of each section are the reports of our increasingly frantic search for the author. At the end of the volume are chronologies of Clemens' lives and a list of the abbreviations of the published works cited.

Winthrop's *Atlantic* article mentions a symposium dealing with the authorship of *Huckleberry Finn*. It was held on 9–11 April 1986. One entire session was given over to the Mark Twain Papers, and I then expounded, for the first time in public, my belief that Samuel Clemens was walking the earth for a second time. It was not my finest hour. I remember the gapes, twitters, and guffaws. I remember one scholar, who will here remain nameless, leaping to his feet during my presentation and calling to the crowd, "There are about two hundred of us here. Let's divide it up. I can swallow one two-hundredths of this yarn, if you can worry down the rest."

I now see that the symposium was not the proper forum for the delivery of a miracle. I only hope that the narrow intellectual pride that seizes us and chokes us when we are in society will, in the privacy of the reader's home, give way to quiet acceptance of the truly strange and wonderful.

I

I Been There Before:
The West

Good-bye, God, I'm Going to Bodie

I have traveled by various conveyances, over the years—womb, baby carriage, family shoulders, slaves' shoulders, toy wagon, hobby-horse (with no real progress to speak of,) raft, canoe, keelboat, flatboat, steamboat, gondola, ark, toboggan, sled, sleigh, horse, mule, ass, camel, elephant, donkey-cart, stagecoach, European diligence, horse-drawn carriages of all descriptions, train, Australian cable-car, jinrikisha, bicycle, automobile, and, at long journey's end, coffin—airborne, thanks to loving hands.

But when I looked around me I saw none of these; nor sign of them —no mark of a wheel, or hoof, and nary a footprint, so I couldn't have walked. Had I dropped from a balloon? The only evidence of my arrival, —if that is what it was—was not helpful. It was a long, scorched swath, about four feet wide, all the way through the snow down to bare earth, beginning somewhere across the frozen plain way beyond where the eye could see in the moonlight and ending right at my feet, where I stood in lonely bewilderment under the stars and the indifferent cold of space. I remembered nothing. No—that is not quite right. I remembered a flash of sparks and a roar of fury. "A train?" I thought. "A train that picks up its rails and takes them along after it has passed over them?"

I dismissed the transportation-question. It was beginning to unsettle my mind. I turned to the riddle of my identity. I touched myself all over, pulled forward on my hair so I could glimpse it at the side of my forehead, puffed my upper lip out for a better look at my mustache—white, like my hair, unless the light from the full moon reflecting off the snow deceived me. So I *seemed* to have a body that matched the dictates of my brain. I sniffed. I sniffed again. No doubt about it—the rankly sweet stench of tobacco throughout my mustache. Both body and brain were saying to me:

"You are Sam Clemens. It don't make much sense, but that's no matter. You are Sam Clemens."

I now felt emboldened enough to tackle the question of my location, in a preliminary sort of way. I gazed up at the stars and saw old friends up there, arranged in a familiar way that gave me no end of comfort. Surely this was Earth. *That* was settled. But *where* on Earth? I gazed up again. Northern hemisphere. Good—I was making progress. But WHERE PARTICULARLY? And when? And why and . . .

I began to walk. I found a road—which is to say I found a place where the snow was more evenly laid down than elsewhere, and stayed that way so long as you stuck to it.

"This is good," I thought. "A road is good. A road will lead somewhere. That is what roads are for." My thoughts were not sublime. They came singly, each one simplicity itself, and each stuck in my brain for longer than it deserved. Perhaps this is the way idiots think. My next thought was this: What did I last remember? My bed—in Stormfield. Pain in my breast—that curious, sickening pain. Slumbering. Then awakening with the thought: "Am I dead yet?" No—so back to sleep. Awake. "Still alive? *Blast!*" Back to sleep. And so on. The recollection came as a comfort, for of course I was dreaming. I was on my deathbed in Stormfield, dreaming I was tramping around in this barren, snowy landscape, dressed only in my night-gown. I neglected to mention this last fact earlier, out of modesty, but there it is now: a night-gown.

I fished around for more bits of evidence to support my dream-theory, and was happy to strike one. I wasn't cold! There I was, unshod, unslippered, the snow licking at my ancles and legs, the wind whipping my hair in all directions, and I was as comfortable as a baby swimming in the maternal fluid. Well, by and by I began to feel I had had enough of this particular dream to suit me, so I tried to wake myself up. I pinched myself—it is a tired phrase, I know, and a tired idea, but my brain wasn't capable of more than this. My pinching didn't answer. It didn't hurt at all; I could *feel* it, and yet it didn't hurt. Then I remembered how a person will wake up if a dream forces a sudden movement upon him. I began to jump and start, throwing my body around like a man with Saint Vitus's dance. But that didn't answer either. It only filled me with worry on behalf of those by the bed, like Clara and Paine, because if my movements had their match in my *real* body, Clara and the others must have thought I was suffering just awfully, priming myself for the last gasp.

Then I ventured a new theory. I decided I was dead. A thought like that—a thought of that, well, of that *magnitude*—doesn't come easy, but I managed to have it, somehow. Dead. This was the afterlife, or the road leading to it. But I found it wanting. It didn't match any of the promises

—or threats. And which place was I in? I could see arguments for both sides of the question. I was dreadfully lonesome and frightened—the bad place—but I couldn't feel pain—the good place. There was nothing to do but tramp on and let the question settle itself.

It began to grow light—this after many hours. "This is good," I thought in my dull, idiotic way. "Sunshine is good." Then I came to a fork in the road. "This is bad," I thought. "A fork in the road is bad." Tedious, oafish thoughts they were. I would have been awful company, if anyone had been with me. Then I saw a road sign. Yes, I thought it was good, but I shan't quote it at you. I wiped the snow off it and read—

AURORA—18 MILES

"Aurora!" I thought. "What a beautiful, heavenly name! I am in the good place after all! This is the dawn of my new life, my reward!" I began to look at myself and the course of my life with genuine fondness and approval. Maybe I hadn't been so bad after all. Maybe I had been very, very good—or as good as I could be. The Deity was probably proud of me. He probably felt sorry for me, on account of my having to struggle so hard all those years not to be bad. He probably recognized that my sins were none of *my* doing—they were *His* doing, because He made me. Maybe my writings on the subject had influenced Him. I had taught God! Standing there in the road, puffed up and swelling, I was the vainest, proudest man dead.

But there was a catch. The arrow on the sign pointed back down the road whence I had come. I had been going the wrong way! Take it all in all, it seemed just like me to blunder at such a critical time—you couldn't strike a more critical time than this one, no matter how long you thought about it. And if heaven was *that* way, then I had been walking toward . . .

I grew uneasy. I suddenly viewed my mysterious warmth with suspicion. I looked ahead, beyond the fork in the road, casting my eyes to all sides. What I saw, far across a flat waste of white, did not suggest hell, but it was still not encouraging. I saw desolation. I saw dozens—no, *hundreds*—of ramshackle, abandoned buildings, their wooden walls aged and cracked and splintered, their crazy, tilting angles and blasted windows mutely testifying to the fact that, whoever may have once walked those streets, none but ghosts did so now.

As my feet took me toward that empty town, I discarded the idea that this was the afterlife. I confess it was a foreign idea to me anyway; it hadn't taken true hold; it was easy to cast aside. I had a new thought, which I muttered to myself, over and over, as I slowly walked toward the town:

"This is the end of the world. This is the end of the world." Some plague had erased all life. I began to pity the human race. I addressed the desolation:

"Men have walked these streets and cheerfully greeted one another and paused to shake hands and pass the time of day; they shall do so no more. Women have shopped in these stores and gossiped and laughed; they shall no more. Children have chased and giggled and frolicked on these boardwalks; no more, no more." I chanced to look up high,—perhaps I was casting my eyes upward imploringly, seeking a divine explanation—and I saw a strange sight—strange in the sense of being unexpected. It was a mine, with what was no doubt a mill, surrounded by tailings spilling down the mountain. I couldn't *see* the tailings, on account of the snow, but the shape of the slope told me they were there. Why, I thought, this was nothing but an abandoned mining town, whose silver or gold must have played out long ago. I promptly ceased pitying the human race, feeling privately thankful that no one had been on hand to hear my poetry. What a chucklehead I had been to think the Deity was mixed up in this, or that the world had ended. I did what any reasonable man embarrassed by a foolish thought would do—slapped myself on the side of the head and called myself a muggins.

I thought of the sign again. "Aurora." Of course! We mainly called it "Esmeralda" then, but it was the same place. Heaven? Hmph. End of the world? Your granny. I was high in the mountains of Nevada, or California—I didn't know which, because of a border dispute that had everyone yelling and shooting back then.

But,—as the careful reader has observed—there remained a lingering question, to wit: how did I get from Stormfield, away across the continent, to *this* place?

Right nearby, I spied a little stand with a sign that promised me I should get something if I put fifty cents into it. Well, it is easy to fall back on old habits, no matter what the circumstances, and just because that something was locked up behind that glass window, I had to have it, even if the price did seem rather dear. I searched the single pocket of my night-gown for coins. No silver—just some old bills. I peeked through the glass and read the cover of the pamphlet inside: "Bodie—State Historic Park."

I wanted one of those pamphlets. I would have one, or die. I found a board and began to beat at the glass. It was the confoundedest glass I ever struck; it just wouldn't break, no matter what I did to it. Finally it tore away from its supports, and I snaked out the reading material. It was a guide to the ghost town, chock-full of pictures and history and . . .

I have always been interested in dates. Remembering them fills a body with pride; rolling them around in the head can give no end of comfort. But the interest I took in *these* dates laid over *any* interest that ever I took in *anything* before. I didn't find them exactly comforting, either. The last year I had recollection of, there in Stormfield, was 1910. Here I read that the Bodie Bank was robbed in 1916! It took my breath away. Then I read that a certain church burned down in 1928! I lost my breath again, but got it back, and put it to good use right away: I began to moan. I read that another church had closed up shop in 1932! Something else happened in 1957! Would it never end? In 1962 this prime piece of real estate became a State Historic Park. That was the latest date I found. I wasn't wishing for a later one. Fifty-two years was plenty to suit me. *I wasn't complaining.*

I went back to the beginning of the pamphlet. My eyes fell on the first sentence—"Bodie State Historic Park is best visited during the summer."

I smiled.

Second sentence—"At other times the weather is unpredictable."

"Oh?" said I. "Is that *all* that's unpredictable?" I began to laugh— but I didn't get beyond the beginning. My laughter became a bitter stream of curses, of such richness, and variety, and conviction, that even *this* town had never heard its like before. The ghosts came out of the saloons to see what the noise was all about, then went back in, blushing and shaking their heads over this strange new creature who presumed to give the Deity spiritual advice.

I collected myself and looked at the map in the pamphlet. It showed me that if I walked west for 13 miles, I should reach a large road. I heaved a sigh; I turned my back to the sun; I shook the snowy dust of death out of my night-gown; and I left that frozen graveyard in search of the living.

Notes on p. 67.

The Ormsby House Phenomenon

I come fresh from an encounter with true excellence. Such a thing is always uplifting—the butcher who can slice your meat just so, or the cobbler who salvages a favorite pair of shoes in half the time you expected, and at half the cost you were willing to pay, and who thereby endears himself to you so powerfully that you want to take him home with you and install him in your family. The man I met yesterday, then again today —under astounding circumstances—is neither a butcher nor a cobbler. He is a liar.

I was getting my hair cut in something called a "hair salon" on the third floor of the Ormsby House. It's awfully handy having a shop like that so near to your room. You never know when an emergency may arise —when the need for a sudden haircut will seize you so mightily that a two-block walk down the street would be fatal. The barber was a woman named Millie. She pronounced my hair "lovely" and exhibited great reluctance to shear me. But I insisted, for I was grown weary with my own notoriety. It is no joy to constantly be told you look just like Mark Twain, especially when you *are* Mark Twain and you prudently refuse to submit yourself to the humiliation of trying to prove that you are. There is no real credit to merely *looking* like a famous person; in fact there is a debit to it, because you are a species of freak, a human nonentity wearing another man's face. I wanted my *own* face.

I had seen a terrifying film on the television the night before, about some vile youths who misbehaved in school. Why, they made my youthful self look as good as pie by comparison. But what interesting hair styles they had! My favorite, sported by one goggly lad, was short on the top, with an invitingly bristly look to it, and long, sweeping stretches of hair on either side meeting at the back. Millie called what I wanted a "duck's ass." I said, "Better a duck's than a horse's," and she giggled—which is to say, she barked six times, her barks rising in tone and then abruptly stopping. It reminded me of someone hurrying up the stairs but then suddenly halting, tragically arrested in her optimistic ascent by a dagger.

I watched my trade-mark drop to the floor around me in a gentle snowstorm of fine white curls. Millie decided to try some singing. It won't hurt the language to call it singing. The language is strong. It can suffer stretches of application and recover right away. Here is what she sang:

> Frosty, the snowman, was a bibbidy-bop boop ba-doo,
> With a dup-bup-bup and a rip-rip-rip
> And a doo-wah doo-wah doo.

The song was unknown to me. I believe the song was unknown to Millie as well.

"I'll want a shave, too," I said, hoping to ring the curtain on her serenade. "I want you to remove my mustache."

"Ooh," Millie exclaimed. "I ain't never done that before."

I frowned and said, "This is a barber-shop, isn't it?"

She climbed the stairs and got stabbed again. "What an experience this is," she said. "It jist goes to show you. Every day you get up thinkin' this day'll be jist like the last one. Every day you think that. But look at me now. Jist *look* at me. Here I am doin' a flat-top with a d.a. and a shave. Life's more surprisin' than we think."

Get ready now, dear reader. Here he comes.

"You call *that* surprising?" bellowed a fat man seated in the shop. "Why, that's *nothing* compared to what just happened to *me.*"

I could see him without turning around, in the large mirror near where Millie kept all of her tools and potions. I waited for him to go on, because your average mortal *will* go on after saying something like that. But this man, I was to learn, spurns the average. He just took to leafing through his magazine, as he had been doing before.

"I reckon maybe it's too surprising for words," I whispered to Millie.

He must have heard me. He went on:

"I was walking down the street," he said, still looking at his magazine but filling up the room with his booming voice, "yesterday morning, just outside the casino, and what do you think I saw lying on the sidewalk?" A mighty pause. I heaved a mighty sigh and said—

"What did you see?" The fat man looked up from his reading with surprise. Liars will do that—pretend to be surprised all the time, even when it doesn't matter, just to stay in practice.

"Oh, it wasn't much. Nothing *too* interesting." He worked up a yawn. "It was only just a human finger."

"My *lands!*" shrieked Millie.

I watched the man in the mirror. He was smirking and making his big head dance in short little nods. He was immensely pleased with himself. I spoke:

"A finger, you say?"

"That's right."

"Which one?"

"Which . . . Which *one?*"

"Yes. Pinkey? Ring? Which one?"

"Well, I . . . I suppose it was an index finger."

"Good. Now—which way was it pointing?"

"Pointing?" He frowned. He looked to Millie, as if for an explanation, but she was busy with my hair. "What possible difference could that make?"

"Maybe no difference. I just want to know."

"But why?"

"I just do."

He shifted a bit in his seat—with annoyance. "Very well, although I must say I . . . Never mind. If you must know, it pointed to the west."

"Mm-*hmm*. What did you do about it?"

"Do about it?" he said. "Why, I went straight to the police."

"And what did *they* do?"

"They confiscated it."

"Did you take the finger with you to the police station, or did you assume it would remain in place, undisturbed, while you fetched the police?"

The fellow shifted again in his seat. "I must say, stranger, that I've never seen a body as purely *interested* in a subject as you are in this finger. It is singular and altogether strange to me. But—to answer your question —yes, I assumed it would not be disturbed, and so I left it. My assumption proved correct, as it turned out. I am quite a student of human nature."

"Had a crowd gathered by the time you returned?"

"Yes—a large crowd, as a matter of fact."

"What was the mood of the crowd?"

"The . . . The *mood?*"

"Yes. Agitated? Melancholy? Resigned? Or festive, perhaps—something on the order of hail-fellow-well-met?"

"Well, I . . . I can't really . . . the crowd was . . . it was just sort of *there.*" He gave a wild, helpless gesture as he said this, don't ask me why.

"And the barometric pressure?"

He sat immobile for a long moment, as if I had whacked him on the head with a board. *"The barometric pressure?"*

"Never mind. Let it pass—for now. I have a more pressing question. Did anyone in the crowd claim the member?"

"No."

"You're quite sure?"

"Yes. "

"Very well. Now, listen carefully, sir. Did you at any time thereafter proceed to the west?"

"No, I didn't," he said—and with such charming innocence that I almost pitied him. "Why do you ask?"

"Why?" I said, working up to my grand finale. *"Why?* Because the finger *pointed* west." My sentence produced the hugest frown I had ever seen—huge in its profundity, but huge also in that there was lots of face for it to find lodgings in. I continued: "I want to tell you I'm mighty glad to have met you, sir. *Mighty* glad. What you've told me clears up something that's been puzzling me for some twenty-four hours. It concerns a little discovery *I* made yesterday, out on the sidewalk, a block west of the casino. It was a hand—quite a nice-looking hand, too, as hands go, allowing of course for the mournful, cast-off state I found it in; but there was a certain something lacking about it—I mean besides a wrist, a forearm, and the like. I mean it lacked *an index finger.* And—poor thing—it's hard to point without an index finger, but it did try. Kind of stuck its pinkey out, pointing to the east. What a pathetic scene—a fragmented organ yearning to be whole again. I do hope the police put those clues together. I plumb missed it. So did you, sir. We have something in common there —*in addition to our being liars. "*

The fat man quietly set his magazine aside and rose to his feet. I observed him closely, but I couldn't make out what he was thinking, or feeling. He transported his bulk up to my chair and said, in a calm, even voice:

"You've had your little fun. But you'll be sorry you ever took me on, stranger."

I grinned and watched him walk out the door. "I hope I didn't lose you a customer, Millie," I said. She waved a hand and said—

"Oh, pooh. It's no matter. You two got me so flustered with your crazy talk that I'm gonna need a break anyhow. I think you're *both* insane. Set still now so's I can finish."

That was my first encounter with the man. You may be thinking, "You call that lying? You call that excellence?" You're probably skilled in the art yourself, and you're probably making up lies of your own, right now, that the fat man's lie can't hold a candle to.

Just wait.

The next morning—I mean *this* morning—I was seated near the Keno corner, watching the action. The management covers blackjack tables not in use with two large partitions, and I am grateful, for this makes a huge table, just the right size for your morning paper, your cup of coffee, and all of your smoking equipment. My paper was open before me, but as I said, my eyes were elsewhere—on the Keno board. I had placed my bet some time earlier—a *long* time earlier, in fact; the game is the slowest-paced amusement on God's earth—and when I placed it the nice lady behind the counter said that although I no longer looked like Mark Twain, I was still "cute." Now, wasn't that nice?

But back to business. My bet was for thirteen over seven—a cautious bet, fitting for a newcomer to the world. If, of the twenty numbered balls to be drawn, thirteen were in the top half of my card and seven were in the bottom half, I would win twenty-one dollars on my two-dollar bet. At the eighteenth ball the lights on the board were perfect: twelve in the top half, six in the bottom, and two more balls to go. I experienced that little tingle you will get, along with the unwarranted burst of pride, when you smell victory in a game of pure chance. But I lost. The top half went lazy on me and stayed at twelve, while the bottom half went up to eight.

I crumpled the Keno ticket and threw it away. When I turned back to my newspaper, I was surprised to see, instead of the San Francisco *Chronicle* I had opened up, a much more familiar local product—the *Territorial Enterprise.* My bulky adversary from the barber-shop stood at my side, grinning triumphantly.

"See that?" he said, a finger jabbing at the scare-head. "See that?"

I saw it: "Finger Found on Carson City Sidewalk (Story Inside)." I looked at the man's face closely. I hadn't done so before, and I realized right away that my previous policy had much to recommend it. His face was not a pretty one. His skin looked like the full moon in the last stage of smallpox, and his lower jaw stuck out like the forecastle of a steamboat. I shuddered and looked back to the paper. I picked it up. There was only one page to it, its back side was blank, and it didn't *feel* like a newspaper.

"This is bogus," I said. "You had it printed up. And a low-quality job it is, too."

In one swift motion, the fat man seized the page out of my hands and crumpled it. "Stranger," he said—he seemed to think that was my name —"the day will come, and *this* is that day, when you will wish you hadn't trifled with me." Without further ado, he stalked out of the casino.

I puzzled over things a bit. By 1910 standards—my most recent experience with the race—the fat man was an odd one. And yet, I thought, there were probably things that people did in 1910 that would have been viewed as odd in 1835. So maybe he wasn't odd by 1985 standards. Maybe he was as dull as the Sabbath. This set me thinking about standards generally. A week earlier, when I had first arrived, I was astonished to see bulk like his masquerading as humanity. The entire country seemed to have gained about twenty pounds per capita. For all I knew, there might have been a similar transformation, or evolution, in human wilfulness—the desire to have one's own way—which seemed paramount with this Leviathan.

Readers are a cocky, demanding, pugnacious breed. You're probably thinking, "Call that a lie? A bogus newspaper?" No, I don't. And I would be grateful if you showed a little patience, though I know it doesn't come natural to you.

I dismissed the man from my mind and turned my attention back to my newspaper. I was pleased to find a few stories I could understand from start to finish. But I began to grow uneasy. I knew it was coming, sooner or later: a crossword puzzle. It never failed. My experience of the past few days had taught me that as soon as I began to feel the smallest morsel of comfortable familiarity with a newspaper, a crossword puzzle would up and smack me in the face. The first time I saw one, I said to myself, "Well, now, what have we here? A little diversion? I like diversions." I quickly deciphered the principle of the thing, and tackled it.

An hour later, I was a whimpering blob of disgraced protoplasm. I had suffered more than a simple intellectual defeat; I had suffered a defeat that *signified.* Those blank squares symbolized yawning chasms of knowledge and language in my brain; those smudged spots told me I was doomed to wander forever in darkness in this new world. I resolved never to mess with one of those things again. (I am still speaking about the past-past, when I discovered my first puzzle, not the more recent past of this morning; I am out of practice, which explains my literary nervousness; I shall try to improve and overcome this.)

But I couldn't keep my hands off them. They were the flame and I the moth. Every day I charged at them, a savage from a bygone era throwing his spear at a bomb. I could manage the Shakespeare quotations. Also an occasional proverb. Monarchs, battles, and politicians up to 1910 —no difficulty. I was right in my element. But "Capital of Yugoslavia"? "Gangster Al _____"? "Moe and Curly's friend"? It was humbling. It was terrifying. It made me want to hop on the next stage over the mountains and go check myself into the Stockton Insane Asylum.

I turned the page of the paper and sighed. (Back to the terrifically recent past. Smooth sailing from here on, I trust.) There it was—that luring cobweb spun for the sole purpose of tying me in knots. I averted my eyes; but then I sneaked a nervous glance back at a clue: "Author of 'The Human Comedy.' "

Could it be? Was I going to get the very first one I tackled right? I counted the squares. There was a passel of them. Would the whole name fit? I tried it: H-O-N-O-R-É D-E B-A-L-Z-A-C. It snugged right in there.

My eyes drifted to another clue: "Popular novelist of the west." Six squares. W-I-S-T-E-R. Just right. I puffed my chest out and glanced around, hoping someone was noticing my progress.

I tried another: "Animal animator." A strange word—"animator." One who animates animals—who brings them to life? Like "Uncle Remus"? I counted the letters, then smiled as I dashed it off—H-A-R-R-I-S. Providence was favoring me, there was no doubt about it. Providence had given me a puzzle calculated to make me feel right at home. I knew the answers, but that was nothing. I knew the *people,* had met two out of the three and shaken their hands.

"General called 'American Caesar.' " It was so easy it was a joke. This one I met more times than I can recall; not only met him, but published his memoirs and presented his widow with the largest single royalty check in history. I looked up, wanting to shout to the sluggish Keno audience, "Listen! I published Grant's memoirs and presented his widow with the largest single royalty check in history—remember?" I counted the squares, just to be sure. There were nine. I hung fire. Then I tried U-.-S. G-R-A-N-T. The periods were a conniving trick. I'd never struck a puzzle with periods before; but I could be flexible—no doubt they would come into play later.

As I searched for an intersecting clue I happened upon another familiar face. "Russian pianist." I counted, hesitated, then boldly pencilled in O-. G-A-B-R-I-L-O-W-I-T-S-C-H. Another period—a fiend had concocted this puzzle, but a friendly fiend, one who liked me, one who knew I was coming, one who knew I would be tickled to find my own son-in-law thus enshrined. This puzzle was a miracle, plain and simple. It was all about *me.*

"Muse of tragedy." I thought a bad word—I shan't repeat it. I hated muse questions. The only one I could ever remember was Clio.

"Stranger?" This was not a clue, but a spoken word. It came from a shaky voice at my side, familiar to me, but without its former punch.

I looked at him. He was all in a sweat. "Stranger," he said, "you'll be reading about a finger on the sidewalk tomorrow." He winced as he spoke. He *gasped* his words rather than spoke them. "You . . . You've driven me to it." He reached up and set his hand on my newspaper: one fat thumb, three big fingers, and a gallon of blood all over my crossword puzzle.

I cried out in alarm and pushed myself away from the table. I stared at the hand and the grisly, bloody stump where the index finger should have been.

"I hope you're satisfied," he spat at me. He seized my newspaper and wrapped it around his hand, which he stuffed under his arm, squeezing it tightly against his body as if to stop the pain. He staggered away and out of sight beyond the rows of slot machines.

I looked wildly around, but the casino was functioning in its businesslike way. The tinkle of betting tokens, the verbal patter at the craps table, the mechanical songs of the slot machines—to my ears these were cold, cold sounds now. To think that a moment of idle joking in the barber-shop could lead to this! And I had thought *I* was a candidate for the Stockton Insane Asylum. The miserable wretch. I hurried after him, thinking he might have collapsed somewhere. Even if he hadn't, he shouldn't be allowed to run loose. If he could mutilate himself on such slight provocation, think what he could do to others. A vision suddenly struck me—of hundreds of 9.00-a.m. gamblers, nursing fresh amputations, sloppily bandaged with newspapers, determinedly betting the weekend away.

He was not in the casino. Nor was he outside. I circled the building, hugging myself for protection against the fierce wind. Back inside, as I wandered through the lobby like a walking dead man, I heard my name —my false name—being called. I turned and saw the desk clerk beckoning. I walked to the registration desk.

"I have a message for you, sir. You look so different, but I recognized you by your walk." The clerk turned to my cubbyhole. "The finger?" I asked myself. "Please, Lord, don't let it be the finger." The clerk handed me an envelope. I thanked him and nervously stepped away from the desk to open it. Inside, torn out of the newspaper and considerably bloodied, was the crossword puzzle I had barely begun. It was completed, even down to the bloody muse of tragedy, Melpomene.

"Good," I thought. "So it *is* a dream." I had been looking for signs, and this was the first clear one in several days. Stormfield, deathbed, morphine struggling against the flames in my chest—*that* was the reality. *This* was a *dream*—and what a staving dream it had been, lasting a week in imaginary time, and thus far so relentlessly undreamlike. But now—this man's finger, the crossword puzzle—a dream! Oh, the relief that conviction brought me!

I looked around. I noticed details: the chuckleheaded desk clerk wincing because the coffee he had just sipped was too hot, and he had swallowed too much of it; the handkerchief tucked up the sleeve of the old woman at the roulette table; the incessantly twitching boot of the bearded fellow seated at the Mark Twain Bar. Just as swiftly as I had decided it was a dream, I concluded it was not. The wealth of absurd trivialities demolished the idea. I swept my eyes around the casino and wanted to cry out in pain. I would have loved to wake up groaning, with true oblivion right around the corner.

I summoned the strength to step back to the desk. I asked the clerk who had left me the message. I was told it was "that large, jovial fellow" he had seen in the casino the past few days. I asked him if he was jovial when he left the message.

"Not particularly," the clerk replied, "but it's early. Some people take a while to get going in the morning."

"That's true enough," I said dully. I wandered away, to the elevator, seeking the comfort and privacy—I cannot say sleep—of my bed. As I waited for the elevator I suddenly felt my head being caressed from behind. I spun around and saw Millie from the upstairs barber-shop, comb in hand.

"Sorry, honey," she said. "Jist touchin' up. Can't keep my hands off my work."

I smiled weakly.

"Say!" she exclaimed, her face suddenly alight with animation. "Have I got a tale for *you*. 'Member that sourpuss in the salon yesterday? How he up and stormed out because you was pullin' his leg a little bit? Well, he come back right after you left. Ca'm as a cucumber. Said he wanted a haircut. I went to work on him, not sayin' much of anything, you know, on accounta feelin' a little nervous, but he seemed relaxed and all emptied outta his wild stories, so I begun to relax too. Then it happened —he reached up to smooth his hair jist as I was trimmin' a little bit of it, and he let out a scream that straightened my curls and made me go all over goose bumps. He leaped outta that chair and begun to wave his hand around, which was all bloody. I figured I nicked him with my scissors and reached for a towel to give him, but when I turn around what do I see but his hand stuck right in my face and a whole buncha *air* where one of his fingers shoulda been. It took the sand right outta me. 'Now you done it, Millie,' I says to myself. 'You've gone and unmembered this man.' All my blood run down to my feet, and I had to grab holt of the chair to keep from goin' under. Then he starts to chucklin', and he says, 'Don't worry, toots. Jist a little joke. I lost this-hyer finger years ago in a sawmill accident.' He grabs my towel and wipes this red stuff off his stump—fake blood, you see.

"Well . . . *mad?* That ain't the word for it. I chased him outta there with my scissors, and it warn't no phantom finger I was after, neither. I wanted his *vitals,* and I told him so. But he moves fast for a fat man, and he got away. Took my other customers with him, too. They'd suddenly lost interest in hair care, I guess, and who can blame 'em? They ain't gonna visit *my* salon in a while, you can bet. Why, they'll look like the Missin' Link before they'll trust theirselves to ol' Millie's clippers again."

There you have it, dear reader. It's been a while since I have "wrotened" a story, as one of my daughters used to say, when she was young, and wrotening this one has made me sweat like an Injun. It's the best I can do, for now. I think it holds together, and the main story is clear: a little joke in the barber-shop—or, as Millie put it, a little leg-pulling—and we've unleashed a fat tornado of vengeance. He got both of us. It was a prime hit both times, and we were sold all the way. Motivation? He's got loads of it. Technique? He's in the same class as the arch-liar himself.

I mean to keep my distance from that gentleman. I have enough problems all on my own. No need to go out of my way looking for people who are only going to confuse me even more.

Notes on p. 68.

Blackjack

The seat at the far left end of the table, to the dealer's extreme right, is the best of all. You are the first to be paid when play ceases—an ideal position for those of a distrustful nature, whose experience has taught them that insolvency lurks everywhere—but I won't embarrass anybody by naming names. In this seat you are also the last to play each hand. Thus not only do you have the advantage of seeing more cards "up" on the table, improving your calculation of the odds of receiving cards of specified denominations, but also *you have time to think.*

This last is very important, because the dealer is no friend of time. To her, time is a thing to be destroyed; if she had her way, time would end right now and the universe would blink right out; she absolutely pines for the end. I know this not because she said so—she never says a word, apart from a crisp bark now and then that only confuses us. I know it just from being in her presence, within the range of her hurrying influence. She has an aura of acceleration. Her dress—severe black and white, like a cleric who is secretly glad Satan exists, for the fear-value of it; her posture; her granitic aspect—all of these condemn the entire table for deadbeats and malingerers, and we flinch and fidget and cast our eyes down in self-disgust and morbid shame.

"Don't touch your cards after play is over, *please,*" she says, and I see that the language has changed since my time: "please" is a new vulgarism I shall have to add to my list to avoid.

"Don't touch your chips after play has commenced, *please,*" she snaps.

"But I want to 'stand,'" I venture, and the rest of the table gasp at my boldness—not in admiration, but in fear that her wrath may come down on them.

"*What?*" she says, scowling at me. She leans forward, thereby showing me even more of her breasts than I had seen before. I cannot take my eyes off them.

"I want to place my chips on my cards to show I mean to 'stand' with these cards," I say, addressing the rounded, sloping masses with an intimation of the infinite, for they show no sign of bottoming out. It beats any amount of bosom I ever glimpsed on the sly in my first lifetime, and by a considerable margin.

Her response is a wordless demonstration of how one can easily slide one's cards under a stack of chips without actually touching the chips. Her feat is withering in its simplicity. But when I try it, the corner of my cards knocks the pile over, making a sloppy mess. I grin sheepishly. My table-mates pity and scorn me, though I notice on the next hand that they are no better at it than I am. On the subsequent hand I backslide and start to go for my chips with my left hand to lift them and place them atop my cards. In a wash of fear I catch myself, yanking my left hand back, almost biting it to show my good intentions. I snuggle the cards in close to the chips, but not quite under them. This is the best I can do. The dealer watches all of this. The look she gives me tells me I am going straight to hell.

"*Please* drink with one hand and play with the other," she says.

My Scotch hangs fire in my throat, and I force it on down with a gulp as I set my glass on the table. "Pardon, ma'am?"

"You're getting the cards wet."

Grins from my neighbors at the table. They feel safer now. She has identified the worst pupil. An easy confidence bathes their faces.

I privately resolve not to blunder any more and take stock, looking for other grounds for potential rebukes. I become aware of my pipe. Its bowl is hot. I must be careful not to smoke and play with the same hand. I may raise the temperature of the cards a fraction of a degree. This is surely forbidden, because she is nuts for those cards. Earlier I saw her caressing them, picking at a minute blemish on one, and finding a hair stuck to another, which she thrust to the floor behind her with an air of one casting out demons.

I sneak another glance. It is amazing. If you gathered together all of the bits of bosom I secretly glimpsed in my first lifetime and created a kind of composite bosom—from Mary, from Betty, from Florence, and so on —and some bits would be pale, some dark, some without blemish, others freckled, and the result would clearly be too various for the average man's taste—but never mind; I am straying from my point—this composite bosom would be *nothing* compared to the dealer's, and it is all there, right now, all at once!

I worry about my pipe some more, then about my drink. I am

burdened with distracting equipment. I will keep my pipe in my mouth, drink with my left hand, play with my right, and focus the remaining morsel of my attention on my cards, because I have lost six hands running.

I am dealt to. A six on top. I peek at the "down" card. A four. That makes ten. I relax a bit; the odds of hitting twenty are good. She works her way around the table, seeming to sigh when she reaches me. I gesture with a short scrape of the bottom of my cards across the table, as if brushing crumbs onto my lap, striving to match her elegant taciturnity. It works! She hits me. A four. "Blast," I think. Her "up" card is a ten. I must be hit again. So I scrape my cards again, thankful that at least I don't have an unlucky thirteen. An eight. "Ah," I think; "thirteen"—the number has stuck in my head, ass that I am—"thirteen plus eight makes twenty-one." I snuggle my cards in, standing with my perfect total, perfect ass that I am. She flips her "down" card over—a queen to go with her ten. She turns to me, flips my cards over, and this time she *does* sigh, emitting a blast that all but rocks me back on my stool. Because of *course* I have busted with twenty-two, and of *course* you are supposed to fess up right away when you bust, not hide your cards like a schoolboy with a dirty little secret.

I feel the need of a drink. I set my pipe down, carefully leaning the bowl against my glass. So far, so good. Concentrating fiercely, with the same hand I pick up my glass. My pipe naturally tips over, spilling ashes and glowing embers, and I scramble to pick it up. But a thin wisp of smoke rises from the table. I brush the mess away, leaving a small black hole in the felt for all to see. My tablemates perch forward on their elbows, licking their chops. I cannot bring myself to look at the dealer's face. My eyes freeze on her iron breasts. I address them:

"I believe that burn was already there."

She smiles. I have read, somewhere, just recently, that the smile originated as an aggressive gesture—a snarl. It is an attractive theory.

Suddenly the "pit boss" is there, right beside the dealer, blowing bubbles with his pink gum in short pops, as if he is shooting at me with a small-caliber weapon.

"Whassa problem?" he says.

The dealer looks down at the burnt hole. The pit boss cannot see her eyes, for he is beside her, staring and popping his pink wad at me, but he senses just where she is looking. He looks down, and they both stare and stare at the hole. He begins to shake his head, ever so slowly. He says:

"Fourteen years I've been in this business, and I've *never* seen such an ass." He looks at my tablemates. "How about you? You feel the same way?"

Well, he's not going to get an argument from *that* crew. They begin to nod and slobber with grins. The pit boss glances to the dealer. He says:

"He's been staring at you, hasn't he?"

She nods.

"At your bosom?"

She casts her eyes down and bites her lip.

The pit boss stares at me. He gives me a final pink pop and says:

"You don't belong here, buddy. Peg out."

I can be very sensitive. I rise from my stool and retreat, not knowing where to, just retreating. Behind me I hear the pit boss:

"Look at him waddle. Jesus H. Christ—he walks like a goddamn penguin! I've half a mind to chase him right out of here."

I hurry over to the Keno corner, drawn to its protective darkness, to the gentle, slow rhythms of the game, to the sweet ladies behind the counter, who always wish me "Good luck" after they have stamped my ticket, and think I am cute besides. I play a few games and lose a few dollars, not caring much, not envying those few players who, upon the conclusion of a game with the drawing of the twentieth number, rise from their seats and strut forward with their tickets to claim their winnings.

I enter my ticket for another game, absent-mindedly staring at the lady behind the counter. She is a skinny, shapeless woman. If she had her head up a stovepipe hole to look into the attic, I couldn't tell her front from her back. She returns my ticket to me and wishes me "Good luck" again. But this time she adds, "Cheer up. You'll win soon."

Unthinkingly, I reach out and clasp her hand with my own. "I don't care if I win," I say, "but you are so nice for saying that." She turns her hand over, so that she can return my squeeze.

When play begins, I notice that she is the one running the machine. She is the one who removes the little white balls from the tube and hands them to another, who calls the numbers out while the board lights up and the players in the audience hunch over their tickets, comparing the numbers they have marked with those that are called out. I have marked ten numbers on my ticket—the months and days of the birthdates of my wife and four children. If I "catch" five numbers I will get back $7.50 on my $3.00 bet; if I am lucky enough to catch six numbers I will get back $60.00.

There are eighty numbered balls in the fish bowl, but only twenty get sucked up to have their numbers called out. So when the second lady is handed the twentieth ball and reads its number aloud, a wave of mild sadness washes over the crowd, for many of them hoped that that twentieth ball would put them in the money. But not me. *I*'m not sad when the last ball is drawn. By then I had caught only two numbers, and wasn't close enough to winning to care.

But the first lady—*my* lady—draws *another* ball out. The Keno audience exchange puzzled frowns. They begin to buzz. "Isn't the game over?" "Isn't that the twenty-*first* ball?" And there she goes *again*, drawing out another. More buzzing. Another draw! And then another! Whoops of delight can be heard with each draw as new players become winners, thanks to this unwonted generosity from on high. My lady draws and draws, working like a somnambulist, until the Keno board is almost completely alight and we are all winners. I have caught nine numbers and will win $15,000.00. When the boss, all in a sweat, rushes on the scene and shuts down the machine, the audience cheer and rise and hustle to the desk to break the house.

My lady works her way back to her station at the counter, a lovely, dreamy smile playing at her lips. I rise and go to the end of the long line at her window, a lovely, dreamy smile playing at *my* lips.

Sometimes, just sometimes, people can be so good to one another.

POSTSCRIPT—I hope the reader enjoyed this happy ending. It has an uplifting quality that just swells me with pride. The truth of the matter is that when the boss arrived he called a halt to the pay-offs and erased all those excess numbers, in reverse order, until he got the total down to twenty. *Then* he allowed the ladies to pay the tiny group of winners. The human race is a sheepish lot, and the rest of us—the losers—didn't raise the kind of clamor we ought to have. Instead, we meekly allowed ourselves to be appeased by the universal Nevada salve and lubricant: five dollars' worth of free betting tokens.

Notes on p. 69.

S. F. Landmark Hollers "'Nuff!"

There is much talk about a new building in San Francisco—no, not really new, just new to me, and there *was* much talk when it *was* new, but not so much lately, because people will grow accustomed to anything and lapse into silence about it, given enough time, so although it is an old subject to San Franciscans, it is fresh to me, and—never mind this warming up. *I* aim to talk about it, and right now. It is called the Transamerica Pyramid.

It stands 853 feet tall, which allows it to look down on every other edifice in the city, with forty-eight stories capped by a 212-foot windowless steeple. While much skinnier than its Egyptian counterparts, it is still technically a pyramid, because its walls slope until they finally meet at the top—*almost* meet, that is; like me, it's got a flat-top. There are twenty-nine windows across one side on the bottom, and only eight on that same side in the top-most row; stated another way, the area at the bottom is 22,000 square feet. The area at the forty-eighth floor is 2,000 square feet. These are all facts.

You will find an "observation deck" on the twenty-seventh floor. Let me put that differently. You will find a row of north-facing windows which you may shuffling approach and gaze out of, all the time wishing you were higher—the twenty-seventh floor is only half-way up the building,—wishing you could look south, where the bulk of the city lies, wishing you could sniff the air and sway in the breeze, and just wishing generally that life could be altogether different. You will forlornly press your nose to the glass and sigh at the lost opportunity. "Observation deck." They might as well have put it down cellar with the furnace.

There are two other ingredients that I must say something about. These are the "wings." They are two protrusions that rise upward, starting at the building's mid point—you remember that, it's where the observation deck is,—and expand as they rise, as if to make up for the narrowing of the rest of the building. But it is no good. They look like ears—

plugged-up ears, too, since they have no windows. When you look at these you ask, just as a Martian would ask about a man's ears, "What are they *for?*" Your guide book tells you that the one on the east side houses an elevator, the one on the west side, a smoke tower. Well, the elevator could just as easily be housed inside the building—I've seen it done before, many and many a time. As for the smoke tower, I'll pass. I'd sooner see a man in Jericho than visit a smoke tower. It sounds perfectly stuffy and unpleasant.

The cooked-up quality of these explanations proves one thing: the wings are there for *show.* This must mean that, at the last minute, the builder regretted the tapering quality of his pile and felt obliged to disguise it by pasting on those wings, pretending they were useful by stuffing an elevator into one and filling the other with smoke. But it is no good. What we are left with is a building without any gumption, a chicken-hearted steeple that tries to hide its true, pointy nature, but only looks worse for it. The real mistake cannot be overcome so simply, for it is a mistake rooted deeply in human nature. Civilization does not value pointiness highly—I mean in many things. In people, for example. Such a person is called pinheaded—a muggins. This is also the shape of a dunce cap, whose point symbolizes a tapering into nothingness of brain matter. This is the sad fact of the Transamerica Pyramid: it looks unintelligent. More than that, it looks stupid. I mean this in a strict, intellectual sense. It looks mentally outclassed by its neighbors, those stately rectangular banks along Montgomery Street. The Pyramid even looks embarrassed. It seems to *know* it is stupid.

I believe those wings *are* ears. I believe that poor pile has been listening to our jeers and censures for these fourteen years, and has gradually grown to look not only stupid but ashamed as well. Some day, perhaps soon, the Pyramid will be able to take no more. I see it heaving up a sigh that would break your heart; then, in the early morning hours, when the janitors are gone and the office workers are still home in bed, dreaming of new ways to make fun of their workplace, I see the Pyramid pulling itself out of its stays and beginning a slow, dismal journey up Columbus Avenue. I see it casting a glance at Coit Tower and blinking back a tear of regret that its own lines couldn't have been as classical. I see it passing through North Beach, where revelers pause and, their lips quivering in mute pity, watch the pile pass. I see it turn up Taylor Street to Fishermen's Wharf, where it accidentally steps upon and utterly flattens the Wax Museum, then on—on to the Bay. It steps into the water between piers 45 and 47, chilled in its cellar and thrilling in anticipation of that final, everlasting chill.

It moves out into the Bay and heads for the Golden Gate, grimly resolved to extinguish its chunk in the cold waters of the Pacific. But it is so stupidly tall! When it reaches the bridge it searches for deep waters, but even in the deepest part of the strait its two top stories and the entire stupid steeple loom above the roadbed of the golden beauty. But there is hope—the Pyramid begins to collapse at the bottom, because far below, the pressure of the water has begun to break the windows, and the floods are gnawing at its fundament. Story after story gives in, and the Pyramid sinks as if slowly dissolving into the Bay. When its steeple is below the bridge, it lurches forward, still sinking. Soon all the windows are submerged. Then the ears. The steeple dips below the waves, and the ripples it has made are soon lost in the general roiling of the fierce currents. Another blast and buckling below, and a dark cloud rising above the waves signifies the end of the famous smoke tower. The winds scatter the cloud into nothingness.

This building has all of my sympathy. I know what it is to be created by a Maker Who gives too little thought to His designs. I know what it is to be jeered at and censured; *I* have been the victim of jeers and censures for seventy-six years. And I know the attraction of the final, everlasting chill.

Notes on p. 69.

Letters

Ormsby House, Carson City
Nov. 30/85

Livy darling, I made it—I got that date written down just a blink before the stroke of midnight. This will allow me to say, if anyone asks, that I managed to get a birth-day letter off to you. I won't mention that it was *my* birth-day, & not yours, when I wrote it. When *yours* rolled around, *I* was rolling around—hurtling across the snow, then coming to a stop in order to sample the unusual pleasure of wondering who I might be. So I was somewhat pre-occupied. It didn't occur to me that it might be your birth-day. I know you will forgive me.

What a joke. Livy, I, who always vowed I would never wish any of the countless number of my friends & loved ones back to life after they had gone, *am back!* I cannot say why. When I was dead, I had no hankerings to return. I did not wish any more of the pie. I didn't even have the consciousness required to wish any more of the pie. It is all a dark, dark mystery to me.

I returned on your 140th, darling. Happy birth-day. What a vicious cosmic prank to turn that day, which I formerly cherished, into something hateful to me.

I love you—so much that I do *not* wish you were here. It is too, too hard.

Saml.

Ormsby House, Carson City
Dec. 1/85

Livy darling, I have spent the day staring out my sixth-floor window at the snow-capped mountains to the east. I am so alone & frightened I could

---

Notes on p. 70.

cry. But crying won't help me. I find that writing *does* help, so again I take this idiotic crayon in hand & call up the vision of your lovely face.

Livy, I landed somewhere near Esmeralda—my old mining camp. Thence to Bodie, a town just full of frolicsomeness & gaiety. I ransacked the empty buildings & found, in an old box, a suit of clothes that . . . well, never mind. They were preferable to my night-gown, anyway, which Someone decided to dress me in before kicking me out of heaven. Actually, I was wearing the very same night-gown when I died. Therefore, I am prepared to venture this hypothesis: If a body comes back to life, he will wear what he wore when he departed. I defy anyone to disprove it.

To resume, from Bodie I tramped farther, to the west, 13 miles. (I have enormous energy; I wish I had less.) I came to a sight that instantly & irrefutably confirmed my suspicion that I had been thrust into an alien future—it was a bewildering, pell-mell rush of automobiles hurtling along at terrifying speeds, faster than trains. I do not exaggerate. I watched this parade from a safe distance, trying to understand it. The speed implied flight. I wondered if they were fleeing some disaster—my thoughts tended toward disaster, you see. But the automobiles were flying both north & south. Was each group fleeing a separate disaster, unknown to the other group? I guessed & speculated & divined & surmised—I do all of these things every minute, trying to understand my world—that the apparent frenzy before me was no other than the familiar human race going about its daily business, only accelerated somewhat.

I walked ahead, wondering whether I should go north or south—or straight ahead, out onto the road, ending my confusion forever. But I rejected that idea—just a coward, through & through. I rejected turning to the south as well. I recalled that Mono Lake lay that way, which is a curiosity, but a lifeless one. To the north lay familiar ground—Genoa, Carson City, Virginia City, unless they too had been abandoned. So I followed the road to the north, walking apart from it, for safety's sake. By & by I grew tired of struggling through the snow, & I noticed the edge of the road was wide, so I inched that way until I found the going easier, though the noise made me want to scream. I expected someone to stop & give me a ride, but no one did. All I got was some jeering hoots now & then, I don't know why. Maybe I looked so cold & friendless that those hooters couldn't resist making fun of me. Cold? No. Friendless? You may say I felt friendless. I wouldn't object.

I found an inn as night was falling. I trusted to Providence & walked right up to the desk to check in. Providence drew from its infinite store-house & supplied me with a drunkard for an innkeeper, who could barely see me. The ancient bill I gave him—a fifty-cent bill, Livy!—was just fine with him, though I could see it didn't match the other bills in his drawer any more than a shekel. I found my way to a room that I shouldn't wish on a Frenchman, & I pulled off my sodden boots & socks & lay down on the bed.

About that bill, Livy—do you remember that silly penny-currency? 10-cent notes, 25-cent notes, & the like, & how the children used them as play money? Well, during one of my last residential upheavals I found a box with several dozen of those notes. I put them away in my room, & fell into the habit of taking them with me when I traveled, to give to children—special children. I liked to see their eyes widen at the sight of those strange denominations. I took some to Bermuda, on my last trip there, & when I came home to die I had some in my night-gown, don't ask me why—Providence again, I suppose. I reckon that innkeeper thought he was getting a 50-*dollar* bill!

I must write that up, Livy. What a gaudy scene it would be—the next morning, still drunk, as he tries to cypher his profits, & he slurs to himself as his befogged mind ties to make sense out of that strange bill.

To resume my bleak narrative—I did not sleep that night. I had been walking steadily for nearly twenty-four hours, but I wasn't fatigued. Since then, three days have passed, & I haven't felt the need of sleep *yet*. It is remarkable. Well, as you may imagine, I didn't exactly have the bulliest time of my life lying there studying my squalor all night; when morning dawned I bid that place farewell & resumed my tramp. I walked steadily, day & night, never pausing for refreshment, because my body takes no stock in *that*, either, & I finally reached my home, for the time being. I had seen signs for the Ormsby House along the road, & I knew that name from the days of yore, so I said, "The Ormsby House it shall be."

I was a little nervous about finding accommodations; by the time I pulled in at the desk, I looked as though I had been in a two-day cat fight, & lost. But I trusted to Providence again. I didn't draw a drunkard this time, Livy—rest your mind, I am not surrounded by drunkards. I drew a chucklehead. We had the following conversation.

"Hi," says he.

Well, that threw me. It set me back. I couldn't figure why he had said it. Then I saw that maybe he didn't mean anything by it, when he said, kind of studying me closely all the while, "Can I help you?"

"I would like a room for the night," says I. He set a piece of paper & a pen on the counter in front of me, & while I made up some lies on it I could feel his eyes running all over me. He says:

"Do you intend to pay with a credit card, sir?"

"Yes," says I, it sounding like the thing that is done, & him looking too sober for my toy money.

"Which one?" says he.

"It makes no difference," says I. "I'm not particular."

"American Express?"

"Why, yes," says I. "That'll answer."

"May I have it for a moment?"

Trouble. I did the brash thing—told him I had lost my wallet. It was brash, because I didn't know if a body carried it in his wallet. For all *I* knew, you needed an elephant to carry it.

But the fellow broke into an easy chuckle. "That's all right," says he. "You see, I know who you are."

My thought? That the game was up. That I was in for it. I said, meekly, "You do?"

"You bet," says he, crowing proudly. "I knew you the minute you walked in. Don't you worry about your credit here, Mr. Holbrook. Your reputation is good enough for me." He gave me a knowing grin. He was just as pleased as punch with himself. He looked at the piece of paper where I had written my name. "C. L. Samuel *indeed,*" he says. "Clever. *Very* clever. Your secret is safe with me, Mr. Holbrook. But, tell me—are you on tour, or just relaxing? Are you here for the festivities, perhaps?"

I have a rule about lying—that is, when I absolutely *must* lie, Livy —& that is to keep things simple. So I said I was relaxing, though feeling no more relaxed than a kitten on a hot stove-lid. I felt obliged to explain my degraded appearance, so I told him my 'mobile went to smash down the macadamized road a ways, & I saw I had maybe pushed too far, because he frowned a bit, but then he just gave me the key to my room & told me to go have a nice hot bath.

I came up & fell into bed, in order to lie there & stare like a dead man. I played a game. I shut my eyes tight, & then popped them open, fully expecting to see Clara or Katy hovering over me. I tried this several times. It didn't work. Then I cried for a while.

Then I took a bath, & I *did* feel better, Livy. But I wish I could sleep. I'm waiting for weariness, *pining* for it, because the days & nights drag on so.

And what am I to do tomorrow? And the next day? And the next? Livy, either I am your beloved Youth, magically restored to some joke of a life after 75 years, 7 months, & 6 days, or I am a lunatic who thinks he is. Unless people are greatly changed, they will not believe the former, so they *must* believe the latter. The idea of trying to convince them that I am who I *think* I am, the idea . . . why, Livy, it is one of my very worst dreams come true, faithful in every detail, even down to the night-gown I arrived in!

If it is a dream, it is a tiresome long one, longer even than *Middlemarch*, & if I don't wake up soon, I shall be all over bedsores.

I must find out who this Holbrook fellow is. But I can't go on being him forever. I need a plan. I need . . . I need *you*, Livy. I need your soft comfort, your sound advice, your warm, tender love washing over me.

I love you dearly,

Saml.

Ormsby House, Carson City
Dec. 5/85

Livy darling, yesterday I erupted. Imagine my hotel room as the bowels of a volcano, filled with rumbling, thundering, boiling lava, weltering, flaming, smoking lava—& *sentient* lava, meditating an explosive escape, weary of sloshing against the confining subterranean walls, until, in a final burst of torment, it erupts. I erupted. I am up & about.

I had been sequestered in my room for 3 days & 4 nights, afraid to come out, just plain afraid. I had been reading newspapers (3 days ago I began ordering them delivered to my room,) & watching the Kinetoscope here in my room, trying to learn about this world I find myself in, trying to understand my monstrous resurrection, studying it & studying it till I grew sick with the futile repetition of my thoughts. I learned a few things. I had privately concluded ("privately" is the foolishest word I could use here—whom could I possibly talk to about it?) that it was my 150th birth-day that brought me back, even though I arrived 3 days before it. But my reading has given me a different idea, one that worries me considerably. I now believe that Halley's Comet is the responsible party. It made its closest brush with the earth the very morning I arrived—your birth-day, darling. (Did you arrange that coincidence, you little rascal?) You know that the comet was midwife to my birth in 1835. But you *don't* know that I cleverly arranged to go out on its next visit, in 1910. It now appears that that infernal snowball has brought me back again, from where I do not know, for how long I *wish* I knew. That is what worries me. Must

Notes on p. 70.

I stalk the earth another 75 years, till it returns again? The prospect sickens me with despair. 75 years, & without you & the children to brighten them! Unless, dear Livy, you too are returned? I shouldn't *wish* it on you if you weren't, but if you were, I would proclaim my arrival to the world, for all to hear, & I would welcome the world's scornful disbelief, just so you would hear of it & know where to find me.

A body normally rejoices to find reasons for strange things, but *I* didn't, not on finding *this* reason, with its threat of a 75-year sentence. I grew warm instead. My eyes roamed over my room—3 days & 4 nights of cramped quarters & the most hellfired loneliness imaginable; I said some unkind things to my room, some *very* unkind things. I was erupting. It felt good. I wanted to erupt some more. So I did. I erupted out into the hall & down the stairs, scorching the carpet all the way, then out the front door, into the open air, so that I could erupt in grand style, without being cramped.

When I became sane again, I took some sensible action. The first thing I did was kill Mark Twain. I lost my mustache & most of my hair to a real "sociable heifer" in the barber-shop here. Livy, now even *you* wouldn't recognize me. Of course, with Mark Twain I also killed Mr. Holbrook, whoever he might be, because I no longer look like *him,* either. The desk clerk is mightily confused. I told him my real name *was* C. L. Samuel, just as I had signed it, & that I had played a little joke on him, letting him take me for the famous Mr. Holbrook. I put his mind at ease by paying up my bill. Where did I get the money? After my shave & haircut I located a rare coins dealer, who paid me an astounding $440 for the ancient bills in my night-gown. I naturally worry about money, because I have just $180 left, & it won't go very far. I don't really *need* money, what with the marvelous indifference of my body to hunger & cold, but I would prefer having a nice room to sitting on a Nevada mountaintop contemplating myself. And I *can* eat, if I want to, which I like for the way it throws some variety into the day, and so I do hope I strike a plan for getting more money. But how? I "cain't git no situation."

This erupting business has its drawbacks. Now that I am out in the world, I feel like a "wanted" man, with pictures of me posted all over the land. You can be certain that whenever I step out of my room I am sort of holding my breath & walking gingerly, just waiting for someone to pounce on me & say, "I know you!" or "What are *you* doing here?" Perhaps I have already fallen under suspicion. I say this because I find that whenever maids & other residents in the hotel see me in the hall, they say

"Hi!" & I always expect them to follow it up with all kinds of accusations & interrogations. But they don't. They just say "Hi!" & go on their way. It is very strange.

Livy darling, Jean is dead. She died Dec. 24, 1909. Clara is the only one who outlasted me. I have noticed many old people here in the hotel & out in the street. Longevity is definitely on the rise. I have yet to see anyone who looks 111 years old—Clara's age, if she is alive—but I have reason to hope it is possible. My reason is this: Outside my window, across the street, is a large sign announcing that Engelbert Humperdinck is to perform here next month. I guess he will conduct *Hansel and Gretel*, but I hope he doesn't strain himself, because he must be 125 years old, at least. Clara's 111 years is nothing to that, you see. Livy, what I would give to see her face, to take her in my arms, withered with age though she must be. Why, I would give ten years of my life for that. This is a joke, you dear little Gravity.

Well, I shall sign this & have another smoke. Then I shall go out & buy some clothes. Mankind dresses in gaudy colors these days, & I mean to go out & acquire a little color for myself. With a world of love,

Saml.

Ormsby House, Carson City
Dec. 10/85

Livy darling, a very odd thing happened yesterday at the Keno counter. First, I must tell you that this is a gambling establishment, but it is *very* respectable, so you needn't worry. Keno is a game in the stupid bingo family. 80 numbered balls sit in a bowl. In the course of a game, 20 of these balls are sucked up a transparent narrow stovepipe & delivered to a woman, who delivers them to another woman, who reads the numbers & calls them out, whereupon a number lights up on the board behind her. Prior to the game, players mark their tickets, which are facsimiles of the lighted board, choosing numbers they hope will be sucked up. An infinite no. of bets are possible. My favorite kind is the "Over & Under" game. You try to guess how many of the 20 balls will be in the top half of your card (nos. 1–40,) & how many will be in the bottom half (nos. 41–80.) A $2.00 bet on 9 over 11, for example, pays $7.50—likewise 11 over 9; same odds, you see. A $2.00 bet on 8 over 12 pays $11.00, on 7 over 13 it pays

Notes on p. 72.

$21.00, on 6 over 14 it pays $54.00, & so on up to zero over 20, which pays $50,000.

It is a fool's game. It's so slow you could marry & raise a family between drawings, & the odds favor "the house," & winners are paid off in proportions not in keeping with the odds. A fool's game—just suited for me.

Now, here is what happened. After studying the board of the previous game—game no. 185 (& please to note that number,) which came out 8 over 12, I decided to try 12 over 8. I marked my ticket & delivered it to the nice lady at the counter. I stood there while she copied my ticket onto *her* ticket, which she always does, don't ask me why. I stood there with my cigar unlit, planning to wait until I sat down again to light it. She sneezed & excused herself. Now, these are small details, I know, but mark them. I returned to my seat, lit my cigar, & waited a few years. The board finally cleared, the game number changed to 186, & the sucking & reading of the balls began. I lost. Had I bet on the winning combination, which was 17 over 3, I would have won the astounding sum of $5,500. I was disappointed, but I did not swear, darling. At least, I am sure I tried not to.

Now the odd thing: I suddenly found myself back at the counter. I mean this literally. I don't mean I rose from my chair & walked to the counter. I mean *I was instantly there.* My cigar was *unlit.* The lady was copying my ticket onto hers. *She sneezed & excused herself.* My head reeled with confusion. In search of a reference point, my eyes went to the board: no. 185; 8 over 12 still lit up. Where had game no. 186 gone? Livy, I'll tell you—*it hadn't been played yet!* And yet it *had,* for I remembered it clearly. 17 over 3 was the winning combination.

Now, once in a great while I have a good idea, & I had one then. I told Bonnie—she's the nice lady—that I wanted to change my bet to 17 over 3. She said fine & handed me a fresh ticket to mark, which I did, & which she copied. I returned to my seat, (I walked—no free ride this time,) I watched the board go blank & no. 186 appear, & off we went. Well, of *course* I won. Bonnie smiled when I went to her window for my winnings —she smiled, but I could tell it didn't taste good, & she asked me if I knew something that she didn't.

What happened, Livy? Did I drop off to sleep in my chair a moment, just after game no. 185, & did I have a dream of premonition about game no. 186, even down to that cigar & that sneeze? Or did the game actually happen twice? I put out a few gentle queries to my neighbors, asking them as naturally as I could if they had found anything, well, *odd* about that last game. The only thing they found odd, I believe, was C. L. Samuel, so I dropped the subject. Did it happen twice only for me? Why?

A curious repetition like this had happened before, just once. I was in the bath-room of my hotel room, shaving. (Yes, I shave; my body is vexingly normal in that regard.) I had gathered my shaving materials before me: the miraculous can that spews forth more soap than it could possibly hold, like a circus barrel from which issue a thousand monkeys, along with the dainty doll-house razor that needs no stropping but is totally useless as a suicide weapon. I went to work, my efforts punctuated with familiar outbursts—familiar to *you,* anyway; you know I cannot shave without verbal helps—as when I knocked the magic can over into the toilet bowl, or, toward the end of my shave, when I cut myself. Again, I am certain I tried not to swear & lo! back to the beginning, face all lathered, can plunking into the toilet bowl. I was bewildered. I stood back from the sink & tried to collect my thoughts. In a half-daze I went back to work. I scraped. I approached the patch formerly cut, very careful, because I knew it was coming, *very* careful now, & *sssst!* into the skin— the same tedious pain, the same messy trickle of red. As I repaired the damage, I thought, "Isn't Providence a dear old thing?" Providence wasn't content to wrest me out of my mouldy slumber & heave me down past 75 calendars. No—that would have been too merciful. Providence had to add some spice to the experience with a new batch of rules. Providence says, "Sam, now & then you're going to repeat an experience. You won't know when or why. Cut yourself shaving, did you? Let's do it again," & there I go, looping over the same dreary track of time.

But now I see it has its advantageous side too. I am willing to endure a double injury shaving if it means I shall win $5,500 a few days later. I am not an unreasonable man. I try to be accommodating. But the awful anticipation of the repetition happening! Will it happen again? When? Is *that* one? No—false alarm. It gives me such a dreadful, tiptoey feeling.

I certainly am chalking up miracles at an impressive rate. I return from the dead: that's one. I fly backward in time: that's another. Catholics consider two miracles sufficient grounds for beatification. I wonder how many are necessary for sainthood?

I have just been seized by a dandy theory about what happened at the Keno counter. A few days back, I wrote a sketch about what I have found to be a drab, cold, heartless institution—modern gambling. It ended with a dreamy flight of imagination in which the Keno lady falls into a reverie

& draws too many balls out, thereby making everyone in the audience a winner. The true miracle that later happened was different from this, but perhaps my writing about the one miracle caused the other.

Livy, I can hear you as clearly as if you were with me. I can hear you improving my thinking. I can hear you saying, "Well, then—what about the shaving can & the toilet? Did you write about *that* too?" All right. Maybe the theory isn't so dandy after all.

My life isn't *too* awful now. I mainly just loaf & smoke & play Keno, & when addressed I smile & nod a lot, agreeing with what people say. If you agree with people they think you're a genius, so no one suspects just how deeply ignorant I am. I've also figured out, at long last, what that devilish little word means. I mean "Hi!" It doesn't mean "Hey!" or "Hey, you!" People still say "Hey!" when the occasion calls for it, when someone is in danger or is somewhere where he doesn't belong, but when they say "Hi!" they don't mean that at all, not any more. It now means, as far as I can tell, "Hello," plain & simple. Isn't it silly how I managed to work myself into repeated states of terror of exposure, when people were just being friendly? Solving this problem has been a mighty comfort to me.

Yes, Livy, I have begun to relax. I even feel the old impulse to see the sights. I've been to Virginia City, for old times' sake, but it was a harsh disappointment. I had forgotten what a strange little town it is, perched so precariously in that unlikely place. As I gazed out from its streets across the Nevada wastes I had an old sense of the power, the cheeky arrogance, of my old youthful self. From that perch I suppose I thought I could write *anything* & get away with it, & it was worth the trip up there to call that old feeling back.

The rest of the tour was not nearly as inspiring. Thirty years ago, Virginia was a ghost town. They have revived it, in a way, with museums of the backwoods variety, & saloons, & gambling halls, but I wish they had left the corpse to lie in peace. They've got no real remnants of my stay there, so they make 'em up. I saw *two* desks, in two museums, at which I was supposed to have scribbled. It's just like my tour of southern Europe, where I saw enough "pieces of the true cross" in the different cathedrals to build a house out of. The race hasn't changed—& never will.

It is half past 3 in the morning. I haven't slept *yet*. I guess it's safe to say I don't. Might as well go down & play some Keno. It is so slow, & dark in that corner, & somehow endlessly comforting to me.

By the way, if you are in heaven,—I mean, if heaven exists, because if it does then I know you are there—& if you meet a man named Fredric March, please tell him he belongs in the other place.

I love you & send you a kiss—there. How was that?

Saml.

Angels Camp
Jan. 22/86

Livy darling, as I write, here in my room, I am bundled like an Arab in an assortment of towels, because my clothes are wet & I am too angry & impatient to fetch dry ones out of my valise. I have had a sort of swim in the Stanislaus River, though when I awoke this morning I hadn't planned on swimming, not at all. I am traveling with a truly remarkable man, a master of many arts. The driving of an automobile is not one of them, however, & he missed the bridge across the river & tried to ferry us across instead. Maybe, like me, he pines for the old times, & old modes of travel. But the modern automobile is a poor ferry. We sank. That is, the automobile sank, but we got out in time. My companion suffered a broken arm, & when I pause to reflect on his misery, it gladdens me no end. He is in the hospital at the moment, though he means to rejoin me shortly—so he said when we parted, I to a policeman's car, he to the ambulance. But he may not find me here. I am considering shedding myself of him. He's just too various for me.

Now, Livy dear, what would you think if I told you that another one of those loops happened to me? And what if I told you that it was a good thing again, not because it brought me profit, but because it saved a life?

Here is what happened. We pulled off the road, onto a viewing area, & got out of the car to enjoy the lovely prospect of the Stanislaus & Jackass Hill on the other side. As a rule, things look smaller when we return to them after an absence, but the Stanislaus looked *larger* to me. I remembered it as a creek you could throw a dog across, if you had one. My companion explained it, however—a dam had been built below, raising the water level, so it *was* larger. End of conversation. We resumed our drive, & my companion, as if struck by the fancy that our vehicle was capable of sprouting wings, suddenly made it soar off the road. As we bounced down a steep bank into the river, we struck a deer right near the water's edge—a doe—killing her. Wet & battered, but alive, I fretted uselessly over the lifeless form of the poor animal, & I suddenly found

---

Notes on p. 72.

myself back in that scenic viewing area, my clothes dry, my companion explaining to me about the dam.

I told him what had just happened. He believed me—& *that* is the reason I have put up with him thus far; he *always* believes me. He laughed & assured me he would drive very carefully this time. But this time was even worse. He ran off the road again—deliberately, you see. He is insane through & through. The deer, at least, was spared the second time, for we lingered longer in the parking area, discussing the first accident, which allowed the deer to wander on through the fatal point of collision unharmed.

These infernal looping repetitions seem governed wholly by chance. They don't follow the calendar in any way I can cypher, & if there is a cause to them, it is known only to the Fiendish Intelligence that brought me back to life.

A second strange thing happened, Livy. It has been a wearying, confusing day. When I was standing in that viewing area, gazing down at the river, musing on old, old times, I saw—both times—a woman dressed in white, dressed for the summer; maybe, like me, she is indifferent to the weather. She was riding a galloping horse across the bridge, away from us. She was an expert horsewoman, & what a thrilling sight it was. She reminded me of Jean, especially in her last days. How she loved animals, Livy! How she loved to dash out of the house at dawn for an athletic ride that would have put me in the hospital for a week. I can't believe that you & I made her.

That is as far as it went, Livy. She *reminded* me of Jean—nothing more than that, nothing at all.

Then, after our second accident, a *third* thing happened. As the ambulance drove off with my various friend, I got into the car of the young policeman who had happened upon us in our wet, miserable state, & had called the ambulance. He had kindly offered me a ride to jail—I mean to my room. He seemed to be a regular sort of fellow, not given to wildness in any form. He seemed regular to the point of dullness, & I didn't expect much in the way of lively talk from him, which was fine with me. But after we had ridden some distance in absolutely unblemished silence, he suddenly delivered himself of this paragraph:

"At luncheon, Father reproved me for using a slang expression & also corrected a grammatical error that I made. Doing that sort of thing before outsiders I consider absolutely inexcusable, & it made me very angry."

He spoke in a dull monotone, never taking his eyes off the road. I said nothing. What did *I* care about his father, or about him? I was naturally somewhat curious about the slang, & about the grammatical error, but I didn't want to encourage him. We rode a ways farther, & he spoke again:

"This morning I happened to go in while he was eating his breakfast & was very curtly told that I shouldn't go into his room while he was breakfasting. I had very lately been told that that time, about eight o'clock, was a very good one to go in & say good morning to him in. Consequently this last & very unfriendly & unaffectionate statement irritated & hurt me considerably."

You cannot imagine the grotesqueness of hearing these words, delivered not whiningly or with self-pity, but in the most excruciatingly flat way, delivered as if the deliverer were unaware of his speech. I noticed that the deliverer was armed with a pistol at his side & a shotgun within easy reach. I wondered if they were loaded.

He spoke again. I had a crawly feeling he was going to. He fell to talking about what would happen if he found himself in love—a subject *I* hadn't broached, & didn't care a fig about. He went on & on & on, as if I had indicated I was just busting to hear about it.

"Of course," he said, "Father would at once raise every objection, no matter whether I were in better health (there it was, Livy—a loony, by his own confession,) or who the man might be, (the *man*, Livy—Lord!) but if I could believe myself in love & loved, I should pay no attention to his desires."

Well, I hate to admit it, but my sympathy was beginning to go out to Father. I was surprised he stopped short at criticizing this idiot's slang & grammar. In Father's place, I would have gone after the boy's utter disregard for conversational decorum, & come down hard on it, & not let up until I saw some improvement. And as to letting him breakfast with me, why, *I* would have bounced my biscuits & sausages off his head as soon as he opened the door.

I struck a plan. I would speak, & shift the subject: "Can you recommend a good restaurant in this town?" His answer:

"That desperate hunger for love does not leave me & doesn't seem to intend to. Doubtless for that very reason no one will ever care for me & I shall have to drag my useless, empty life out by itself. Oh! is there no hope whatsoever for me? What can I do! I feel as though I must find some means to prove attractive to a person that I can also learn to love. Will I have to go on indefinitely leading this empty, cheerless life without aim or real interest? Oh! it does not seem as though I could."

He spoke right to the point, didn't he? Only he spoke in a code, &

I ain't worked it out yet. I made another stab:

"I shall need to dry my clothes," I said. "Can you suggest an establishment where I could do that?" His reply:

"Of course, Father's rude & ungentlemanly ways often make me angry (that "of course," Livy!—how eerie it was to hear that little piccolo note of reason, with which a speaker gives notice that he is advancing logically, in this cacophony of melancholy irrelevance!) But I do believe that I have passed that undesirable stage of not being truly devoted to him."

I didn't think Father would warm to this news. I suspected Father would be able to content himself with the merest morsel of this madman's devotion to him, exhibited no more often than once in a twelvemonth.

"I do often have a sort of hunger to get hold of him & hug him."

"I would put a check on that impulse," I said as I opened my door, for we had arrived at my hotel, or motel, or whatever the blasted thing is called.

This armed officer of the law turned & blinked at me like a robot. I bid him farewell, saying I had a pressing engagement in a place called reality, which I heartily recommended he sample some day, & I hurried away. He drove off—I reckon to a secluded wood, to kill himself. I wish him luck.

It's been a lovely, lovely day.

Lovingly,
Saml.

San Francisco
Feb. 5/86

Livy darling, what a fool I am! I am a much bigger fool than ever you imagined. I have been duped—completely sold. I cannot tell you how—it would break your heart to hear of it. If only I could set it right! The world has *good* people in it, Livy, not just bad; but what an ugly & distrusting nature I have.

You see, Livy, to-day I visited the Mark Twain Papers. Quite a busy little beehive across the Bay, & *I'm* the honey that all the buzzing is about. I heard of the place from a librarian here. He said if I was as interested in Mark Twain as I appeared to be, I *must* go visit the Mark Twain Papers. He wouldn't tell me what was there. He just said *go.* So I went.

Notes on p. 72.

I bought a subway ticket *from a machine,* & then rode in a tunnel *under the water* to Berkeley—unlikely beginnings for a journey into the past. I found my way to the University library & took an elevator to the 4th floor. As I stepped out I saw the sign: "Mark Twain Papers," along with an arrow pointing the way. I made a right turn & came to a large room full of newspapers. Was this it—piles & piles of the dozens of different newspapers I wrote for? No—farther down the hall I saw another sign about my papers. I walked on, past one blue-painted office door after another, & I saw yet *another* sign & arrow, & made *another* right turn. Was *this* the Mark Twain Papers—a devilishly endless circle without beginning or end?

But the hall was not infinite after all. It ended at a closed door & a strangely out-of-place doorbell, which I pressed. After a time, the door swung open; a head peeked out; a rather nice head, with long black hair. She was a young woman, & very tall. When she looked down to me she made me feel very . . . well, short. She didn't mean to, though.

"Can I help you?" she asked.

"So far, so good," I say to myself; then, to her, "I want to see these Mark Twain Papers."

"Which ones in particular?"

"Whatever you have."

"What are you interested in?"

"Anything that has to do with Mark Twain."

She smiled. "*Everything* here has to do with Mark Twain. Do you know anything about the Papers?"

"No."

"Come on in. We don't like to leave this door open." I joined her inside, in a hall so narrow we were thrown together somewhat. The door clicked behind us, making it even cozier. "We have manuscripts, letters, notebooks . . . Are you a Mark Twain scholar?"

"Hmmm," I thought. "No," I said.

"A buff?"

"Hmmm" again. My thoughts drifted to buffalo skin, to light yellow. I warned myself not to be a ninny. I hung fire.

"A fan?"

I wasn't at all warm, so *this* offer puzzled me.

"Hello?" she said, to see if my spirit was still present, I suppose.

"Hi!" says I, hoping this would put us on a modern & friendly footing.

She frowned. It didn't suit her soft face. She asked, as a last resort,

"Do you have any favorites among his works?"

"*Joan of Arc?*" Livy, I don't know why I *asked* it like that, but at least I got that frown off her face—now she was grinning. I was mighty pleased with myself.

"That's refreshing," says she. "Did you want to see the original manuscript? Is that what you want?"

"Yes."

"Come with me." She led me to a narrow room with a long empty table facing the windows, & invited me to sit down. "Do you plan to work with it for very long? We normally ask patrons to work downstairs in the reading room. You can request the material down there, & a page will bring it to you."

"I just want to see it. Just for a moment."

"All right." She left. I looked around. Along the wall behind my chair were rows & rows of books, all by me, though some had been given titles that I didn't use, like *Early Tales & Sketches. I* didn't know they were "early" when I wrote them. As I studied the titles, I became aware of the strangest kind of talk; it came from a room down the hall, & was much muffled by the many corners it had to turn to reach my ears. But I am sure I heard something like this—

"It is figure 2 in the morning calm ampand figure 9 in the evening."

I discontinued my eavesdropping promptly; decyphering that non-sense would have unsettled my reason. I took down a book called *The Mysterious Stranger Manuscripts.* It was a wonder. The very first sentence in it read, "Mark Twain's *The Mysterious Stranger, A Romance,* as published in 1916 & reprinted since that date, is an editorial fraud perpetrated by Twain's official biographer & literary executor, Albert Bigelow Paine, & Frederick A. Duneka of Harper & Brothers publishing company." When I read it I burst out laughing.

The young woman caught me. She had returned, & I could see that my outburst had reinstated her frown, but she just said, with a glance to the book, "It's about time we set the record straight, don't you think? Here —I've got the MS." She set a bright orange box down on the table, opened it, & took out the manuscript.

I turned a few leaves. "This is it," I said, because I didn't know what else to say. "It hurts to look at it. All that labor."

She heaved a sigh. "And such an awful waste."

I looked at her. I meant to indicate that she had my full attention, because she did.

"That's what most people feel, anyway," she said.

"Oh?"

She nodded—slowly, & with an indefinable sadness. "I don't want to hurt your feelings, or anything like that—you said it was your favorite, & to each his own, of course. But I think Clemens tried to be something he wasn't when he wrote *Joan*. He was tired of being the buffoon, so he tried to be high-toned & serious. The result was a very boring book. I think he was his best when he was being funny." She paused. "It's a shame he didn't understand himself better. You study him, & his works"—she waved an arm around the room, taking in the bookshelf, maybe even the entire building—"& you can feel the pain of a man who doesn't understand himself. This whole collection just aches with his pain."

It was strange, Livy. I felt the pain—felt it being transmitted from the surroundings through this young woman to me. My nerves felt exposed, as if I had just been completely stripped—of my clothing, & of my skin as well.

"He loved this work," I said, feebly.

"Even Howells panned it."

I sighed. "I know," I said. I felt as if one of my children had been slandered. I also wondered if the child hadn't deserved it! Still, one must defend one's children. "After *Joan* was published," I said, "Clemens met the Archbishop of Orleans, & the Archbishop assured him that anyone who had written so lovingly about Joan was bound to join her in heaven; she knew the right people & would see to it, without fail."

The woman gave me a tired smile. "I know that story. Clemens used to brag about it all the time. But it's just one more sign of his divided nature. I can imagine half of him wanting to rejoice at the Archbishop's comment, & the other half howling at it & scorning it. He's an endless contradiction."

I sat in silence & contemplated my two halves. Having peeled me, now she had sliced me in two. Seeking to shift the subject & put off her ingestion of me, I threw a glance to the books on the shelf behind me & said, "Do you mean to publish *all* of his work?"

"Yes indeed."

"Because it is out of print?"

"Out of print?" That frown again. I had blundered. "Almost all of it's *in* print. But we're after a uniform, authoritative edition. Quality publication on acid-free paper, with mind-boggling apparatus."

"Apparatus?" I thought. "Mind-boggling?" I let it pass. I didn't want to blunder again. I asked if she had any mementoes from Clemens' life, & she said there was a box of "odds & ends" in the main office. Did I want to see them? I said yes & thanked her for being so extraordinarily helpful. She smiled & said—

"It isn't often we get a *Joan* fan. I may even start re-reading it tonight, looking for something I like, because of you."

This got my spirits back up, & I said, "She's based on Susy, you know."

"Yes," she said with a sigh. "Poor Susy."

Now, Livy, I ask you—what could I say to that?

As I followed her out into the hall, I heard some more of that "ampand" nonsense coming from a room to our left. We turned right. I was going to ask her about it, but I suddenly thought of something else, & said, "You're obviously well-versed in Mark Twain. There's a particular film that interests me. It—"

"The Edison film? Sure. We've got a print. Want to see it?"

It took me a moment to understand her, & when I did I nodded.

"It's back that way." She turned me around & took me down the hall. We passed the den of strange gibberish. As we walked by I heard someone call out, "Check!" Were they playing chess? All I could see in there was a bunch of printed sheets, over which two young fellows were huddled.

"Proofreading," my guide explained to me. "For the *Collected Letters.*" We walked on, down to a very small office, empty save for a desk & a few chairs & a long silvery thing leaning in one corner, which my guide seized hold of in the most aggressive way & transformed, with an impressive flourish & snap, into a white, glittery canvas on a tripod. She turned to me—for a moment I felt like a prospective slave being eyed by an Amazon—but she just said, "Be right back" in a friendly way. She was a curious mixture.

I sat down, dazed, happy to be alone for a moment. I felt as if I had returned to the British Museum after a long absence & discovered that the entire collection—Elgin Marbles, Rosetta Stone, the whole boiling—had been shunted down cellar & the Museum given over to my life & works. But I also felt a little—how shall I say it—distrustful? This woman, for all of her hospitality, seemed to enjoy petting me with one hand & slapping me with the other. I couldn't make it out.

She returned with a large machine. I watched her flip levers & attach spools & wind the film around. The door opened & three men came into the room. One of them nodded to me & sat down beside me. The other two perched on the desk.

"We don't show this too often," my guide said. "When we do, work generally grinds to a halt for a few minutes."

The man seated next to me scrutinized me. "You the *Joan* fan?" he said, & Livy, *he* was grinning. I was about to say something, but the lights suddenly went out, & a rectangle of white appeared on the screen. Then, in the distance, a white-clad figure came strutting down the walk along-side the house. He was smoking a cigar, & he looked irritated—or maybe just pre-occupied. As he approached the camera he alternately looked into it, then away. When he came close to it he blew a cloud of smoke in its direction. Then we saw the same view again—him in the distance, the same walk & turn into the house.

"His famous steamboat shuffle," my guide said.

The next scene was at a table, inside—I on the right, Katy in the middle, & the one I was hoping for was on the left—Jean. When my guide had mentioned the film, I couldn't remember if Jean had been in it or not, but I privately hoped, & now there she was! Katy tried to put on a hat, only it kept slipping. Jean said something. I said something. I looked old. A few more words. Then it was over.

Someone in the room sighed.

"If only we had his *voice*," said another—sadly, I thought.

"Again?" said my guide, & we all said yes, by all means, & we watched it again, in silence. When it was over & my guide had turned on the light, I said:

"Jean looked happy. It was good to see her looking happy."

"Yes," the man beside me said as he stood up. "Poor Jean. There wasn't much happiness in her life."

"Until the end?" I suggested.

The man hesitated, then agreed—but with such reluctance! "Yes. Briefly." He & the two other men walked to the door, & I could hear them talking about the film as they walked down the hall.

I turned to my guide, who was winding the film backwards onto a small spool. "There's another film I wanted to ask you about," I said. "Quite different from this. An *attempt*, you might say, at biography. It's called *The Adventures of Mark Twain.*"

She burst out in the most musical laugh I have ever heard. "Now *that* we don't have. I've seen it, though. It's a monstrosity."

"Would you say it's representative of the way Mark Twain is viewed today?"

"Are you kidding? Good God."

"But . . . But Clara endorsed the script."

"Poor old Clara," she said, shaking her head sadly as she removed the spool from the machine & put it into a little orange box.

Livy, these incessant attributions of poverty to our offspring bewildered me, as I'm sure they do you. I just don't know what to make of them.

"Come on," she said, ordering me around again. "Mementoes time. Then I *must* get back to work."

The proofreaders were still at it—or rather, at it again, because I recognized them from that other office, where we had watched the film. I walked ever so slowly by their door, & heard this—"Point para Livy comm please try to have on hand a bottle of cap Scotch comm a lemon comm some sugar comm ampand a bottle of cap Angostura bitters point." Do you remember that letter, darling? The "comm" in those places means the one fellow was telling the other, with the other page, that a comma belonged there; likewise "cap," "point," &c. It's the confoundedest reading-aloud I've ever heard.

In the main office a woman behind a desk gave me a grin. I didn't know if she was being friendly or if she was gratified to meet the notorious *Joan* "fan." My guide walked behind her & reached up to the top of a bookcase for a metal box. She set it on the desk, opened it, & took out a small marble head. I laughed, then quoted myself, getting it mostly right, I reckon:

" 'Every now & then we were astonished to see, in the grass around the Parthenon, a grim little face staring up at us.' "

My guide said, "I say shame on him for pillaging the ruins & bringing it back, when he spends all that time in *Innocents* making fun of the other tourists for doing that very kind of thing." She laughed then, so I knew she didn't mean any harm by it.

"Here's a lock of hair," she said. "Somewhat yellowed. Ah—this might interest you." She removed several cases & set them out on the desk. "They're miniatures of Livy," she said as she began to open the cases. "One of these is the miniature her brother carried on that cruise—the one Clemens saw when the ship was in the Mediterranean. His first glimpse of her. It really excited him—you know, really lit his fire. We aren't sure which of the bunch it is. I'd love to know."

"It's this one," I said, picking it up & touching it tenderly.

"You think so?"

I looked at your ivory image a long moment, Livy. Then, darling, I don't rightly know what happened, but I *think* I squeezed it in my palm & pressed my hand to my chest, & I *also* think I may have shut my eyes & let out a little groan. As I set it back down I saw that my guide & the other woman were watching me, & no wonder. "She's lovely," I said, but it was a lame explanation for my behavior—compounded the offense, in fact. Just imagine the impropriety they must have sensed in a chuckle-headed stranger like me hankering after Mark Twain's wife!

I decided it was time to leave. I said, "I don't want to trouble you any more. I just want you to know . . . that . . . well, that this work of yours, this institution, this enterprise—it . . . well, it's all just as bully as it can be!"

They worked up a smile for me.

"I'm fine now," I said. "I can find my way out. Please don't bother. Please don't." I left them & hoped for a hasty retreat. But I discovered, out in the hall, that I didn't know how to get out of there after all. I took several steps in the wrong direction, ending up all confused just outside the proofreading room. Those words came out & began to box my ears with their semi-coherence. As I stood there, dazed & unaccountably frightened, my guide came out of the office & began to walk toward me. I stood rooted in fear & confusion, & all the while that musical madness floated out of the room, & my guide came closer & closer, & I didn't know *what* she was going to do. She must have thought I was about to speak, because when she reached me she raised a finger to her lips & inclined her head ever so slightly toward the open door of the proofreading room; she smiled; she whispered—

"It's Clemens writing to Livy, from London, four years after they were married, & he misses her horribly, &—yes, listen, listen to *this* part." Her hand went out to my forearm & lightly rested on it. From the room we heard:

"Cap And I can imagine myself returning late at night comm ampand ringing the bell comm ampand waiting a while dash a long while comm an eternity dash ampand then your gentle quote cap Who is it q-mark close-quote ampand my response ampand then ever so many kisses ampand then up the stairs ampand then everything just as happy ampand jolly as it can be point."

She let her hand drop from my arm & smiled her soft smile. "Isn't that the sweetest thing? Isn't it? Here—this is the way out." She pointed down the hall & said good-bye. I looked away—I *had* to, Livy—& hurried down the hall toward the door, waving a hand in thanks without turning around.

I am a fool, Livy—I say it again & again & again. Not because I embarrassed myself when I clutched that ivory miniature, or afterward, for the day will never come when I am embarrassed to show my love for you. No—I am a fool because I believed—was *led* to believe, was *seduced* & *beguiled* to believe—that no one really cared about me or my life. To believe that without question—isn't that just me all over?

Then, on my way out of the building, whom do I meet? That co-author of darkness himself, that cask of rancid guts—

No. Let me stop, Livy. Let me end this where I should have, for if you knew what I have done, it would break your heart. Let me close with that ivory image, in Charley's room on board the *Quaker City,* in the Bay of Smyrna. Let me hold that image close to my chest, & be silent. Lovingly,

Saml.

Notes on p. 72.

Notes

Given the unprecedented circumstances in which Clemens found himself in 1985–86, and given the uncertainty that must have plagued him as to the audience for the works he wrote in this period, one must pause and ponder a basic question: Why did Clemens write in his second life? The answer, I believe, is essentially the same as the answer to this question: Why did Clemens write in his *first* life?

The record of Clemens' sense of himself as a writer, like the record of many other aspects of his personality, is ambiguous on the surface but fairly clear under close analysis. For public consumption Clemens could speak glibly of his writing career as one he had stumbled into, with his popular success giving it a life independent of his desires and unwarranted by his talent; but this was probably one of his many self-deprecating poses. In an early letter to Orion (19 October 1865), he writes of his having experienced a "call" to literature, one so strong that in a postscript he urges his brother to burn the letter, showing uncanny prescience when he says, "I don't want any absurd 'literary remains' & 'unpublished letters of Mark Twain' published after I am planted"—this from a twenty-nine-year-old writer virtually unknown outside California and Nevada, a writer of a kind of literature he terms, also in this letter, "of a low order —*i.e.* humorous"—literature, in other words, that he could not have expected posterity to value unless he did great things with it (see *MDB*, pp. 6, 9).

To be sure, Clemens could find writing an onerous, hateful task, especially when he was under contractual pressure, as in the writing of *A Tramp Abroad* and *Life on the Mississippi*. He was also no stranger to frustration when he wrote, as this passage from a 16 August 1898 letter to Howells shows, written in Vienna:

> Speaking of that ill luck of starting a piece of literary work wrong —& again—& again; always aware that there *is* a way, if you could only

think it out, which would make the thing slide effortless from the pen
—the one right way, the sole form for *you,* the other forms being for men
whose *line* those forms are, or who are capabler than yourself: I've had
no end of experience in that (& maybe I am the only one—let us hope
so.) Last summer I started 16 things wrong—3 books & 13 mag. articles
—& could make only 2 little wee things, 1500 words altogether, succeed;
—only that out of piles & stacks of diligently-wrought MS., the labor of
6 weeks' unremitting effort. (*MTHL,* p. 675)

Most of Clemens' books stalled in the course of their composition—
roughly, *The Prince and the Pauper* for two years, *The Adventures of Tom
Sawyer* for two periods of a year each, *A Connecticut Yankee in King
Arthur's Court* likewise for two periods of a year each, and *Adventures of
Huckleberry Finn* for seven years. But, in time, he came to accept this need
to pigeonhole a work in progress as a necessary and even beneficial feature
of his artistic method. Now and then Clemens would threaten to abandon
his literary career altogether, but such threats were short-lived, and he
would soon be back at work on a manuscript, or writing notes for future
use. Also, he often spoke of the intrinsic pleasure he found in writing; this
sentence in another letter to Howells is typical: "I have reached (MS) page
326 on my historical tale of 'The Little Prince & the Little Pauper' & if
I knew it would never sell a copy my jubilant delight in writing it would
not suffer any diminution" (*MTHL,* p. 290). He wrote even through
periods of intense emotional pain. Six months after the death of his beloved daughter Susy, he wrote to Howells, "I don't mean that I am
miserable; no—worse than that, indifferent. Indifferent to nearly everything but work. I like that; I enjoy it, & stick to it. I do it without purpose
& without ambition; merely for the love of it" (*MTHL,* p. 664).

Over forty books and pamphlets, 4,000 pieces of journalism and short
fiction, 8,000 surviving letters—the sheer quantity of Clemens' writing in
his first life corroborates his personal testimony to Howells: he wrote
because he loved to write.

But for whom did he write in 1985–86? Clemens addresses and toys
with his reader here and there in *I Been There Before,* and he directly
addresses the question of audience in "A Dispatch from the *Delta Queen* "
in Part II, where he celebrates its nonexistence in a mood of jubilant
anarchism. Thus the issue was a real one for him, but it seems not to have
inhibited him at all. Also, by the time Clemens began writing the eastern
portion (Part III) of *I Been There Before,* he had sent Parts I and II to the
Mark Twain Papers, implying a desire for the preservation of his manu-

scripts, if not their publication, and in his letter accompanying Part III he encourages their publication.

But the question of audience is especially problematic for his letters, their recipients being "planted" and not subject to being uprooted. Again a letter to Howells sheds some light on the matter. Late in his life (17 April 1909), Clemens wrote, "My mind's present scheme is a good one . . . It is this: to write letters to friends *& not send them*. . . . the *scheme* furnishes a definite target for each letter, & you can choose the target that's going to be the most sympathetic for what you are hungering & thirsting to say at that particular moment" (*MTHL,* pp. 844–845). Clemens' 1985–86 letters to Livy (and, later, to Howells and to Susy) may owe their existence to a rediscovery or recollection of this scheme. Certainly Clemens would have found Livy "the most sympathetic" audience for what he was "hungering & thirsting to say" in his most lonely, frightened, and bewildered moments. We must assume that, just as he could write literature in both lifetimes with no eye to publication, he could write personal letters with no expectation of their ever being read by the addressee. Indeed, judging from the apparent chronology, he was immediately attracted to the letter format upon his return. He appears to have written at least two, and perhaps three, letters to Livy (30 November, 1 December, and perhaps 5 December) before he wrote for a more general nonexistent audience ("The Ormsby House Phenomenon").

Two more comments are in order here—one about terminology, the other about Clemens' writing tools. We are using the somewhat loose term "sketch" for Clemens' travel pieces. They are not really "tales" or "stories." They more closely resemble chapters from a travel book, but we hesitate to use the term "chapter," because the manuscript lacks the continuity of any of his several travel books. Clemens seems to have written these pieces as the spirit moved him, with little concern about any resulting gaps in the narrative.

Clemens cursingly struggled with a variety of writing devices in his first lifetime; in his second, he must have rejoiced at the advances since 1910 that aid a writer to put ink on paper. In 1985–86 he favored a ballpoint pen with blue ink. (There is no evidence that he ever used a word processor.) The few sketches and letters not written with a ballpoint pen are so identified in the notes. In his second life, as in his first, he favored small sheets of paper. Almost all of his 1985–86 writing was done on plain white sheets measuring 6 by 9 inches (15.2 by 22.8 centimeters) without watermarks—the type of paper one finds in inexpensive writing tablets. Below, if no comment is made about the paper, the reader may assume this type was used.

Good-bye, God, I'm Going to Bodie

This sketch was written completely on small-sheet stationery from the Mark Twain Hotel in San Francisco, which places its date of composition somewhere between 23 January and 7 February 1986, fully two months after the event it describes. Clemens must have kept the Park pamphlet with him (published by the State of California Department of Parks and Recreation in June 1979), either as a memento or with an eye to the writing of this sketch, for the sentences and dates ascribed to it are faithful quotations.

Bodie State Historic Park is located twenty miles southeast of Bridgeport, California. Gold was first discovered there in 1859, and the population of the town grew to 10,000 before it began to decline in the 1880s. In its heyday, Bodie was one of the wildest of the boom towns. Its reputation gave rise to a common lament in that area, "Goodbye, God, I'm going to Bodie," which Clemens borrows for his title, the circumstances of his "visit" investing it with a uniquely appropriate meaning. Eighteen miles to the northeast of Bodie is the site of Aurora, Nevada—a former bustling mining town of which not a trace remains. Clemens mined for gold and silver in Aurora (or Esmeralda, as the mining site itself was called) in February–August 1862. It is evidently here, or near here, that he first touched down in the early morning darkness of 27 November 1985.

Stormfield is the name of Clemens' last home, an Italianate villa in Redding, Connecticut, where he lived from 18 June 1908 until his first death there on 21 April 1910; the house burned down in 1923. The "pain in my breast" is a reference to angina pectoris, which plagued Clemens from June 1909 until his first death. Clara (1874–1962) was the only one of Clemens' four children to survive him. She was at his bedside on 21 April 1910. Also by his deathbed was Albert Bigelow Paine (1861–1937), Clemens' official biographer and literary executor. On the strength of his 1904 biography of cartoonist Thomas Nast, Paine called on Clemens in January 1906 and proposed that he write his biography. After what Paine describes as a "long and ominous" silence (*MTB*, p. 1263), Clemens agreed, and the two men were nearly constant companions until Clemens' death four years later. Paine wrote the first complete biography (*MTB*, 1912), and edited Mark Twain's unpublished works (*Mark Twain's Speeches*, 1923; *The*

Mysterious Stranger, A Romance, 1916; *MTA,* 1924) and personal papers (*MTL,* 1917; *MTN,* 1935). As a critic, Paine was seldom penetrating; as an editor, he was given to occasional bowdlerizing and silent tinkering; as a biographer, he sometimes distorted or suppressed unpleasant facts. Still, his editions have served a useful purpose, and his biography will always be valuable.

The Ormsby House Phenomenon

This sketch was written on Ormsby House small-sheet stationery. If the "yesterday" of the third sentence can be taken at face value, its date of composition (or at least the date when Clemens began composing it) is the same as that of the third Livy letter: 5 December 1985.

The "terrifying film" that inspired Clemens' hair style is presumably *Blackboard Jungle* (1955), which aired on local television the evening of 3 December (Carson City *Nevada Appeal,* 3 December 1985, p. 8); a "goggly lad" with the coveted coiffure can be spied on the fringes of a few early scenes of the film.

In 1900 Clemens met Owen Wister (1860–1938), the father of the modern western novel and author of the immensely popular *The Virginian* (1902); he met Joel Chandler Harris ("Uncle Remus"; 1848–1908) in 1882. In 1884, frustrated by what he saw as repeated mishandling of his books by publishers, Clemens established his own publishing firm under the management of his nephew by marriage, Charles L. Webster; the firm's first publication was *Huckleberry Finn* in 1885, and later that year it brought out the highly successful two-volume *Personal Memoirs of U.S. Grant.* Ossip Gabrilowitsch (1878–1936), a Russian-born pianist, married Clara Clemens at Stormfield in 1909; from 1918 to 1936 he was conductor of the Detroit Symphony Orchestra.

Clemens' five answers to the crossword puzzle questions were all incorrect. The correct answers are, in order, "William Saroyan," "L'Amour," "Disney," "MacArthur," and "Anton Rubinstein." If Clemens' nine-fingered antagonist in fact completed the puzzle for him, then Clemens no doubt learned just how far off the mark his answers were and wrote of his performance with conscious irony. But if that portion of the sketch in which he receives the completed, bloodied puzzle is pure invention (a possibility to be weighed heavily in everything he wrote), then he may have remained ignorant of his ignorance.

Blackjack

Three of the seventeen pages of this sketch are on 'Ormsby House small-sheet stationery; the remaining fourteen pages are on small plain sheets. In his 10 December 1985 letter to Livy, Clemens mentions a sketch he wrote "a few days back." The sketch referred to is clearly "Blackjack." On 5 December he was busy writing a Livy letter and some, or all, of "The Ormsby House Phenomenon." Thus it is probable that "Blackjack" was composed no earlier than 6 December and no later than 8 December.

The "insolvency" referred to may be Clemens' own bankruptcy of 1894.

S.F. Landmark Hollers "'Nuff!'"

This sketch was presumably written during Clemens' stay in San Francisco (23 January–7 February 1986). For reasons which will become clear in Part III, the final paragraph of the sketch suggests a more likely *terminus ante quem* of 4 February, the day before his visit to the Mark Twain Papers.

"S.F. Landmark Hollers "Nuff!' " summons up ghosts from Clemens' past in a way not obvious from the text itself. First, the location of the Transamerica Pyramid was fraught with significance for him. In its immediate vicinity were the offices of most of the journals and newspapers to which he contributed while in San Francisco—the *Golden Era*, the *Californian*, and the *Morning Call*. A few blocks to the south, at Pine and Montgomery Streets, stood Maguire's Academy of Music, where Clemens gave his first formal lecture on 2 October 1866, and just to the south of this were his two favorite hotels, the Occidental Hotel and the Lick House. At the site of the Transamerica Pyramid itself (Washington and Montgomery Streets), the "Montgomery Block" formerly stood—a business building with a saloon and billiard room, both of which Clemens almost certainly frequented. Most of the buildings on Montgomery Street were destroyed in the 1906 earthquake and fire, and Clemens must have found the area unrecognizably changed in 1986. (In his first life, he never returned to San Francisco after 1868.) If he was disappointed in the change he found, his critique of the Transamerica Pyramid may have been colored by angry nostalgia.

The sketch also picks up the "wandering building" motif of several of Clemens' articles for the *Morning Call* (*CofC*, pp. 46–48), in which he humorously complains about congestion in the streets of San Francisco caused by houses being moved. In these 1864 articles, Clemens humanizes the houses with a melancholy temperament—a treatment echoed in "S.F. Landmark Hollers "Nuff!" "

Finally, the sketch treats in a disarmingly comic fashion a subject that was evidently very much on Clemens' mind in 1864–66: suicide. Several of his *Morning Call* articles deal with suicides and attempted suicides; also, in his 19 October 1865 letter to Orion (the same letter in which he refers to a "call" to literature), he wrote, "If I do not get out of debt in 3 months, —pistols or poison for one—exit *me*" (*MDB*, p. 9); and in 1909, Clemens wrote, "I put the pistol to my head [in 1866] but wasn't man enough to pull the trigger. Many times I have been sorry I did not succeed, but I was never ashamed of having tried" (*MTLR*, p. 426).

Letters

To Livy, 30 November 1985

This letter is written on Ormsby House small-sheet stationery in black crayon. Ricky Olivieri, our editor who was later on the scene, has pointed out that black crayons are used by gamblers to fill out Keno tickets in the Ormsby House casino. Presumably Clemens arrived at the hotel without a writing instrument and took one of these to his room the night he checked in.

Clemens was born in Florida, Missouri, on 30 November 1835. By an odd coincidence he first put words to paper in his second life on the sesquicentennial of his first birth. His wife, Olivia Langdon Clemens, was born in Elmira, New York, on 27 November 1845; she died in Florence, Italy, on 5 June 1904.

To Livy, 1 December 1985

This letter is written on Ormsby House small-sheet stationery in black crayon.

The fractional currency Clemens writes of was printed in five issues, from 1862 to 1875, in 3-, 5-, 10-, 15-, 25-, and 50-cent denominations (Chester L. Krause and Robert F. Lemke, *Standard Catalog of United States Paper Money*, 2nd ed. [Iola, Wisconsin: Krause Publications, 1982], pp. 168–176).

The Ormsby House is named for Major William M. Ormsby, a

principal founder of Carson City; in Clemens' first life there was an Ormsby Hotel in Carson City.

Hal Holbrook (b. 1925), in addition to having performed in many roles on stage and screen, has been the most famous dramatic impersonator of Mark Twain since his 1959 off-Broadway debut in *Mark Twain Tonight!*

"C. L. Samuel" was the alias Clemens used, with complete failure, in an attempt to travel incognito on the Mississippi in 1882, when he was gathering material for the second part of *Life on the Mississippi.*

The festivities the clerk refers to are probably the celebrations of the sesquicentennial of Clemens' first birth in nearby Virginia City.

"Katy" is Katy Leary—Livy's personal maid and a devoted servant to the Clemens family from 1880 to 1910. Her close tie to the family is perhaps best illustrated in the fact that she was present when two of Clemens' daughters died: Olivia Susan (Susy) Clemens, 1872–1896, and Jane Lampton (Jean) Clemens, 1880–1909; when Livy died; and, finally, when Clemens died.

"Youth" was Livy's pet-name for Clemens.

Clemens' reference to "one of my very worst dreams" apparently concerns one of three recurring dreams he told Paine about (the first dream is that reduced circumstances force him to take up the life of a Mississippi pilot again; the second is that he is giving a lecture full of "silly jokes" to an audience that is not amused and that finally rises and leaves him alone in the auditorium):

> "My other dream is of being at a brilliant gathering in my night-garments. People don't seem to notice me there at first, and then pretty soon somebody points me out, and they all begin to look at me suspiciously, and I can see that they are wondering who I am and why I am there in that costume. Then it occurs to me that I can fix it by making myself known. I take hold of some man and whisper to him, 'I am Mark Twain'; but that does not improve it, for immediately I can hear him whispering to the others, 'He says he is Mark Twain,' and they all look at me a good deal more suspiciously than before, and I can see that they don't believe it, and that it was a mistake to make that confession. Sometimes, in that dream, I am dressed like a tramp instead of being in my night-clothes; but it all ends about the same—they go away and leave me standing there, ashamed." (*MTB*, pp. 1368–1369)

George Eliot, author of *Middlemarch,* was one of Clemens' least favorite authors. In a 21 July 1885 letter, Clemens, inspired by a reading of Howells' novel *Indian Summer,* wrote to him, "You make all the motives

& feelings perfectly clear without analyzing the guts out of them, the way George Eliot does. I can't stand George Eliot, & Hawthorne & those people; I see what they are at, a hundred years before they get to it, & they just tire me to death" (*MTHL,* p. 534).

To Livy, 5 December 1985

This letter is written on Ormsby House small-sheet stationery.

Engelbert Humperdinck (1854–1921) is best known for his opera *Hänsel und Gretel* (1893). It is impossible to determine if Clemens' confusion of the composer with the British-born singer of the same professional name (Arnold Dorsey, b. 1936) is genuine.

To Livy, 10 December 1985

Virginia City, eighteen miles northeast of Carson City, is where Clemens, formerly a sporadic writer, became a full-time one, serving on the staff of the *Territorial Enterprise* from September 1862 to May 1864.

In chapter 17 of *The Innocents Abroad,* Clemens writes of his tour in Genoa, "We find a piece of the true cross in every old church we go into."

Fredric March (1897–1975) played the title role in the 1944 film *The Adventures of Mark Twain.* The film is important to understanding Clemens' behavior in December 1985 and January 1986; he returns to the subject briefly in his 5 February Livy letter and in more detail in "Portrait of a Usurper," where its significance is finally made clear.

To Livy, 22 January 1986

Of all of the Livy letters in this section, this is certainly the most confounding. For a full discussion, see "On the Trail of Samuel Clemens: The West."

To Livy, 5 February 1986

On 5 February 1986 two editors at the Mark Twain Papers were indeed reading proofs of early 1874 letters written by Clemens when he was in London. The quotations from the letters in this sketch are slightly inaccurate, presumably because Clemens misremembered exactly what he had overheard. The full sentences that he partly quotes read as follows: "Livy darling, it is 2 in the morning here, & about 9 in the evening in

Hartford, or half past 8" (3 January 1874; *LLMT,* p. 189); "Livy my darling, I want you to be sure & remember to have in the bathroom, when I arrive, a bottle of Scotch whisky, a lemon, some crushed sugar, & a bottle of *Angostura bitters*" (2 January 1874; *LLMT,* p. 190); and "And I love to picture myself ringing the bell, at midnight—then a pause of a second or two—then the turning of the bolt, & 'Who is it?'—then ever so many kisses—then you & I in the bath-room, I drinking my cock-tail & undressing, & you standing by—then to bed, and—everything happy & jolly as it should be" (2 January 1874; *LLMT,* p. 190).

Paine's edition of *The Mysterious Stranger* was indeed a literary fraud. Late in life, Clemens worked on four different versions of a tale about an angelic/Satanic character visiting the earth, but he was evidently unhappy with all of them and never published them. After he died, Paine took one version—the best one, it must be said—substituted a major character in it with a character from another version, changed some names, omitted some incidents he found offensive, and attached a concluding chapter to it from a different version, publishing the result with no hint of his editorial handiwork. In the words of William M. Gibson, Paine "secretly tried to fill Mark Twain's shoes, and he tampered with the faith of Mark Twain's readers" (*Mark Twain's Mysterious Stranger Manuscripts* [Berkeley and Los Angeles: University of California Press, 1969], p. 3). Clemens' quotation of the first sentence of the introduction to the volume is accurate; we assume he acquired his own copy shortly after his tour of the Papers.

Nothing better illustrates Clemens' feelings about the label "humorist" than his labor on *Personal Recollections of Joan of Arc.* Marking the culmination of a lifelong interest in Joan, the book was to be Clemens' triumphant demonstration of his capacity to write serious—even sublime—fiction. But history has proven wrong the prediction made by Paine in his 1912 biography, "A day will come when there will be as many readers of *Joan* as of any other of Mark Twain's works" (*MTB,* p. 1226). Howells' unenthusiastic review of the novel appeared in *Harper's Weekly* (30 May 1896) and is reprinted in *MMT,* pp. 129–135. Clemens' report of his conversation with the Archbishop of Orléans is discussed in James J. Walsh, "Mark Twain and Joan of Arc," *The Commonweal,* 22 (23 August 1935): 408.

In 1909 a crew from the Edison Company made the very short film of Clemens at Stormfield that he describes here.

On 15 August 1867, when the *Quaker City* lay in quarantine off Athens, Clemens and three shipmates slipped ashore for a midnight visit to the Acropolis, risking severe punishment if they had been caught by the quarantine patrol. In chapter 32 of *The Innocents Abroad* he describes the detached marble heads near the Parthenon: "It startled us every now and then to see a stony white face stare suddenly up at us out of the grass with its dead eyes"; his notebook entry reads, "Grim marble faces glancing up suddenly at you out of the grass at your feet" (*N&J1*, p. 390).

Charles Langdon, Livy's brother, was one of the passengers on the *Quaker City* tour. Clemens saw the ivory miniature of Livy on board ship in early September 1867, and met her in New York on 27 December of the same year.

Clemens' tour of the Mark Twain Papers is discussed further in "On the Trail of Samuel Clemens: The West."

On the Trail of Samuel Clemens:
The West

As stated in the Introduction, our search for the Mark Twain "impostor" began on 12 March, the day Parts I and II of *I Been There Before* arrived at our doorstep. It began on our own turf, with a re-creation of the author's visit to the Mark Twain Papers, which we confirmed as having occurred on the date cited in the Livy letter, 5 February 1986. The tour was very much as described in the letter, with two exceptions. Gloria Wilson, our 6′1″ editor whose height so impressed Clemens, recalled being even more violently outspoken about *Joan of Arc* than reported in the letter. In particular, Wilson remembered placing special blame on Livy for that noble failure of a work, telling her visitor that if Livy, who exercised so much influence over her husband, had only seen that his greatness lay in his river books, especially *Huckleberry Finn* (note: the tour occurred almost two weeks before we learned of the new notebook), and not in some superficially "respectable," unhumorous work of literature she imagined issuing from his pen, she would have encouraged him to stick with what he did best. Imagine another book like *Huckleberry Finn,* only even better! But no—Livy had to urge him toward refinement, which in his hands became pretentious tedium. Wilson said all of this to the visitor, and yet in what is in most respects a faithful record of that visit, the writer (i.e., Clemens, but we did not know that then) made no mention of the charge of Livy's heavy responsibility for his literary misfire.

The other departure from fact was in the description of the final moment in the main office, when the writer claimed to have clutched Livy's ivory-framed miniature image to his breast. Wilson and Pamela Higgins, who was also present, recalled no such clutching. They did recall a hasty exit, but no demonstration of emotion. We noticed that both deviations from fact in the Livy letter showed keen sensitivity to the imagined reader of the letter: the first appeared calculated to spare Livy pain, the second, to give her pleasure. Could an impostor possibly take his craft this far? We decided to broaden our hypothesis about the stranger.

He might be an impostor, but he could also be a man suffering from a severe delusion of identification with Mark Twain.

As to the visitor's personal appearance, he was reported as being of average height (between 5'8" and 5'10"), somewhat slight of build, in his mid-fifties, clean-shaven, with brilliantly white hair in an Eisenhower-era style—a fact that aided all those involved in the tour in recalling it. Another feature aiding recall was a purple novelty T-shirt worn by Clemens, with a maxim across its front that will not be found in any of Pudd'nhead Wilson's calendars: "LIFE IS A BITCH. THEN YOU DIE." This shirt, Clemens' hair style, and, above all, his somewhat otherworldly air of confusion combined to create a certain uneasiness in Wilson's mind, which explains her zealous hospitality toward him—a rare quality in what we in Room 480 have come to call, perhaps uncharitably, "nuisance tours."

In addition, the visitor drawled. According to Wilson, "He drawled as if he were *imitating* a drawl, telling a joke in which the character is a Southerner." In the words of Ned Scully, the editor who sat beside him during the screening of the Edison film, "Imagine Gomer Pyle at sixteen RPM." Katy Leary, Clemens' maid in his first life, once said of him, "I heard him tell once, that that drawl would find him out anywhere—even in the Desert of Sahara. He said even if he was to put on a green wig, and red spectacles, and lose all his front teeth and walk with a cane—as soon as they heard him speak and heard that drawl of his, they'd know who it was" (Mary Lawton, *A Lifetime With Mark Twain* [New York: Harcourt, Brace and Co., 1925], pp. 242–243). This may have been true in Clemens' first lifetime, but it certainly was not true in 1986. Not a soul at the Papers who met him that day (I, alas, was not among the group) suspected for a moment that he might be Samuel Clemens. Also, the stranger's behavior gave no obvious hint of who he thought (alternatively, wanted us to think) he was. His delusion (alternatively, imposture) was so complete that it comprised a desire to remain anonymous.

We were especially puzzled by the stranger's questions during the tour. He seemed to have entered our chambers in a peculiarly half-informed state. Though well versed about some aspects of Clemens' life and works, he knew nothing about the Mark Twain Papers; he was apparently unaware of our edition of *The Mysterious Stranger;* he wondered if *The Adventures of Mark Twain* was representative of the way Mark Twain was viewed today; and he thought Mark Twain's works might be out of print. If the man was pretending to be Mark Twain, to what end did he contrive such a tangled web of apparent misconceptions? If he was genuinely deluded, why did his delusion take such a complex form?

Thus rather confused, Ricky Olivieri set out for Carson City on 13 March 1986. I chose Olivieri for the assignment primarily because as the newest member of the staff (he had been hired just two months earlier) he was still in his editorial apprenticeship and could be spared more easily than anyone else. However, Olivieri was positively qualified as well. While a somewhat shy person, he had shown enough imagination in the detective work that is often part of literary editing to lead me to believe that if the new manuscript had any basis in any actual experience, and if any clues to that experience were lying around in Carson City, he would find them.

Before leaving, Olivieri checked back issues of the San Francisco *Chronicle* and, somewhat to his surprise, found the same crossword puzzle as the one reportedly begun by our author and then completed and bloodied by the Ormsby House Phenomenon. All of the puzzle questions in that sketch appear in the puzzle of the 5 December 1985 issue, with the exception of the question on the muse of tragedy—an embellishment for heightened effect, perhaps. Then he called the Mark Twain Hotel in San Francisco, on whose stationery "Good-bye, God, I'm Going to Bodie" was written. Although the hotel staff could recall nothing at all about the guest, their records showed that a C. L. Samuel had indeed stayed there recently—from 23 January through 7 February. These discoveries were important at that stage, for they established a factual basis underlying the content of the manuscript. Without such a basis, Olivieri would have been on a fool's errand.

Olivieri took copious notes of his investigation. Many of these led nowhere, but others led ultimately to answers to many of our questions. Only the latter are reproduced here. "Quarry" is Olivieri's private name for the object of his search. Square brackets enclose my explanations of possible obscurities.

We begin with Olivieri's notes of his first day in Carson City:

> 3-13—Checked in. Clerk unhelpful. Refused to show me register. He wasn't working here when Quarry on the scene. Hair salon closed for the day. Back to casino. Blackjack dealers (the female ones) *are* buxom; gamblers *are* old—Ormsby House a spot more for gentle retirees than for high-rollers; $2.00-minimum tables humming, while the $10.00-min. table draws no more business than a Young Republicans table in Sproul

Plaza. Bar *is* the "Mark Twain Bar." Asked a few dealers if they remembered a Hal Holbrook- or M.T.-lookalike here in Dec. I said he was an old friend of the family I was searching for. Got zero response. Got chased off by pit boss. Asked same question at Keno counter. Told them he was my uncle & I urgently needed to find him. Got same response, same treatment. A bust. Went to bed.

3-14—Went to hair salon, determined to be clever. Would get a haircut and *glide* into interrogation naturally. Got scalped by a gloomy woman who knew nothing, said less. All the time I thought, "This can't be Millie. Nobody, not even the *real* SLC [= Samuel Langhorne Clemens], could render this sullen creature as Millie, that 'sociable heifer.'" Then, amazingly, in she bounced, the unquestioned original of that sketch. Filled the room with her chatter, talking about her rattle-trap trailer and how it nearly got "blowed over" in a storm last night. Talks ungrammatically, but not really "Pike County." Talked about herself in 3rd-person—Dixie this, Dixie that. (Name change of Dixie to Millie in MS consistent with SLC practice—our mimic knew *this* too.) When Dixie saw my blond hair on the floor she stopped in her tracks and put a cork on her speech. Burst into song: "Oh! Tie a yellow ribbon / Die-die-dot die-dee." My grim hairdresser showed some life and chuckled. A joke? "Yellow"—was Dixie singing about my hair? She got a broom and dustpan and gathered up my locks and took them into a back room. Heard a rustle of paper—a paper bag? Dixie came out of back room the picture of contentment, singing again: "It's been rup long years / Rup-rup-rup die-dee." My hairdresser chuckled again. Whole scene very weird.

Dixie began to work on a customer in next chair over. I introduced myself to her. Asked her if she ever heard of people on a quest for their long-lost father. Yes indeedy, she said. Told her *I* was on such a quest. "Oh you poor thing." Told her my dad *may* have been in O. House in Dec. Looked like Mark Twain, until he got a shave and haircut. Dixie went ape-shit: "Why-I-met-him-he-was-here-three-four-months-ago-did-his-hair-why-right-here-in-this-chair-what-a-nice-man-your-father-you-say-don't-that-beat-all-don't-it." Too much attention from customers, so I offered to take Dixie to lunch. We arranged to meet in coffee shop. Went back to my floor (same as Quarry's—6th) to look for maids. Found one. Scared her when I walked into room she was making up, and put her off from answering questions. She said she didn't remember Quarry. Decided to drive to Va. City—just enough time to squeeze it in before lunch.

Four pages of notes recount Olivieri's search for Quarry's trail in Virginia City. He found nothing there of substance, save for useful confirmation of two facts implied or mentioned in the manuscript: there is a shop where one can have a bogus front page of the *Territorial Enterprise* printed, and two different museums boast "authentic" Clemens desks.

We pick up Olivieri's record at his luncheon meeting with the hairdresser:

> Dixie said my dad ought to be on Johnny Carson. Said he was "a stitch." I asked her what he talked about. She said, "Lordy, what *didn't* he talk about?" He told her of people he'd known, exotic places he'd been. Told her stories, one about his hair ("it bein' a natural subject for the occasion, you see"), about his having it all shaved off once "on accounta lice." She said he scared his children—they thought a stranger had gotten into the house. She said he seemed to *enjoy* the fact that he'd scared them. She asked me if *I* was one of those he had scared. Confused me at first, then I got it—said no, I was only a year old at the time he disappeared. She ranged far and wide in her autobiography then: Provo, Winnemucca, Elko, Carson City. I asked her what she did with my hair. She blushed and called me "a quick one" to have noticed her stashing it. But she declined to tell. She scrutinized me with a frown and told me Ruth (my hairdresser) "sure butchered" me. "Lucky most a our customers is just passin' through," she said, "or we'd be in real trouble." Then she gave me Ruth's biography, which I didn't need. I steered her back to Quarry. Asked her if anything *unusual* happened that day. Anyone else in the shop that he talked to, etc.? She then volunteered the story of the fat man who bragged about having seen the finger on the sidewalk. (I didn't suggest the story at all.) She also pointed out that, to her surprise, once he got in the chair she saw that *he* was missing a finger. She figured he had this thing about fingers. But that was the whole story, evidently. No evidence of Quarry "topping" fat man with his story about the hand, nothing about fat man pretending to have lost his finger to Dixie's scissors.
>
> On the way out of coffee shop Dixie spontaneously told me her plans for my hair. She's an artist, she said—makes embroidered portraits and landscapes out of her customers' hair, "like they used to do with dead people's hair." She does scenes from well-known stories, fairy tales, songs. "You're 'Tie a Yellow Ribbon,' Ricky," she said with an air urging me to feel flattered. "Leastways, you're the ribbon." I asked her what she was going to do for the green leaves, and she called me a

simpleton and said of *course* it would have to be an autumn scene. "You see any redheads in the casino, you tell 'em they need a haircut so bad they oughta be ashamed. You send 'em right up to Dixie." I asked her if she ever displayed her artwork. No, she said, a little huffily. L'art pour l'art.

As far as "The Ormsby House Phenomenon" is concerned, where does this leave us? My opinion—not shared by any of the other Papers editors, incidentally—is that the fat man did surprise Clemens with a fake-bloody stump in the casino, roughly as told in the sketch, even though he evidently did not surprise Dixie in the same way. The fat man's obsession with never being "topped" is what leads me to make this claim —an obsession of which we shall see further evidence in "Portrait of a Usurper" (in Part III of Clemens' manuscript). We are far from having seen the last of the fat man.

Olivieri again:

Said goodbye to Dixie and went up to room. Got address of Carson City Public Library. On my way out, almost bumped into the maid as she came out of a room. "Say," she said, "do he smoke a lot?" I said yes —maybe ten cigars a day. She said more like twenty. Said she'd just found a cigar in an ashtray, and it'd reminded her of Quarry and my questions about him. Said he was "awful nice." Said after he'd been here a while he stopped her in the hall. "He was all excited because he'd just learned people are supposed to tip the maid, and he felt bad because he hadn't, an' I say, 'Some does, some doesn't,' an' he say, 'Well I *does*,' an' he give me a twenty-dollar bill, to make up for before, you know, only he hadn't been here more 'n a week. He asked me what was my name an' about my family an' all. He was the sweetes' man." Did he look like Mark Twain? "For a while. Then he got this *strange* haircut." I asked her if she knew where he had gone when he checked out. No idea. Did he have any friends here—anyone he spent a lot of time with? An awkward look came over her face. She asked if I was *sure* he was my daddy. I said I thought so. She wasn't so sure. Why not? I asked. " 'Cuz he was a . . . a funny one," she said. She went on to tell me about some "funny doin's" in his room, which he shared with a fat man. I pressed her for details. She hesitated, and finally said, "I'll tell you then, if you really lookin' for the truth. One mornin' I was about to knock on the door, an' I hear some yellin'. I listen real close. The fat man is yellin', 'Ride me! Ride me, Sam! Come on! Ride me!' " She distinctly remembered the "Sam" because she knew him by a different name, which she couldn't recall. I asked her what happened then. "Oh, Lord. *Awful* noises. Like they was rompin' on each othuh, an' the fat man gigglin' an' callin' out, 'Go, Sam. Ride me!' " Did she enter the room? *"Me?* I don' mess with none a *that.* Nn-*nnh."* I asked her if she remembered anything else. She responded with some bitterness against the fat man. He was always in the room, she said, when she made it up, and was in the habit of saying to her, "Come on in, sugar, and do your stuff" in a way that insulted her. Then she remembered one such occasion, as she was cleaning up, when both men were in the room, and the fat man suddenly shouted, "Caught you nappin'!" Napping? I said. "Yeah. Nappin'. The othuh one—your daddy, *may*be—he say, 'No you didn',' an' fatso, he say, 'Yes I did.' Daddy—'No you didn'.' Fatso—'Yes I *did.'* Daddy—'Didn'!' Fatso—'Did!' Daddy—*'Didn'!'* On an' on, back an' forth like that, like a coupla kids. I wannit to whop the both of 'em with my mop, they was bein' so silly. Then they settle down, an' daddy asks fatso to learn him how to blow bubble gum. Imagine that—a growed man an' he don' know how to blow bubble gum. Fatso didn' seem too interested in learnin' him, but your daddy kep' after him till he finally give in an' showed him how." I asked her if she remembered anything else, anything at all. She shook her head, then said I should watch out for that fat man. "He ain't no good." I asked if she noticed if he was missing a finger. She said she hadn't and then gave a huge belly laugh. "Why you ask that?" she said. "You think maybe he lost it rompin'? *Where*'d he lose it, thas what I wanna know." She laughed and laughed while I thanked her and backed away down the hall.

To the library. Looked through back issues of *T. Enterprise* and *Nevada Appeal* for TV listings of late Nov. and all of Dec. No listing for *The Adventures of M.T.* Local theatres seem to show only new releases. Letter to Livy damns F. March, so Quarry must have seen it during stay here—but where? (Unless he saw it long ago, somewhere else, and worked it in as if he'd just seen it?) Happened by accident on article in Nov. 28 issue of *Appeal* telling of "a strange light in the sky" seen by some citizens in Bridgeport just after midnight on the 27th. One follow-up story in Nov. 29 issue—mentions some UFO groups showing interest, and quotes a U. Nevada (Reno) physicist calling it "a meteor or space debris," and saying Halley's proximity probably a coincidence. (Quarry could have read this and exploited the coincidence, using it as the "explanation" for SLC's return.) Wandered over to Mark Twain section of collection, just to see how well the MTP [= Mark Twain Papers] editions were represented (not badly). Spied Paine's ed. of *Myste-*

rious Stranger. Looked at the checkout slip in back—infrequent recent use: one 1979 due date, another in 1981, and nothing until Dec. 24, 1985. Looked through *all* the MT books (by and about) and found about 30 with late Dec. 1985 due dates. Browsed them, looking for marginalia. Found some—e.g., "Yes" and "Could use this," written in a small, crabbed hand very different from Clemens' (but it might have been Quarry's *real* hand, when he wasn't forging). Marginal marks and comments esp. heavy for intro. to *N&J1*, which deals with SLC's note-taking habits. Found a Xerox machine and copied some of the marked pages. Went to front desk and asked if anyone there remembered a MT lookalike, or a white-haired, flat-topped, d.a.'ed man in his fifties with a drawl, or a fat nonadigitarian. Drew blank looks. Also, no C. L. Samuel in file of borrowers. Had another idea. Found a video equipment cum videotape rental store in yellow pages and drove there. Too late—closed. Went back to O. House, to write up notes and think and sleep.

3-15—Drove to video store. List of films for rent showed *Adv. of MT!* Talked with several people (used lost-Dad story again, it had worked so well with Dixie). Talked with manager last of all. Didn't take much to jar his memory. He said "a fat turkey" had bought a VCR in Nov. or Dec. and rented "a shitload" of tapes, all adult films. Was he *sure* they were all adult films? "Pretty sure," he said. Said fat man came back next day with VCR and tapes, demanding a refund. Said he was outraged at the filth he'd seen on the screen. Manager said, "I said to the guy, 'What the hell? *You* rented 'em. What'd ya' think?' " Fat man said he had been cruelly misled by the titles. Thought *Pussycat Ranch* would be a western. Thought *American Pie* and *Honey Buns* were cooking shows. Manager said the guy "talked a good line," was impossible to argue with, stubborn as hell, so he gave up and gave him a refund. (I figure fat man—the Ormsby House Phenom.?—*could* have also rented *Adv. of MT*, which manager forgot.) Manager's final words to me: "My advice to you, son, is to drop this search of yours right now. If that man's your dad, you're better off bein' an orphan."

Olivieri's notes up to this point are conscientious and forthright. But a twofold complication arose. First, Olivieri developed an unfortunate and unjustified distrust of me and began to withhold information. Olivieri was the first of us to suspect that our "impostor" was no impostor at all, and, perhaps fearing ridicule or obstruction of his work, he began to pursue a private investigation proceeding from that premise parallel to his official investigation under my supervision.

The second complication (of which the first might have merely been one consequence) was that Olivieri became what can only be called unbalanced. For the cause of this we turn to a set of notes kept by him in his secretive phase, unseen by me until late in April, two weeks after Clemens had departed. Note that Olivieri's report thus far gives the impression that he had but two meetings with Dixie, one in the hair salon, the other in the coffee shop. Olivieri's private notes show, however, that a subsequent crucial conversation occurred:

> Out of further ideas [presumably after the visit to the video store], I became a tourist and walked to Orion's old house on Division St. Now a law office, of all things. I hoped the firm's practice was more successful than Orion's. Summoned up a mental image of him—dark hair. I wondered if it ever turned white, like brother Sam's. Some sort of digging in progress on front lawn, with a row of stakes marking off path of pipe to be laid, or something. Orange ribbons on stakes. Reminded me of Dixie's artistry ("Yellow Ribbon"), and then it happened: I could actually hear her singing "Frosty the Snowman" in Quarry's ear. I dashed back to Ormsby House—caught her out in hall on way to coffee break. Asked her if she had made an art object out of "Dad's" hair. Her response surprised me. Threw her face into her hands and began to sob. Said she was "no good, just no good at all." Bewildered, I assured her she was very good. She said she should have come right out in the beginning and told me about it, him being my dad and all, and so naturally I would want this remembrance of him. Said she was so proud of it she'd been too selfish to tell me about it—afraid I'd want it. Said she was now going to give it to me. I said just a lock would suffice. No—she wanted to give me the whole thing. During her lunch hour I followed her in my car to her trailer—not exactly "The House Beautiful." Over a dozen hair-objects that make you itchy just to look at them. She gave me "Dad's" white protein, an II × 14 snowy landscape beyond description. I thanked her. More tears and self-reproach. I got out of there.

At this point, I jump ahead to a later note, also withheld from me at the time, which Olivieri made on his return to Berkeley:

> 3-17—Filched pieces of true SLC hair from MTP box in office. Put in Baggie and labeled "Sample A." Snipped pieces of hair from Dixie's "Frosty," bagged them and labeled "Sample B." Called U.C. Med School forensics lab, claimed Fred [i.e., Frederick Dixon, this editor] wanted comparison of the two; I said "A" was known Mark Twain hair and "B"

was a questionable sample from a Va. City museum, which a curator there had sent to Fred with request that comparative tests be run. I said Va. City museum should be billed—ha! that'll throw some confusion into things. I told them to deal only with me—said Fred was ticked off at his precious time being taken up with horseshit like this. Sent samples off.

I, of course, knew nothing of all this. Much later, on 22 May 1986, a letter from the lab addressed to Olivieri arrived at the Papers. Inside was this report:

> Portions of human subject hair samples A and B were washed with ethanol to free them of superficial contaminants. They were then placed in separate polyethylene vials and irradiated for 18h at a thermal neutron flux of 2.5×10^{11} N cm^{-2} s^{-1} for neutron activation analysis, following standard protocol, as in Lewin, P. K., *et al.*, *Nature* 299, 627–628 (1982). The samples were analyzed for elements with radioactive half lives of 12.5-67h (K, Na, As, Br, Au, and Sb) by counting the emitted gamma rays. Concentrations of K, Na, As and Sb in samples A and B matched closely and were within range of standard values. Concentration of Br was low in samples A and B, compared with standard values. Concentration of Au was strikingly high in samples A (2.66 p.p.m. ±0.06) and B (2.52 p.p.m. ±0.06) compared with standard values (0.0006–1.36 p.p.m.); see Takeuchi, T., *et al.*, *Radioanalyt. Chem.* 70, 29–55 (1982).
>
> Therefore, based on closely matched concentrations of K, Na, As and Sb in samples A and B, and based on below-normal Br and above-normal Au levels for both samples A and B, I conclude there is a strong probability that samples A and B derive from the same human head.
>
> Mr. Olivieri, could I possibly keep the rest of sample B? Here's my problem. I'm taking care of my girlfriend's schnauzer while she's out of town, and the damn dog got out of the apartment and got his butt bit up by a Doberman that belongs to the Nazi downstairs, and my girl is going to bitch bitch bitch when she sees the nick in little Pfeffer's ass, and sample B matches the white hair there *perfectly,* if I can figure some way to stick it on. I hope you'll give me permission to cover his ass, and mine as well, until his hair grows back. The dog is so goddamned dumb he won't know the difference.

The letter continues for eight more pages, which demonstrate beyond any reasonable doubt both the stupidity of the animal in question and the temporary mental imbalance of the pathologist. With our help, the pathologist recovered. However, Bay Area readers with remarkable memories might recall a brief report in the San Francisco *Chronicle* of 23 May 1986 of a small gray and white dog seen jumping from the Golden Gate Bridge the day before, with a follow-up story by *Chronicle* columnist Herb Caen the next day, calling for a crackdown on rampant canine suicide in the city.

What is the meaning of all of this? Just this: that in the course of his four-and-a-half-month stay on earth, Samuel Clemens' hair had a literally maddening effect on anyone who came into contact with it, a fact of which Clemens seems to have been unaware the entire time. For one more example, with which I shall end this excursus, we turn to the aftermath of Clemens' incognito visit to the Mark Twain Papers. When he arrived at our door, over his pessimistic T-shirt he wore a pullover sweater, which he removed shortly after arriving and, presumably suffering from the same absentmindedness that plagued him in his first life, left behind. Later that day, one of our editors, Jeff Langford, found the sweater on a chair, inquired about it, and put it high on the top shelf of a bookcase. Luckily, no one else touched it—and then only with gloves—until after we fully understood the power that lay in the fallen hairs lodged in it. But for the next two days, until he experienced a spontaneous recovery, Langford was out of his mind. Rather than pursue his assigned labor on our edition of *Life on the Mississippi*, Langford shut himself away in his office and obsessively studied notes and drew models for an old invention of Clemens'—a clip to prevent sheets from sliding off a baby's mattress—oblivious to the fact that contour sheets had filled this need in the marketplace in the intervening century. All the while, Langford, normally a quiet worker, constantly muttered, "A buff trip slip for a six-cent fare, a pink trip slip for a three-cent fare, punch in the presence of the passenjare"—part of an idiotic jingle of Clemens' day whose haunting quality he wrote about, to the delight of *Atlantic* readers, in "Punch, Brothers, Punch" (1876). Upon his recovery, Langford had no recollection of his behavior of the preceding two days. In fact, he was unaware that two days had passed, and when we finally convinced him that they had, he took a week off from work to sort things out.

This "delirium Clemens," as we later came to call it, raises difficulties in interpreting the behavior of Clemens' companions and even brief acquaintances as portrayed in the travel sketches and letters. With the nine-fingered "Ormsby House Phenomenon," for example, are we dealing with a chronic eccentric or a normal man who happened to touch Clemens' hair and became infected? The same question can be asked about the maid on Clemens' floor, who may well have come into contact with Clemens' hair and whose verbal behavior, as reported in Olivieri's notes, strikes this writer as slightly out of true. As for Dixie/Millie, the hairdresser, our later investigation at Carson City (a follow-up to Olivieri's, in preparation for this edition) produced the information that she became a hair artist the very day she cut Clemens' hair, and that she gave up her hobby and threw out her works of art in disgust shortly after she gave the "Frosty the Snowman" landscape to Olivieri.

And Olivieri? For the next month he carried that landscape with him, to Hannibal and then to New York, often fondling it in desperate yearning for the head to which it had been attached, and all that time it drove him mad (see "On the Trail of Samuel Clemens: The Mississippi River" and "On the Trail of Samuel Clemens: The East"). With regard to the potent triggering mechanism in Clemens' hair that causes delirium Clemens, we will be forever ignorant; under rather urgent conditions, I personally destroyed the work of art and Clemens' sweater on 21 April 1986.

We can now return to Olivieri's investigation in the west. We pick up his activity in Angels Camp. His first interview was with the highway patrolman who arrived on the scene after Clemens' plunge into the Stanislaus River. As the reader may have already observed, given the date and circumstances of that accident, we are dealing with a certain intersection of two of our investigative paths: the driver of the car (Clemens' "too various" companion mentioned in his 22 January letter about the accident) was Arthur Laufbahn, the ostensible bird-watcher who discovered the 1861–64 notebook.

Olivieri made the following notes available to me upon his return to Berkeley the next day:

> 3-16—Talked with CHP [California Highway Patrolman] Ed Leonard. His report tallies with newspaper accounts of Laufbahn's accident, and with the Livy letter account. Leonard said Laufbahn was "a weird duck." Said he ranted and raved about "some kid who had busted his toe." ???? Leonard said he saw Laufbahn find the box, but didn't pay much attention. Laufbahn didn't open box then. Just took it. I asked Leonard about Laufbahn's appearance: fat and ugly (= Asquith's description of him [i.e., Charles Asquith, the antiquarian who purchased the notebook from Laufbahn]). Leonard saw no horsewoman on bridge, and doesn't know of any woman who habitually rides there. Leonard not

at all the melancholy space cadet portrayed in Livy letter. Just an average Joe. Never been to MTP, never read Hill [i.e., Hamlin Hill, author of *MTGF*; see below], never heard of Jean.

The last sentence of this entry needs some explanation. It will be recalled that in Clemens' Livy letter of 22 January, the highway patrolman enlivens Clemens' ride back to the motel with some rather weighty talk about problems with "Father" and about his projected love life. The words attributed to him in that letter are taken verbatim from a poignant diary kept by Jean Clemens in 1906 and 1907, and their occurrence in this context defies explanation according to known laws of cause and effect. Portions of the diary are quoted in *MTGF* (pp. 160, 167–169), but the bulk of the patrolman's words can be found only in a typescript copy of the diary in the Mark Twain Papers. Clemens' visit to the Papers occurred two weeks *after* the date of this Livy letter. Also, Clemens did not examine Jean's diary during his visit. We therefore have no explanation for the mode of transmission of the diary passages into the letter. It should also be noted that in the letter Clemens gives no indication that he is aware of the ultimate source of the patrolman's words.

We pick up the trail at Olivieri's next notebook entry:

Drove to river. *Very* steep bank. Don't see how they survived the crash. Drove across bridge and up to Jackass Hill cabin [where Clemens resided from 4 December 1864 to 23 February 1865]. Checked register inside for Jan. signatures. Quarry had signed it, in SLC hand, with the early nom de plume, "W. Epaminondas Adrastus Blab." Dated Jan. 22. Right below this, in a small script, was "Oscar Umlauf." Um*lauf* = *Laufbahn*? Register has a special column for tourists' comments. Most are bland. But Quarry's was "I don't see no p'ints about this cabin that's any better 'n any other cabin." Umlauf's was "It sucks." Tore page out for files. Checked Umlauf's signature and comment in register against handwriting in margins of Carson City Library books. *They matched.* Went to Pineview Motel, where CHP Leonard had driven Quarry after accident. Register showed that a C. L. Samuel and an Arthur Laufbahn stayed in adjacent rooms the nights of Jan. 21 and 22. Manager remembered Laufbahn, because of the accident and, later, the publicity when the notebook story hit the papers, but couldn't remember C. L. Samuel. Crucial point: Laufbahn had 9 fingers. Manager *sure* of it. Recalled Laufbahn scaring his grandkids in coffee shop with a moralistic tall tale (moral: "Don't bolt your food, kids") about how he had eaten his breakfast so fast he ate one of his fingers, thinking it was a sausage.

When Olivieri returned to Berkeley (at which time, incidentally, I detected nothing strange in his behavior), he informed me of his progress and made a copy of most of the notes he had taken for my files. A phone call to the Mark Twain Hotel in San Francisco confirmed that an Oscar Umlauf, like C. L. Samuel, had spent the nights of 23 January through 7 February, and on the same floor as C. L. Samuel. Desk clerks had no recollection of him, however.

Where did this leave us? Confused but encouraged. Remember that our goal was to prove the 1861–64 notebook fraudulent. Umlauf/Laufbahn's name-switching, whatever the purpose behind it, looked suspiciously like the behavior of a man with something to hide. His association with Quarry had the appearance of a conspiracy. And his research at the Carson City Public Library and probable rental of *The Adventures of Mark Twain* looked like a search for material suitable for the notebook. Quarry's remorse in his Livy letter dealing with his tour of the Mark Twain Papers made sense if *he* was the author, or a co-author, of the notebook. That letter closed with a reference to his meeting, outside the library, "that co-author of darkness himself, that cask of rancid guts." Umlauf/Laufbahn? A check of the register for the reading room of the Bancroft Library answered that question. Oscar Umlauf had worked there almost daily from 27 January through 5 February, using *our* resources so that he might thoroughly hoodwink us when he appeared in Charles Asquith's rare books shop. Asquith, incidentally, recalls no missing finger, but he remembers that Laufbahn wore gloves, indoors and out, "in deference to the delicacy of the manuscript," he recalls Laufbahn saying. If Umlauf and Laufbahn were one and the same, then Laufbahn was far from a shy bird-watcher from Munich who innocently happened upon a metal box on the Stanislaus and innocently made $215,000 from the sale of its contents.

Olivieri's request for tests of the hair sample he had acquired in Carson City indicates how strong his suspicion was that Quarry might be the real Samuel Clemens. His suspicion quickly developed into a firm conviction. Immediately following his notes about the tests, he wrote the following, also unseen by me until over a month later:

1. Umlauf did the research for the notebook, so that he could watchdog SLC's progress; SLC did the writing.
2. Note this, from *N&J1*, intro., heavily underscored in Carson City Library copy: "Clemens occasionally wrote in his notebooks while on horseback or aboard ship, in a carriage or a crowd, or in very

bad light. Such passages may be chaotic scrawls." Consider maid's report of "Ride me, Sam! Ride me!" Notice description of Nevada "horse" in 1861–64 notebook. [This is quoted in the *Atlantic* article; see above, p. 12.] "Wilfulness" a key word for horse; "wilfulness" a key word for Ormsby House Phenom. Ergo, in that hotel room in the Ormsby House, where SLC must have written some or all of the notebook, Umlauf played horsey for Sam, for the sake of verisimilitude, and Sam took advantage of the occasion to describe his "beast."

3. Did Umlauf know his companion was SLC? Maid says he called him "Sam." And Umlauf saw him in salon before trimming. And "Caught you napping!"—SLC may have told him about his eternal wakefulness. Or Umlauf could have thought him insane, and humored him throughout. Either way, once Umlauf got a sample of SLC's penmanship and compared it with samples in Carson City Library books, he must have known he'd struck a bonanza.

4. Why did SLC make up stuff about Orion writing *Huck Finn?* To enhance value of notebook, probably. The more earthshaking the contents, the better price it would bring.

5. After MTP visit, SLC had regrets. Was it too late for him to cancel scheme? Or did he go ahead despite regrets? At any rate, he skipped town, then came back with, or sent, new material to MTP when *Atlantic* story broke, as his way of saying, "Look, I'm back and I wrote that notebook all right, but obviously I wrote it this time around, not the first time around." He signed that letter "Poor Mark Twain." Fred says the writer was mocking the "Poor Susy," "Poor Jean," and "Poor Clara" from his MTP tour. I know better. He *is* poor Mark Twain—he's in pain. The poor bastard's out there somewhere, lying awake, smoking, settling in for the long, miserable, lonely wait until dawn. Got to find him. Got to.

Except for his assumption that Clemens was motivated to participate in the notebook hoax for money, Olivieri was right on target. (For more on Clemens' motivation, see "Portrait of a Usurper.") A glance at the western portion of *I Been There Before* shows a significant gap in composition—between 10 December 1985 and 22 January 1986. During this period Clemens was no doubt working on the notebook, a project which compunction prohibited him from mentioning, except obliquely, to his wife.

Meanwhile, Olivieri kept his counsel and pretended to believe he was still searching for an impostor. Then, a new development: on the day before Olivieri was to leave on the next leg of his search, the following story appeared in several national newspapers. Below is the version we first read, from the San Francisco *Chronicle* of 18 March 1986:

"Mark Twain" Returns

FLORIDA, Mo. (AP)—A man who claims he is Mark Twain was taken into custody by police yesterday, then released without charges being filed. Responding to citizens' complaints of a noisy vagrant camped in a city park—the site of the birthplace of Samuel Langhorne Clemens, better known as Mark Twain—police arrested and questioned the man but were unable to determine his true identity. The man, who police say bears no physical resemblance to Mark Twain, stated he had been in the country since November 27, when he claims to have arrived in Carson City, Nevada. On being released, "Mark Twain" reported he was on his way to nearby Hannibal, Missouri, Twain's boyhood hometown, where he said he hoped to receive better treatment.

When we read this in the office, Olivieri bitterly exclaimed, "They think he's a crank!" Our general reaction was "Don't we all?" and Olivieri, whose guard had slipped a little, recovered and said he had just been joking. At the time, I gave his outburst no more thought. Olivieri booked a seat on the night flight to St. Louis, bound for Hannibal, and bid us farewell.

II

I Been There Before:
The Mississippi River

A Dispatch from the *Delta Queen*

The river! The river!

The river can wait. First I must talk about the people. The cast of stowaways—I mean passengers—embraces the entire human race. Intellectually, we have the literary "buffs"—this includes the Mark Twain "buffs," and I am King of that particular buffdom—the Civil War "buffs," the nature "buffs," the life-in-the-antebellum-South "buffs," the great-days-of-steamboating "buffs," and the art-of-modern-navigation "buffs." We also have the odd passenger who asks if we are heading upriver or downriver, or when we shall reach Arizona.

Economically, the passengers range from those who have pinched their pennies all of their lives in preparation for this trip, to those who have sailed the seven seas and have wedged this cruise into their busy schedules of rapacious leisure just so they won't have to sit in jaw-grinding silence when the *Delta Queen,*— or the *Mississippi Queen,* its more modern sister ship—becomes the topic of discussion at the next posh affair they attend. The first group are forever bustling about, drinking in the sights, counting every leaf on every branch of every passing tree; because I, in both of my incarnations, am part of their once-in-a-lifetime experience, they can't get enough of me. The second group, though, lie abed in their pajamas and let the steward bring them coffee, emerging on deck late in the day for a patronizing glimpse, with which they seem to say, "Well, this isn't *too* awful." They seem to view me the same way. "You don't stink *too* awfully," they seem to say. Don't ask this bunch for comparisons with other cruises. They are so full of themselves that they pay no heed to how they talk, thinking that *if* they talk, that ought to be enough. But it ain't. There is no more horrible bore than the well-traveled man who brings no art to the telling of his travels.

Which of these two groups, you may ask, do I like the least—the wide-eyed babes in the woods, or the yawning sophisticates? Perhaps you have already perceived a prejudice. But the question is more difficult than it might appear to be. It is such a tough question, that I shall ignore it. But I *can* say, and *will* say, that the first group loves life too much for my tastes; the second group too little. There.

I have come to know some of the passengers very well. There is Milton Tibbett, for example. Milton is plagued by women—a sorry state for an unmarried man, who pays the piper all day but enjoys no jolly melody of a night. Traveling with Milton (we are all on first-name terms here, but then I suppose so is everybody these days, everywhere,) are his spinster sister, his spinster sister's spinster friend, and two younger girls whose connection with him I haven't yet determined. They all hound him to death. It's enough to make a sensitive man like me drop to his knees and cry. They chronically complain about the voyage, painting a picture so bleak and fraught with hardship that if I closed my eyes I would think they were describing a donkey journey through Palestine. Milton, being the man of their retinue, is expected to make the necessary inquiries and demands to assure their comfort. It is heart-wrenching to see him "take on" a steward or a waiter. All of these fellows are paragons of subservience already, just dying to bring you John the Baptist's head on a platter, if only you would ask for it. But Milton—poor Milton!—feels obliged to assume a bullying role as foreign to him as to a mouse, one which obviously pains him through and through. He eventually gets what he wants, but the cost is considerable. After such a campaign he will mope off by himself for long stretches, or sit down morosely with his camera, poring over its mysteries with dark sighs. That camera is another nemesis of his. He bought it not long ago and unwisely delayed familiarizing himself with its operation until this trip was under-way. His sister orders him to "shoot this" and "shoot that." Milton's lips tighten. We know what he would really like to shoot. I have studied his instruction booklet with him—something in him touches me, I want to *help* him, *save* him, bring an ounce of *joy* to his life—but I am small assistance. The camera is as baffling to me as it is to him, and the instruction booklet is the work of a sadist.

As for the river, it— But wait. There is another fellow who has my pity, and I must say something about him. Hermann. Hermann the German. He is a student from Heidelberg, a zealous observer, and an undertaker of that most mortal of enterprises—the travel journal. He wears American clothes, even down to a cowboy hat he bought somewhere and occasionally sports on deck, but because of his obviously Teutonic frame, his pale face, blond hair, and strange spectacles, that hat is as out of place on his head as a buffalo in Berlin. Hermann *tries* to have fun, but he is so dreadfully alone—as lonesome as a German verb. His English is perfect. This is his undoing. His speech, in its bookish striving for perfection, is even slower than mine, and at least with *my* article the listener gets to hear drawn-out vowels to keep him occupied between the thrilling stretches. With Hermann the listener gets nothing but dry, deadly silences, Sahara-like pauses while Hermann forages in his mental dictionary for the precisely correct word—only that will do, you see. Yesterday I saw him hang fire for three minutes in search of a preposition. His listener grows weary and eventually wanders off to get drunk, proud to have done his diplomatic duty by enduring a chat with the foreigner. I have tried a bit of my German on him, and I don't think I injured him too badly with it. But he prefers English, for the sake of his education. He is here to learn, to experience new things, to taste life. He is the saddest man I have ever met.

The river! How can words possibly describe its grandeur, its majesty, its—

But there's another fellow on board that I want to write about. I like him. I like him so much I wish he were in Yugoslavia, or anywhere far away, so that I wouldn't have to yell at him and hurt his feelings. He resides in the cabin next to mine, and he loves music. He wants to share his love. This is good. He wants to share it with me. This is bad. He *makes* me share it, for I can hear it, as I write, coming through the wall. Presently I must go next door and yell at him. I believe the poor fellow has the mistaken notion that, through repeated exposure, I will become a music lover. For my part, I love enough music as it is. I love marches, spirituals, and *very carefully selected* compositions of a higher-toned sort, like Beethoven's Fifth Symphony, and one of Schubert's impromptus—I forget which. That's enough love for me. I don't want to be promiscuous. I'm happy just the way I am.

My neighbor leans toward "the moderns," as he calls them. I do not like "the moderns." I don't trust 'em. Just when they get pretty and favorable to humming with, they turn ugly. Imagine a pretty woman with golden hair, and you draw closer, as politely as you can for a better look, and she suddenly snatches off her wig, pops out her teeth and glass eye, and thrusts her face up close to yours so you can gaze into her caverns. The moderns will get you every time, just like that. On the occasion of my last verbal eruption, my neighbor invited me into his room for a personal concert from his tape recorder. For some reason that I still can't fathom, I went in and sat down. He played *The Creation of the World* for me, which was composed by I-forget-what-his-name-is. It was a treat—for a deaf man. *Creation of the World?* If that tune was played for Adam,

I can understand why he fell on such hard times. It would affect *any* man's judgment.

The river! To return to the river after an absence of eighty years is, I find . . . not as interesting as Mabel. I must tell you about Mabel. She is joviality itself. You could call Mabel an "open" person. There isn't a bit of "hold-back" to her. Just say the smallest little thing and her mouth will fly open, her arms fly apart, her legs spread, her breasts separate, and if you don't duck you're in danger, because she isn't shy about aiming that laughter right at you.

What would it be like to be a writer and have Mabel as a wife, a critic, a first audience for your manuscript? In another life, perhaps . . .

"Mabel, I've written a—"

"Oh, read it, Sam, read it! Eee-hee."

"Well, I aim to, Mabel, but just let me tell you—"

"Eee-hee."

"—what it's about first. It's about this little girl who goes to visit her grandmother—"

"*Eee*-hee, it's prime, Sam."

"—and in the woods she meets a wolf, and—"

"A *wolf!* Oh! Oh!"

"—and they talk for a while—"

"A *talking* wolf! Why, the things you can think up!"

"—and the wolf learns where she is going and humps it to the grandmother's house before the girl can get there—"

"Eee-*hee.*"

"—and the wolf eats the grandmother and dresses up in her clothes—"

"Dresses up in her clothes! Oh, carry me home to die!"

"—and then—"

"There's more? *More?* How can there be more?"

"—and the little girl says, 'Grandma, what big eyes you have,' and—"

"*What big eyes!* Oh, Sam, it's National Book Critics Circle, First Prize, without fail!"

"—and—"

"There's *more?* If there is, the Pulitzer's yours, Sam!"

"—and—"

"More yet! Oh, Sam, if there's more, if there's one word more, then—"

"—and—"

"That's it! Pack your bags, Sam. You're bound for Stockholm. The Nobel is in your pocket just as sure as—"

"—and the wolf says—"

"Eee-hee. Stop, Sam. Stop!"

"—and the wolf says . . . Are you listening, Mabel? Mabel?"

Well, Mabel would miss the wolf's snapper, because she'd be stretched out on the floor. Death by merriment.

The river! The river's ceaseless, ever-flowing, eternal tide is . . . is . . . is . . . is navigated by the Captain. He is a peculiar mix of the old and the new, as is fitting on this modern floating monument to the past. He has a Yale degree of some kind and speaks perfect English without a trace or even a promise of profanity. That is his new side. He wears mutton chops, just as I did on the river, and that is his old side. His age is about sixty-five.

Until recently, I was curiously shy about the Captain. If I spied him strolling on the deck, I would turn and hurry away. Once, I had a chance to dine with him, but I fled the dining room. I struggled to understand this shyness, and I came to a strange conclusion: I was avoiding this man because I was too much like him. I saw that this was an unaccountable basis for shyness, and resolved to treat him as if he were my grandson. If there had been no Civil War, I would have piloted all of my life; I would have married some Memphis belle; I would have passed my river-lore on to my son; and he would have passed it on to his son, the good Captain Mutton of the *Delta Queen.*

Well, being a blood relative, nearly, he shrank to human proportions. I dropped in at the pilot house. But I saw right away that I had picked a bad time. The boat had fallen behind schedule. Captain Mutton and his assistant, Mr. Veal, were discussing this in low, troubled tones. The boat had to get somewhere before nightfall—I wasn't able to hear where,—and to do that we had to clear a certain obstacle, a treacherous patch of water, and again I didn't catch the name, but . . . Wait. I heard it, and my blood ran cold, every cell in my body was charged with horror, &c. Hat Island. We had to clear Hat Island. But darkness was closing in, and the Captain squinted ahead at the black expanse of water, as if wondering whether to try it, but then his shoulders sagged and he said:

"Well, yonder lies Hat Island. I guess we can't make it. We'll have to lay to."

"Pardon me," said I. "I used to know this stretch of the river, and it is miraculously unchanged since that time. May I?" I pointed to the wheel. Captain Mutton eyed me closely, his manly judgment seeming to take in all of my strong and weak points in a single manly glance, &c. He said:

"Well, if you think you *can,* by all means. You do seem to have a pilot's look and manner about you. Go ahead. But remember: *No man has ever tackled Hat Island in the dark and lived to tell about it &c.*"

I sucked in my breath, thrust my chin forward, and checked my fly. I seized the wheel. At my fingertips lay an impressive array of levers, buttons, and switches. I ignored them and gave a yank on the bell rope. The Marine Band Radio cackled and chattered; I reached out and snapped it to silence, preferring to listen to the sweet ancient whistle of the steam through the gauge cocks. My eye fell with scorn on the shifting digits of the fathometer. "Damn the fathometer!" I said under my breath, and with a vicious yank on the knob I turned it off. I heard the leadsman calling, from away far off. Says I to myself, "I shall heed the leadsman's old, old cry and steer this ornery tub the old, old way."

"*Quarter-less-twain!*" called the leadsman.

"She's coming up to the reef," whispered Captain Mutton.

"*Quarter-less-twain!*"

"Now she's in the marks," he whispered.

"*Eight-and-a-half!*"

"There," Mr. Veal whispered. "She's on the reef now. She only draws eight, so—"

"*E-i-g-h-t feet! . . . E-i-g-h-t feet!*"

"She'll not make it," whispered a third voice. I became aware of a crowd of voices murmuring behind me. It was a gang of pilots on holiday, experts all, drawn to the pilot house to witness my brash assault on Hat Island.

"*Seven-and-a—*"

We touched bottom! I instantly set the bells ringing and shouted through the tube, "*Now,* let her have it—every ounce you've got!" and the boat hung upon the apex of disaster for one brief moment, and then lurched free.

"*Quarter-less-twain!*"

The handkerchiefs came out. Brows were mopped. &c.

"We're out of it!" said a grizzled voice behind me, unable to disguise its relief.

"Oh, it was done beautiful," said another. "*Beautiful!*"

"I don't know who he is, but by the Shadow of Death, he's a lightning pilot!"

"*M-a-r-k twain! M-a-r-k twain!*"

"Mark twain," echoed Captain Mutton. "Good. Good." Suddenly he bolted forward and looked closely at me, bending at the waist and cocking his head at all angles, like a bird, as he scrutinized my face. "By George, I've been sold!" he shouted. "There's only one man who could steer a boat like that, *and that man's name is Mark Twain!*"

The other pilots gasped and gaped, then broke spontaneously into song: "*M-a-r-k Twai-ain . . . M-a-r-k Twai-ain,* " making two melodious syllables out of my last name, and wasn't it just lovely!

"Fess up now, sir," said the Captain, beaming and clapping me on the back. "Your incognito is exploded."

I fell to chuckling and cast my eyes down shyly and allowed as maybe he was right, and didn't we all have a gay old time talking about the river, and about how I conquered Hat Island! We sang "Jolly, Jolly Raftsman's the Life for Me," and just as the song was dying and we were about to pass the jug around, the purser peeked his head in the door and said:

"Captain, the swimming pool is full up to mark twain now. You may take a swim whenever you like."

"Yes, thank you, Beasley," said the Captain. "I heard the announcement."

The announcement! Why, all that time I thought I was steering by the soundings of the river, it was just some idiot measuring the swimming pool and calling out its progress as it filled! Lightning pilot your granny. It was blind luck.

Well, the Captain saw that my smile was kind of frozen now, and suddenly *his* smile froze, and he said to me, in the most suspicious, ominous, unpleasant, old-fashioned way, "Hi! . . ."

I believe I shall end this story right here. The remainder is too painful.

The river!

Why don't I want to write about the river as it is now, in 1986? I shall tell you why. I wrote about the river in a series for the *Atlantic,* and called it "Old Times on the Mississippi." That was in 1875, and it was fun. Seven years later, wanting to get a book out of the subject and knowing that my earlier work was not sufficient to fill up a book, I went back to the river and sailed its length again from St. Louis to New Orleans, then back upriver, all the way to St. Paul. I squeezed a heap of words out about that trip, much of it stolen from other books (though credit given), pasted it onto my earlier writing for the *Atlantic,* and called the queer hybrid a book—*Life on the Mississippi.* I loathed writing about the river in 1882, and that loathing is still with me. The river can dry up, for all I care. The reader will search in vain in these pages for masculine prose about the hard life of the bargemen and "river rats," and for flowery descriptions of the scenery—especially *those*. I loathe that old business of working up an atmosphere. I refuse to devote a single word to a single drop of water, or to a single stupid bird winging into flight and flashing its bright colors against a single stupid purple sunset. Why should I, when I don't want to and don't have to? I am not bound by any contract to put these words down on paper. I am not writing for any publisher, or any audience. I am writing for myself—which is to say, I am writing for the audience I always imagine when I write, which I can almost see sitting upon my desk, all around its edges. Diminutive figures they are, irreverent dwarves, with their legs dangling over the edge of the desk and scissoring back and forth in the air, and they alternately applaud and snarl, and I have to please them even if I don't much like them, on account of their rudeness and eagerness to condemn my every pen-stroke. It is just me and my dwarves, this time around, and when I am done with this trip on earth I shall pack up my writing and pack up my dwarves and take them all with me back into the void.

So, you savage, nonexistent reader, don't look for birds and sunsets. "I shall leave it to the reader to imagine the manifold splendors of . . ." That is a phrase that used to get my blood boiling whenever I came across it in a book, especially if the book was one I had hopes of drawing from, by which I mean stealing from it and rehashing the plunder. It's awfully hard to steal and rehash from a description that the author leaves to the reader's imagination. Well, no one will ever steal and rehash from *my* description of the river, not this time around. I shall leave it to the reader to imagine the manifold splendors of that stupid bird winging up and flashing its stupid bright colors stupidly in the stupid purple sunset.

Notes on p. 142.

The Twain Man

How Slowly Did He Speak?
What Famous People Did He Meet?
Was He in Every State of the Union?
What Did His Body Look Like?
Mind If I . . . Tag Along?

These and similar questions have been filling the air around me of late. There is a person on board the *Delta Queen* who is not content with the standard, run-of-the-mill biographies of me; he has attacked my history with his tool box, he has disassembled it, and he now hopes to rebuild it according to a unique plan. But he should speak for himself. Here is a specimen:

"Don't you think there are far too many unaddressed questions in Twain studies? Don't you? Wouldn't it be interesting to explore highly focused questions, following them wherever they may lead us, even if the end point is something we hadn't anticipated—or, if we had, we feared we might lack the courage to face? But isn't such courage the essential armor of the biographer? Do you think it presumptuous of me to believe that the world would not find unwelcome a wholly fresh treatment of Mark Twain, the man? Can you imagine a collection of modest little pieces, each of which treats a small subject, which in its totality is a final summation of Mark Twain, the man? Would you like to see a sample? Are you headed for the Texas Lounge? Mind if I . . . tag along?"

Can you imagine speaking to such a man? Wouldn't you expect his customary mode of expression to contaminate your own? Wouldn't you begin to utter *everything* with a question mark? Wouldn't you soon find yourself bereft of all other modes—the declaration, the command, the exclamation—to the extent that, if you were to see a fire break out in the auditorium, you would call out (humbly, always humbly,) "Shouldn't we flee, lest we burn?"?

He calls himself a "Twain man." Because my literary lectures on board ship favor Mark Twain over other writers who are perhaps equally meritorious (but, on reflection, are perhaps *not*,) he spied me right away as a kindred spirit, albeit a mere cub when it comes to out-and-out dedication to Mark Twain, *the man.* He began to seek me out wherever I might be, always sidling up to me with his unanswerable "Mind if I . . . tag along?" But I didn't like him. It was a simple matter of personal taste— he didn't taste good. I disliked his voice, his ideas, and his aura of being fresh from a bath in salad oil. He was also impenetrably obtuse about how others feel about him. I tried treating him with Christian charity, and succeeded—for twenty seconds. Then I began to treat him with mockery, sometimes gentle, sometimes harsh. Gentle or harsh, it had no effect on him. He could not get enough of me.

I saw samples of his work. He claimed to have published some of it, or to have come close to publishing some of it, "here and there," though where these places may be I don't know. He insisted that I read them, ignoring my repeated statements that my criticism would be irrelevant, that the open marketplace must be the final judge of the worth of his work. But I have formed a sort of opinion about his essays. They are detailed —there is that to be said for them. "How Slowly Did He Speak?" *does* answer the question for all time, drawing from all existing descriptions of my speech, from modern language theory, and from close analyses of contemporary speech rates across the nation. The modern Yankee, for instance, averages . . . I have forgotten, but he averages many words per minute; the average Southerner . . . well, I forgot that one too, but my point is that those are facts—facts you can take home with you and chew on, or they would be, if only I could remember the figures. Contemplating facts like those can be sufficient inducement to get out of bed in the morning, if one needs one, and many people do. So the essays aren't altogether empty.

As evidence of my speech he relates the charming story of Susy and the doll's hat. I've related that story in my autobiography, but it will lift my spirits to relate it again. When Susy was three or four years old, she and I took a walk. This was in Hartford—a lovely day in early spring. She pushed a carriage with two dolls in it, one of which wore a straw hat. The hat repeatedly fell off the doll onto the ground, slowing our progress in a way that was irksome to me, so I said, "You walk ahead. If it falls off, I'll pick it up." A few days later I chanced to hear Susy talking to her nurse. She said, "Can you talk like papa? When my dolly's hat fell off, papa said, 'I-f i-t f-a-l-l-s o-f-f, I--l-l p-i-c-k i-t u-p.' " What a state of affairs!

A three- or four-year-old girl imitating—no, *mocking*—her father's speech! One can only conclude—as my Twain Man does, though lamely, clouding the issue as much as he can—that my speech must have differed greatly from that which Susy was accustomed to hear from her Yankee mother, or from her nurse. The Twain Man also duly notes that my very own dear mother commented on my drawling habits—"Sammy's long talk," she called it. I was just surrounded with ridicule.

Now, I am grateful to the busting-with-questions Twain Man for rendering this anecdote about Susy. I can go on to say that I am *generally* grateful for his profound interest in me. I am touched by it. But how pathetically his enthusiasm misfires!

"What Famous People Did He Meet?" Well, there were loads of them—

MONARCHS—Alexander II, Wilhelm II, Franz Josef, Edward VII, Oscar II (Sweden,) and Queen Elizabeth (Roumania)

AMERICAN PRESIDENTS—Grant, Cleveland, T. Roosevelt, Wilson—before his term, so he had to get along in office without my advice; the same goes for another, F. D. Roosevelt, who was just a cub of 5 years of age when I met him

ENGLISH PRIME MINISTERS—(most of these crossed my path before they took office) Lord Salisbury, Balfour, Campbell-Bannerman, and Churchill

WRITERS AND POETS—Lord! a long list; I do not have my man's list before me, and it had some gaps anyway, so I give it from memory, in the order as they happen to occur to me: Howells, Kipling, Emerson, Longfellow, Holmes, Whittier, Lowell, Aesop—did that wake you up?—John Hay, Bayard Taylor, James Whitcomb Riley, Harte, Oscar Wilde, Cable, "Uncle Remus," (the bashfulest grown person I ever met,) Lewis Carroll, (the second bashfulest,) Harriet Beecher Stowe, Mary Mapes Dodge, C. D. Warner, Henry James, John Bunyan, Robert Browning, Louis Stevenson, H. G. Wells, Trollope, Conan Doyle, G. B. Shaw, Penelope Ashe, Matthew Arnold, George Ade, Lew Wallace, Edmund Gosse, Gorky, Tourgenieff, Bram Stoker, and Sholom Aleichem

DRAMATIC LUMINARIES—Adah Isaacs Menken, John T. Raymond, Sir Henry Irving, Edwin Booth, William Gillette, and Oscar Umlauf

MUSICAL LUMINARIES—Leschetizky, Gabrilowitsch, Schnabel, Dvorak, Paderewski, W. S. Gilbert, and Saint-Saens

MISCELLANEOUS BIG BUGS—Mommsen, William James, Henry Stanley, Darwin, Herbert Spencer, Henry Adams, Rodin, Whistler, Thos. A. Edison, Stanford White, "Gentleman Jim" Corbett, Frederick Douglass, Booker T. Washington, Gandhi, Arthur Orton, Oscar Umlauf, P. T. Barnum, Buffalo Bill, Generals Pope, Sherman, and Sheridan, Brigham Young, H. H. Rogers, John D. Rockefeller, Andrew Carnegie, Horace Greeley, and Helen Keller.

Now, after I pause to catch my breath and let my blush fade, I must ask you, is any of this so surprising? Is it? If these Olympians kept such lists, wouldn't *I* be on *theirs?* Let me cancel that sentence. Let me put it less interrogatively, more forcefully. *They* met *me.* Famous people meet famous people. Could we not say that this is one of the extra benefits of fame? Or is it right to call it "extra"? Couldn't it be that . . . Blast! I am totally infected.

Or take "Was He in Every State of the Union?" The answer is a blunt no. In a flesh-raking preamble devoted to what he calls "methodology," The Twain Man eliminates Arizona, New Mexico, Alaska, and Hawaii, on the grounds that they were not states until after I died, and he agrees to allow himself ("but not without some reservations; but are not reservations the inevitable pebbles in the biographer's shoes?") to count as states those territories I visited, like Nebraska, that became states before I died but which I never actually visited when they *were* states. (If you find these distinctions painful, imagine what they were to The Twain Man; they cost him plenty; you can see the blood and sweat on the very page (My man is also an ass for parentheses; he even uses that dam to fluidity, that blockage of rock-hard constipation—the *re*parenthesis (But I sha'n't let him influence *me.*).).) Having arrived, a shell of his former self, at the body of his text, my man is left with the following states I never visited (where "visit" means "set foot on" or "ride a train through"): Alabama, Georgia, North Carolina, Oklahoma, South Carolina, South Dakota, and Texas. He is not sure about West Virginia. His deliberations over that state cost him ten years of his life, his good temper, and his manhood. He would like to blow West Virginia out of the Union, or reunite it with its mate, which he knows I *did* visit. If you ever see my man in conversation, looking happy (which you won't,) or if you catch him whistling as he strolls along the deck (also unlikely,) just mention West Virginia and watch his face go ashen and listen to him heave up a sigh that sums up centuries of suffering.

I like facts as much as any man. I *love* facts. Though I am afflicted with a leaky memory, give me a juicy fact and I will roll it around on my tongue all day. But this man of mine has his emphasis all wrong. He goes after the fag-ends of biography, the incidental residues, and exalts them into his chief topic.

"What Did His Body Look Like?" Well, the camera came along at a good time, as far as that goes. It's my impression that people don't need much help in this area. (And those titles! He is so smitten by me that he assumes everyone else is as well, so naturally a mere pronoun will do, for whom *else* could he be talking about? Capitalized as they are, those pronouns give me a godly feeling with which I am almost uncomfortable.) In this particular "modest little piece," he tells us I was five feet, eight and a half inches tall, weighing 145 pounds, with a fairly slight build and somewhat sloping shoulders. Hmph. My mouth, he says, was "as delicate as a woman's." *Hmph.* (He got that fact, and that phrase, from Kipling; I know this, because I've read it in Kipling; The Twain Man doesn't *say* he got it from Kipling, though; he is severely in arrears when it comes to paying debts like that.) My fingers, the author continues, were delicate as well. I was just as delicate as can be.

I had no obvious marks upon my body, other than faint scars on one hand from a Keokuk printing press that tried to eat it one day. (After reading this, I got in the habit of concealing this hand in The Twain Man's presence—one can't be too careful.) My hair was auburn, then gray, then pure white. The precise dating of the periods of transition gives my man some trouble; his sailing prose takes on a little water at those points. It absolutely founders on the rocks when it comes to my eyes. Were they gray? Blue? Agate-blue? Gray-blue? Blue-greenish? Or was Clara right when she said they changed color, going from gray (in calm) to pale blue (mild irritation,) then to light sea-green (outrage)? I do not know; I am not in the habit of fetching a mirror when I become irritated or outraged. My man, though, obviously hates my eyes. He would like to pluck them out. They are worse than West Virginia to him.

What was my health like? he asks. Did I ever have quinsy, the heaves, bone-rot, or the itch? What about dropsy, the glanders, erysipelas, and the botts? And you may rest easy, for of *course* he takes up brain fever, St. Vitus's dance, and the blind staggers. His inventory does not stop there. He is a pioneer. He explores corporeal territory where no white man has ventured before: my teeth, my aorta, the inside of my lungs. He lays me out on his examining table, and I am just a bucket of organs by the time he is through with me. He even dives after my private parts, though I can tell it didn't come natural to him. He hints in the most uncharitable way at a certain reluctance of a certain piece of God's handiwork to rise when called to duty, especially late in my life, and he does so simply on the basis of some idiotcy I dashed off without thinking about it in *Letters from the Earth.* If my man has a wife I must track her down and put some questions to her. I must do publicly for his member what he aims to do for mine, if he ever finds a publisher.

"Mind if I . . . tag along?" Two days ago, I was standing on the deck, a foot placed on a chair, elbow resting on knee, chin nestled in palm, fingers curling around my pipe bowl, for warmth, when he sidled up to me and oozed this greeting. Being the very picture of tranquil immobility, I could not imagine what he meant. I nodded assent, and immediately felt obliged to hump myself into motion, so that I might be literally faithful to his request.

"May I?" he said, reaching into his coat pocket. I nodded again, assuming he was reaching for a cigar or cigarette—though I had never seen him smoke. He pulled out a sheaf of manuscript.

My eyes turned blue.

"A little something I've been polishing?"

My eyes turned light sea-green. I wished I was back in West Virginia, making some famous person's acquaintance.

"What do you think of this topic?" says he. " 'How Much Time Did He Spend on the Water?' "

My teeth clenched around the bit of my pipe. "I'd go for something along a different line," I said. "When he was out west, they said he'd fill a drunkard's grave. I'd address that subject, only with a clever, indirect title. I'd call it 'How Much Time Did He Spend *Making* Water?' "

His face went through several contortions. "Isn't that a little . . . irreverent?"

"An irreverent man deserves an irreverent treatment."

He laughed his version of a hearty laugh and glanced around. What was he looking for? As I saw an expression of mild disappointment cross his face, I suddenly knew. He was searching for witnesses to our comradeship. It occurred to me that I had never seen him in the company of any passengers but me. I alone had allowed him to . . . tag along, and I had comforted myself in the task with cruel mockery. The heart is a changeable organ, and mine began to waver. Our bond—which I was prepared to sever at any moment with a cut that went just too deep—was perhaps the closest this wretch had ever come to true friendship. *This* was his idea of affection, of people joining together! It was pathetic. I had treated him just about as low-down as I could have. I wanted to weep. I wanted to embrace him and declare, "People oughtn't treat each other so." I did not go this far. I *did* ask him, however, with heart-felt enthusiasm, if I might read his new essay. He blushed, stiffened, threw his gaze down to his feet, and handed the manuscript to me with a quick, awkward forward thrust of his arm. I hurried off to my cabin.

It is amazing what reform can do to a person. In the light of my new sentiments, his style was altogether transformed. What had been vapid, flat, shopworn dullness now appeared as manly directness. His punctuation, which I had formerly cursed for its distracting wrongness, now charmed me with its originality. His stale metaphors I saw as new wine in new bottles; his dementedly mixed metaphors I delighted in as altogether happy conjunctions. And the subject! It was endlessly enchanting. I turned the last page of the manuscript thirsting for more.

I jotted down a few notes on a separate sheet of paper and made some quick calculations. Then I dashed out in search of him. He was where I had left him—hadn't moved an inch. He threw me a look of abject terror, which is the look he always threw me when he awaited judgment of his work.

"It's pure garbage, isn't it?" he said.

"What?" said I.

"It's a crime, isn't it? I should be drawn and quartered, shouldn't I?"

"What are you going on about? It's a block-buster! It's a fascinating statement about Mark Twain, casting a fresh light on his relentless traveling! It's just prime!"

His face—well, it looked like an envelope without any address on it. He backed away from me a step. "Do you really think so?"

"It's a pure delight from beginning to end," I said, edging in close to him. "I made a few notes—paltry little things, just a couple of additional points you might want to consider. Mind, I'm not saying the piece isn't finished and damned near perfect as it stands, but there are a few small items I'd like to bring to your attention. If I may, that is." Seeing no resistance—seeing only nervous agitation—I said, "Now you've got a figure here for the total days in his life: 27,153. That's fine. And you've divided that into, let's see, 2,133 days on water—I take it your only requirement is that he spent at least *part* of a day on water for a day to count as a water day?"

"Don't you think that was sound? Should I change it?"

"Oh, no. By no means. So—2,133 days spent entirely or in part on the water. You've excluded swimming, I trust?"

"Isn't '*on* the water' self-explanatory, as opposed to '*in* the water'? Should I make that clearer?"

"No, no. It's quite clear. Now, thus divided, you get a rounded-off figure of 7.9% of his days on earth spent on water. You've got his four years as a river pilot. Good. You've got his Sandwich Islands tour. Fine.

You've got his twenty-seven Atlantic crossings. Good, good. You've got his around-the-world tour of 1895–96. Excellent. And his several trips to Bermuda. Good thinking. Now, have you included his 1891 boat trip down the Rhone?"

He gasped.

"I thought not. No problem there. We haven't gone to press yet. It was a ten-day trip, so we can add ten to your 2,133, for 2,143. Now, how about little ferry trips in California—say, across the Stanislaus, or on San Francisco Bay?"

He shook his head—sadly.

"Well, let's throw in, oh, twenty-five for the lot, giving us 2,168. Now, if we divide that . . ." I hunched over the railing and made the calculation, working at fever-pitch. "Blast! Still just 7.9%. Not enough to bump it up to eight. I'll work on it some more. You've got me fired up over this. May I keep your manuscript, for reference?"

"Do you really think it's worth all the trouble?" he asked, the epitome of humbleness and lust for failure.

"Of course! Of course!" I clapped him on the shoulder,—he recoiled a bit—and hurried off in search of more days on the water.

Later that afternoon I spied him in a deck chair. When I walked up close to him I saw that he was asleep, but it was a fitful sleep, with much twitching of the muscles and tossing of the head. I leaned down close to him.

"Mono Lake?" I whispered into his ear.

His eyes snapped open. He looked wildly at me.

"Lake Tahoe?"

Understanding dawned on him. He pressed his lips together and gave a curt shake of the head.

"Sailing up the Ganges?"

His Adam's apple began to roam up and down his throat.

"Add a day for each of the first two," I said, "and two days for the third. That gives us 2,172. One more day and we'll clear eight percent." I hurried off to do some more remembering.

The next day I caught sight of him in the gift shop. He was sullenly browsing along, picking up one item and studying it without affection, then moving on to another. His lack of good cheer confounded me. I sidled up to him and said:

"Yachting with Rogers?"

He froze as if I had stuck the point of a knife into his ribs. He turned around and faced me with a haunted look.

"I didn't *think* you'd counted it. I cyphered it out. About fifty-five days altogether. That brings the figure up to 8.2%. But we ain't finished —oh, no." I scuttled off.

That evening, as I entered the dining room, I spied him just settling into a chair at a table, an empty chair beside him. I began to make my way toward him. He looked up in my direction and bolted, almost knocking his chair over as he fled out a rear door. I took the other chair at the table, expecting him to return. The conversation among the others seated with me was entertaining enough, and I took part, but my heart wasn't in it. I found myself pining for my man's society. I excused myself before dessert and went out in search of him. He was on the deck, gazing forlornly upon the dark water.

"Mind if I . . ." I caught myself.

He turned to me. A soft whimper escaped his lips.

"His boyhood on the river," I said, "excluding his youngest years, of course—on a raft, a skiff, a canoe, floating over to Glasscock's Island, or down to the cave. He was nuts for the river. There's also the time he stowed away on a steamboat, though he didn't get very far, and then a trip he took with his father and brother. Just throw all that in together, and kind of average it out. Let's say ten years times fifty days per annum, and what do we have? Five hundred more days on the water! Think of it! And just a short while ago we were satisfied with increases of a paltry few days. Five hundred! Oh, I know what you're thinking. You're worrying about the summers he spent inland, on his uncle's farm. Well, you can put your mind at ease, my friend. Salt River! Remember? Right nearby, and of *course* he was on it. You couldn't keep him away from water with a shotgun. Now, hold on to your socks, because I've an announcement to make. The percentage now comes to 10.04! We've topped 10 percent! Why, there's no end to it. If we dig, and dig, and keep on digging, why, we might even top eleven! Yes, that's it—I shan't be happy until we've topped eleven."

I left him there to contemplate his good fortune. I retired to my cabin to smoke and think, settling atop my bed. By and by, something about his figures began to bother me. I looked at his essay again. I pulled a notebook out and did some calculating.

A knock at the door.

"Come in," I called.

He was a changed man. A wild, murderous gleam in his eye momentarily froze me to my bed. Breathing heavily, and with difficulty, he stalked forward and seized his manuscript out of my hands, along with my jottings. I was speechless—but not for long. I was too full of my discoveries. With a hint of rebuke, I said:

"You didn't deduct any days from his four years as a pilot—a horrible blunder. What were you thinking—that he piloted without a break for four years? No—the evidence shows that the average length of a round-trip tour between St. Louis and New Orleans was twenty-five days, with six of these days devoted to loading and discharging cargo. We must cut down his 'on-the-water' time in those four years by six-twenty-fifths. I've worked it all out. The figures are there in your hands.

"Another thing—your number for his total days on earth is wrong. You neglected taking into account the fact that he lived through eighteen leap years. I know what you're going to say—you're going to say he lived through *nineteen* leap years. I can see you were mentally cyphering it out and were coming up with nineteen. But look to your modified Gregorian calendar, my good man. Leap years are those divisible by four, except centesimal years, which are ordinary years unless divisible by 400, which 1900 isn't. So we must add eighteen days to his life total, which further reduces the percentage of days on water. I hate to do this, and I can tell by looking at you that you hate to do it too, but we must ask ourselves if we want to do this thing right or not. These two changes combine to crush the figure down to 8.7%. It's a cruel blow, I know, but you yourself have written eloquently about the biographer needing thick armor, and having pebbles in his shoes, and—"

The door slammed. He was gone.

When I began writing this piece, I said that The Twain Man was on board. I have just learned otherwise. This morning, he asked to be put ashore. I shall probably never see him again. It depresses me that he didn't think to say good-bye.

I ask you—how do you figure a man like that? I had genuinely warmed to him, and look at how he rebuffed me. He was an odd one, take him all around. But I still feel a certain fondness for him. I have obtained his address from the purser. When I disembark and am finished with *this* "on-the-water" experience, I shall send him a reckoning that is right up to date. I am sure he will appreciate it.

Notes on p. 143.

A Glimpse: I

Milton Tibbett sighed mournfully, squirmed into a less uncomfortable position on the cold wooden bench, and began to fuss with the gears of his new Sashimi Kamikaze X-208/Y-49/f-1.2 camera. He swore softly. He swore because he hated his camera. He swore *softly* because his sister or aunt or aunt's female friend or aunt's female friend's niece might suddenly burst from the crowd of tourists in the Becky Thatcher Book Shop and overhear him. He had driven them all down from Keokuk for a tour of "Mark Twain Country," and weren't they a pathetic little group, though. All the way down, his sister had shot belittling sarcasms at him about the photos he used to take with his old Kodak, a plastic thing with a little bar that flew up into the viewer when there wasn't enough light, which is to say, whenever he wanted to shoot anything but sun spots—or so it seemed to him. It also had a red vinyl case that wrapped around it, with a long, snapping flap that you had to remember to hold out of the way or it would show up in your pictures, leering at you like an obscene tongue sticking out at the bottom. The worst of it was you couldn't tell if the flap was in the way when you snapped the picture, because you weren't really looking through the lens when you snapped. God knows what you *were* looking through. It was all a dirty trick. What gay times they had had looking at the slide-pictures after their Vancouver trip. "Yes," said his sister, "and here's a *particularly* nice shot Milton took of the Canadian flag on the bow of our ferry boat, with a seagull perched atop the flagpole, and some kind of red sea monster emerging from below. Well done, Milton."

She had chucklingly told this story in the car, to their aunt (a bitch,) their aunt's friend (slowest-moving behemoth in the Middle West,) and their aunt's friend's niece (a bored teen-aged girl who sat in the front seat in rebellious silence and who Milton had decided, with pleasure, was suicidal,) going on to say, with false good cheer, "Well, at least your new camera doesn't have one of those *flaps*, Milton."

"That's right, Evangeline," Milton had weakly replied, taking a corner of the river road at a speed calculated to throw the three occupants crunchingly to one side. "No flap," he had said. "But I *do* have a flap of another sort," he added to himself. "I keep it in the glove compartment for people like you, Evangeline. If you'll just bend your head forward I'll be happy to . . . muzzle, you say? Oh, I wouldn't call it a muzzle, really. That's an awful nasty word—muzzle. I wouldn't like to call it a muzzle."

The pity of it was there was no one to share his wit with. His best jokes were always of this sort. They just rattled around in his head. But some day . . .

He finally managed to latch the perforation in the film onto the sprockets of the baby gears inside, while a single drop of sweat rolled under his spectacles and off the end of his nose somewhere into the bowels of the camera. He suspected this couldn't be too good for it and closed the back of the camera fast, lest anything else go wrong. He shuddered with the sudden thought that the film might not be truly engaged on the little gear. With mocking superiority, his instruction booklet had warned him against such a blunder, for then one's cocking of the camera had no effect at all, and one could ignorantly shoot one picture after another of mere air.

"Oh, yes," he could hear her saying. "You *must* see Milton's pictures of our Hannibal trip. They delightfully leave *so* much to the imagination."

"Yeah?" he'd say. "Oh, yeah? Well imagine this!" *Pow!*

He staggered to his feet, almost dropping the camera in the mistaken belief that the strap was around his neck. Then he angrily shoved the strap over his head, catching the edge of his spectacles in the process and shoving the frame painfully against the bridge of his nose. He studied the numbers atop the camera as he moved slowly down the sidewalk, bumping into hordes of loud tourists, wondering if the camera was on "automatic" or "over-ride" and, if the latter, just what he was over-riding. Milton wasn't accustomed to over-riding things, and the notion filled him with momentary terror. Oh, what a fool he had been to "make the move to SLR."

He wanted to get a picture of the house, if only that passel of screaming schoolbrats would get out of the way. Wait—here came their teacher, a dashing, tanned, blond-headed son of a bitch they all probably loved. "Kids love school too damned much these days," Milton muttered to himself. "Something wrong in that." There—they were going into the museum. Now—no, here came some more imbeciles, adults this time, lingering in front of the building as if they were the only ones in town. "*Hey,*" Milton wanted to shout, "I don't know you. I don't want your dumb faces in my living room." He gritted his teeth, then cleared his throat in a loud, annoyed whine. One of them heard this, looked up at him, and hurriedly pulled the group out of the way. Milton, seeing what he had wrought, blushed with fear of reprisal and nervously raised his camera, partly to take the picture, and partly so that he could hide. He groped for the shutter button. There it was—no bigger than a pin-head, designed for a Japanese midget's finger. He squeezed slowly, slowly, then faster, lest some other pedestrian intrude, and, sure enough—wasn't it his god-damned luck? Wasn't that the dreadful story of his rotten life? Just before the shutter snapped, some bastard suddenly appeared, slouching as if he owned the place, right in front of the door.

Milton looked up from the camera at the man, who seemed to have popped into his view-finder out of nowhere. Bushy white hair and mus-tache. White suit with vest and black bow-tie. Slight list to the east, toward the river, with a bow in the legs. A defiant look, then a half-smile in Milton's direction. Milton gasped and raised the camera again, but this time there was only the house.

"By *God!*" he exclaimed. In a daze, he cocked and snapped, cocked and snapped. He wanted plenty of plain house shots to stuff down Evangeline's throat. But that first one he'd got—that was *his* secret. By *God!* There was magic in the air.

Notes on p. 145.

A Glimpse: II

Nobody knows how to tell a story.

Aha! thought Jimmy. An *idea*. It was the first he'd had in three months. There was hope yet for him—hope that this blasted period he had set aside for having "experiences" wouldn't be a total waste. Why, that idea could be the heart of a short story. It would feature Skaggs, his foreman, whose narrative incompetence had inspired the idea and who was presently off befouling the woods while Jimmy dragged his empty trash bag around the historic cabin in search of bottles, cans, and . . . Historic cabin—of course! It was no wonder he had had such an idea, on this spot, hallowed by the residence of that greatest storyteller of all time —Jim Gillis. Why, if it hadn't been for the yarns Jim Gillis spun around the fire, Mark Twain would have spent the rest of his days pocket mining in his own little corner of obscurity.

Skaggs would be the central character of his story. Jimmy felt good. He *always* felt good when he had hit upon a central character, because he thought a good story needed one, even though he had never put this notion to the ultimate test by actually writing a story down. Now, in his story, Skaggs would bore everyone he spoke to. People would fall asleep on their feet. People would drop dead. Once dead, they would decay more rapidly than neighboring corpses—still under the lingering influence of that boredom. It would be a killingly funny tale.

And so true to life! Skaggs certainly had the material to be a story-teller. He was a veteran of Korea, and had lived a varied life of odd jobs and travel before settling down with the California State Parks system, but he lacked the *art*. He made ghastly blunders—he would announce he was going to tell a story before telling it, he would make apologies for his tale right in the middle of it, he would put his snappers in the wrong place or forget them altogether, or until two days later, and he had absolutely no sense of the all-important pause. It was a hellish torture riding around the foothills with him.

Skaggs had experience, but he lacked brains. Jimmy had brains, but he lacked experience. It often struck him that his brains were supposed to protect him from bad experiences, but those were the only good kind for a writer to have. How he loathed that skein of cruel contradiction. So what had he done? He had given up good friends and a decent job as a librarian in San Francisco and moved back in to live with his father in Angels and deliberately chosen pain, just to see what would happen. Pain, pain, pain—he had plenty of it. The painful boredom of eight-hour days with Skaggs, and the brand-new, unexplained pain in his cod, which he could feel right now, right now! He had told Skaggs about it, on an impulse, just because he was so lonely and had nobody else to talk to, and of course Skaggs had roared and joked and warned him about the women in the local saloons, in response to which Jimmy had grinned with the air of a man of the world, even though his pain could not *possibly* have the explanation Skaggs gave for it. And of course Skaggs had gone on to tell him some mangled stories about his own Army adventures, which (he told Jimmy) he had always carefully backed up with a dose of penicillin, which he urged upon Jimmy with warnings viciously calculated to keep him awake at night, unable to think of anything but his persistent pain and his certain doom to the Stockton Insane Asylum.

Yes, he would have to get Skaggs down on paper. But then couldn't Skaggs sue him if he did? No, not if he didn't know about it. But—another damned contradiction!—how could Skaggs *not* know about it if the story (though yet unwritten) were as popular as Jimmy knew it would be, to wit: *adored by every living American.* Jimmy decided he would have to throw in some flattering hogwash about Skaggs, to appease him. As he bent down for an empty beer can he tried to think of some. He could feel his new story dying even as it was aborning, all because Skaggs was thoroughly bad. His exuberant feeling of inspiration was gone, blown away into nothingness. Hallowed ground your granny. Tell it to the marines.

Jimmy stopped abruptly as he rounded a corner of the cabin. An old man stood there, wiping his face with a towel and squinting into a small mirror wedged in the crotch of an oak tree. He wore a blue woolen shirt, and his pants were sloppily crammed into his boot-tops. What now? Jimmy thought. Some deadbeat who had taken up residence in the cabin? He would have to shoo him off, politely, before Skaggs showed up. Skaggs would enjoy doing it too much.

"Good morning," Jimmy called out.

The man turned around. He wasn't quite as old as Jimmy had first thought. The whiteness of his hair had fooled him. The man squinted at Jimmy, then reached down to the ground for his pan of lather-filled water. As he cocked it back to throw its contents across the ground, he snarled:

"I don't see no p'ints about this mornin' that's better 'n any other mornin'."

Then he vanished, pan and all. Nothing was left but an arc of lather and water curving through the air and plunging to the ground.

When Skaggs walked up, grunting with organic satisfaction, Jimmy was studying the puddle and trying to catch his breath. Skaggs belched, scratched himself, stepped up to where Jimmy stood, and looked down.

"No urinatin' on the premises, Jimmy boy," he said with a chuckle. Then, catching sight of the shaving lather mixed in with the water, he gasped and said, "Boy, you *got* to get your urine checked."

Notes on p. 145.

St. Peter Helps Me Feel Good About Myself

A curious thing happened to me in the middle of a long letter I was writing. I got waylaid. I got abducted.

I was sitting at my desk, churning out the words, when two burly fellows stormed into my motel room without so much as a by-your-leave. I recognized them right off: hench-angels, sent down by St. Peter, and a rough-looking pair they were, too. They seized me and dragged me, kicking and screaming all the way, to that court of last resort. I had been there before, but my memories of it were dim, and so when I saw the judge's bench and the slide to the left of it, I had only a vague, ungraspable feeling of familiarity with the place.

I must tell you about the slide. It was a long, spiraling device, such as you will find in a playground, only this one didn't taper off gradually, with regard for youthful backsides. It plunged straight into the floor, though I couldn't see the actual end of it, on account of the fog or mist that swirled about the place from knee-level down.

I had to wait my turn. Peter, seated high up on the bench, was listening to some fool of an inventor describe the thousand working parts of some machine of his; the fellow was going on about how despite repeated break-downs, especially at critical moments when prospective investors had been invited for a show, he was optimistic,—unstintingly optimistic—that one day, one day *soon*, that machine would function perfectly, and how he did go on and on. Peter listened, his eyelids drooping at times and then snapping back up. Now and then he would dip his fingers into a bowl he kept handy, and sprinkle a little liquid on his face. At first I took it for a species of holy water, but by and by I decided it was regular water, and he did that to keep awake.

Finally, Peter interrupted the gentleman, who was beginning to sound uncannily familiar to me, and he made a little sputtering or spitting noise with his mouth, so quiet you could barely hear it. It must have been some kind of signal, for the two hench-angels—bailiffs, I should say—

swooped in and carted the inventor over to the slide and up the stairs to the top of it. All the way up the stairs, this fellow, who I now saw with astonishment was none other than Paige, studied the structure of that slide, and bent down and felt the metal stairs, and wondered aloud if his machine could benefit from that particular alloy, only he never finished his sentence, because the bailiffs gave him a shove, and he let out a couple whoops—which I could hear quite clearly, when the spiral of the slide brought him around into view—and then he was gone, with no trace of him other than a little turbulence in the fog at the bottom of the slide. Damned. No doubt about it. I had damned him, myself, many years before, and I took a little pride in getting the bulge on a saint in the judgment.

Peter said to the bailiffs, "His tongue's hung in the middle, ain't it?" and they had a good chuckle over that. Then he spied me. His face seemed to brighten and he said, "Come on up closer so I can have a good look at you."

I approached the bench. Peter picked up a thick pair of spectacles and began to shuffle through some papers, pausing to read something now and then, and occasionally frowning. Finally, he sighed and looked at me over his spectacles, which sat low on his nose. He said:

"This business of the drunkard in the Hannibal jail—the one you gave the matches to. Let's attend to that first."

I had been afraid something like this would happen. Peter was going to review my past and come to some sort of judgment about me. I could see it was going to be a long, tough morning. And if his verdict proved to be what I *thought* it could be, I was in for a long, spiraling slide to . . . As I thought about it, that slide suddenly seemed more familiar to me than before. Had I been on it? But where had I landed?

"Well?" said Peter.

I fidgeted. "I'm not sure what to say, sir. He was a harmless, pathetic fellow—the drunkard was—and one chilly evening he was wandering around asking for a match, and I took pity on him and gave him some. Later that night he was arrested, and he accidentally burned down the jailhouse and perished in the fire."

"It's nothing. Forget it."

I looked at Peter, wondering if I had heard him correctly.

"Forget it. You meant well."

"But—"

"Forget it."

I forgot it. His words seemed to *make* me forget it. I still remembered all the details, but in a way that brought no remorse. Pity, yes—remorse, no. It was a thrillingly cleansing experience.

"Now," said Peter, "I reckon we should take up the question of Henry next."

I shifted my feet nervously. "Henry . . . Clemens?"

Peter kind of snorted through his nose. "I sure don't mean Henry the Eighth." He suddenly looked to the rear of the room. "Just a moment," he said to me; then, calling out more loudly, "What have you got there, Gabriel?"

I turned around. Corraled into a small herd by a third bailiff I hadn't noticed was the sorriest collection of humanity I had ever seen. They were all yoked together by ropes tied about their waists. The bailiff—Gabriel —read their names out from a sheet of paper:

"Charles H. Webb, Elisha Bliss, James R. Osgood, Charles L. Webster, Fred J. Hall, Frederick A. Duneka."

"Oh," said Peter. "Publishers' Row, eh? Good. This is real handy, them arriving in bulk like this. Line 'em all up, boys, and give 'em a ride together, toboggan-style, right into the void."

The two burly bailiffs walked to the rear and hustled the crowd over to the slide and up the steps. They went uncomplainingly—all but Bliss. He caught sight of me when he was mounting the steps and called out my name, imploringly, and he took handfuls of bills out of his coat pockets and waved them in the air, indicating the money would be mine if only I would put in a word for him. I remained silent. The money was probably mine to begin with; more of it ended up in *his* pocket than in mine. With cold pleasure I watched the tribe coast down into the foggy floor.

"Good," said Peter. "Now. Henry."

"Well, sir, Henry was my younger brother, and he was awfully good. He was just as good as—"

"I know, I know," Peter said wearily. "He was as good as pie. He was exasperatingly good. But what's this flapdoodle about his death?"

"Well, it was in 1858, May or June of 1858, when I was an apprentice pilot. Mr. Bixby had lent me to Mr. Brown, and I was steering for him on the *Pennsylvania*, a boat on which Henry served as 'mud' clerk. Brown and I got into a fight, and—"

"What was the fight about?"

"It was about his cruel mistreatment of Henry."

"Duly noted. Please go on."

"Well, on account of that fight, when the *Pennsylvania* reached New Orleans, Mr. Brown threw me off the boat and insisted I stay off. So when the boat went back upriver three days later, Henry was on it but I was not. I was on another boat,—I forget which—just a few days behind him. Just below Memphis, the *Pennsylvania*'s boilers exploded. Henry was badly scalded, and inhaled steam, and he lingered in awful pain for many days, and he *appeared* to be about to recover, but a young doctor gave him too much morphine, and he died." I paused. Peter seemed to be waiting for more. I knew what it was. I sighed and lurched on with my tale:

"I was there at the end, with Henry. The chief physician, before leaving for the night, had instructed me to ask for an eighth of a grain of morphine, and when the time to administer it came, the young doctor in charge protested that he had no way of measuring it, but I urged him to *try,* for Henry's sake, because he was suffering so! And so he measured it in the old-fashioned way, on a knife blade, but it was too much, and . . . and so I killed him."

Peter did a strange thing. He grinned. "Henry was the original for Sid, Tom Sawyer's prissy brother, wasn't he? And you were Tom, the mischief-maker?"

"Yes, but—"

"Wasn't Henry the one who pointed out to your mother that the thread she'd sewn your collar together with, to keep you from going in swimming, had changed color by the end of the day?"

"Yes, but—"

"Now, considering that your mother played favorites—"

"That's a lie! She was the dearest, sweetest—"

"—it should come as no surprise to you to learn that somewhere in your heart, you harbored murderous impulses toward Henry—"

"That is the sheerest nonsense, the most out-and-out—"

"—which led you not to kill him, but to believe you had, on account of your bizarre, but basically guiltless, connection with his death. My advice to you is to forget it, forget it, forget it."

I forgot it. That Peter—he had a way with words, all right. He didn't just make a suggestion in the conventional way. He *performed* the suggestion.

"We're going to leap ahead now," said Peter, "to June the second, 1872."

"I'd rather not."

"Your son—your only son—Langdon. Tell me about it."

"Why should I? You seem to know all there is to know about me already."

"Hold on a minute." Peter looked to the rear of the courtroom again. "What is it?"

Gabriel called out, "Bret Harte, drunk—as usual."

I turned around with considerable interest. There he was, as foppish and dandified as ever, filling the room with the smell of liquor. On each arm he sported a giggling, painted tart.

"The void?" asked Gabriel.

"You bet," said Peter. "Give 'em a ride." And over to the slide and up and down they went. I liked Peter. I liked his *judgment.* I said to him, hoping for a laugh—

"I reckon Harte didn't have The Luck with him this time." Peter contained his amusement remarkably well. He said:

"Tell me how Langdon died."

"Well, I killed him."

"Oh, I'll *bet* you did."

"I *did.* He was a weak, sickly boy, and I took him out for a drive one day—he was twenty-two months old—and I fell into a reverie and neglected the boy. The blankets fell off him, and by the time the coachman discovered it and pointed it out to me, Langdon was frozen to death."

"You're saying he died right there? In the carriage?"

"Well, not exactly. It was a few days later. Maybe several days later."

"And are you saying he died of pneumonia?"

"Not exactly. More like diphtheria."

"More like? It *was* diphtheria, wasn't it? And you don't catch diphtheria because your blankets fall off, even if your father *is* a daydreaming muggins. You should read *Mr. Clemens and Mark Twain,* Sam. It's a book made by a man named Justin Kaplan. He calls you 'a lifelong guilt-seeker.'"

"He does? Why, I'll have his hide for that. What gave him the right to call me that?"

"*You* did. You gave him the evidence, anyway. *You* didn't kill Langdon. Diphtheria did."

"Why did I *think* I did, then? Are you going to say I wanted *him* to die, too?"

"Well, Livy almost died giving birth to him, and she almost died with continual worry over him, and it wouldn't surprise me if you saw him as a threat to her, and—"

"Oh, to perdition with your theories. You're a pompous, all-knowing ass."

"I don't want to argue with you, Sam," he said in a disarmingly pleasant way. Then he suddenly laughed. "I don't have to, either. Forget it, forget it, forget it."

A fresh wind blew over me. "I like you, Peter," I said. "I like what you do for me. Do it some more, won't you?"

"I can't."

"You can't? Why not?"

"I've done three already. That's all I can do, by way of illustration. The rest are up to you—according to my calculations, three hundred and thirty of them."

"Three hundred and thirty of *what?*"

"Sins of the past that ruin your present."

I swallowed hard; the number seemed improbably large; and yet, as I thought about it . . .

"You're on your own now, Sam. I've shown you how easy it is. I call it 'aggressive forgetting.' You call up the blunders of the past, give them a fresh, hard look, and forget them forever."

"Forget them? Just like that? It's impossible."

"Why, *I* did it, Sam. If I can do it, anybody can."

"But you're a saint. You've got some kind of power working for you."

"No, no. You don't understand. I did it for my *own* sins, and long before I died. I did it when I was just a bumbling mortal. And if *I* can do it—"

Some voices from the rear of the room drifted toward us. Peter looked up in annoyance and said:

"Gabriel, put a hold on those candidates. Close the door and tell 'em to cool their heels in the waiting room. I've got something important to do here." He looked back to me. "You know me, Sam. Why, I was the Tom Sawyer of the apostles—brash, impulsive, a backslider, a hooky player, and, more often than not, a muggins. There I am, in the gospels, for all to read, trying to walk on the water and then getting chicken-hearted, and Jesus having to pluck me out with a rebuke that made my ears burn. There I am, asking Jesus to explain a parable and getting snapped at again for being such a punkinhead. And there I am *again*, trying to get on His good side, trying to cheer Him up when He was forecasting His crucifixion; says I, 'No, Lord, this isn't going to happen to You.' Know what He said? It wasn't too flattering. He said, 'Get thee behind me, Satan.' Well, when the Lord says something like that to you, it takes the sand right out of you. Try it some time, if you don't believe me.

"Then I tackled it again. I couldn't do without His respect. I tried to get it back by asking Him how many times I should forgive a man who had sinned against me. 'Seven times?' says I—you see, I wanted to show

Him how generous-hearted I could be, because I knew He was just nuts for forgiveness. Well, He never let up; there just wasn't an ounce of give to Him. He said, 'Seven? Hmph. More like *seventy times* seven.' So I came away a loser again. Even worse, the other apostles were down on me for a long time after that. They'd heard it, you see, and they'd been struggling with this notion of forgiveness too, and here I'd gone and provoked the Lord into giving us a rule *no*body could live up to. Seventy times seven —it was too many for them.

"The last days were the worst. It was one blunder after another. Jesus took me up to Gethsemane, and He was awful blue. He asked me to be with Him—you know, for support, as you may say. 'Sure, Lord,' says I. 'You can count on me. I'm Your man.' What'd I do? I fell asleep. When He saw me laid out He woke me up and gave me a real dusting off, but my hide was pretty hard by then, and I just fell back asleep. To read about that now, you wonder how He ever put up with me.

"When they came for Him I sprang into action and smote off an ear that belonged to one of the high priest's servants. That was just my way —sleeping on the job one minute, and then inflamed with a brand-new, red-hot enterprise the next. There's a little something I should mention here. Luke, when he wrote about this incident, got the notion that Jesus put that servant's ear back on. That's a stretcher. Think about it. If Jesus had done that, don't you think the priests and others who came to arrest Him would have had second thoughts about it? Of *course* they would have.

"Well, you're probably thinking that relieving that fellow of his ear wasn't an example of brilliant military strategy. Jesus wasn't too pleased with it Himself. He gave me that tired look of His, that I was used to by now, and He snapped at me again, saying His cup had been given to Him and He'd just have to drink from it, which I was able to understand, for all of my dim-wittedness when it came to parables, and I sheathed my sword. The priests fell into an easy chuckling and elbowing of one another over Jesus' rebuke of me, as if to say, 'Oh, *this* religion'll go far all right, with disciples like this fellow. Oh, you bet.'

"You know what happened next. All four of the gospelers wrote about it—not a one let me off; and I can just see them sighing and shaking their heads and muttering with disappointment over their pens. You know the story. After Jesus was arrested, I hung around the palace, warming myself by a fire, just biding my time and kind of keeping to myself, you know, and up comes this woman and says, 'Hi! You were with Jesus of Galilee.' It kind of threw me, and before I knew what I was doing, I denied it. Then another woman comes up and says the same thing. There was a big crowd of rubber-necks showing interest by then, and I got hot and ripped out something brisk and denied it again. Well, they left me alone for a while, but there was this bummer who'd had his eye on me the whole time, and he was studying me, and studying me, and finally *he* comes up and says, real loud, 'Of *course* you were with Jesus. I can tell by the way you talk. You're a Galilean through and through.' Well, what I said then laid over any swearing that ever I'd done before, and I denied it again—three times, you see, just as Jesus'd foreseen I would, and, sure enough, I don't know where he came from or what he was doing there, but a rooster that'd been laying for me commenced to crow his head off, just throwing my betrayal back into my face and calling everybody's attention to it, in case they hadn't noticed, which wasn't likely, since it seemed to me that every deadbeat in the Holy Land was on hand to watch me squirm.

"Now, I ask you, have you ever heard of such out-and-out gumption-lessness? If you have, I want to know about it. You can bet I was pretty low after that. Matthew and the rest say I 'went out, and wept bitterly.' That's true, as far as it goes, but none of them followed up on my story the way they should have. Instead, they all start talking about Judas, and how he hanged himself. The truth is—Judas stole my rope to do it with; stole the rope, and *the idea.* I was on my way up this hill, my eye fixed on a redbud tree and a coil of rope slung over my shoulder, when up comes Judas, all in a sweat, and he knocks me down and takes my rope from me. When I come to my senses, I look up, and there he is, swinging in the breeze, with a real unhealthy look to his face and his tongue sticking out in a way you couldn't really call natural. One look at him and, says I, 'On reflection, I do not wish any of the pie.'

"But for days after that—depressed? That's not a strong enough word for it. All I could think about was how I had been with Jesus every day, and seen Him perform miracle after miracle, and seen His love,—a love so perfect it just had to be divine—and then, in the end, I had let Him down. I felt as if *I* had crucified Him. That's right. I thought *I* had killed Him. But I got over it. You see, I got to thinking about the way Jesus'd said I would deny Him. He didn't say it in a mean way, or with any kind of bitterness. He didn't snap it at me either, for a change. He said it just as calm as you please. I think I know why. He was saying, 'Peter, you're human; that means that you're a blunderer; here's an example—you're going to deny me; that's just the way people are.'

"Well, thinking along those lines cheered me up considerable. By and by I stopped kicking myself. I even began to feel *good* about myself. I went on to have a real gaudy career—got published in the Bible, got canonized, and got put in charge of the keys to the gates here. Why, Jesus even went and built His church on me, 'the rock'—it's the only joke He ever told, really, and He'd been so sober, all along, that it caught us all by surprise, and it didn't occur to us to laugh, but looking back on it, I think it's a prime pun. Now, doesn't that tell you something, Sam? Of all the apostles, He singled out the blunderingest as the cornerstone of His church."

I nodded. I had been attending to Peter's tale very, very closely. I found it immeasurably comforting. I felt myself swelling up. I, too, began to "feel good about myself." I had heard someone on the radio use that phrase earlier in the day—a lady who answered the phone on the radio and made everybody who telephoned her feel awfully good about themselves. To my Presbyterian ears, the words sounded strange, even comical. But the more I listened to her talk, the more I wanted her to do that for me. And now here Peter had gone and done it even better than she could have—besides which, he had considerably more authority.

"Aggressive forgetting, Sam," said Peter. "That's the ticket. Utter self-complacency—that's the spiritual state to aim for. You didn't quite get there in your first life. Now and then you *approached* it, though. Do you remember those Kodaks that Paine took of you on the porch in New Hampshire?"

"Yes, I do."

"And the captions you wrote on them? I believe there were seven pictures, and you arranged them in a sequence, and numbered them. On the first one you wrote, '*Shall* I learn to be good? I will sit here and think it over,' and the rest of them show you in thoughtful poses, each with a caption showing you thinking about your goodness. And the last one, giving the result of this long contemplation of reform? 'Oh, never mind. I reckon I'm good enough just as I am.' Now, *that's* the kind of thing I'm talking about. If only you could have hung on to that thought instead of lapsing into your old, old habits of morbid self-rebuke, then we wouldn't be having this chat right now. There'd be no need for it. I'd just send you directly into—"

"But surely there are *some* sins," I said,—or rather, the Presbyterian in me said—"that I *can't* forget, that I *oughtn't* forget, on account of their hideousness. Why, I've done things that no right-thinking man with an ounce of conscience could *ever* forget."

Peter seemed to grow restive. "When you authors write down ideas," he said, "I've always assumed you *believed* the ideas, and you were instructing the rest of us. In your *Huck Finn* you've written all about the devilish pangs of conscience, and its cunning capacity to nag a body for a course of action just as much as it would have nagged him if he'd chosen the *opposite* course. You have your boy, Huck, say, 'If I had a yaller dog that didn't know no more than a person's conscience does, I would pison him.' You wrote that. Don't you *believe* it?"

"Yes, but . . . it's not at all a simple matter. One can struggle with an idea, and write about that struggle, and . . . and yet . . ."

"It's no good," said Peter. "You're too stuck on your old ways of thinking. Try this—go home, and *read*. You're luckier than most people, Sam—you're dead and famous; heaps of books and essays have been written about you, and with no special regard for your feelings. I've loafed around in some of them, and I've learned that your biographers can be quite forgiving. Why, I read a sockdolager of an essay that helped me understand you and Henry—called "Why I Killed My Brother," by somebody or other. And I saw a title that intrigued me, though I didn't read any of the book. It's called *Mark Twain: God's Fool.* You might try that. Judging from the title, it just might put the blame for your actions . . ." Peter's voice trailed off; he hunched down a bit over his desk and spoke again, but in a whisper: "It just might put the blame where it belongs."

"I'm all for *that,*" I said. "Should I keep on writing, too?"

"Hmph. Judging from *Huck,* it don't seem to do you a whole lot of good; I mean, you don't seem to *learn* from doing it; but I suppose it can't hurt."

"How about my letters? Shall I keep up with them, too? You see, I want to do the right thing, according to your lights. I want my reward."

"Oh, you might as well. Livy seems to enjoy them."

He'd said it so carelessly that it took a moment to sink in. "She . . . She *enjoys* them? You mean, they actually reach her?"

"Sure," said Peter. "Didn't you know that? As soon as you sign your name to a letter, we get a copy here, and I call her back from the void and read it to her."

"Why, that's the most heart-warming news I've . . ." A chill gripped my heart. "Back from the *void?* You mean she's . . . she's with Harte, and Paige, and Bliss, and those other rascals?"

"That's right."

"But she was the purest, best, most unselfish and innocent—"

"That's right. She was just as good as she could be; what's more important, *she knew it.* She was at peace with herself, just like Harte and the others. She got our Lord's message all right, in her own way, even if her faith in Him went to smash, on account of your influence. So I rewarded her, just as I did the others."

"You *rewarded* her?"

"Yes—I sent her into the void."

A thousand questions rushed upon me. "The void is the reward? What kind of reward is that?"

"It's better than the alternative."

"You talk as if Livy got a different fate from mine; but I distinctly remember going down that slide."

Peter said, "I'm afraid you're mistaken there, Sam. You rode down *this* slide." He turned to his left, and there, looming up out of the fog, was the twin of the slide on the other side of the bench. I was amazed I hadn't seen it until now.

"Where does that one go?" I asked, pointing to the new one.

"I think you know where it goes." Peter looked to the rear of the room. "Gabriel? It's time."

"Aw," said Gabriel. "He's more fun than most. He's guilty as all hell. Just a little longer?"

"No. Come on now."

I felt Gabriel's hand close around my upper arm. I began to wriggle, but I might as well have tried to give the slip to Goliath. As he led me to the slide I began to shout to Peter, in protest, but the noise from a fresh influx of candidates from the rear of the room drowned me out. Then, just as Gabriel set me down on the top of the slide and gave me the gentlest little nudge, I heard Peter call out to me over the din:

"I don't want to see you again until you know that you are just as good as pie!"

Notes on p. 146.

[Untitled Sketch (Working Notes)]

I lock myself in my room with 40 books, all about me. I read them all. At week's end, I am a slobbering idiot. I cannot act without watching myself. "Yes, this confirms what Billson says about me," or "My, that certainly raises the dickens with Blatherskite's hypothesis."

I go on a rampage, calculated to prove them all false.

Or two columns, consisting of paired summations of my *essence,* by different authors. Each contradicts the other—just line 'em up like front ranks of opposing armies, & let 'em mow each other down, leaving the field empty.

A list of all the quotes that say I am "contradictory," or "inconsistent," or "a dual personality."

Have the first writer who used the word "dual" (or his heirs) sue the thousands who used it after him, for copyright infringement.

Draw a portrait based on descriptions of me—hair 6 times bigger than head, which is 6 times bigger than body. Hands like a new-born babe's.

Use McDowell's Cave—use map outside, which shows modern tour route—a safe, illuminated tour, with no surprises, except when the guide says, "I'm now going to turn out the lights so that we can experience total darkness. Does anyone object?" & if you did object she wouldn't do it. Map also shows side-passages, sticking out at crazy angles like the branches of a sagebrush, places where you can get lost & go mad. Moral: The cave is *my life,* crazy side-passages & all. The safe, well-lit tour is *the summation of my life* by biographers, who know it's partly a lie, but they are slaves to their readers, who cry, "Give us the tour! No crazy side-passages, & for God's sake, don't turn out the lights! Give us the safe, well-lit tour!"

Notes on p. 150.

Letters

On board the *Delta Queen,*
just off Baton Rouge
Feb. 14/86

Livy darling, it is no mistake. Baton Rouge. And you thought I was back
in Ceylon. No, darling. Providence didn't want me there, I suppose.
Providence thought I was having too much fun. But I got the bulge on
Providence, because I'm having just as much fun now—high times on the
river, lecturing about myself with a breadth & depth of knowledge that
absolutely astounds my audience, then lying abed & smoking in my cabin
when I grow fagged out from the charade, or strolling along the deck &
watching the changing colors of the river & sky. Every mortal soul on this
boat *loves* me,—I mean my old self, Mark Twain. My present self is still
C. L. Samuel—make that C. L. Samuel, *Lecturer.* You should see the way
I feed their love with anecdote piled upon anecdote. One fellow on board,
who seems to know a great deal about me, told me Mark Twain is the only
writer he knows of who was so fervently loved both in his lifetime &
afterward as well. He says that his detractors—both then & now—have
been impotent in their attacks on him. Well!

Last night, I gave a reading from my work in the ship's auditorium,
bringing Mark Twain to life, as you might say—only *I* ain't sayin'. I read
the passage about Huck wrestling with his conscience, & the scene with
the bragging, loud-mouthed raftsmen from "Old Times on the Mississippi," & then finished up with Huck & Jim on King Sollermun, & oh,
the pure joy of it! *I* ain't havin' much fun, Livy. Oh, no, I reckon not.
It's somebody else. Must be "the gentleman in the wagon."

We are three days out of New Orleans & have just left Baton Rouge,
Natchez-bound. After that, we chug back to New Orleans. Then—I don't
know. I don't care! I may do this the rest of my life.

Imagine me standing on the moonlit deck & firing a Cupid's arrow
high into the night sky, up the Mississippi, then up the Ohio, across the

Alleghenies to the heart of Elmira, to the heart of my love who lies beside me. Ich liebe dich. Happy Valentine's Day, my darling.

Saml.

New Orleans
Feb. 12/86

Livy darling, "I am the master of my fate. I am the captain of my soul." What I mean is that I have solved the riddle of these infernal loopings of time. I mentioned the bewildering repetition of events at the Keno counter, which I brilliantly turned into a profit. I mentioned the twice-occurring accident on the Stanislaus. And then there was a breath-taking leap from late March to early February, from the Indian Ocean all the way back to San Francisco. All of those redundancies were thrust upon me. I was caught in the reverse-spin of the world, with no say in the matter at all. But now—you'd better sit down, Livy. I have big news—*I know what causes them & I can command them at will.* Here is how it works—

3.15 a.m.—I place 3 matches on the table before me.
3.16 a.m.—I call myself a "muggins"—that's right. I say, "You muggins," or "You're such a muggins," or "What a hopeless muggins you are, & always will be." The key word is *muggins.*
3.17 a.m.—I remove one match from the table, leaving two.
3.18 a.m.—I say, "Damnation!" It is suddenly 3.16 & lo! there are 3 matches on the table.

It is easy as pie. "Muggins" throws all events that follow into a horrible vulnerability to being *erased,* as if they had never transpired; the erasure comes into play with my utterance of "Damnation!" & at that moment, time returns to the "muggins" point of departure. Like this—

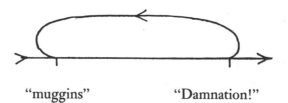

"muggins"   "Damnation!"

Notes on p. 151.

I command time with my vocal cords, with those two words!
It gets stranger—

3.15—3 matches.
3.16—I call myself a muggins & remove one match.
3.17—I say I'm a muggins again & remove another match. So—one match on the table, & two mugginses registered.
3.18—I say "Damnation!" It is suddenly 3.17, & 2 matches on the table. Immediately, I say "Damnation!" again, & it is suddenly 3.16, & all 3 matches on the table.

I tried to draw this one, Livy, but nearly lost my reason in the attempt, so you will have to get by without a picture.

It reminds me of an old river story, Livy—about an ancient pilot with fading abilities. He was a visiting pilot, on board the *Skylark,* I believe, & the chief pilot, seeing an easily navigable "chute" approaching, gave the ancient mariner the wheel. The old fellow went up the chute, then ignorantly came down the other side of the island, up the chute, then down again, & on & on. Three hours later, when the chief pilot returned to the wheel, he was astonished to see the boat hadn't progressed an inch in all that time. What that old fellow did in the realm of space, *I* can do in the realm of time. I can loop over the same course as many times as I wish, & not a soul on board this earth-ship knows about it.

I have illustrated the power of these words, with my matches, with intervals of mere minutes, but there seems to be no limit to the size of the chunk I can wipe out. Mercifully, a "muggins" all by itself is not fatal to time. It must be twinned with a "damnation." A "muggins" all by itself is just a word in the air, & time goes merrily along. I could always come back to it, if I wanted to, with a "damnation." Usually, though, I don't want to.

It is a wonderful gift, Livy. I strongly doubt that I possessed it during my first trip on earth. I certainly must have used those words in combination, & I never found myself heaved into the past, not in my first life, & something like that doesn't happen without your noticing it. I reckon the gift is part of my equipment for *this* trip. I am glad to have it. I need it —I more than anyone. I needed it last evening. By "last evening" I don't mean the evening of the 11th, despite the date on this letter. I mean—oh, it's too blamed hard to figure out. Here is what happened—

I was on the *Delta Queen,* a day out of Baton Rouge. But I must tell you how I came to be on that boat—something I neglected to do in my last letter. In San Francisco I met a professor from the University of Chicago in the hotel restaurant. For a lark, & also because I don't like to be showed up, I told him I was a professor from Oxford University. I did not attempt an English accent—just claimed an American birth & English education. With a lie like that you've got to plunge right in & talk up a storm, & that's what I did, claiming as my special area of knowledge the life & works of Mark Twain, & I unloaded an encyclopedia of opinions about myself on him. He was truly amazed. He said that many of my views weren't exactly supported by what he called "the existing literature," but that they had the ring of truth to them nonetheless. When he tried to steer our talk into channels I couldn't swim in—did I know this scholar, had I attended that meeting, did I study under so-and-so,—I would swipe the floor back & talk some more. He said he was bound for New Orleans in a few days, where he planned to board the *Delta Queen* as a sort of resident expert & lecturer on the literary & historical importance of the Mississippi. I told him it sounded like rattling good fun, & I wished him a good trip, & we parted on very friendly terms.

Then Providence barged in. The professor's wife gave birth to a baby girl much earlier than expected—*dangerously* early, but that's the way Providence works. Providence likes to kill Peter—kill him painfully, if possible—to save Paul. I ran into him at the hotel desk just after he had learned about it, & he was in a state, hurriedly checking out & on his way home. The *Delta Queen* trip was out of the question now. He expressed some concern that the management of the boat wouldn't be able to find a substitute for him. Well, I clapped him on the shoulder & told him *I* would do it. The way he hesitated & frowned & puzzled over the idea was a wonder to behold, but then he suddenly agreed, saying he would telephone the *Delta Queen* folks & explain everything to them & urge them to take me on.

I am delaying the narration of the catastrophe. Very well—full speed ahead. I shan't mince words. The *Delta Queen* went to smash. We ran aground. Several injuries resulted, maybe even some fatal ones. Cause of the accident? A siren.

We were booming along in a clear channel, no danger in sight—even if there *were* danger in sight, the pilot has enough equipment on board to render it harmless; I wouldn't be surprised if he could pull a lever & *fly* the boat over an obstacle, if he had a mind to. But his equipment couldn't help him in this case. What he needed was something very primitive: he needed cotton. He needed cotton in his ears. I was in the pilot house—had talked my way inside—& was trading yarns with the gang & enjoying the company, when the chief pilot suddenly began to cock his head, as a dog will do when it hears a noise. I heard nothing, & went on talking, but the pilot distracted me with another cock of his head & an eerie, far-off look in his eyes. Then he spoke, as from a great distance:

"Both my sisters died in their twenties after enduring a variety of distressing illnesses."

My thought? It was, "What in the devil do this fellow's *sisters* have in common with channel-dredging—the topic under discussion?" But I tried to be polite. I said, "That's too bad."

The pilot gave another twitch of his head & dropped another bombshell of irrelevance:

"My sisters & I were presented with atrocious nervous systems & a marked propensity for hyper-emotionalism."

I began to get a crawly feeling.

"Hypersensitivity of nerves is a baneful attribute."

"That's so true," said I, "& well-phrased. Now about the channel. You mentioned—"

"I used to suffer a great deal from shyness."

I decided to humor him. "Don't let that bother you, my good man. I confess to being a little shy myself, about making your acquaintance. So, you see, it's a small matter—a trifle."

"I am nothing but a bed-occupying senile, a mistake from beginning to end."

"I wouldn't be so down on myself like that. You're an expert pilot of a mighty fine boat, &—"

"I am strong with the sap of the Universe."

"*Yes.* My point exactly. That's more *like.*"

"Stand porter at the door of thought."

"Beg pardon?"

"Why must Dick always have grease spots on his waistcoat?"

I looked around. If "Dick" was among the tribe in the pilot house, he didn't seem to take notice. All the men were gazing shoreward, open-mouthed. I became aware of singing in the distance.

The pilot's voice-box continued to crank out words: "I would like to discuss Mr. Holbrook & his eyes."

Mr. Holbrook! That name again. *Damn* his eyes. What was going on?

The singing suddenly became louder. It was "Ich weiss nicht, was soll es bedeuten." You know it well, Livy. I heard it as clearly as one hears a tower bell in the dead of night. It came from a bluff on the starboard side. I found it rather pretty. I liked it. The pilot liked it, too. It is not an exaggeration to say he liked it. He liked it so well that he decided—though "decided" may be the wrong word—to steer his vessel thither. He must have felt obliged to explain his action, for he said:

"Hostility towards the unfamiliar is a common weakness in human nature. Only a lively instinct for adventure moves man to plough into unknown areas—most especially in metaphysical realms where the visible is discarded for the invisible."

Well, I wasn't about to dispute that, but I couldn't bring myself to voice approval of the unknown areas *he* was ploughing into. He was taking us straight to the shore, & at full speed. I lodged a mild protest. I was ignored. I lodged a loud & violent protest. Same treatment. I seized the wheel. The pilot cuffed me back, sending me sprawling to the floor. From my new position, I looked up at the other members of the crew. Loonies to the core, all of them, gazing up to that bluff like a bunch of puppies awaiting a biscuit.

Well, of course we met with disaster, ploughing into a row of rocks sticking up like an alligator's teeth. And of course there was massive confusion & carnage. In despair, I out with a "Damnation!"—quite by accident, for I was ignorant of the mechanism of the thing then. I am proud to say, Livy, that my choice of that particular word saved every soul on board by heaving the boat back downriver to New Orleans, reversing the flow of time by three whole days.

You see, Livy, at the time of boarding in New Orleans, I ran into some trouble with the purser, who hadn't been informed of my substitution for the lecturer originally booked for the trip, & I grew impatient & cursed him roundly, & *he* cursed *me* & stalked off, leaving me on the wharf wondering if I would ever get on board. By & by I began to regret my words,—not because they were unkind, but just because they hadn't advanced my cause any, & had probably wrecked it, & so I called myself a muggins. A few minutes later, the purser came back, newly enlightened from some quarter & just gushing apologies, & he conducted me to my cabin.

Now, if you can follow this, you will see that my "damnation" sent us back to this very moment—me biding my time on the wharf, the passengers eagerly boarding, the purser on the boat & making inquiries about my legitimacy. I watched the passengers. I studied what had just happened to me—the singing from the bluff, the crash, the flight three days into the past. I silently bid those passengers a safe bon voyage & went to a park to think about it some more, & to conduct a few experiments. The purser, meanwhile, no doubt returned to the wharf in a vain search for me. They'll just have to get along without my wit & wisdom this time. They're well upriver now, & I'm sure they'll have smooth sailing; Dick Allbright, that pathetic jinx, has jumped ship.

But I did enjoy being on the river, & I have a mind to buy me a little boat & make the trip alone. If I meet with disaster, at least I sha'n't have anybody else's blood on my conscience. I have a new mission in life, you see. It is this—I shall studiously avoid killing anybody. When—*if*—my sentence on earth comes to an end, I want to be able to say to myself, "Well, at least I didn't kill anybody."

To be on the safe side, I suppose I should post another muggins now. There. (I just said it.) If I make it through the day, I shall post another one next morning. In this way I shall tiptoe forward, like a man working his way across a frozen river with the ice breaking up, stepping from one chunk to the next only when he is certain of the soundness of that next chunk. Lovingly,

Saml.

Hannibal
Mch. 10/86

My Dear Howells:

When I examine my paid exercises in lying, I find them wanting in some respects. Listen to these opening sentences, if you can:

> In compliance with the request of a friend of mine, who wrote me from the East, I called on good-natured, garrulous old Simon Wheeler, & inquired after my friend's friend, Leonidas W. Smiley, as requested to do, & I hereunto append the result.
>
> —from "The Jumping Frog"

> The following curious history was related to me by a chance railway acquaintance.
>
> —from "The Stolen White Elephant"

> "Yes, I will tell you anything about my life that you would like to know, Mr. Twain," she said, in her soft voice, & letting her honest eyes rest placidly upon my face, "for it is kind & good of you to like me & care to know about me."
>
> —from "The Esquimau Maiden's Romance"

Notes on p. 152.

Do you perceive a dreary sameness to these openings? So do I. As tale-teller, I always seemed to be the one of the three that the Ancient Mariner stoppeth.

Now try these:

> I was told by the physician that a Southern climate would improve my health, & so I went down to Tennessee, & got a berth on the *Morning Glory & Johnson County War-Whoop* as associate editor.
>
> —from "Journalism in Tennessee"

> Thirty-five years ago I was out prospecting on the Stanislaus, tramping all day long with pick & pan & horn, & washing a hatful of dirt here & there, always expecting to make a rich strike, & never doing it.
>
> —from "The Californian's Tale"

> When I was twenty-seven years old, I was a mining-broker's clerk in San Francisco, & an expert in all the details of stock traffic.
>
> —from "The £ 1,000,000 Bank-Note"

> I was spending the month of March, 1892, at Mentone, in the Riviera.
>
> —from "Is He Living or Is He Dead?"

These certainly "set the stage," don't they? The reader knows right where he stands, & right where the teller stood, & when, to the year, even to the month. There's not an ounce of nonsense in it.

Sometimes I set my stage as if writing a play, like this:

> [*Scene—An Artist's Studio in Rome*]
> "Oh, George, I *do* love you!"
>
> —from "The Capitoline Venus"

> The first scene is in the country, in Virginia; the time, 1880.
>
> —from "A Double-Barrelled Detective Story"

> A great beer-saloon in the Friedrichstrasse, Berlin, toward mid-afternoon.
>
> —from "The Belated Russian Passport"

I suppose I fancied I was being pretty brash & original, using openings like these. Hmph.

And then there are these chestnuts:

It was at a banquet in London in honor of one of the two or three conspicuously illustrious English military names of this generation.

—from "Luck"

It was summer-time, & twilight.

—from "A True Story"

It was a time of great & exalting excitement.

—from "A War Prayer"

It was 1702—May.

—from "The Chronicle of Young Satan"

It was many years ago.

—from "The Man That Corrupted Hadleyburg"

Oh, it was, was it? Hmph. Do you see my drift, Howells? Isn't there a strait-jacket sameness here? I wrote as if I were a prisoner, with just four windows to look out of, & every morning I could take my pick, but always from the same four views. And isn't there a kind of trumpet-blare about them, as if I took the gentle reader for an idiot?

Now, feast your old, old eyes on *this:*

Milton Tibbett sighed mournfully, squirmed into a less uncomfortable position on the cold wooden bench, & began to fuss with the gears of his new Sashimi Kamikaze X-208/Y-49/f-1.2 camera.

"What?" you shriek. "Who is Milton Tibbett? Where is he? When does the story take place? What is the meaning of this infernally presumptuous *the* in 'the cold wooden bench'? I ain't familiar with this bench. Never sat on it in my life. And how did Tibbett, whoever *he* is, come to be sitting on this famous bench?"

Relax, Howells. Don't be such a dinosaur. I'll fill in this information, by & by. I'll do it with a leap further into the past, with the verb *had*— I don't know what the tense or sex of it is called; I know grammar by *ear*, not by label. Like this—"He had driven down from Keokuk for a tour of 'Mark Twain Country.' " There. Are you feeling cozier? You'd better get used to it, Howells, if you want to be modern. Everyone's doing it.

Everyone's doing another thing as well. Before I show you what, first cast a tired eye on the way the Lincoln of our Literature scooped samples of thought from his characters' brains:

From *The Prince & the Pauper*—

A smile twinkled in Hendon's eye, & he said to himself, "By the mass, the little beggar takes to one's quarters & usurps one's bed with as natural & easy a grace as if he owned them." (He goes on for 6 more sentences—likes to listen to himself, I guess.)

Hendon muttered, "See now, how like a man &c" (No one's listening to his muttering—just the reader.)

"Yes, sire," Miles replied; then observed to himself, "If I *must* humor the poor lad's madness &c" (A versatile fellow, Hendon—he talks to others & himself.)

From *The American Claimant*—

"How grand that is!" said Tracy, as he wended homeward. (Why did he *say* it? He's all alone here. Eccentric, I suppose.)

A shudder went quaking through him, & he exclaimed—
"What have I been thinking of! &c" (He exclaimed it to the walls; I hope they found it interesting.)

Tracy said to himself, almost shouted to himself, "I'm glad I came to this country &c" (Goes on for 28 lines—a sockdolager of a thought.)

The colonel was startled, & said to himself . . . At length he said to himself . . . The Englishman made this irrelevant remark to himself . . . The artist said to himself . . . (All four of these are on the same page!)

He said—*to* himself, but *at* his conscience &c (A nice distinction, just brimming with artfulness.)

Nobody heard this remark, because Hawkins, who bred it, only thought it, he didn't utter it &c (What crippled clawing after variety!)

The shady devil who lives & lurks & hides & watches inside of human beings & is always waiting for a chance to do the proprietor a malicious damage, whispered to her soul & said &c (This means "She thought" in undemented English.)

From *Pudd'nhead Wilson*—

"Great Scott!" Then he added to himself, "That's &c"
"What is you mumblin' 'bout, Chambers?" (Ha! She caught him—

it's about *time* one of my characters complained about all this mumb-lin'.)

What an embarrassing load of groaning, creaking machinery. A drunken surgeon could lay open a brain with greater deftness than this.

Now hitch up your bulging trousers & listen to this. It's about a camera:

> The worst of it was you couldn't tell if the flap was in the way when you snapped the picture, because you weren't really looking through the lens when you snapped. God knows what you *were* looking through. It was all a dirty trick.

That's *thought*, Howells. Or rather, it's description heavily colored by thought, & finally shading into it, & if you do it right, why, the reader is drawn right into your character's soul without being the least bit aware of it. Isn't it fetching?

I have a plan. I mean to use this style in a new book I am writing, one I have been pegging away at the past two days. It will be a fantastical-ized yarn about my return to this orb. It will begin with three brief sketches, wherein Mark Twain is merely glimpsed for a fraction of a moment before he disappears. The characters who glimpse me will also appear in the story later, re-entering the world of the book for very good reasons of their own, & the reader will be lulled along, gradually becoming acquainted with each of these "new" people, & then it will strike him like a thunderbolt: *I know this character!* he will think (or say to himself, or mutter, or exclaim to the walls.) That moment of recognition will be delightful to him.

I am stretching things with these "glimpses," because they didn't really happen, but that's no matter. It's the spirit of these things that counts—the spirit of lowly, miserable wretches experiencing a thrill that lifts them out of their drab lives. I have already written one of the glimpses & am fooling along with another, which takes place on Jackass Hill, & I mean to shift abruptly from one glimpse to the next, just as modern as can be, instead of . . . well, instead of *this* sort of thing, just dripping with gumptionless apology:

> Now to return to Tom & Becky's share in the pic-nic.

> We left John Canty dragging the rightful prince into Offal Court, with a noisy & delighted mob at his heels.

It is necessary, now, to hunt up Roxy.

None of that. Just *shift*, & let the reader work it out for himself.

I am puzzling over the rest of the book. I haven't really hit on an over-all plan that satisfies me. This much I *do* know—there must be *magic* in it, & there must be *hope* in it. Mark Twain will do great things in this tale. He must have powers that will steer destiny out of its perilous course. He will be known as "Comet Man," & he will wreak no end of benevolent confusion. I shall have him infiltrate the minds of a Presidential committee assigned to investigate our mission in Central America; he will confuse those statesmen & scholars; they will suddenly go fuzzy on geography & think Central America means the center of America, which is to say somewhere in Kansas, only they're not exactly sure where, & they'll argue about it, & eventually they'll agree on a spot, & go there & look into revolutionary activity, & an old farmer will scratch his whiskers & say, "No, they ain't been no rebels in these h'yer parts since the Civil War," & they'll fly back to Washington with the news & raise no end of confusion in the White House. Or Comet Man will infiltrate the weapons—go right into the missile silos & turn them into *real* silos, full of wheat, & he'll do the same in Russia, & when there's a war all the missiles will veer off to Africa & explode over-head & rain manna down on the starving souls there.

But Comet Man will be a perfect saphead too. He will get into all sorts of scrapes & awkward circumstances,—just brimming with assfulness, on account of his Rip-Van-Winkle-like ignorance. On an airplane, he will ask if they are over land or water. "Why?" the lady conductor will ask. "Because I want to use the bathroom," he will say. He will wonder what an "I.Q. Test" is—then take one, to see how intelligent he is. But, being such an anachronism, he will get the score of a moron. He will audition as a comic in one of these open-stage places, but he will fail miserably—speech too damned slow, jokes old-fashioned, & too chaste. Along *that* line, he will catch wind of a "sexual revolution" having taken place in his 75-year absence, & he will doubt it, but then he will take a look around—at the clothes & the glimpses they afford, & he will listen to the frank talk of sexual matters, & notice that now even *women* may swear in public (a development that Mrs. Clemens would have greatly appreciated,) & he will see famous films like *Pussycat Ranch* & *Honey Buns*, & he will say, "I believe I shall have some of the pie." But he will mistake society's mere *modification* of the rules for utter *abandonment* of them, & he will make a grossly indecent suggestion to the next pretty woman he sees, & then— But it is too painful to write of *twice*. I shall save it for the MS.

In this yarn I must bring Mark Twain out of hiding. But what would that be like? What kind of reception would I get? Should I do it & find out? Sometimes I want to; other times, the idea makes me cringe & shrivel like a spider. But if it would serve the book, wouldn't it be worth whatever embarrassment it caused me?

No. It wouldn't.

Damnation, I wish you were here to help me plan this book. We could have roaring good times talking about it into the late hours, & you could help me *imagine* what my reception would be like.

You will be pleased to see my lovely face on the cover of the April *Atlantic,* just out. If you come across it, don't bother to read the innards. It's a pack of lies.

Ys Ever
Mark

Notes on p. 155.

Notes

A Dispatch from the Delta Queen

In his Livy letter of 14 February 1986, Clemens states that he has been working on the *Delta Queen* since 12 February as a lecturer-in-residence. One's first impression is that he wrote this "Dispatch" in this period. However, the events described in his 12 February Livy letter suggest that any manuscript he had written while on board may have been lost. Thus the instant sketch may be a post-hoc reconstruction, perhaps written during his stay in Hannibal, of work written while aboard the *Delta Queen.*

No record of Clemens' presence on the boat is extant. But our investigation into this cruise has produced the following data: the description of "Captain Mutton" jibes with the physical characteristics of the chief pilot on the *Delta Queen* for the 12–17 February "Dixie Promenade" cruise, Captain Walter A. Jensen; a real-life counterpart to Milton Tibbett (a fictitious name) was on the cruise; likewise a real-life counterpart to Hermann the German (also a fictitious name). We have chosen to honor these men's requests for anonymity. We have been unable to identify either the lover of modern music or the mirthful Mabel. We are grateful to the Delta Queen Home Port Office in Cincinnati for their assistance in our investigation.

The Creation of the World is probably the 1923 ballet, *La création du monde,* by the French composer Darius Milhaud (1892–1974).

Clemens' account of his turn at the pilot's wheel draws heavily from the language of chapter 7 of *Life on the Mississippi,* where he describes a true feat of daring navigation by his mentor, pilot Horace Bixby. Hat Island was a particularly dangerous stretch of the Mississippi above Cairo, Illinois; in later years, long after he had quit the river, Clemens was repeatedly troubled by nightmares of wrecking his steamboat at Hat Island. Clemens takes severe liberties in this scene—in the location of his navigational triumph (the northernmost point reached on the "Dixie

Promenade" cruise is Natchez, Mississippi), with the invention of a swimming pool on the *Delta Queen,* and with the leadsman's cries, for if he were truly filling the pool, the water level would not drop from quarter-less-twain (ten and a half feet) to seven and a half feet before rising to mark twain (two fathoms, or twelve feet).

Clemens' sentiment about the tendency of certain authors to leave descriptions to the reader's imagination echoes an entry in his notebook, made in August 1866 during his return voyage to San Francisco from the Hawaiian Islands:

> "Can be better imagined than described"—d--n the man who invented it. Often, with 100 island books before me, I have thought, "now this piece of scenery is described in these, & I can steal & rehash—turn & find them shirking, with that hackneyed expression.
>
> (*N&J1,* p. 159)

The Twain Man

This sketch was ostensibly written during Clemens' *Delta Queen* cruise (12–15 February), but like the "Dispatch," it may date from his later stay in Hannibal.

The Twain Man was destined for an even more important role in Clemens' second life than either of them could have suspected on their first meeting; see "On the Trail of Samuel Clemens: The Mississippi River," and "On the Trail of Samuel Clemens: The East." The five essays described here are in the Mark Twain Boyhood Home and Museum in Hannibal (copies are in the Mark Twain Papers); Clemens' treatment of them in this sketch is quite fair.

Clemens' story about Susy's imitation of his drawl is not in his autobiography, as he claims here, but in an unpublished manuscript titled "A Record of the Small Foolishnesses of Susie and 'Bay' Clemens (Infants)." Portions of the manuscript are in *S&MT;* for the drawl-imitation story, see p. 42.

Although not exhaustive, Clemens' list of famous people he met is accurate, save for the obvious exceptions of Aesop (fl. 6th c. B.C.), John Bunyan (1628–88), and Penelope Ashe—the last being the pseudonymous author of the 1969 novel *Naked Came the Stranger,* a work composed by twenty-five reporters and editors for the Long Island newspaper *Newsday,* in a conspiratorial parody of bad writing; the book ranked seventh on the 1969 best-seller list (New York *Times,* 7 August 1969, p. 28; Alice Payne Hackett and James Henry Burke, *80 Years of Best-Sellers: 1895–1975* [New

York: R. R. Bowker, 1977], pp. 205–206; Mike McGrady, *Stranger than Naked, Or How to Write Dirty Books for Fun and Profit* [New York: Peter H. Wyden, 1970]). It is not known how Clemens came to learn of this novel.

Oscar Umlauf's appearances on the list—once with famous actors and actresses of Clemens' day and once in the miscellaneous category, where his name is significantly framed by those of P. T. Barnum and Arthur Orton (the Tichborne Claimant sentenced in 1874 to fourteen years in prison for perjury)—constitute the only direct acknowledgment in Parts I and II of *I Been There Before* that Clemens was familiar with this name.

Rudyard Kipling (1865–1936) visited Clemens in Elmira, New York, in the summer of 1889. The first American publication of his account of their meeting was in the New York *Herald*, 17 August 1890; it is reprinted in *Mark Twain: Life as I Find It*, ed. Charles Neider (Garden City, N.Y.: Hanover House, 1961), pp. 310–321.

Letters from the Earth was written in 1909 and was prepared for publication in 1939 by Bernard DeVoto, but, owing to objections by Clara Clemens, it was not published until 1962. The "idiotcy" that Clemens "dashed off" unthinkingly is probably the following passage, which is of uncertain autobiographical significance, from Satan's Letter VIII:

> During twenty-three days in every month (in the absence of pregnancy) from the time a woman is seven years old till she dies of old age, she is ready for action, and *competent*. As competent as the candlestick is to receive the candle. Competent every day, competent every night. Also, she *wants* that candle—yearns for it, longs for it, hankers after it, as commanded by the law of God in her heart.
>
> But man is only briefly competent; and only then in the moderate measure applicable to the word in *his* sex's case. He is competent from the age of sixteen or seventeen thenceforward for thirty-five years. After fifty his performance is of poor quality, the intervals between are wide, and its satisfactions of no great value to either party; whereas his great-grandmother is as good as new. There is nothing the matter with her plant. Her candlestick is as firm as ever, whereas his candle is increasingly softened and weakened by the weather of age, as the years go by, until at last it can no longer stand, and is mournfully laid to rest in the hope of a blessed resurrection which is never to come.

A Glimpse: I

According to the register at the Tom 'n Huck Motel in Hannibal, Missouri, a "Dick Allbright" (an almost certain Clemens alias; see notes to Livy letter of 12 February for an explanation of the name) stayed there from 25 February to 12 March 1986. One of the desk clerks, Homer Stubbs, remembers him very well—for his drawl, his bushy white hair (evidently grown back; but he was still sans mustache), his friendliness, and his studious habits. Clemens spent most of his time in his room, reading and writing. We assume "A Glimpse: I" was written in this period. Clemens discusses the purpose and style of this and the immediately following sketch in his 10 March letter to Howells.

In mid-November 1839, the Clemens family moved from Florida, Missouri, to Hannibal (the St. Petersburg of *Tom Sawyer* and *Huckleberry Finn*), which was to be Clemens' home until 1853, when he began a four-year career as an itinerant printer in the midwest and east. Most of his Hannibal years were spent in the family home at 206 Hill Street, just two blocks from the Mississippi River.

The reader will recall Milton Tibbett as the *Delta Queen* tourist with the new camera who was harried by his female companions. We assume Clemens' transporting of him upriver to Hannibal is purely imaginary.

A Glimpse: II

Though set on Jackass Hill, near Angels Camp, California, this sketch, given its location in the manuscript, certainly dates from Clemens' Hannibal period: 25 February–12 March 1986.

From 4 December 1864 to 23 February 1865 Clemens resided in a cabin on Jackass Hill with miner Jim Gillis, a natural storyteller of superb talent, to whom Clemens would later give credit for some of his own stories (*MTE*, pp. 358–366).

The "unexplained pain" in Jimmy's "cod" (penis) is a curious matter. In his first lifetime, Clemens may have experienced such a pain. John Henning, in his exhaustive (but still short of conclusive) essay on the subject, "Clemens' Clap" (*IMT*, pp. 78–132), argues that Clemens probably contracted gonorrhea in the fall or winter of 1866. As evidence he cites five notebook entries in December 1866 and January 1867, during Clemens' return voyage from San Francisco to New York, in which Clemens refers to a lingering illness but, uncharacteristically, does not identify it; for example, he writes, "Nearly everybody seasick. Happily I escaped—had something worse," and "I am in bed all day to-day (2d Jan)—same old thing" (*N&J1*, pp. 245, 268). Clemens also abstained from liquor during the trip—"for obvious reasons," he says mysteriously (*N&J1*, p. 275); Henning argues that liquor would have increased the frequency of urination, which Clemens would have found painful. Henning also claims that Clemens' recurring rheumatism later in life might actually have been gonococcal arthritis. The "unexplained pain" in this sketch is of uncertain evidential value. Clemens may be recreating once-experienced symptoms, giving them to a character in the west, where *he* was infected, *if* he was. But he may simply be setting up the joke at the end of the sketch. We shall take up this subject again below, in "On the Trail of Samuel Clemens: The Mississippi River."

St. Peter Helps Me Feel Good About Myself

Among the personal effects recovered after Clemens' 11 April departure from the earth were the two books referred to in this sketch: Justin Kaplan's *Mr. Clemens and Mark Twain* (New York: Simon and Schuster, 1966), and *MTGF*; the former still bore the price tag used in the Becky Thatcher Book Shop in Hannibal, and the latter contained a bookmark from the store. (Both books show very heavy marking by Clemens; for a discussion, see the report by one of our editors, Gloria Wilson, "Some Recent Clemens Marginalia," *American Literature,* to appear in May 1988.) We assume that Clemens, during his stay in Hannibal, purchased these books, read them, and, perhaps inspired to reassess certain aspects of his life, wrote this sketch. If the "long letter" referred to is his 10 March letter to Howells—the only extant letter written in Hannibal—the sketch was presumably composed about the same time as the letter; we say this not because we truly believe Clemens' composition of the letter was interrupted by two "hench-angels," but because mention of the letter in the sketch suggests a close temporal association between the two.

James W. Paige was a Hartford inventor who induced Clemens to invest over $200,000 from 1881 to 1894 in a typesetting machine under development; the machine was ultimately a complete failure.

Clemens gives the story of the death of the drunken tramp in the Hannibal jail fire in chapter 56 of *Life on the Mississippi* and in his autobiography (*MTA*, 1:130–131).

The gang yoked together by a rope are Clemens' publishers from 1867 to 1910. Their stormy tenures with the demanding and distrustful author were as follows: Webb, 1867; Bliss, 1869–80; Osgood, 1881–83; Webster (Clemens' nephew by marriage and the manager of Clemens' own publishing firm), 1884–88; Hall (Webster's successor in Clemens' firm), 1888–94; and Duneka, 1895–1910 (i.e., Harper and Brothers; Duneka's association with the firm began in 1900).

Henry Clemens' death is treated in chapter 20 of *Life on the Mississippi* and in *MTA*, 1:307–312.

Clemens met Bret Harte in 1864 in San Francisco. In the early years of their relationship, Harte advised Clemens on his writing and frequently published his sketches in the *Californian*, as well as chapters from *The Innocents Abroad* in the *Overland Monthly*. Their 1876–77 collaboration on an unsuccessful play, *Ah Sin* (about which Clemens once said it "had a run of one consecutive week" [Anon., "More About Twain," *Bookman* 31 (July 1910): 458–459]), marked the beginning of a decline in their relations. Clemens would ultimately condemn Harte's life as one of squandered talent and moral turpitude. Clemens' joke about "The Luck" is an allusion to the last sentence of the famous Harte story "The Luck of Roaring Camp" (1868).

Clemens recounts Langdon's death in his autobiography (*MTA*, 2:32, 230–231), where, as in this sketch, he incorrectly gives Langdon's age as twenty-two months; when Langdon died he was just under nineteen months old. In his memoir, Howells writes, "There had been a boy, and 'Yes, *I* killed him,' Clemens once said, with the unsparing self-blame in which he would wreak an unavailing regret. He meant that he had taken the child out imprudently, and the child had taken the cold which he died of, but it was by no means certain this was through its father's imprudence" (*MMT*, p. 12).

Immediately following the sentence "Do it some more, won't you?" is a passage that Clemens canceled by drawing a wavy line down each of five consecutive manuscript pages. There are several possible reasons for his choosing to exclude the passage: misgivings about the criticism of Howells contained in it; desire to retain the focus of his discussion with Peter on incidents from his past involving deaths for which he felt responsible; desire to adhere to the prevailing numerology in the sketch, in which the number three plays such a large role; or any combination of these reasons. That Clemens canceled the passage so lightly is evidence that he parted with it with some reluctance; in a sense, because he included the five pages in the manuscript transmitted to us, he did not part with it at all. The passage is given below:

"All right. I shall. Let's leap far ahead now, to December 17th, 1877."

"I'd rather not."

"The Whittier Birthday Dinner." Peter suddenly guffawed. It was a very irreverent guffaw. "Tell me about it."

I sighed. "Well, the occasion was John Greenleaf Whittier's seventieth birthday. I was one of many speakers. It was at the Hotel Brunswick, in Boston, and the whole shebang was put on by the *Atlantic* staff. At the head table sat Emerson, Longfellow, and Holmes. Howells, also at the head table, introduced me. It was a very warm, personal sort of introduction. Then . . . then . . . I shall quote his memoir: 'And then the amazing mistake, the bewildering blunder, the cruel catastrophe was upon us.' He means, I gave my speech. It was a burlesque, set in a mining camp in the California foothills, in which three rough fellows try to pass themselves off as Emerson, Longfellow, and Holmes when they drop in on a miner. They play cards, cheat, drink, swear, fart, misquote their poetry—"

"Don't exaggerate."

"All right. They don't fart. But if I'd had them do it, my tale couldn't have been any more coldly received than it was. A glacial silence set in when I was just a few minutes into it, and I struggled through it, somehow, and when I finished, every man in that room was silent—save for one, who cackled and brayed in celebration of the purity of the blunder I had made."

"Couldn't he have been laughing because he found your tale genuinely funny?"

"No."

"Don't be so sure. What do you think happened? Why was everyone else silent?"

"Because they were shocked that I could portray those august Brahmins in such coarse terms. I showed my native colors that night. It was a case of the Missouri rube misbehaving in the big eastern city."

"You apologized though, didn't you?"

"Oh, yes. I wrote letters of apology to the three men I had insulted."

"And their replies?"

"Very polite."

"That's all? 'Polite'?"

"Yes."

"Didn't they absolve you of all guilt and say they hadn't been offended at all?"

"They were just being kind."

"You're a stubborn one, ain't ya'? What do *you* think of the speech —as a literary work, I mean?"

I shrugged. "I'm beyond being able to judge it."

"Well, *I* read it, and I think it's prime. You read it, didn't you, Gabriel?"

"Yes!" he shouted from the rear. "It's killingly funny."

"How about you, Harte?"

Harte's head mysteriously shot up through the fog covering the floor. "When I read it in the Boston *Evening Transcript,* I burned with envy. Clemens, you've surpassed me, but I shall catch you. Posterity will eventually—" He suddenly sank from view.

"Call 'em back from the void and you can't shut 'em up," said Peter. "Listen, Sam. Howells exaggerated the disaster—plain and simple. You really shouldn't go around quoting him about it. He was a rube, too, you know—an Ohio rube. He felt *contaminated* by you, especially after he gave you such a tender introduction. You shouldn't have let him interpret the event for you the way he did—and still does, from the grave, in that memoir of his. Forget the whole thing. Forget it, forget it."

I burst into laughter. "You know," I said, "as I think about it, it *is* an awfully good speech, isn't it?"

In Clemens' mind, the Whittier speech was without doubt the greatest public-speaking disaster of his life. Six days after the dinner, he wrote to Howells,

> My sense of disgrace does not abate. It grows. I see that it is going to add itself to my list of permanencies—a list of humiliations that extends back to when I was seven years old, & which keep on persecuting me regardless of my repentancies. . . .
>
> It seems as if I must have been insane when I wrote that speech & saw no harm in it, no disrespect toward those men whom I reverenced so much. And what shame I brought upon *you,* after what you said in introducing me! It burns me like fire to think of it.
>
> (*MTHL,* p. 212)

A few days later he wrote,

> I haven't done a stroke of work since the Atlantic dinner; have only moped around. But I'm going to try tomorrow. How could I ever have—
> Ah, well, I am a great & sublime fool. But then I am God's fool, & all His works must be contemplated with respect.
>
> (*MTHL,* p. 215)

But in his definitive essay on the subject (" 'That Hideous Mistake of Poor Clemens's,' " *Harvard Library Bulletin,* 9 [Spring 1955]: 145–180), Henry Nash Smith, having surveyed the evidence bearing on the contemporary reception of the speech, concludes, "The two friends [Clemens and Howells] churned themselves into a state of mind which bore little relation to external reality at the time and distorted their memories of what happened" (p. 156).

The series of captioned photographs referred to by St. Peter were taken by Paine in Dublin, New Hampshire, in the summer of 1906. The photographs are in the Mark Twain Papers and appear in *The Autobiography of Mark Twain,* ed. Charles Neider (New York: Harper and Row, 1959), following p. 164; in *MFMT,* following p. 266; and in John Seelye, *Mark Twain in the Movies* (New York: Viking, 1977), pp. 37–39.

The "yaller dog" sentence is in chapter 33 of *Huckleberry Finn.*

"Why I Killed My Brother: An Essay on Mark Twain," by Forrest G. Robinson, first appeared in *Literature and Psychology,* 30 (1980): 168–181; it was reprinted in *IMT* (pp. 46–60), a book regularly stocked by the Becky Thatcher Book Shop and Clemens' presumed source for the essay. However, the book was not found among his personal effects after his departure.

[Untitled Sketch (Working Notes)]

These notes for a sketch were written on both sides of a single small sheet of stationery from the Tom 'n Huck Motel. The sheet was folded in half and wedged between pages two and three of the St. Peter sketch. Given this location and the shared concerns with biographical treatments of him, the St. Peter sketch and the notes were probably written about the same time. In light of its haphazard placement, Clemens probably did not intend to send the sheet of paper along with his manuscript; he may even have searched for it vainly at a later date. At any rate, the sketch itself is not extant.

McDowell's Cave, now known as the Mark Twain Cave, lies two miles south of Hannibal and was a favorite boyhood haunt for Clemens. In *Tom Sawyer* it is here—renamed McDougal's Cave—that Tom and Becky become lost and Injun Joe dies.

Letters

To Livy, 14 February 1986

"And you thought I was back in Ceylon"—this sentence initially bewildered us at the Mark Twain Papers, as did a related sentence in the Livy letter immediately following: "And then there was a breath-taking leap from late March to early February, from the Indian Ocean all the way back to San Francisco." Our confusion on this point ended when we received Part III of *I Been There Before.* In the cover letter accompanying that portion of the manuscript (given below in "On the Trail of Samuel Clemens: The Mississippi River"), Clemens informed me that from early February to late March he had been on a pleasure cruise in the South Pacific. His pleasure was interrupted, however, when he suddenly found himself back in San Francisco and back to 4 February, for his largest leap back in time yet. Although no record exists of his presence on board the ship that he playfully misnames in that letter, the dates and ports of call of its voyage in this period correspond with Clemens' briefly sketched itinerary; that is, the Norwegian-registered *Björnstjerne Björnson* (Clemens calls it the *Bejesus Bejohnson*) departed San Francisco 10 February for an around-the-world tour closely paralleling the route of Clemens' 1895–96 lecture tour. Clemens wrote during this sea voyage (he mentions this in his cover letter, and the sentence in this Livy letter quoted above implies previous correspondence with her about the voyage), but none of this work is extant.

On the back of the last sheet of this letter are seven completed tick-tack-toe games and a tally immediately below them, arranged as follows:

Name	Age	Games Won
Rebecca	5¼	4
C. L. Samuel	150¼	3

We have established that a Rebecca Flowers, then aged five years, two and a half months, accompanied her parents on the "Dixie Promenade" cruise.

To Livy, 12 February 1986

Although dated earlier than the letter of 14 February, this letter was composed *after* it, i.e., after the erasure of the 12–15 February loop during which the 14 February letter was written.

The opening quotation is the conclusion of "Invictus," a poem by William Ernest Henley (1849–1903).

The story of the aged visiting pilot on board the *Skylark* is given in chapter 30 of *Life on the Mississippi.*

The lecturer originally scheduled for the lecture-residency on the *Delta Queen* is Byron Blyleven, Professor in the Department of American Studies at the University of Chicago. On 6 February his wife gave premature birth to a girl, and he arranged for Clemens to take his place on the "Dixie Promenade" cruise, just as Clemens reports. Blyleven, it should be noted, has gone on record as fervently denying the possibility that the man he met in San Francisco was Samuel Clemens (Chicago *Tribune,* 29 April 1986, p. 1), even though his testimony confirms Clemens' report of their association.

In his account of the *Delta Queen* accident, Clemens seems as unaware of the "presence" of his daughter Clara (whose words the pilot hypnotically quotes, and who was a concert singer of, among other works, German Lieder) as he was of his daughter Jean's "presence" at the time of the Stanislaus River accident (Livy letter of 22 January). The sentences uttered by the pilot can be found in two books by Clara, *Why Be Nervous?* (New York: Harper and Brothers, 1927), and *Awake to the Perfect Day* (New York: The Citadel Press, 1956), and in Caroline Thomas Harnsberger's *Mark Twain's Clara, or What Became of the Clemens Family* (Evanston, Ill.: The Press of Ward Schori, 1982), as follows: "Both my sisters ..." (*Awake,* p. 24), "My sisters & I ..." (*Awake,* p. 23), "Hypersensitivity ..." (*Awake,* p. 45), "I used to suffer ..." (*Why Be Nervous?,* p. 15), "I am nothing ..." (*Mark Twain's Clara,* p. 192), "I am strong ..." (*Why Be Nervous?,* p. 18), "Stand porter ..." (*Awake,* p. 48), "Why must Dick ..." (*Why Be Nervous?,* p. 12), "I would like to discuss ..." (*Mark Twain's Clara,* p. 197), and "Hostility ..." (*Awake,* p. 20).

"Ich weiss nicht, was soll es bedeuten" is the first line of the Heinrich Heine poem "Die Lorelei" (1824), about which Clemens wrote, "Germany is rich in folk-songs, and the words and airs of several of them are peculiarly beautiful,—but 'The Lorelei' is the people's favorite. I could not endure it at first, but by and by it began to take hold of me, and now there is no tune which I like so well" (*A Tramp Abroad,* chapter 16). In this same chapter he also writes, "I have a prejudice against people who print things in a foreign language and add no translation. When I am the reader, and the author considers me able to do the translating myself, he pays me quite a nice compliment,—but if he would do the translating for me I would try to get along without the compliment." Taking our cue from Clemens, we give both Heine's text and a translation—Clemens' own, whose chief virtue he claimed was that it could be sung to the melody.

Die Lorelei

Ich weiss nicht, was soll es bedeuten,
Dass ich so traurig bin;
Ein Märchen aus alten Zeiten,
Das kommt mir nicht aus dem Sinn.

Die Luft ist kühl, und es dunkelt,
Und ruhig fliesst der Rhein;
Der Gipfel des Berges funkelt
Im Abendsonnenschein.

Die schönste Jungfrau sitzet
Dort oben wunderbar,
Ihr goldnes Geschmeide blitzet,
Sie kämmt ihr goldenes Haar.

Sie kämmt es mit goldenem Kamme
Und singt ein Lied dabei;
Das hat eine wundersame,
Gewaltige Melodei.

Den Schiffer im kleinen Schiffe
Ergreift es mit wildem Weh;
Er schaut nicht die Felsenriffe,
Er schaut nur hinauf in die Höh'.

Ich glaube, die Wellen verschlingen
Am Ende Schiffer und Kahn;
Und das hat mit ihrem Singen
Die Lorelei getan.

The Lorelei

I cannot divine what it meaneth,
This haunting nameless pain:
A tale of the bygone ages
Keeps brooding through my brain:

The faint air cools in the gloaming,
And peaceful flows the Rhine,
The thirsty summits are drinking
The sunset's flooding wine;

The loveliest maiden is sitting
High-throned in yon blue air,
Her golden jewels are shining,
She combs her golden hair;

She combs with a comb that is golden,
And sings a weird refrain
That steeps in a deadly enchantment
The list'ner's ravished brain:

The doomed in his drifting shallop,
Is tranced with the sad sweet tone,
He sees not the yawning breakers,
He sees but the maid alone:

The pitiless billows engulf him!—
So perish sailor and bark;
And this, with her baleful singing,
Is the Lorelei's grewsome work.
          (*A Tramp Abroad*, chapter 16)

Terence FitzWilliam, Chief Purser on the *Delta Queen*, confirms the angry conversation with, and subsequent disappearance of, a man whom he describes as "a white-haired, hot-tempered, foul-mouthed son of a bitch," during the boarding in New Orleans on 12 February.

Dick Allbright is a character mentioned in a scene originally written for *Huckleberry Finn* (in chapter 16), but deleted before publication because of its length and its previous publication in *Life on the Mississippi* (in chapter 3). In the scene, Huck sneaks aboard a nearby raft and hears one of the raftsmen tell a tale of a previous river voyage fraught with disasters because of a haunted barrel that persistently floated alongside the raft. The barrel was finally seized and opened, and the corpse of a naked baby was found inside. One of the raftsmen, Dick Allbright, confessed that the child was his, killed by his own hand and buried in the barrel, which had followed him for three years on the river. Allbright then took the baby up in his arms, jumped overboard with it, and was presumably drowned.

To Howells, 10 March 1986

This is the only letter from Clemens to Howells in *I Been There Before*. Much of their voluminous correspondence in Clemens' first life (661 extant letters by one or the other of them, spanning thirty-eight years of very warm friendship) concerned literary matters, and this no doubt explains the shift from Livy to Howells as the preferred audience for his message.

In his memoir, Howells calls Clemens "the Lincoln of our literature" (*MMT*, p. 84).

The three unidentified quotations dealing with a shift of scene are from, in the order given, *Tom Sawyer* (chapter 31), *The Prince and the Pauper* (chapter 10), and *Pudd'nhead Wilson* (chapter 8).

Judging from this letter, Clemens intended to write a book—a novel, evidently—distinct from the travel book/letter collection he had been working on up to this point. But apart from the two "Glimpses" in Part II and two more in Part III (i.e., one more than he had planned on when he wrote Howells), no manuscripts or notes related to the projected book are extant. It is possible, of course, that some of the material in *I Been There Before* besides the four glimpses was intended for the projected book; while we consider this doubtful, we leave it to the judgment of the reader as to whether any other of the works in *I Been There Before* depart so strongly from the style or narrative thread of the rest of the work to suggest they were conceived as part of this other projected book.

No doubt Clemens went through a "perfect saphead" stage on first arriving to this world for a second time. Indeed, we have seen a few examples of his misconceptions in his sketches and letters. But it is not known how many of the blunders listed here he actually committed.

The cover story in the April *Atlantic* was William Winthrop's article about the newly discovered 1861–64 notebook.

On the Trail of Samuel Clemens: The Mississippi River

In the manuscript left at our doorstep, Clemens' trail ends with the last piece of writing in the collection—the 10 March letter to Howells, written in Hannibal. In retrospect, Hannibal, rather than Carson City, would therefore have been the logical *first* place for me to send Ricky Olivieri in search of the author. But at the outset we had no idea that the manuscript was anything but a work of fantasy. Although we had confirmed that a tour of the Mark Twain Papers much like the one described in the 5 February Livy letter had indeed taken place, there was little or no expectation on our part that Olivieri would find any further correspondence in reality to the events chronicled in the manuscript; when one's working hypothesis is that nothing interesting will be discovered, one pursues the quickest and least expensive means of discovering nothing: thus my dispatching of Olivieri to Carson City rather than to Hannibal. Naturally, when Olivieri returned to Berkeley with his rich array of evidence showing that the manuscript actually chronicled its author's travels, we were chagrined that we hadn't begun our investigation where the trail was warmest.

At that precise moment, the trail unexpectedly heated up with the 18 March newspaper report of the arrest of our presumable quarry in Florida, Missouri, and with the report of his vow to go to Hannibal, "where he said he hoped to receive better treatment." That night, Olivieri flew to St. Louis, where he rented a car and drove to Hannibal, arriving at a timely moment.

However, it will be recalled that when Olivieri concluded his western investigation, (a) he was mildly insane, and (b) he was firmly convinced that his quarry was in fact Samuel Clemens. No doubt he saw the rest of us at Berkeley as hopeless skeptics. He turned against us. He stopped taking notes, and his telephone reports became willfully obscure.

Thus, for a record of what happened in Hannibal on the day Olivieri arrived there, we must turn to other sources. The first of these is fortunately a very reliable one. It is a transcript of a taped recording of what has come to be called "The Debut Speech." The recording itself, which was taken from a public address system set up on Hill Street directly in front of Clemens' boyhood home, no longer exists; but a transcript of it was immediately made by one Herbert Hummel (about whom much more below) and was donated to the Mark Twain Boyhood Home and Museum the next day. My belief in the fidelity of the transcript is based on reports of witnesses to the event, newspaper articles written by local reporters who were on the scene, and the word-for-word agreement between the last two pages of the transcript and four minutes of a videotape record of the conclusion of the speech, filmed by a late-arriving WGEM-TV (Hannibal) cameraman.

Judging from Hummel's transcript, the audio recording failed to pick up the audience's responses clearly, and Hummel rendered these—perhaps speculatively, perhaps from his memory of the event—in square brackets. Here the transcript may well depart from fact. Witnesses to this speech recall an audience considerably more skeptical, and less mirthful, than the one reflected here. Nonetheless, I have retained these bracketed remarks, as I have all of Hummel's somewhat idiosyncratic and inconsistent punctuation. The transcript reproduces the entire speech, omitting only some apparently casual banter while the crowd gathered.

The Hummel Transcript (19 March 1986)

"—will take me a while to get the hang of—" Pause. Crackling sounds and squeals from the public address system. "There we are. My, isn't this handy, though? How my voice *booms* down the street. Makes me feel like the Lord addressing Adam and Eve. I bet they can hear me all the way to Jackson's Island. *Jim?* You, *Jim!* You hear me, Jim? Come on back. Put down that catfish you're chewin' on and come home. You're a free man, Jim—been free for more 'n a hundred years."

[Laughter]

"What I was saying was how proud I am of what you have done in the way of keeping my memory alive here. I've been through the museum, I've been through the home, I've been up on Holliday Hill, and I . . . I just can't tell you how much it all means to me." Pause. "But there's another side to this business. I know. Sometimes there can be too much of a thing—even a *good* thing, like yours truly. Maybe there's too much of *me* here. Mark Twain this, Mark Twain that—a body grows weary of that sort of thing. Why, I was in the Mark Twain Dinette this morning, and as a joke I says to the waitress, 'I'll have Mark Twain eggs,

Mark Twain bacon, Mark Twain toast, and Mark Twain coffee.' I was commiserating with her, you see, because I *knew* she was a native, she just had that *look* about her, and the tired smile she gave me just summed up worlds of misery. Now, you other folks with deep roots here—as I look out I seem to see, faintly outlined and but dimly reflected, the countenances of my childhood, and I'm looking forward to climbin' down off this bench and shaking your hands, because I just *know* that many of you are the grandchildren and great grandchildren and great great grandchildren of my old playmates—those few, at least, that weren't so harum-scarum to break their necks and pass on without issue. Those of you with those kind of roots, I want you to come up here and see if I can guess your name—guess if you're a . . . a McCormick, or a . . . a Dawson, or a Nash.

"But what I was saying, was . . . well, I'm *sorry*. I'm deeply sorry that you come from a town you just ought to plain be proud of bein' from, in its own right, and all anyone can ever think of when they think of Hannibal, Missouri, is Mark Twain. I know it's been awfully hard on you. Let me say this—*I* didn't put Hannibal on the map. It was here before I came along, and it will be here long after all memory of me has faded, as it is sure to do, and your children, and your children's children, will go on living their honest, hard-working, God-fearing lives. Hannibal is on the map because of *you*, not because of me."

[Applause]

"I've been touring this fine town. I've been to your grain terminals and seen first-hand where the *real* glory of this town lies. I've seen your fine new mall, your fine highways, your lovely cemetery. I was struck by the pretty fence runnin' around the cemetery. Funny thing—a fence around a cemetery. I can't see the real *need* of it: those who are inside can't get out, and those that are *out* don't want to get *in.*"

[Laughter; then an indistinct shout from crowd.]

"Your fine mayor, who I am proud to have standing beside me here, is an entertaining man, and a perfect host. He is also a golfer—or *thinks* he is. We were up early this fine spring morning, out on the links, and I saw just how fond your mayor is of your prime Marion County soil. When he swings at a golf ball, he likes to bring a heap of it up—why, he seems to favor the *soil* over the *ball.* After our game, when he asked me how I liked the course, I had to say that after standin' in the neighborhood of a golfer like him, it was absolutely the best golf course I'd ever tasted."

[Much laughter. Then another shout]

"There is a certain . . . gentleman, I suppose I should say, who has been dying to ask me a question. I suggest we allow him to speak before he busts. Sir?"

[Shouted question about Mr. Twain's body]

"Well, there ain't much to do in heaven, you know. I never really took to playin' the harp they gave me, so I got to snackin' and put on a little weight. I'm only joshin', of course. I'd like to ask this man a question. Are you a Christian, sir?"

[Single shout—affirmative]

"Good, good. I like the frank way in which you speak. Well, then, if you're a Christian, you know the *body* doesn't count for a thing. It don't mean shucks to the Lord. It's the *spirit* that counts. The Lord got the notion in His head to send me back, I don't know why, and He wasn't going to be fussy about a silly old body, so He picked a model He had handy and wrapped me up in it for mailing. He got the hair wrong, He forgot to give me a mustache, and just look at this face. Whew! I hope there aren't any small children present; don't let 'em get too good a look at me, if there are. And look at this belly. My lands! And another thing—the Lord wasn't dealing from a full deck when it came to my digits. Look at this: I ain't got but nine fingers. So, as you can maybe guess, I ain't exactly delighted with the frame I been assigned to this time around. But I guess I oughtn't complain. Maybe I even ought to look on the bright side. After all, at least I ain't a nigger."

[Laughter, quickly becoming silence; shout from same man in crowd]

"Well, now, that's a first-rate idea, sir, and you're right—there *is* a pile of samples of my handwriting in the museum. But it wouldn't do as a true test, I'm afraid. My handwriting just ain't what it used to be. After all—" (Holds hand up for crowd to see again)

[Much laughter]

"You're a Dunlap, ain't ya'?"

[Some hubbub]

"I thought so. And I think I see a daughter of the Kerchival clan out there. How about it, ma'am?"

[More hubbub]

"I thought so."

[Shout from crowd]

"My, my. Will Mr. Dunlap *never* be satisfied? But it's all right—he honors the name he wears, with his questioning spirit. It's a spirit that as much as calls me a liar, but that's no matter. The truth is, I want *all* of you to consider me a liar, and try to think of ways to prove I am not your own Sam Clemens. Your good mayor, though he can't hit a golf ball a lick, has been kind enough to open the Ice House Theatre, where I will take the stage tonight. Doors open at seven-thirty, and the trouble starts at eight. Come armed to the teeth with your ugly questions. Bring a dead cat or two, and boil up some tar, and pluck your chickens."

[Shout from crowd—about Mr. Twain's death]

"What's that? I couldn't hear you."

[Same shout]

"Yes, I *did* die. I don't dispute that. My . . . return, my . . . reawakening, baffles me no less than it baffles you. I've spent four months bein' baffled—that's how long I've been back, tiptoeing around and getting the lay of the land, looking out for a prime opportunity for my debut. I hit upon the date—March 19th. My Susy's birthday. She's up in heaven, munchin' on her birthday cake and watchin' over me. I can *feel* it, I can *feel* her eyes on me. As to the *place* of my debut, well, there wasn't ever any question about it. I reckoned I'd cast my fate into the hands of the people of Hannibal. This is where I got my start in my first life, and it's where I mean to get another start, with your blessing. It's in your hands. So . . . until tonight. At this time I would like to step down and renew my acquaintance with the Dunlap line, and the Kerchival line, and I do believe I spy a RoBards out there. Come on up. Come on up, all of you, and shake my poor, disfigured hand."

[Shout from crowd]

"What? What's that I hear? Give us a sign, you say? Oh ye of little faith . . . (Laughs.) Well, I met some of you last night, and I've chatted with some others of you this morning, and all of you did the natural, mean, human thing, which is to say, you tried to catch me in a mistake. But you didn't, did you? Isn't it enough that I can answer any question you can put to me about my life or my books?"

[Shouts of "No!"]

"Well, then—isn't it enough that I have recognized several of you as descendants of my boyhood contemporaries?"

[Shouts of "No!"]

(Laughs.) "I'm not surprised. No. I know the human race. Very well, then. I *shall* give you a sign. It's not much of a sign. I'm afraid I can't wave my hand and mumble something impressive and make that new bridge over yonder fall into the river. I can't hypnotize my boyhood home and make it rise six feet off the ground—besides, it's old and rickety and probably couldn't stand the strain. But I do have a little something for you. It isn't much." Pauses. "As a matter of fact, as I think about it, maybe I'd better not tell you what it is. You're bound to be let-down. No—I think I'd better not."

[Several shouts]

"My, my. You *are* a demanding bunch. You don't have to tell me where I am. I *know* where I am: in the 'Show-Me State.' "

[Cheers]

"I'll give you the sign, then. Don't be disappointed, now. It ain't much. (Chuckles.) It's only just this: right now, at this precise instant, high overhead on the other side of the world, *Halley's Comet is splitting in two.* "

[Much hubbub]

"Astronomers are just now starting to see it. In a half hour or so, ordinary folks will begin to see it with opera glasses—I mean the ordinary folks that are down under. We up on this bulge of the earth will have to wait until tonight to see it, but as sure as I'm standing here, when you cast your eyes to the south, sometime after midnight, you're going to see that old Halley has gone and twinned itself. Half of that comet said to the other half, 'I don't like your style. I'm gonna secede.' Now, word travels pretty fast in the world these days, so I wouldn't be surprised if we caught wind of this development sometime today before we actually *see* it, but that doesn't mean you can't have your own *personal* thrill, like in olden times, because you can. After midnight, just grab some opera glasses and take a boat and go out to the middle of the river for a nice, clear view, and look south. You'll see it, all right. Now, I suspect that some of you—maybe *all* of you—are thinking, 'This dead-beat knows an astronomer somewhere with a good, powerful telescope. That's how he knows.' Well, now, just look at me; I've been in plain view for nearly an hour. I haven't been in communication with *anyone*, here or on the other side of the world. And if that's not good enough, I reckon *this is.* Mr. Mayor?" Pause. "That's right—step right up. Go ahead. Read it."

Pause. Mayor speaks: "Umm, let's see, it says here, 'On March 19th, 1986, at 11:00 a.m., Hannibal time, my heavenly carriage will commence to split in two.' It's signed 'M.T.' "

"And would you tell us, Mr. Mayor, what you read that from?"

"It's a personal ad in the *Courier-Post*, dated February 19th."

"Thank you, sir. You may step down now. Well done. Yes, ladies and gentlemen, I placed that ad there one month ago. Now, I challenge anyone here to find an astronomer that knew a full month ago that Halley was going to split. You won't find a one, as much as they've got their eyes glued on it. Even those foreign spaceships that have been ogling it up close didn't see it. I got the jump on *them,* too. And I'll tell you why. That comet brought me back here, as I was explaining to some of you last night. That comet and I are old friends. That comet is sentient. It *thinks.* It telegraphed its thought to me that it had the notion to split. Oh, I telegraphed back right away, urging him not to do anything rash. But you just can't argue with a comet—I've learned that. Once a comet gets it into his head to split, he's going to split, whether you like the idea or not. That's just their way." Pause. "So, after my talk tonight at the Ice House Theatre, we'll all break for refreshment and we'll stroll down to the river for a nice clear view, and we'll behold that twin marvel soaring over this great land of ours, and then, ladies and gentlemen, you just might find yourself turning to me and saying, 'Mark, I'm glad you're back.' Now, come on up and shake this poor, disfigured hand."

Ricky Olivieri, "our man in Hannibal," filed the following cryptic report from a pay telephone on Hill Street while the crowd broke up. The conversation went something like this; the first speaker is this editor:

"Hello?"
"It's the fat man."
"Hello? Who?"
"It's the fat man. The one with nine fingers."
"What? Ricky? Is that you?"
"It's the liar. The *phe*nom."
"What?"
"The bird-watcher. The notebook peddler."
"What? You mean Laufbahn? What about him?"
"Laufbahn, Umlauf, whatever."
"What about him? What are you saying?"
"Umbahn, Lauflauf—"
"What?"
"—Hofbräu, Oberammergau—"
"Ricky? Hold it. Hold it."
"—Übermensch, Unter den Linden—"
"Ricky, what the hell? Are you drunk?"
"Auf Wiedersehen."

Needless to say, Olivieri's report fell somewhat short of putting me on top of the situation in Hannibal.

But let us consider Umlauf—this seemed to be his favorite name—

and his astonishing debut. Like Caesar, he was ambitious. It is not clear at what point he decided to extend his reach from the notebook fraud into the realm of fraudulent impersonation, but I suspect the idea had taken shape by the time he was in San Francisco and Berkeley. He spent far more time in the reading room of the Bancroft Library, perusing Clemens material, than was necessary to ensure a successful sale of the notebook. No doubt he was industriously preparing for his transformation into Mark Twain—or, as he came to be called in the respectable press, "The Hannibal Claimant."

On the face of it, the plan seemed doomed. True, Umlauf had managed to gain the apparent support of the mayor (a loyal Hannibal booster, who now claims he never saw Umlauf as a resurrected Mark Twain, but only saw him as an opportunity for unusual publicity); also, while singing a song that sounded something like Mark Twain's song, Umlauf had managed to hold the attention of the crowd of townspeople gathered on Hill Street. But he faced a number of obstacles:

1. his body;
2. mankind's reluctance to believe in miracles;
3. the trail he had left behind in the west, especially under the name of Arthur Laufbahn.

Umlauf never effectively solved the first problem. His prophecy of the splitting of Halley was his attempt to solve the second. As to the third, if his scheme succeeded at all, his unforgettable face would be displayed across the nation, where there were many (Dixie the hairdresser, rare books dealer Charles Asquith, hotel desk clerks, et al.) who could say they knew this man under another name. How would he handle it?

For an answer, we turn to the WGEM-TV videotape record of an impromptu news conference held on Hill Street immediately after Umlauf finished pumping the hands of the citizens of Hannibal. Although the videotape shows only Umlauf, its audio portion clearly renders the voices of the reporters; among them can be heard Ricky Olivieri, who after filing his "report" to me joined the circle of questioners, perhaps posing as a member of the press. Below is our transcript of that news conference. We have chosen to identify the reporters only by numbers, for the sake of simplicity. We strongly suspect Reporter Number One was an Umlauf plant:

> UMLAUF: That's right. Gather around now. *(Lights cigar. Puffs on it meditatively.)* As you know, I was once a newspaperman myself. Fire

away, gentlemen—I say "gentlemen," because I fail to see any ladies in your group. This surprises me. From what I have been able to learn in my four months on this earth, womankind has penetrated practically every sphere formerly limited to man. This is good. This is very good. I have always been a woman's rights man, as well as an ardent scholar of the achievements of the ladies. I recall the great tidal wave of mourning that swept over Europe when Joan of Arc fell at Waterloo; I still admire the dulcet strains of Sappho—that sweet singer of Israel; and I stand in awe before Cleopatra's ingenious conquest of George the Third. I see some smiles. Good. I'm glad you're alert. Now, if you boys have any questions, start askin' 'em. I've been silent for seventy-five years, and I've got a powerful urge to talk.

REPORTER No. 1: Sir, what do you think of our Missouri weather?

UMLAUF: Well, we're starting off gentle, aren't we? *(Smiles.)* I find the weather just fine, just fine. I'm tempted to say that everyone talks about the weather, but no one does anything about it, because I have seen that remark attributed to me, but I never said it. A friend of mine did —Charles Dudley Warner, a newspaperman. That explains his clever way with words. *(Eyes twinkle as he surveys the press; puffs on cigar.)*

REPORTER No. 2: Sir, what is the basis of your prediction that Halley's Comet will split?

UMLAUF: Not *will* split. *Is* splitting. It's doing so right now.

REPORTER No. 2: Very well—*is* splitting. What is the—

UMLAUF: I've told you what the basis is. I know the comet. We communicate.

REPORTER No. 2: Isn't that a little far-fetched?

UMLAUF: Talk to me tonight. On the river. Ask me that question then.

REPORTER No. 3: What if Halley *doesn't* split? Won't you look pretty foolish?

UMLAUF: It's splitting. *(Smiles.)* I am satisfied that it is splitting. I don't resent your doubts, by the way. I've always believed it were not best that we should all think alike; it is difference of opinion that makes horse races.

REPORTER No. 4: Mr. "Twain," what have you—

UMLAUF: Just a minute, sir. *(Scrutinizes reporter who just spoke.)* Do you have a condition of some kind?

REPORTER No. 4: A condition?

UMLAUF: Wigglin' two pairs of fingers in the air around my name like that. You got Saint Vitus's dance? *(Grins.)* By the way, do you know what the worst possible affliction is?

OLIVIERI *(in a loud, bored tone):* Rheumatism and Saint Vitus's dance.

UMLAUF *(eyes twinkling):* I see I shall have to work up some new material. But you, sir, with your finger-wigglin'—are you impersonating an ant? Are those your antennae?

REPORTER No. 4: I just wanted to ask you what you had been up to in the past four months, since your alleged return.

UMLAUF *(frowning):* "Alleged"? Sir, I want to like you. At the moment, I don't, but I *want* to. I truly do. But you *must* choose your words more carefully. *(Grins.)* Speaking of words, it's always been my belief that the *right* word is all-important. Why, the difference between the *almost* right word, and the *right* word, is—

OLIVIERI *(in a very loud, bored tone):* —the difference between the lightning-bug and the lightning.

UMLAUF *(jaw slightly set, showing the strain):* That's exactly right, young man. You don't know what pleasure it gives me to know my words have survived me so well. But I believe there was a question— Oh yes, what have I been doing in the past four months. I'll tell you. I've been loafing. I made a bit of money playing blackjack in Carson City, and I have mainly spent my time reading in cheap little hotel rooms. History and politics. Trying to catch up, you see.

REPORTER No. 1: Fiction too, sir?

UMLAUF: No, no. *(Puffs at cigar, which has gone out.)* I don't read much fiction—never did. And the modern novels—well, with their language and all, I positively *blush* to read 'em. *(Grins.)* You know, I always said—

OLIVIERI *(drawling in an extremely loud and bored sing-song):* Man is the only animal that blushes—or needs to.

UMLAUF *(not missing a beat, but with testiness):* Right you are again, sonny boy.

REPORTER No. 2: What about the afterlife? What is it like?

UMLAUF: I shall tell you if you will stop smiling, sir. Your colleagues know that your question is facetious. You needn't telegraph it to 'em like that. *(Studies reporter.)* Good. Now, it's a curious thing about the afterlife. I have no recollection of it. If there *is* a heaven, and if I've been there, I cannot remember it. *(Looks around, sweeps his arm out.)* As far as I'm concerned, this simple, innocent town drowsing in the sunlight—*this* is heaven *(looks at one person in particular, probably Olivieri, and points at him),* so *you'd* better make the most of it.

(Mild laughter from reporters greets this remark; as it dies down, Olivieri's laughter stands out as a hollow, mocking laugh, snapping to an end with a barking exclamation of the name "Umlauf," as shown below.)

OLIVIERI: HAHAHAhahahahmmmm*um*lauf.

REPORTER NO. 1: Have you met any ladies, sir? Would you consider remarrying?

UMLAUF: No, no. Oh, I've met some ladies—some lovely ones, in fact—but just look at this face of mine. A body can't get no show with a face like this. I'm awful bitter about it, and it pains me to talk about it. But never mind that. Besides, you must remember that I've already been married once, and I have always been convinced of the truth of the biblical assertion that a man cannot serve two masters.

(Mild laughter from reporters.)

OLIVIERI: HAHAHAhahahahmmmm*um*lauf.

UMLAUF *(raising a hand to silence further questions while relighting his cigar):* I would like to return to an earlier question—the one about my activity over the past months. I don't believe I did it justice. I arrived in Carson City in November, and I stayed there, in a hotel called the Ormsby House, until late in January. Thence I traveled to San Francisco, where I stayed, naturally, in the lovely Mark Twain Hotel. But I found life in California too . . . too various. The sensible people of the Middle West will know what I mean by that. So I traveled east, by train and by bus, stopping frequently along the route I had followed in the opposite direction way back in 1861, retracing my steps, as you might say. I can give you the names of the hotels I stayed in on my way here, with dates, if you like. If you examine the registers you will find the name I used all this time: "Oscar Umlauf." That's U-M-L-A-U-F. *(Eyes twinkle, wandering over reporters, coming to rest on Olivieri.)*

REPORTER NO. 1: Sir, would it be safe to stay that the report of your death has been greatly exaggerated?

(Mild laughter from Umlauf and other reporters; raucous, mocking laughter from Olivieri, who ends his laugh in a new way.)

OLIVIERI: HAHAHAhahahahmmmm*lauf*bahn.

UMLAUF: You know, back in my former life, on the day when those reporters came flocking to my door, on account of that rumor, I noticed one of them looking awful sheepish. I asked him why he looked that way. He handed me the cabled instructions from his editor, which read, "If Mark Twain dying, send five hundred words; if dead, send one thousand."

(Laughter.)

OLIVIERI: HAHAHAhahahahmmmm*lauf*bahn.

REPORTER No. 3: Given your appearance, how—

UMLAUF *(hand upraised):* Allow me, if I may, to say a little bit more about my . . . my recent past. Please. *(Pauses; struggles for words—or perhaps only seems to.)* I . . . I stretched things a bit when I told the crowd I had no idea why I had been brought back into the world. I do have an inkling—*more* than an inkling, really. I reckon I *know* why I'm back. It has to do with an instance of bad behavior on my part, unknown to the world at large until just recently. You're probably familiar with this dispute over *Huck Finn,* the one that got started when one of my old notebooks was discovered. I want to say for the record, right here and now, that the notebook is genuine; that my brother, Orion, who taught me the printer's trade in this very town, was the author of the bulk of *Huck Finn,* which he wrote while we were in the Nevada Territory; that I persuaded Orion to delay his attempts to publish it until well after the bitterness from the War had passed, because of the book's abolitionist sentiments, which would have just murdered sales in the South; that Orion, true to his nature, subsequently forgot about the manuscript in the heat of manifold new enthusiasms; that I, having retained the manuscript, took it up again much later, in 1876, fiddling with it here and there with the intention of publishing it under my own name, only to pigeonhole it out of shame; and that—conscience being a weak, fickle, changeable thing—I ultimately demolished my principles on this point and took up the work anew in 1883 and brought it to its conclusion. *Huck Finn* is ninety percent Orion's book, gentlemen. The world has been ignorant of this fact for all these years. Providence, unhappy with the unearned praise heaped upon me for the book, sent me back. Why? I shall tell you why. Providence sent me back—*to find that notebook.* Yes, it is shocking news, but it is the truth. Gentlemen, *I am the discoverer of my own notebook.* You will remember the name I used, on that chilly day on the Stanislaus: "Arthur Laufbahn." That's L-A-U-F-B-A-H-N. *(Nods head slowly, with deep self-satisfaction, eyeing Olivieri all the while.)* You can go ask that fellow, what's his name . . . yes, I have it—Asquith. Charles Asquith. He's the one I sold the notebook to. Show him my picture. Ask him if I'm not the same man. I know what you're thinking—you're thinking what an amazing coincidence it is that *I* of all people found the notebook. Coincidence—hmmmmph. 'Twas Providence, my lads, Providence. *(Puffs at cigar, which has gone out again.)* You know, an uneasy conscience is a hair in the mouth, and this particular hair tortured me for the last twenty-five years of my life. *(Sighs.)* Confession tires a body so—I do believe I am out of wind. *(Looking off to one side.)* Herbert? *(A short man sidles up to him—Herbert Hummel; they privately exchange a few words.)* Gentlemen, I shall now retire to my room for a rest, in preparation for the evening's events. I hope to see you in the Theatre, and then later, outside, for that celestial surprise. I thank you, one and all.

REPORTER No. 3: Sir, excuse me, but there are still a few points—

UMLAUF *(hand genially upraised)*: No, no.

REPORTER No. 2: But sir—

UMLAUF: No, no. You've got enough to fill a couple of columns, especially if you pad your story with "background" material—the notebook problem, previous appearances of Halley's Comet, choice selections from my Sandwich Islands lecture, names of my cats, names of *your* cats —just heave in anything you've a mind to. I'm sure you're experienced at that sort of thing. So, until tonight. *(Waves; walks through group of reporters, brushing their questions aside; shakes hands with a few townspeople still gathered around, claps a few on the shoulder, then is free of the crowd, with Hummel beside him; Olivieri appears in the picture, hurrying after them; videotape ends.)*

The last segment of tape shows Olivieri clearly in pursuit of, and gaining on, Umlauf and Hummel. What happened from that point on is not known and, as of this writing, cannot be determined. One is initially tempted to think the following: that after Umlauf had deftly parried Olivieri's futile sallies during the press conference and had even worked them around to his own advantage, Olivieri, in a fit of pique, overtook him at the foot of Hill Street and challenged him outright, telling him that he knew Umlauf was a co-conspirator in the notebook hoax and that he knew, just as Umlauf knew, that the real Samuel Clemens was afoot. One reason for such a confrontation would be to learn from Umlauf, if possible, just *where* Clemens was afoot. But considering that Umlauf apparently tolerated Olivieri's presence in his growing entourage for at least a week following the moment in question—an unlikely eventuality if Umlauf knew how fully informed, and therefore how dangerous, Olivieri was— there was probably no such confrontation. Olivieri seems to have chosen to swallow his anger and bide his time. Likewise Umlauf, who must have kept a wary eye on this stranger who had mysteriously barked his recent aliases at him during the press conference.

Olivieri's next telephone report to me sheds some light, but not a glare, on what happened after the press conference; it tells us that Olivieri at least made his identity known (though not necessarily the full extent of his knowledge) to Umlauf's assistant. To my recollection, his report went as follows:

> "He's got this creep with him."
>
> "Ricky? Now slow down. Just—"
>
> "A little creep. God, I'd like to belt him one."
>
> "Let's back up a bit, Ricky. We're here, and you're clear out there, and we—"
>
> "The creep has gone ape over him. Gone ape over the ape."
>
> "Let's just take it a step at a time, Ricky."
>
> "He says, 'You're from the Mark Twain Papers? You're one of those possessive perverts?' "
>
> "What? 'Perverts'?"
>
> "He says, 'You're just like Howells, aren't you? *My* Mark Twain, *my* Mark Twain. Listen to me,' he says, the little creep. 'He's not *your* Mark Twain. Oh, no. And he's not Howells' either. He's *mine.* He's *my* Mark Twain.' "
>
> "Ricky? Ricky, you're going to have to walk me through this again."
>
> "I'm gonna go belt him one. Bye."

A rational word about Umlauf's assistant is in order here. In the opinion of this editor, Herbert Hummel's association with Umlauf was an innocent one. His later refusal—perhaps ill-judged—to cooperate with Umlauf's biographers has of course cast suspicion on him, but his refusal springs from an understandable desire to disassociate himself from Umlauf altogether. Hummel is no confidence man. He is simply a Mark Twain devotee whose devotion led him to champion a false cause.

Having said this much, I must, somewhat regrettably, say something more. Readers of this volume have met Hummel before. Several weeks after Clemens' second sojourn on earth was over, I visited Dan Harris, Curator of the Boyhood Home and Museum in Hannibal, to obtain his version of the events narrated here. When I mentioned Hummel, Harris smiled and went to his files. He pulled out, first, the transcript of Umlauf's debut speech, given above, and, second, a thick wad of manuscripts— essays that Hummel had written and wished to see added to the Museum archives. Their titles had a familiar interrogative ring: "What Famous People Did He Meet?," "How Much Time Did He Spend on the Water?" and so on. The essays confirmed something that Clemens told me in his last communication with me (letter of 11 April 1986, given in "On the Trail of Samuel Clemens: The East"), namely that Herbert Hummel is The

Twain Man. Immediately upon learning of the arrest of "Mark Twain" in Florida, Missouri, Hummel evidently rushed south to Hannibal from his home in Muscatine, Iowa. He met Umlauf and instantly put himself at the great man's disposal. Thus, after having been in the presence of the real Samuel Clemens without knowing it, Hummel suffered the additional irony of allying himself to a charlatan. As Clemens wrote of him in "The Twain Man," "how pathetically his enthusiasm misfires!"

To return to the 19 March events in Hannibal, after his press conference, Umlauf napped, dined, and then lectured in the Ice House Theatre. Readers will recall that the news that Halley's Comet had in fact split, as predicted by Umlauf, first reached the United States in the early afternoon, and satellite-beamed pictures appeared on the evening television broadcasts across the nation. As a result, the Ice House Theatre was packed to overflowing. A complete transcript of Umlauf's speech is on file in the Mark Twain Papers. Suffice it to say here that after three hours of standard Mark Twain stories and derivative imitations, interspersed throughout with unctuous flattery of his audience (the *real* Clemens would have condemned it as "rot and slush" and "soul-butter and hogwash"), Umlauf capped the evening by leading the audience in the singing of "Happy Birthday," in celebration of Susy Clemens' birthday.

It would be a mistake to take the size and festive mood of Umlauf's audience as a measure of its belief in his claim to be Mark Twain—a mistake that was made by one wire-service reporter, whose widely printed story simultaneously exaggerated the gullibility of the citizens of Hannibal and gave early impetus to Umlauf's rise to brief national notoriety. Similarly, festiveness—but not necessarily credulity—reigned when, after the lecture, many members of the audience hauled their boats out of winter dry dock and went on a midnight cruise. The river became glutted with boats, there was much drinking, and at least two accidents resulted, fortunately neither of them causing serious injuries. By order of the mayor, Hannibal's streetlights were turned off, to allow a clearer view of the sky. When, shortly after 2 A.M., Halley rose above the southern horizon and shone in its twin glory, the raucous cheers rolled across the waves.

Much of Umlauf's story from this point on is well known. (See the highly partisan, and therefore unintentionally comic, *The Return of Mark Twain*, by Albert Syler [Boston: Billfinger Press, 1986], and the more objective *I Get Around: The Strange Career of Oscar Umlauf,* by Ingrid Thorsten [New York: Damrell, 1987].) Thus there is no need here to chronicle Umlauf's day-to-day activities. However, I shall touch on Umlauf's story where previous writers have been silent or in error, and where it intersects with Clemens' story. One such matter I shall take up immediately: the famous incident of the Mark Twain Party Barge.

Umlauf concluded his speech in the Ice House Theatre by announcing that henceforth he would travel only by water. (Herbert Hummel, if he showed Umlauf his essay on the subject—a reasonable assumption—may have inadvertently originated the notion.) "Mine is a watery planet!" declared the impostor. The announcement served its intended purpose: it captured everyone's attention. "Travel only by water?" one thinks. "How odd." Reporters on the scene dwelt fondly on the announcement, and, in the following three weeks, they monitored Umlauf's circuitous progress after leaving Hannibal with the zeal of preservationists tracking the lumbering migration of a resurrected dodo. But Umlauf's "fluvial commitment," as it came to be called, served him in another way as well, one that he could not possibly have foreseen but, once espied, that he milked for all it was worth. At some point during the river revel, Umlauf spoke with the mayor of Hannibal about his need for a boat. Could the mayor recommend where he might purchase or rent one? The mayor, forever forthcoming, said he could help him there all right: the City of Hannibal had recently impounded a boat that had turned up at the wharf and had sat there, unclaimed, for three weeks. The City would count itself proud to let Mr. Twain borrow it for as long as he liked. Mr. Twain would like the boat's brand name too, he added; it was a "Mark Twain Party Barge." They arranged to meet at the riverfront the next day at noon.

According to several witnesses to the event, Umlauf and the mayor boarded the boat—a thirty-foot pontoon deck boat equipped with a 110-horsepower motor—while reporters and hangers-on stood at dockside. Umlauf studied the vessel's lines, declaimed ponderously upon its riverworthiness, and delivered himself of a few chestnuts about the golden days of steamboating. Then he worked his way to the storage compartments under the rear seats. He lingered there for some time, while the mayor, seated behind the wheel, tested the engine and the accessories. Umlauf suddenly spun away from the compartments in what one observer recalls as "a monstrous pirouette," and he let out a howl of some kind—of ecstasy? Of anguish? No one could tell. He then staggered the length of the boat, fell forward against a railing, and collapsed in a heap on the bow.

The observers sprang aboard to assist him. When he finally came to, he was muttering incoherently. Eventually his mutterings became intelligible. "The change!" he said. "The change!"

"The change, Mr. Twain? What change?"

"The change! The change! Oh! It came over me. Sometimes I

. . . Oh, the change!" Umlauf glanced up to the stern of the boat and snapped out, with unexpected clarity (but a crisis had arisen; he *had* to speak), "Get away from that compartment! Don't touch anything!" Seeing that his command had been obeyed, he fell to swooning and muttering some more, again becoming coherent by stages. He haltingly explained that every now and then his present body became exactly like his first body—not all over, but just in parts. Sometimes it happened to his face, other times to his feet, and *this* time it had happened to his hands. "It's a blessing, in a way," he managed to say, "painful though it was. It's a blessing because I know there are still those who don't believe I am who I am. *One* sign is not enough, astonishing as it is. They want more. I know the human race. They always want more. All right—I'll give you more —one more, and then *no* more. You will find some fingerprints and palm prints on various items in that compartment that I touched as I was browsing through it. Call your police force, Mr. Mayor. Let them put their very best men on the job. In the meantime, I suggest you seal off the area. I must go to my room now and nap. Herbert!"

There are no existing prints of Clemens' fingers. Umlauf certainly knew this. There is, however, a photographic print of Clemens' entire right hand, which was taken in 1907 and reproduced in the New York *World* on 21 August of that year. The negative of that print shows just a few whorls in the fingers, but it captures the palm lines, which are equally useful for identification, in striking detail. Umlauf certainly knew this as well. One of his disciples (not Hummel; there were many others by this time) called the attention of a reporter to a reproduction of the 1907 palm print on page 151 of Milton Meltzer's *Mark Twain Himself* (New York: Bonanza Books, 1960). The reporter passed the word on to the Marion County Sheriff's Office forensic experts, who were busily studying the "various items" in the storage compartment that Umlauf had "touched" —that is, that he scrupulously had *not* touched. These consisted solely of six empty beer bottles (Bass Pale Ale), four of which yielded clear portions of palm prints, each bottle showing a part of the palm not wholly represented on any of the others. Working with these four bottles, the forensic experts produced a composite palm print with fine detail to it. They compared this print with the print in the Meltzer book and announced that the two bore "a resemblance approaching identity." They added that they would need the negative to speak with absolute certainty. In his book, Meltzer properly credited the print to the Mark Twain Estate, which now bears the name of the Mark Twain Papers. Our phone rang right away.

We hung fire. Here is why: in a mere matter of four days we had experienced from afar, with mounting amazement, the following:

1. the arrest in Florida, Missouri, of "Mark Twain," whom we assumed to be our quarry, going public with his delusion or imposture at last;

2. the revelation that the arrestee was the nine-digited Ormsby House Phenomenon (= Oscar Umlauf/Arthur Laufbahn);

3. Umlauf's accurate prediction of the splitting of Halley's Comet, an apparent miracle that we were unable to explain;

4. the matching of the beer-bottle palm prints with the print in the Meltzer book.

The second event forced us to modify our view of things, insofar as we had one. We knew we were in search of a Clemens-claimant. Umlauf's debut forced us to contend with an apparently new, different Clemens-claimant—moreover, one that our original claimant had written about, but with no hint that he shared our original claimant's delusion. But could this new claimant be our original one? That is, could *he* have authored the manuscript left at our doorstep, in a portion of which he portrayed himself as a person distinct from the person he claimed he was? But then who was the man who toured the Mark Twain Papers? Certainly not this new claimant; the body was all wrong. Our new theory, such as it was, was that there were indeed two claimants, perhaps in league with each other.

The third event, I confess, made us wonder about Umlauf precisely as he intended us to wonder about him. Given his gift of prediction, perhaps he *was* a being of a different order. Perhaps he was *Mark Twain*. And if his body was subject to "the change" (the fourth event), and if he had toured the Papers when under its sway, his closer resemblance to Clemens at that time could thereby be explained.

But there was, of course, another possible explanation for those beer-bottle palm prints. Our original quarry had stated, in his Livy letter of 12 February, "I have a mind to buy me a little boat & make the trip [upriver] alone." We obtained a list of dealers in the New Orleans area who handled the Mark Twain line of boats, and we made some phone calls. We found one Amos Nickerson, owner of Nickerson's Boats and Motors in New Orleans, who possessed a receipt showing a 13 February purchase of a Mark Twain Party Barge by a Dick Allbright, whose address was given as "Mark Twain Crater, lat. −10.5, long. 138.5, Southwest Quadrant, Planet Mercury"—a detail Nickerson had overlooked at the time of purchase and commented on perplexedly during our phone conversation. Nickerson had no trouble recalling the transaction, in part because the purchaser had paid in cash, and in part because the purchaser, in Nickerson's words, "was the most ignorant fool about boating equipment of any damned fool I ever met."

As Clemens might have said, "Now this was something more *like.*" Hannibal police had impounded the Mark Twain Party Barge shortly before 19 March, after having seen it lie idle for some three weeks. That is, the boat first appeared at the Hannibal wharf in late February, a time that corresponds with the 25 February check-in date by Dick Allbright at the Tom 'n Huck Motel in Hannibal. If Clemens departed from New Orleans on, or shortly after, 13 February, he could easily have reached Hannibal by 25 February, especially if sleep continued to elude him. I use the name "Clemens" advisedly at this point, for this is what we began to call our quarry from this moment on. His purchase of the boat, and later of the bottles of Bass Pale Ale, and his journey upriver, combined to make for a far more plausible explanation of the palm prints than the nine-fingered man's pretensions to spontaneous bodily metamorphoses. Ultimately, then, while to many people Umlauf's second "sign" confirmed his claim about his identity, to us it confirmed his fraudulence.

Regarding the negative of the palm print, we certainly did not want to lend support to Umlauf's imposture, but at the same time we were not quite ready to go public with our version of the story. We admitted to possession of the negative but insisted that it could be examined only at the Papers. We would not send it to Hannibal. This passed, as we hoped it would, for mere archival crotchetiness, and bought us a little time. A group of specialists and reporters came to Berkeley, and when Umlauf was chugging down the Mississippi toward Cairo, Illinois, the word went out: a perfect match. Umlauf was on a roll.

How did he know that Clemens had touched those beer bottles? All I can say is that in addition to the bottles, there must have been some other evidence that Clemens had been aboard, perhaps some written notes or discarded manuscript, which Umlauf could have surreptitiously pocketed before going into his swoon. (Given his complicity in the notebook hoax, he would certainly have recognized Clemens' handwriting.) It was a bold stroke, to be sure. No doubt an examination of the entire boat would have produced prints in places Umlauf hadn't touched, but no one thought of suggesting that. (By the time *I* thought of it, Umlauf was on the river, traveling with a rather unwieldy retinue of true believers and reporters, and the prints would have been obliterated.) And no one thought to ask, at least publicly, why Umlauf had bothered to touch the bottles in the first place. Had the question arisen, I am sure he would have had an answer —"I was thirsty and was looking for an unopened one," or "I was interested in the label. I always liked English beer, you know. The English were always good to me, too—why, when I received my honorary Oxford degree in 1907 . . ." I am sure he had something handy. He was probably disappointed the question never came up.

Olivieri was not on the immediate scene when Umlauf experienced "the change." We know this not directly from Olivieri, but indirectly, from police reports and court records of 20 March, which indicate that at that hour he was being arraigned on charges of breaking and entering into the Marion County Department of Public Health. Why did he do this? Note that his quest for Clemens was directed at every turn by the manuscript of *I Been There Before*. "A Glimpse: II," which was probably written in Hannibal, features a character with an "unexplained pain in his cod"; thus Clemens was interested in this subject, perhaps even preoccupied with it. In another sketch of likely Hannibal provenance, "St. Peter Helps Me Feel Good About Myself," an essay is referred to—"Why I Killed My Brother"—which is contained in a book evidently purchased by Clemens in Hannibal—*IMT*; that book also contains the essay "Clemens' Clap," cited above (p. 145). Olivieri's keenly mad reasoning was that if Clemens was interested enough in himself to read the former essay, it is likely that he also read the latter. Upon reading it, either (a) Clemens wondered with astonishment if the thesis of the essay could possibly be true, or (b) Clemens ruefully acknowledged its truth. Whichever was the case, he might have feared his affliction persisted into his second life, which would naturally prompt him to seek a diagnosis. Thus Olivieri raided the clinic in the predawn hours of 20 March, seeking evidence of such a visit, perhaps in the hope of finding a local address or phone number for his quarry.

Olivieri used his one phone call from the jail to file his final report from Hannibal, roughly as follows:

> "He went to a clinic."
> "Ricky? Now listen to me. Just—"
> "He wanted to see if he had it."
> "Ricky . . . Had it? Had what?"
> "I saw the form—the medical history he filled out. It's his handwriting. I *saw* it, *held* it, *pocketed* it—but the bastards took it away."
> "Ricky, I don't know what—"

"I'm so *close.*"

"Ricky—"

"He used an alias, but he didn't fool *me.*"

"There's a large question of responsibility, Ricky—to me, to the Papers, to scholarship itself. Frankly—"

"He used Twichell's name. Isn't that just like him?"

"Twichell? Twichell?"

"Isn't he a dear old thing?"

"Ricky—"

"The results were negative, thank God. He's got enough problems. Me, too—I'm off to Death Row. Bye."

This is the closest I have come to the evidence of Clemens' visit to the clinic, for which he evidently assumed the name of his Hartford minister, Joseph Twichell. During my own research in Hannibal, and for several months thereafter, the Marion County Department of Public Health steadfastly refused to divulge its records to me. Then one day the Twichell file simply disappeared—presumably either stolen by someone with an eye to its commercial value (in which case it may surface someday), or destroyed by a devotee who found the subject threatening to Mark Twain's reputation.

One wonders exactly what prompted Clemens to seek this diagnosis. Was he symptomatic? If asymptomatic, did he just want to satisfy his curiosity? Or was he sexually active, and did he fear he might be infectious? Or maybe he intended (or hoped) to become sexually active, assuming he could conquer his Victorian inhibitions and also avoid the blunders of the "perfect saphead" sort described in his 10 March letter to Howells. Clemens returns to the subject, but not altogether reliably, in his final communication to me of 11 April.

I should note here that the Twichell file and the evidence of the presence of "Dick Allbright" at the Tom 'n Huck Motel are the only certain indications of Clemens' 25 February–12 March stay in Hannibal. Whatever chats or encounters he may have had were evidently not memorable enough to be recalled by townspeople in the quiet, early phase of my investigation; as public interest in the issue grew, many later testimonies were enthusiastically volunteered. (These are of doubtful validity; the complete file is in the Mark Twain Papers.) Consider Clemens' productivity in this period. In addition to the reading he did, he wrote two "Glimpses," the St. Peter sketch, the Howells letter, and very possibly the two sketches purportedly written while he was aboard the *Delta Queen.*

In contrast to his adventurous boyhood, Clemens' stay in Hannibal in his second life was apparently quite studious.

Olivieri, whom I earlier labeled a "shy" person, had become quite irrepressible by this point. Shortly after his arraignment, he bolted through an open courthouse window and eluded pursuing policemen in the woods to the south of town. That evening, at Lock 22 on the Mississippi River (about ten miles south of Hannibal), he boarded Umlauf's Party Barge; a Hannibal reporter who had ridden on the first short leg of the cruise disembarked at the lock, thereby making room for Olivieri, who the reporter says boarded without any particular notice by Umlauf or anyone else.

Olivieri went entirely underground at that point. We at the Mark Twain Papers charted Umlauf's progress as well as we could—by reading the weekly tabloids, where he was an instant sensation after his debut speech, and by reading frequent stories in the mainstream dailies, where Umlauf had become a subject of fairly enduring quizzical interest and somewhat futile critical inquiry. We followed his progress south to Cairo, Illinois, then east, up the Ohio, his ultimate destination unknown but much speculated about in the press.

We also read fragments of his speeches, delivered at river towns where he docked to take on supplies or to spend the night. Since the new "Mark Twain" seemed to have no recent history apart from the one he had described in his Hannibal press conference, reporters focused heavily on these speeches, searching for the Mark Twain "style"—or rather, its antithesis. Special attention came to rest on Umlauf's comment on his strange body, originally made in Hannibal but repeated on several occasions afterward—it seemed to be a favorite of his: "At least I ain't a nigger." The impression of reporters and the early consensus of Mark Twain scholars was that the real Mark Twain would never have said such a thing. Scholars cited Mark Twain's financial support of several black students in their college educations; his fond words about Frederick Douglass and other black leaders; and his affection for his black servants in Hartford and Elmira. (They also would have cited *Huckleberry Finn* for its loving portrayal of Jim, but that book was a shaky document—certainly not because of the charges of a year earlier that it was somehow racist, but only because the 1861–64 notebook had raised questions about its authorship.) The opinion of this editor was solicited, and from the many documents that sprang to mind I cited a rather out-of-the-way one, valuable because there can be no question of its being an instance of public posturing. It was an 8 January 1885 letter to Livy, in which Clemens recounts, in simple language rich with indignation, this incident during a train ride through Southern Illinois:

> A small country boy, a while ago, discussed a negro woman in her easy hearing distance, to his 17-year old sister. "Mighty good clothes for a nigger, *hain't* they? *I* never see a nigger dressed so fine before." She *was* thoroughly well & tastefully dressed, & had more brains & breeding than 7 generations of that boy's family will be able to show. (*LLMT*, p. 225)

Unfortunately, Clemens never shed the word "nigger" from his vocabulary, using it with apparent ease and thoughtlessness throughout his life, and this fact was cited by some of Umlauf's champions, who also uncovered an equally thoughtless remark in a June 1872 letter to Howells; Clemens, thanking Howells with relief for his favorable *Atlantic* review of *Roughing It*, wrote, "I am as uplifted and reassured by it as a mother who has given birth to a white baby when she was awfully afraid it was going to be a mulatto" (*MTHL*, pp. 10–11). Sadly, the scholarly community was forced to counter with the weaker claim that the real Mark Twain would never have said Umlauf's infamous sentence *publicly*.

While this debate was being conducted, a black woman in New York City suddenly announced, or was reported to have announced, that (a) she had met Mark Twain in New York, (b) they had fallen in love with each other, and (c) she was now carrying his child. At the time, the woman's announcement was widely viewed as some sort of offbeat contribution to the public debate over Mark Twain's racial views. Umlauf, when informed of her claim, did a curious thing. He hedged; he temporized. Perhaps he was waiting to see if he could benefit in any way from confirming it. The woman, who never revealed her name to reporters, disappeared from public view as suddenly as she had entered it, but other mother-claimants, black and white, came out of the woodwork. Umlauf, evidently seeing that trouble lay that way, denounced "the whole tribe" as impostors.

Shortly afterward—perhaps with an eye to sexual opportunity—new Clemens-claimants announced themselves: a schoolteacher in Milpitas, California, an accountant in Sydney, Australia, and a professional clown in London, who at least had on his side a sentence uttered by the real Clemens in 1907, while he was en route to England to receive his Oxford degree: "I may never go to London again until I come back to this sphere after I am dead, and then I would like to live in London" (*MTS*, p. 554). Umlauf ranted and fumed and threatened these three with lawsuits. Privately, though, he must have been pleased that Mark Twain's prediction of his return to "this sphere" had been unearthed.

While we were monitoring these events, we prepared to go public with our side of the story. Although we still had no explanation for Umlauf's prediction of Halley's splitting, we were confident in the strength of our evidence on all other points. We had the manuscript—Parts I and II of *I Been There Before;* we had a photocopy of Amos Nickerson's sales receipt for the Mark Twain Party Barge, showing Dick Allbright's signature in Clemens' hand; we had eyewitness testimony from desk clerks in San Francisco and Hannibal. (Unfortunately, we were unable to find a trace of Clemens' stay in New Orleans; he may have stayed in a hotel we failed to contact, or he may have used an alias unknown to us.) In addition to desiring to sink Umlauf's Party Barge, we were motivated by the ominously approaching "Who Wrote *Huckleberry Finn?*" Symposium, scheduled for 9–10 April in New York City. Advance copies of the papers to be presented had been trickling into our office—ingenious arguments that Orion could have written *Huckleberry Finn,* and equally ingenious arguments trying to explain away the 1861–64 notebook. Given our strong sense of where the truth lay, it would have been unforgivable if we allowed the meeting to go forward.

But Umlauf's speeches took a bizarre turn, causing us to hang fire once again. Some examples:

> I'm certainly chalking up miracles at an impressive rate. I return from the dead: there's one. My body changes back and forth between my former beauty and my present mud-fence article: there's another. I understand that Catholics consider two miracles sufficient for beatification. Will someone please tell me how many are necessary for sainthood? (Speech in Cincinnati, 27 March 1986)

> You don't know what pleasure it gives me to be here at the birthplace of the most famous general, and one of the most famous Presidents, in our land. I knew President Grant well. Why, I published his *Memoirs* and presented his widow with the largest single royalty check in history. I knew *many* famous people in my former life. Why, I hardly know where to begin in listing them—there's Grover Cleveland, Thomas Edison, Kipling, Longfellow, Emerson, Holmes, Aesop, John Bunyan . . . I am glad to see you are awake. I admire that in an audience. (Speech at Point Pleasant, Ohio, 28 March 1986)

These are close paraphrases and fragmentary direct quotations of material in *I Been There Before.* Reading these words, so precious to us by then, with attributions to Umlauf, was a cruel and confusing blow. How did he know what "our" Mark Twain had written? The two men had been together in the west, so it was possible that Umlauf had read and even copied the western works from which he quotes (the 10 December Livy letter and "The Ormsby House Phenomenon"), but the second passage also draws from "The Twain Man"—a work written by Clemens after the two men had presumably parted.

But *had* they parted? Could they have traveled upriver together, despite Clemens' evident disgust with Umlauf after his tour of the Papers (he had vowed to rid himself of Umlauf before, and failed) and despite the total absence of any mention of Umlauf as a traveling companion during the writing of the Mississippi portion of the manuscript? Could Clemens have been in Hannibal during Umlauf's debut, unobserved—even by Olivieri—in his shorn state? Could Umlauf and Clemens have been together even now, aboard the Party Barge, with Clemens watching Umlauf's progress with amusement and feeding him lines? But then what were we to make of the evidence that reporters had uncovered of Umlauf's stays in Salt Lake City, Laramie, Wyoming, and Kearney, Nebraska— evidence he had invited them to seek out that showed that he had taken an overland route to Hannibal? Or, to resurrect another theory (one we did resurrect then), could Umlauf be Mark Twain after all? Could he have made the journey upriver that the manuscript chronicles, while a confederate (for obscure reasons) sprinkled a trail of "Umlaufs" across the continent?

In this storm of conflicting theories, we reluctantly canceled our plans to go public and decided to wait for new developments. And as we waited, the "Who Wrote *Huckleberry Finn?*" Symposium approached, day by day, until it was upon us.

The Mississippi River section of our report threatens to end now with Umlauf in ascension and Clemens in total eclipse. After Umlauf's debut, three frustrating weeks would pass before I would hear from Clemens again. Something in me resists allowing Umlauf's star to shine so brightly, even for a moment, and so I shall close this section with the cover letter from Clemens that accompanied the third, or eastern, installment of *I Been There Before:*

April 8/86

Dear Mr. Dixon—

Can you believe the cheeky impertinence of that base scoundrel? His rascality deserves a place among the fine arts. He "predicts" that

Halley will split, therefore he is Mark Twain? There's logic for you. *What about his body???* If I looked like *that,* I would have extinguished my chunk long ago.

Well, then—you are doubtless wondering—how *did* he predict it? I'll tell you. First, he didn't predict it. *I* did. Second, I didn't *predict* it. I *saw* it happen, saw that comet split, from the deck of the *Bejesus Bejohnson,* six hours out of Melbourne. If you have carefully read my earlier work composed during this sojourn,—which you have my encouragement to publish if, as I fervently hope, I depart this second life as expected; I suggest the title *Very, Very Late Tales & Sketches*—then you know about my peculiar & damnable knack for putting back the clock. Well, back on February 4, the day before I visited your establishment, I reckon I logged a "muggins." The next day I did *not* visit your establishment. I can't remember what I did—probably moped around the hotel room, waiting for my ugly pal to make his sale of my "notebook." He eventually did, & I lit out for balmier climes—the South Seas, New Zealand, Australia. Lazy, pleasant days of butterfly idleness, take them all in all, though I did have a few pangs of conscience (I can't even say "a hair in the mouth" now—I'd sound as if I were quoting that bastard,) about the filthiness of the lucre that sponsored my voyage. Then—I shall skip details, the days blend into one another so, on the ocean—on March 20, high overhead in that southern sky, Halley split. This was March 19 in Hannibal—it's always been a slow, backward place. A few more days passed, maybe as much as a week, & I inadvertently blurted out a "Damnation!" & was back in San Francisco, back to February 4th.

Now, when time throws you around so, when it obliterates one & a half months of history, you naturally want to share the news with someone, & so I told my goddam—I mean *quondam*—pal, Mr. Oscar Umlauf—ain't it a belchy name? Told him all about my loops, though I didn't understand the causes, not then, not until I got to the river. Also, idiot that I am, I told him about Halley. He expressed an ever-so-mild interest & asked me, ever so casual-like (casual-*like;* nothing is ever *truly* casual with that lying machine,) about the particulars of the comet-split. "Are you *sure* it was six hours out of Melbourne? My, my. And what ship did you say you were on? Oh, you didn't say? Well, what ship was it? &c &c." Of course, all he had to do was check the *Bejesus Bejohnson*'s schedule for that cruise, & he would know when to time his "prediction." How was I to know he was storing up material to spring on the innocents of the world?

I'm afraid posterity will forever be denied the works I wrote on that ocean cruise. I didn't have them on my person, you see, when I out with that "Damnation!" To make up for that loss, I enclose herewith the third, &, I desperately hope, FINAL installment of my work. I have a strong sense I will bid the planet adieu on April 11th (you must see "A Curious Encounter," enclosed here, for the details,) & you can bet that ever since I established the link between those two words & their power to drag time out, I have been very, very careful in my speech. When in a self-rebuking mood, I now call myself an "Umlauf." I also swear with his name. It is a great comfort. I recommend it to you.

Yours truly,
Mark Twain

P.S.—In looking over the above, I see I may have confused you. When I came back to Feb. 4th, the next day I *did* visit your sweat-shop, & I *did* see what a blunder I'd made, & I *did* try to foil Umlauf's scheme, but of course I botched it, just because I'm such a stupid Umlauf. After giving him some spiritual advice, I threatened to expose him if he went through with the scheme, but he knew I was bluffing, & I'm such a cowardly Umlauf I couldn't bring myself to kill him, so I left—went to New Orleans, &c—but you know about that, I reckon, from my writing. Umlauf got it in his head to work up a binding for the notebook. I assume this, since I read about the binding, & it's something he & I never discussed. I figure that was the reason he sold the notebook so much later than he did the first time—the time that didn't count because I canceled it. Understand? I'd better stop—I'm getting confused myself. Or maybe he delayed the sale because he thought it would be "cute" to time it with the 101st anniversary of the publication of *Huck*. He's quite a showman, ain't he? A master of timing.

P.P.S.—I should have sunk that godumlaufed boat instead of just leaving it tied up like that, godumlauf it to umlauf. Let us hope there is a hell, for this impostor's sake, who carries his bowels in his skull, & when they operate, works the rank discharge into "Twainian" mush-&-milk & brings shame upon me.

P.P.P.S.—If you publish, you may use the title I mentioned, or this one, which just struck me—*I Been There Before*. Either will answer.

III

I Been There Before:

The East

The Contest

I had pulled into the forlorn, decrepit dock of the small town of Pikesville to buy the only absolute essentials to my second livelihood. I was concluding my purchase—cigars, a new pipe, tobacco, pipe cleaners, lighter fluid, and flints—when I spied a handbill:

World's Championship Pipe-Smoking Contest
Pikesville Town Hall
February 14, 1986, 1.00 p.m.

Are you a pipe smoker? Do you enjoy a long, cool smoke? How long? How cool? If given 0.1 oz. of quality tobacco, how long could you make it last, provided you smoke continuously and no rekindling is allowed? Come show us what you know about drawing, tamping, and back pressure. Match your puffing against the world's best. *Make it last.*

NO GREENHORNS NEED APPLY.

I asked the druggist what day it was.

"Why, it's St. Valentine's Day!" he exclaimed. "And a happy one to you, sir!"

I looked at my watch: 12.45. I hesitated. If I entered this contest, what new catastrophe would I cause? Would the roof cave in? Would the river suddenly rise and engulf us? Would my pipe explode and blow us to Memphis, causing widespread carnage and destruction? No, I thought. Surely there could be no safer place on earth than the Pikesville Town Hall. Maybe Providence had thrown this handbill in my path for relief, for the sheer fun of it. I was long overdue for some fun.

I obtained directions to the Town Hall and hurried off. I arrived somewhat short of breath from the rush—not the ideal state in which to undertake a campaign of long, cool smoking. But by the time I was signed in and given a plastic bag containing my morsel of tobacco, along with two wooden matches, I was perfectly tranquil. I took a seat at a long table, around which sat the other contestants—twenty or so, and four of them women. The rules were explained to us. Both matches could be used, but both would be collected by the judges after thirty seconds of "play" had elapsed; if a contestant was unable to "emit smoke" upon being asked by a judge to do so, said contestant was eliminated; anyone who burned a hole through his pipe would also be eliminated. We all laughed to hear that—not a greenhorn among us, you see. The last man or woman to keep on puffing would be declared the winner.

We loaded our weapons. My adversaries, I noticed, took great care with this. Some favored the dense tamp, others a loose, aerated profusion. The chief judge surveyed our preparations with barely contained excitement. He said:

"Ready?"

We nodded and reached for our matches.

"*Play.*"

We lit up. A sour-faced fellow across the table from me was connivingly slow about striking his first match—he was going to get the most out of that first thirty seconds. He caught me watching him and his eyebrows shot up in surprise. Then he gave me a long, cold stare before finally looking away with a mysterious smile. There was a certain indefinable something in the way he looked at me that chilled me. Also, his complexion was haunting; it had a faint greenish tinge that was almost other-worldly. As I studied him I saw that he was small; he was smaller than small; he was a dwarf—or as close to that article as a man can come without being billed as one.

It would be pleasant to say that fragrant clouds of richly dense smoke billowed upward and mingled above our heads, and that the exhalation of our innermost selves entwined in glorious harmony, where no man knew an enemy, and, and, and. But, alas, our mouths were tight little sphincters, out of which painfully constricted wisps of smoke struggled for release. It was a pathetic sight. No pipe should ever be smoked so. We nursed our pipes like mothers fretting over sickly babes. We timed our puffs with clock-watching diligence, treading the narrow line between excessive fire and total extinction. Control! Discipline!! Relentless attention to the Golden Mean!!!

Once we had our pipes under-way and our matches had been collected, conversation developed. At first, all the talk was of pipes and tobacco, with emphasis on the ideal equipment for our present engagement. I noticed I was the only one there with a brand-new pipe, and I am sure others noticed it too. It was a fool's equipment—not sufficiently carbonized, and so it would burn fast and hot. Some contestants favored the straight-stemmed article, others the bent-stemmed; some argued for moisture dripping down into the bowl, others against. The anti-moisture faction concentrated their arguments against a slender youngster with a pipe that gurgled as if he were sucking the remnants of liquid from the bottom of a glass. He sucked and struggled, interrupting his red-faced efforts only long enough to throw out lame justifications for his dampness, then sucking and gurgling some more. Finally, in a fit of temper and frustration, he seized his bowl and snapped his pipe sharply in the air, flinging a stream of brown-stained saliva out of his bit in a dotted line across the table. Howls arose, and a judge hurried over with a towel and a stern admonishment.

An uncomfortable pause followed, which was finally broken when a kindly-faced old gentleman at the far end of the table ventured a morsel of home-grown philosophy: he pointed out that every bowl of pipe tobacco had its distinct character, like people. Some bowls were friendly—cool, free of debris, endlessly alight; others were the opposite—defiant, hostile, enemies to pleasure. Just like people. We nodded. It was a happy conceit, and we were gratified for it. The contestants fell to discussing previous meetings of this august body. Then, suddenly:

"I was in a stone-skipping contest once." This came from the dour pygmy sitting across from me. We turned our attention to him. He sat in silence. We waited, puzzled. It was easier to imagine Job skipping stones than this fellow.

"Lost," he finally said, and we all sighed in relief at this long-awaited dropping of the other shoe. Another man spoke up—

"Our boy Buster was in the Tom Sawyer Fence-Paintin' Contest up to Hannibal once. Didn't win, but Mabel here was runner-up in the San Diego Laughin' Contest."

I was about to congratulate Mabel, a large woman with a large face and a very wide-open manner, when I heard a "Hmph" from the other end of the table. This came from a round-faced woman wearing spectacles. "Runner-up," she said, her lips snarling around a huge curving pipe bit. "Hmph. There just *happens* to be an annual Bed-Makin' Championship Meet, that just *happens* to be at the Marriott Hotel in Philadelphia, and I just *happen* to be the winner two years runnin'."

Mabel was unleashed. She produced a long, loud bray, which she followed up instantly with six or seven rapid-fire snorts of derision. I thought the conversation was taking an altogether odd turn.

"Stuff," said a young fellow with a meerschaum. "Bed-making. Hmph." We watched him examine the ash in his bowl a moment. Then he said, "You folks might be interested to know that you're sittin' with last year's winner of the International Spittin', Belchin', and Cussin' Triathlon up to Central City, Colorado."

This aroused a good deal of interest. "How far did you spit?" "Give us a burp." "What was the winning curse?" But he was a coy one. He just sat back and concentrated on his pipe.

"Well, now," said a burly man in a mackinaw jacket, "maybe you're settin' with the winner of the Southern California Exposition Cow Chip Throwin' Contest, and maybe you ain't."

"I once raced a jumping frog in Calaveras," I said in a voice gone girlish with enthusiasm.

Mabel burst into a singing laugh that ranged all over the bass and treble clefs.

"*Did* you now?" a skinny fellow snapped at me. He was nothing but a bag of bones, as if he had been fasting in preparation for the day's event. "Did you enter the Juneau Vomit Festival of '84? And did you win top scores in all three areas—quantity, distance, and texture? Did you? Tell it to the marines."

"*Go* way!" said a petite, rather attractive woman. "How you talk! Why, at the annual meetin' of the Fundamental Sigh Society, I let out a rip that made Vesuvius look like somethin' that jist throws little kisses into the air. You know that crazy winter of '83, with all them freaky floods and storms and droughts? Wasn't no El Niño that done that. Was *me*. Why, you shoulda seed it—when the smoke cleared enough for folks to see, and when the judges finally come to, they jist flung that trophy at me and clumb all over each other tryin' to git outta the buildin'."

A silence descended on the group as we contemplated this scene. By stages, the sour-faced, Martian-colored manikin attracted our attention, through a series of sighs, throat-clearings, and unwarranted scowls up and down the table that forbade further speech on any subject but the one he was warming up to.

"I suppose," he said at last, "I shouldn't be surprised that it has come to this. I know you're all just trying to egg me on."

A chorus of denials: "Egg you on?" "What do you mean?" "What?"

"I suppose," he went on wearily, "you know about me and want to hear my version of what happened that day."

"*What* day?" "What the devil?" "What *are* you talking about?"

He raised a hand and silenced us. He smiled—it was a rather lippy, unpleasant smile. "All right, all right. I'll play along. I'll pretend you don't know."

"But we *don't* know!" we shouted as one.

The little man frowned and seemed to withdraw into himself. "You *seem* to be speaking truthfully, hard though it is for me to believe. I . . . I'm very confused."

"Perhaps," I said, "if you would just *tell* us what it is, our memories would be jarred into recognition."

His greenish face split into an even wider smile, and lippier than before. The effect was like seeing a frog's lips break the surface of swamp water. "Perhaps they *would* be jarred," he said. "Perhaps they would." He held that eerie smile a moment longer, then, with a resounding slap on the table, he launched into his narrative:

"It was at the Annual Hell Hole Suicide Jubilee. I was one of the four finalists admitted to the 'Room of No Return,' and I was the only one to emerge. The three others—well, they took the easy way out and swallowed the cyanide capsule with which they had been provided."

"*What?*" we shouted. "*What the devil?*"

He quieted us with another raising of his hand, palm outward. "The rules are these. To gain admittance to the room, each contestant must submit a detailed autobiography to the judges, in which at least one disgusting sin is spelled out—preferably more, but one will do. Each contestant must also have a proven talent for self-blame—without that, the Jubilee would be a sham. When the chief judge calls, "Play," you try to guess the sins of your competitors and you . . . talk about them. Lying is strictly forbidden. The judges are listening, you see, from the next room, and they know all about you, and if you lie you're disqualified and yanked out. You're washed up as far as future competition goes, too.

"After the introductions and handshakes and pleasantries were over, the four of us settled into our chairs around the table and began to peck away at one another. I held back, at first, content to let the others grope and stumble with feeble questions like 'Does your sin involve money?' and 'Does it involve sex?' and 'Is it bigger than a bootjack?' When I saw that everyone was feeling the comfort that is to be had in the presence of flimsy opponents, I went to work. I started in on a fellow I like to call 'Johnny-off-the-spot,' because he was never where he should have been. I talked about how he didn't have the decency to go to his own daughter's debut as a concert singer, and about how he was even a no-show when she gave a concert at their home—the guests could hear him, between songs, rattling billiard balls around up-stairs. I didn't *guess at* these facts, mind. I *talked about* them. I talked about how he decided to be off the spot and go abroad just two months after his infant son died, leaving his still-grieving wife behind. Well, I knew I'd hit a nerve there, because he kind of flinched when I touched on that subject, so I went for his sockdolager of a sin right away. I approached it in a disarmingly general way—like this:

"When someone is fatally ill—a woman, let's say—she needs to be with people she loves. If she has been married for a long time—let's say thirty-two years—and still loves her husband, and if she must spend the last two years of her life bedridden, at death's door, his daily bedside presence would be of inestimable value. It would naturally be *assumed* that he would be *there.* Well, this Johnny-off-the-spot of mine, he had such a wife, who lingered in just such a way, and he *wanted* desperately to be with her, but things didn't work out that way. Seems she was a 'delicate' woman and he was an 'agitating' man, so the doctors banished him from her room for long stretches. Three months would pass without him catching so much as a glimpse of her, and then he would be granted a five-minute visit. When she rallied he could be with her more often, but then she would slip and Johnny'd be left pawing at the door again. This went on for two years, until she died. Johnny-off-the-spot. But it was the doctors' orders, you might be thinking; it wasn't *Johnny's* fault. It wasn't? I ask you—what the devil kind of love did they have if his presence only made her more ill? Why could he not *comfort* her? Why could he only *agitate* her?

"Well, I heard a crash and saw feet flying upward as my adversary sprawled back on his capsized chair. His agitating days were over. The judges were Johnnys-on-the-spot and had him out of there in no time.

"I turned to the next fellow. I quickly established that he had a brother, ten years his senior, whose life was a pathetic history of failure from beginning to end. His mother thought him pathetic; his wife thought him incompetent; his cat thought him a disgrace to the household and moved across town. But his brother—*my* man—who was successful, whose success was so great that had it been divided in two, and half given to his brother, *both* would still be in the history books, *he* not only thought him pathetic. He thought him *comical.* He figured the world would also find him comical, and urged him to write an autobiography. Why, you may ask, would anyone want to read an autobiography of a failed nullity? Because it would be funny—that's why. My man's advice to his brother about the work was this: 'If, when you shall have finished, the reader shall say, "The man *is* an ass, but I really don't know whether *he* knows it or not," your work will be a triumph.' Imagine yourself an acknowledged failure and trying to write up your life according to those specifications. Imagine it!

"The project failed, of course. But my man had to do *something* with that brother of his. He urged his friends to work him into their books and plays; possessing more sensitivity to feeling than my man—that is, possessing more than an ounce of it—they declined. But my man had one more chance at this literary gold mine. He concocted a hoax, for the sheer fun of it, consisting of evidence he made up that his incompetent brother was the true author of his own most famous book.

"Well, I didn't have to say more than what I've said just now. My man saved me the trouble. His head hit the table with a thud, and the judges hustled in and carted him off. That left me with one opponent. He was an odd case. He proved to be the toughest of the lot, even though the facts against him were staggering—absolutely damning. Here is his story.

"He was a success in many things, and rather well-off, for a time. But he was a frustrated inventor, an absolute nut for gimmicks. He took out many patents in his lifetime—one for a special kind of suspenders, another for a history game, and another for a self-pasting scrapbook, which contained its own strips of ready-to-moisten stickum. This was all harmless enough, but he also had *money* and was obsessed with acquiring *more money,* so he threw it all at a newfangled typesetting machine that promised, at first, to revolutionize the industry and that proved, at the last, to be worth no more than a mouthful of ashes. By the time it went totally to smash, he had wasted over $200,000 on it.

"But he had another source of money, this fellow did. He was a platform speaker—and a good one; he worked out a long, around-the-world itinerary, the income from which would restore his finances and his reputation. A problem: what to do with the family? The wife would go with him, as would one daughter. Two would stay behind, don't ask me why, and one of these two was the *favorite,* the *darling*—the *acknowledged* favorite and darling. So—off they went, in a westward circuit—to Australia, New Zealand, India, South Africa, and England, and him dragging his tired, ageing body up to one podium after another. What a hard worker he was! What a prince! But oh! how he and his wife pined for their *favorite,* their *darling.*

"Well, after a full year on tour, they were in London, eagerly awaiting the arrival of the rest of their family, scheduled to meet them there for a glorious reunion. But no such luck. They get the news from the

States that the *favorite*, the *darling*, has taken sick. Not to worry, say their friends back home. She'll get better and be along by and by. They wait. The mother and daughter, consumed with worry, finally head for home, leaving papa behind. Why didn't he go with them? Search me. Economizing, maybe. Then, while they're in transit and he's just hanging out in the dining room, with nothing particular going on in his brain, he gets a cable: 'Susy was peacefully released to-day.'

"It was meningitis, and it killed her. Now, it was bad enough that this *favorite*, this *darling* of the family, had died at the cruelly young age of twenty-four. But she died just as they were about to see her lovely face after a year's separation. From *their* point of view, it was as if she had died a full year earlier. And she died *alone*—all the poor girl had for comfort was a housekeeper, whose face she stroked, delirious and blinded from the illness, crying in confusion, 'Mamma . . . Mamma.'

"Well, the old guy, still stuck in England by himself, took up his pathetic pen and wrote letters to his friends, saying it was a great comfort to him that she had died in the home in which they all had spent so many happy years. Oh, *that* meant a lot to her—you bet. He wrote, 'To us, our house was not unsentient matter—it had a heart, and a soul, and eyes to see us with; and approvals, and solicitudes, and deep sympathies,' and hogwash. What an unmitigated ass he was to think that a building could substitute for loved ones at such a time. Then he wrote to his wife, saying it was good that the girl had died rather than live and remain demented from the illness. Oh, you bet. Better still if she hadn't become ill in the first place, don't you think? He went on to write that he had learned the girl had jotted down some notes on scraps of paper in the fever of those last days. He wrote, 'I wonder if she left any little message for me, any little mention, showing that she thought of me. I was not deserving of it, I had not earned it, but if there was any such word left behind for me, I hope it was saved up in its exact terms and that I shall get it.' Sorry, papa. You're out of luck. Nary a word for you.

"Maybe he should have been thankful for that. If she *had* written him a note, she might have thrown the whole ugly sequence of events in his face: the money lust, the speculation, the bankruptcy, the resulting need for that tour, and the long separation at such an untimely moment. She wasn't able to do this, but I was glad to help her out there and speak for her, laying it all out, step by step—'in its exact terms,' as you might say.

"He still hung on, though, gripping the edge of the table with his jaw set. He was a tough nut, all right. I shifted my attack a bit. I leaped ahead a year—to the first anniversary of the girl's death. The chap and his wife were in Switzerland at the time. It was a day they had been dreading, and you would expect your average couple to face it together. But not this pair. Here's the way it went. The wife rose early and slipped out of the house with a small bag, destination unknown. She took a ride on a boat across the lake, to a small, peaceful-looking inn. She checked into a room and passed the day quietly reading old letters written by the daughter she had lost. She spent the day alone, returning late to a husband frantic with worry. She knew him well. She must have known he would worry. She was a mild, gentle, tender-hearted creature; in its indirectness and its ever-so-quiet effectiveness, the punishment she chose matched her character perfectly.

"As punishments go, it wasn't bad. I know just how good it was, because this mere reminder of it had induced my man to bring his cyanide capsule up to the edge of his lips; he was rolling it between his thumb and finger as he stared at the table.

" 'There's more,' I said to him. 'Shall we talk about it?' He declined. He popped the pill into his mouth and just stared at me until the end came. He went rather quietly—just sort of slumped in his chair, with his chin resting on his chest—'peacefully released,' as you may say. It's a shame he had to die in that barren little room, instead of at home, where his sentient house would have cheered him up no end."

The dour pygmy gave a quick, short puff on his pipe and gazed into the distance. "And that's how I won. You might be wondering what *my* sin was. Well, I'll tell you. I cheated!" He let out a huge roar of laughter. "I had access to the judges' files, and I was completely prepared for the contest. I knew as much about those people as they knew about themselves. I even seemed to know *more*, what with the way I could point out motives for their behavior, and connections between incidents, and unacknowledged aggressive impulses, and the like. It wasn't a fair contest at all. I feel just horrible about it." He chuckled. "Just horrible."

I looked around. Half of the pipes in the room lay on the table, or sat cupped, forgotten and neglected, in a cold palm; dead, the smokers eliminated. The other half were blasting out smoke like steamboats burning pitch pine—another form of neglect, dooming them to certain elimination within a few minutes. Meanwhile, the sour-faced manikin puffed on, just as he had been doing all through his tale—the epitome of cool moderation. I had to give him credit. He had accomplished at this very table what he *claimed* to have accomplished at that made-up suicide table of his. Using the instrument of cunning distraction, he had so absorbed the other pipe-smokers in his tale that they had killed their chances in the contest.

The fellow gazed around the room with satisfaction, his eyes coming to rest on me. His calm smile faded, and was replaced by a scowl of surprise, for I was placidly puffing away—gently, ever so gently. I believe he must have identified me early on as an experienced smoker, one he had to worry about, even with the handicap of a new pipe. Had he really thought his tale would affect *me?* How could he have thought that? It was such a contrived patchwork of ugly lies. Who would ever believe such horrible examples of humanity could be gathered together in one room?

The sour little fellow won, though. It was a close finish, but he won. It was that confounded new pipe that was my undoing.

Notes on p. 239.

A Glimpse: III

Hermann the German cast his eyes down to his feet and sighed. *Nein,* he thought, pressing his lips together with determination. "I must fight this melancholy. Ich *muss* es." He forced himself to take an interest in some aspect of his surroundings. Since he was already looking downward, he started there, with the rug beneath his feet, and he privately resolved to study its intricate design and so distract himself from the fatiguing sadness of his perennial loneliness that he might once and for all . . . *verdammt!* He had bumped into the tour guide, who had suddenly stopped in the hall. Hermann hoped the guide took him for a metaphysical fellow inclined to per . . . peri . . . peripatetic—that was it, that was the word—revelries, and . . . "Revelries?" Nein, *reveries.* . . . given to peripatetic reveries and therefore somewhat inclined to collide frequently with his fellow man.

"I think," said the guide, "it might just be warm enough for us to step outside for a view from the balcony. That's right, come along. And could the last one out close the door behind you, please? The heating bills are not to be believed, and this house has already experienced one bankruptcy, ha, ha! Yes, that's it, thank you very much indeed. Now, it's awfully gray and overcast today, but even so, I think you will be able to appreciate the view from up here, especially if you imagine that perfectly hideous high school replaced by woods, and . . ."

Yes, thought Hermann. Gray. That was his color, durchaus. Through and through. Inside and out. From top to bottom. "The whole kit and caboose," as they said in Amerika.

". . . a favorite little nest for the family, and Sam and Livy would sometimes spend hours at a time up here, just loafing, or reading, or enjoying the sights and sounds of nature—*together,* for remember, as Clemens says in *A Tramp Abroad,* 'Even the finest scenery loses incalculably when there is no one to enjoy it with.' Now, down there to the left you can spy . . ."

What could he have been thinking when he set off for Amerika all alone? Did he think he would meet interesting travel companions and join up with them? Did he think he would have adventures? Romance? Yes, he had to admit that he did think that. How could he have forgotten the lesson of his English travels two years earlier? They had produced nothing of the kind—only this all-too-familiar gray loneliness. Why couldn't he learn from his mistakes? Why did he have to be such a . . . such a . . . what was that word, the one the Hasenlippe called Huck? *Muggins*. That was it. Hermann had tried it on a pretty waitress the other day. He had spilled his coffee and called himself a muggins in front of her, but she hadn't seemed impressed. It hadn't "rattled her cage," as they said in Amerika.

". . . and on those occasions when Clemens wished not to see any friends or visitors, because he was working, he would step out here and hide while George the butler called out in vain for him. . . ."

He wasn't a friendless person. He was popular back home. He just couldn't start a friendship *here*. The entire New World at his feet, and he was still alone! His thoughts, uninspired by the stimulus of companionship, tended toward repetition, and he now concluded what he had concluded a hundred times before: it was the language that isolated him. Then, a new thought, or a new way of thinking it—The Awful English Language! What a tremendous joke! He had to share it with someone! But with whom? Certainly not the tour guide. Hermann had already tried a little joke on him downstairs; what a wretched failure it had been. After telling the group about the beautiful piece of stained glass that once separated the front hall from the drawing room, now evidently lost forever, the guide had sighed and lamented, "Of all sad words of tongue or pen," and Hermann had finished it for him! And in German! And in Mark Twain's German, for Hermann had read it somewhere! It went like this:

> Of all sad words
> Of tongue or pen,
> The saddest are these:
> Es hätte sein könn'.

Hermann was no Dummkopf. He had "gotten" Mark's little joke. The last line translated the original poem, but, more than that, all those verbs at the end of German sentences made the language especially hard for Mark, and so *those words* made him sad. And naturally Hermann had assumed this tour guide, who seemed to know so much, would like it. But he didn't. Too urban. Wait! thought Hermann. "Urban" seemed wrong. *Urbane*— that was the word. *Urbane*. What a verdammte Sprache. *Also!* thought

Hermann, desperately tracking down his thought in hopes of concluding it before sunset, the tour guide was too urbane. Didn't like the idea of being upstaged by a Kraut—didn't "cotton for it," as they said in Amerika.

Hermann had had but one blissful moment in the past two months, and it had been brief, and had ended cruelly. On the bus from New York to Hartford, he had fallen asleep and dreamed he was back home, in a Weinstube, with friends, and someone asked him, *in German,* about his American travels, and Hermann answered, *in German,* and they listened and laughed and understood every subtlety of language, delighting not only in his uncanny selection of the precisely right word, but also in his talent for the *unusual,* the *unexpected,* word. And was that a knee pressing against his leg? Yes—Grete's knee, under the table. Now her *hand* on his knee! Gott sei Dank—he had finally begun to win her over, and it was his silver-tongued speech that had done it, his mastery of his beautiful native tongue! Then he had awakened. Next to him on his seat, the crazy lady who had ceased talking only because he had closed his eyes had started up again, swinging her knees back and forth and jabbering English at him as if someone had hired her to torture him, pouring out her speech in such a liquid form that he could not detect the joints between the words.

". . . down there was the stable and house for Patrick McAleer and his family—beloved coachman of the Clemenses for many years. It was in that building that, one day, Clemens' daughters Susy and Clara became locked up in a bin of oats, and it was Patrick who heard their faint cries for help and rescued them before they suffocated."

Hermann sighed. Every time the tour guide mentioned Mark Twain's children, he seemed to single out Hermann with his gaze and fix his eyes on him, as if to say, "I know you're just a cold and lonely Kraut, and I know it hurts you to hear these tales, but my subject is Mark Twain, and Mark Twain was, above all, a family man."

Aber ich auch! Hermann wanted to shout. He adored children too. On the *Delta Queen* he had loved playing hearts with those charming young girls. And he couldn't "fill his bucket," as they said here, with those Mark Twain family stories, like the one the guide had told about little Susy, on the porch below, bursting into a song she had made up and astonishing her parents: "Oh Jesus are you dead, so you cannot dance and sing!" or the one about little Jean, "besshy Mish Chain," and her blackbird, even though her tenses weren't of the sort Hermann had encountered at the university. Yes, those family stories were "right up his sidewalk!"

". . . beneath the laughter. So—shall we go back in? If you will be so kind as to turn to your right . . ."

"Beneath the laughter?" Where had Hermann heard those words before? He couldn't remember. But he did remember that they had something to do with Mark Twain's melancholy, which lay *beneath the laughter* he aroused in others. Hermann suddenly had a dizzying thought. He felt as if *he* were Mark Twain, abroad, fighting genders and declensions and moods. Why, Mark had suffered just as he was suffering, and he had written about that suffering in "The Awful German Language," and again in *Meisterschaft,* a play Hermann believed demonstrated Mark Twain's true brilliance as a dramatist. Yes—Mark had suffered, and had joked about his suffering, and soon Hermann would be able to do the same, when he returned to his beloved home.

As for that other business, why, Mark hadn't married until he was thirty-four, and Hermann was only twenty-six, so, as they said in Amerika, "What's the deal, hunh?"

With a smile he turned to join the tour group filing back into the house. Something caught his attention. He squinted into the bright sunlight reflecting off the snow-covered ground. Sunlight? Snow? *Mein Gott!* He gazed, transfixed, at the slope down to the large brook—an area that only seconds before had been a paved parking lot. *Gott im Himmel!!* He watched in stupefied amazement as the man in the sealskin coat helped each of the three children onto the toboggan, while three collies pranced about, barking and snapping playfully at the snow their paws kicked up. He heard a voice—the man's voice—intoning some sort of ceremonial chant as he stood over the toboggan in an attitude of exaggerated officiousness. Then he launched the toboggan, and how he laughed to see the children fly down the hill, their brightly colored snow suits flashing blue, yellow, and red in the sun. He waited until they had reached the bottom of the hill and had looked back at the course they had run, and back at him, and *then* he took off his cap and waved it in the air over his head, giving out hurrah upon hurrah.

Hermann thought he heard a woman's echoing hurrah from directly below, and he leaned forward over the railing and looked down, but he saw nothing, and when he looked back to the hill again he gave out an audible *Ach!* to see nothing but American automobiles parked on the gray parking lot under the cold, gray sky.

"*Mensch!*" cried Hermann, worrying up another Amerikanism: "I must by all means tell the marines about this!"

Notes on p. 240.

A Glimpse: IV

Recipe: Take one tolerably well-behaved child and place him in a car and
when he asks, "When are we going to get there?," answer, in the
most musical way, "Pretty soo-oon."

Result: A monster.

Yield: Serves one cannibal.

Gus smiled at his words and then hastily placed the postcard back in
his pocket, because Elizabeth was throwing him nasty glances for his
inattention to the tour guide. He had scribbled down the "recipe" while
waiting for this tedious trek to get under-way; now he had to decide which
of his like-minded, kid-hating friends he should send it to.

Eight days on the road. Eight "family" days, rich with bickering,
bellowing, barking, and biting—the last between Bobby and Johnny, each
of whose dental impressions could now be found liberally distributed over
his brother's forearms. What better way to pass the time on the highway?

Gus had wanted to go to Atlantic City and deposit the kids in a game
room that would turn their brains into oatmeal and render them soft and
pliable in the evening, while he would pass his days drinking and gambling. But Elizabeth had insisted on a "culture tour" of New England.
This was supposed to be one of the many "high points" she had promised
when she mapped out the trip: Mark Twain's home in Hartford. Hartford? Gus had been doubtful. Wasn't Mark Twain from Missouri, or
someplace like that? He had hoped she was wrong, and his hopes had
mounted to an expectation of victory when they had had such a hard time
finding the place. But she was a stubborn one, was Elizabeth, and in spite
of his best efforts to make wrong turns in apparent innocence, she had
finally guided them into the parking lot below the house. Bobby and
Johnny had leaped out of the car as if vomited by it and were on their way
up the hill, almost out of sight, before Gus had managed to get out and
work the stiffness from his limbs. Perhaps the kids would get lost up there,
he thought.

As they climbed the wooden steps from the parking lot to the top of the hill, Gus noticed another family within earshot just behind them, so he broke into riotous song:

> Let's do *Elizabeth!*
> Elizabeth, Elizabeth, Bo-belizabeth,
> Buh-nannuh-nannuh-no-nelizabeth,
> Me-my-momelizabeth, melizabeth.
> *Elizabeth!*

Gus grinned to see her hurry up the stairs. He chalked another point up for his side. Revenge—it wasn't sweet at all. It was bitter through and through. That was the joy of it. But as to the kids, he was out of luck. When he arrived at the front door, there they were, wrestling on the front lawn and taking fresh samples of each other's flesh. Elizabeth was ogling the outside of the house, ignoring them.

The house seemed calculated to heap shame on Gus's worldly goods, which consisted chiefly of a two-bedroom bungalow in Buffalo. The tour was also designed by no friend of the common man; it was calculated in its portrayal of a family life of seamless perfection to depress every normal father who endured it. Mark Twain loved his perfect wife with a perfect love; Mark Twain played charades with his perfect daughters right here in this room; Mark Twain told stories to his perfect daughters, using these very jimcracks on the mantel-piece as his props and characters, running them through all sorts of lively adventures, and he did it *every goddamned night.* Mark Twain taught his perfect daughters how to shuffle their feet on this very carpet and work up a spark on dry winter days, and then to touch the gas jet and ignite it with their fingers, as if by magic; Mark Twain let his perfect daughters turn him into an elephant and ride him all over Kingdom-Come when they played "jungle," using the plants in *that* very conservatory for background, where they hunted for the tiger —actually their black butler, George, who was also reported as just slobbering after the chance to join in the frolic. By the time Gus dragged his monumentally bored bones up to the third floor, he felt positively damp from the tour guide's bucketfuls of goody-goody sentimental gush. Gus wasn't depressed, though. He didn't believe a word of it—not a word. He knew a white-wash job when he struck one. He was willing to bet even money that Mark Twain never got out of Missouri.

The billiard room. They stepped inside it, at one end, but the rest of it was roped off. Bobby and Johnny fingered the rope. Gus privately hoped they would lean forward on it and bring down the wobbling posts supporting it, just so that Elizabeth would see once and for all what little beasts they were. What was that? A desk? The tour guide explained: Mark Twain had moved his study up here, converting his original study on the second floor into a schoolroom for the children. Schoolroom? thought Gus. Good God—weren't those kids *ever* out of the house?

Gus looked at the desk. Nothing special about it, he thought. The chair—there reposed the authorial buttocks. Big deal.

"Of course," said the tour guide, "not all was rosy in the Clemens family."

"Clemens?" thought Gus, with disdain. Why didn't they say "Mark Twain" like everybody else did? Did they have to show off like that?

"At this very desk," said the guide, "Clemens once wrote a letter to his good friend, William Dean Howells, that tells something of the other side of the story. The letter is somewhat mysterious, in that the incident it alludes to was never raised by either man again in their correspondence; nor is there any other reference to it in the family records. And yet Clemens speaks of the incident with a depth of feeling that . . . but never mind. I shall let Clemens speak for himself and read the passage to you. The letter is dated December twelfth, 1886 . . ."

Gus had actually found himself interested in what the guide was saying, and so he had looked at him. His eyes wandered back to the desk now. He grinned. Some idiot from their group had sneaked over to the desk and installed himself in the chair. He was hunched over, as if writing. Gus could see nothing but his white hair.

". . . Clemens was fifty-one when he wrote it; his three daughters were six, twelve, and fourteen years of age at the time. Here it is . . ."

The guide was going to go nuts when he saw the guy, thought Gus, who knew this for a fact, because the guide had coldly told him to remove his posterior from a sofa in the drawing room. Gus hadn't minded. He had managed to embarrass Elizabeth, so *he* was satisfied. He now looked around for the family attached to the white-haired man. He was surprised to see that no one was looking particularly mortified.

" 'Your recent experiences,' wrote Clemens, 'have been hard, very hard . . .' "

Gus looked back to the desk. The idiot was writing as the guide read —as if he were writing the very words the guide was reading aloud. It was a prime idea. Gus wished he had thought of it.

" '. . . and yet yesterday a thunder-stroke fell upon me out of the most unsuspected of skies which for a moment ranged me breast to breast and comraded me as an equal, with all men who have suffered sudden and awful disaster: I found that all their lives my children have been afraid of me! have stood all their days in uneasy dread of my sharp tongue and uncertain temper. The accusing instances stretch back to their babyhood, and are burnt into their memories: and I never suspected, and the fact was never guessed by *anybody* until yesterday. Well, all the concentrated griefs of fifty years seemed colorless by the side of that pathetic revelation. That list is closed, that record is ended; if I live seventy-five years yet, it will still remain without an addition.' "

Gus watched the man address an envelope, set his pen down, and fold the letter. The man then lifted his head and gazed forward. The tour group began to file out of the room. Gus stood rooted in place. He watched the man gazing—at the billiard table. The man sighed deeply. Gus looked at the billiard table. It was piled high with presents gaily decorated in Christmas wrappings. He looked back to the desk. The man sealed his envelope, affixed a stamp, and stood up. He walked the length of the room, directly to Gus, and drawled:

"If you're going by the post office, would you be so kind to post this melancholy missive for me?"

Gus pitched forward across the rope barrier, falling unconscious in a heap that brought down the metal posts with a noisy clang.

_____

Notes on p. 243.

The Kingdom of Heaven
(Working Notes)

Boy who prays to his twin brother, who is dead.

Stranger in Wash. Sq., father of twins, one died at age < 5 > 6. Surviving twin injured < years later > , father drives boy to hospital— the very one where twin died. Tries to shield son from this knowledge —fails, *but doesn't know he fails,* until end. < How does boy > Use < Benton > Balducci free calendar—one of the 6 portraits is a kodak of the dead child—B. printed it before boy died, or didn't know—it's a big city. That calendar *haunts* the family. It is *everywhere.* Druggist shops, libraries, father impatient for year to end, & it is in the hospital, in < waiting room > hall outside w. room. F. doesn't see it, boy does, & thinks it's there because his brother died there.

"Papa, do people die in this hospital?"

"Sometimes they do, but never from getting stitches. Nobody ever dies getting stitches."

"Papa, does God want them to die?"

"No, I'm sure he doesn't."

"Why doesn't he save them < then > ?"

"I believe he has a rule about letting people save them."

"Can you pray to people, papa?"

Papa, trying to divert son, tells him about Catholic prayers to saints —a variety of people. Doesn't say "saints"—says "good people who die & go to heaven."

Boy steps out for drink of water. Sees calendar over fountain. F. doesn't know this, & *we* don't know it. Returns & says, "This is a nice hospital." F. puzzled—they've been waiting < 4 > 2 hours,—*he* doesn't think it's a nice place. Dr. takes stitches. Son very brave—f. can't account for it, at first. Then he fancies boy learned to trust Drs. from experiences with him, removing splinters &c. Swells with pride.

Dr: "Do you have any bros. or sisters?"—during stitching.

Boy: "I had a bro. He died in this hospital."

Dr: < To father, "Is > "I'm sorry."

Boy frowns—he privately takes Dr's statement to mean *he* was the one who failed to save his bro. Boy's lips move—silent prayer. F. puzzled. After, boy runs ahead to fountain. Gets drink, steps back & looks at calendar, gets another drink, steps back again—a form of religious rite. F. sees this, sees calendar. Understands all.

"And we think we understand our children, sir. We think our superior intellects can fathom their inferior ones. I tell you, sir, we are wrong. All that time I thought I was following his thoughts, & I was on a different track altogether. And the boy's bravery & manliness? From *my* training, *my* gentleness? Far from it, sir. He was praying to his saintly brother, whose death he thought the "nice hospital" had memorialized with that portrait." Rises from bench to leave, says, "We needn't worry about our children, sir. Of *such* is the kingdom of heaven."

< Ask Cocoa for name of the hospital near W. Sq. > Ask Walter & Darrell if they believe in God, prayer, & praying to good, dead people.

Dr. Grabow a hell-fired article. Ask Cocoa about pipe shop.

Write a < McW > sketch about Cocoa & her ex-husband meeting by accident at a party. Work in Cocoa's blush—how you *feel* it, like a change in temperature, more than see it. Make it *serious*—about *love* & *sex* & all that, just to leave behind proof that I can do it.

Notes on p. 244.

Portrait of a Usurper

It is well-known how delicate and woman-like my ever-so-tiny little mouth and hands are. With the right costume, and with practice, I calculated I could pass for a woman, though I shouldn't stop traffic with my beauty—not even a passing mule train. I acquired a flamboyant dress, in the multi-hued gypsy style, and cultivated a flamboyant, artistic manner, and I contrived, through diligence and feminine wiles, to arrange a special sitting for Mr. Oscar Umlauf, also known as "Mark Twain," so that I might paint his portrait. Mr. Umlauf has a face that is best suited to artistic talents of my sort, which is to say that with *this* subject, the inability to render a face "like unto nature" is a positive strong point. You don't want to come too close to the real thing in portraying him. Just a hint will answer. Anything more could be fatal.

After I guided him to his chair and positioned his face so that I could view his profile in its full glory, I stepped back to my easel and studied him. Something was amiss. He wasn't ugly enough. I knew why. He had fallen on hard times, recently—there had been that near-scandal with those two country girls in Pennsylvania, and then his river had dried up on him in western New York, which *seemed* to surprise him—but only *seemed* to, for everything is *seems* with this *tub of rotten offal*, this *animated barrel of saturated fat*, this—

But I am forgetting myself. I am a portrait artist, an ever-so-gentle one, and I am studying my subject's profile with disappointment. I knew from my earlier experience just what that face was capable of. I knew just how far outward it could thrust, when the mood was right—*that* was the expression I wanted. I hit on an idea. As I mixed my paints, I told him I thought he looked a little pale, a little expressionless, and I wondered aloud if perhaps the thrill of his wonderful return to life had lost some of its splendor. I intimated that his face could do with a little animating, for the sake of the portrait, and I encouraged him to recall some recent achievement of his.

"I don't care what the achievement is," said I. "Just talk it up, and don't hesitate to be proud of it, because I'm sure you've done some splendid things."

"Oh, splendid enough," he said, a grisly smile of self-congratulation beginning to flicker at his lips.

"Your big speech in Hannibal, for example. It must have taken a great deal of courage and confidence for you to announce your return like that."

"Courage?" said he. "Confidence? You don't know the *half* of it."

"Oh, I'm sure I don't," I piped, sounding so meek and mild. "The labor that goes into your preparation for a lecture—why, it must be immense; especially so, considering your audience is so different from the one you were accustomed to, from before."

He scoffed. His lower jaw eased forward half an inch. "Madam, you cannot give compliments to a man without knowing the full extent of his achievements."

"Oh, that's so true, so true," said I.

"*No*body knows what I've accomplished," he said testily. "That's the penalty of my vocation."

"Oh, the color is coming into your face ever so nicely. But, if I may be so bold, I would say you're wrong there. Most folks know quite a bit about Mark Twain; their respect for your accomplishments is well-informed."

"Mark Twain—hmmmmph. He couldn't hold a candle to what *I've* pulled off."

" 'He'?" I giggled and waved my hand limply at him, all flustered. "I don't understand—"

"Of *course* you don't. Because you don't know who *I* am."

"That's *good,* " I said, staring at his face with mounting wonder. The lower half of it stuck out as if he had half-swallowed a frying pan, handle first. "You're really projecting now, Mr. Twain."

He muttered something under his breath. I believe it was "ninny," but I let it pass. Then he spoke more loudly:

"I shall tell you something, Madam. I shall tell you the entire story, because this portrait *is* important to me, and I can't abide the thought of being down-in-the-mouth for it. But I must say something first. If you repeat what I say here, it won't matter to me, because no one will believe you. But if you repeat what I say here, it *will* matter to *you,* because I shall kill you."

I giggled nervously, as if pretending he were kidding.

"I am not Mark Twain," he said. "My real name—the one I use more often than others, I mean—is Oscar Umlauf. I met the genuine Mark Twain in Nevada, four months ago. I stole his act. What do you think of that? Doesn't that take more courage, not to say imagination, than simply *being* Mark Twain?"

I oohed and aahed, professing great astonishment. Then I went to work, sketching furiously, letting him know with my industry how beautiful he was beginning to look, so that he would continue talking. And he did:

"We were in the casino of the Ormsby House, in Carson City, playing Keno, and after exchanging handshakes and names,—false names, on both sides—we fell to chatting, to pass the time between games. By and by, we began to swap stories about unusual experiences we had had. I told him I had once eaten human flesh. He seemed not to believe me. I didn't like that. I did what I always do when that particular offense is committed against me—I upped the ante. I told him about my 'verge of death' experience. You've read about these things, of course. Someone is in an automobile accident, or they're on an operating table, and they die—temporarily. They sort of rise out of their bodies and are actually able to look down on themselves, and on the fuss being made over their lifeless shell. You've heard of such experiences."

"No, I haven't," I said absent-mindedly, for I was sketching like a demon.

"Of course you have," said he. "The people, in their new state of consciousness, are always drawn to a blinding light of some kind. I'm sure you've read about such things."

"I don't believe I have."

"Sure you have. Then, just at the moment of supreme joy and exaltation,—the blinding light does that to them, you see—they get sent back to their bodies. Turns out they were summoned prematurely, and they have to live a while longer. They always raise a howl at that point. They don't *want* to go back. You've heard of that part of it, too."

Now, I knew this bird well enough to know that this was just his way. Once he got a notion into his head, you couldn't get it out. He would have gone on for an eternity insisting I had prior familiarity with his subject, if I went on saying I hadn't, so I just said:

"Perhaps you're right."

"Good," said he, chalking up a point, and with that victory his jaw edged forward still more. "That's settled. Well, I told him that precisely such a thing had happened to me."

"Were you lying?"

My boldness caught him by surprise. "Lying?" he said. "That's such an ugly word. I wouldn't want to call it lying."

"What *would* you want to call it?"

"Practicing."

"Practicing? Practicing what?"

"Practicing lying."

I thought this a distinction too fine to go unremarked, but then I remembered I was supposed to be a ninny, so I simply said, "I see." But I added, "May I safely say, though, that your story about your 'verge of death' experience was not true?"

" 'True' is a difficult word. Truth is a difficult concept."

"I don't feel that way. I've always believed that some things are true, and some aren't, and that's all there is to it." I was become quite emboldened. My mask of humility was beginning to slip off.

"No. No. The whole issue is much more complicated than that. I think, deep down, you agree with me there."

"Agree with you? With what you're saying right now?"

"Yes."

"But I don't!"

"Sure you do. May I please finish? You did ask me a question, you know."

"I suppose I did. But the way you've been trying to speak my thoughts for me, and investing me with opinions I've never—"

"Calm down, now. Just let me talk. I told the gentleman, as I've already indicated, that I had had such a 'verge of death' experience. He claimed not to believe me."

"You mean he didn't believe you."

"No. He *claimed* not to believe me. Deep down, of course, he did. My challenge was to help him admit that he did."

I couldn't resist the strong attraction of sarcasm. "You're very noble, putting yourself out like that, just to help a man understand his own mind. Most people would content themselves to take a man at his word and leave him to wallow in ignorance about his real beliefs."

"Most people *would* do that, yes. But I am unlike most people." This bird actually took my statement for a sincere compliment! He continued:

"What happened next is that he became aggravated at my gentle insistence on the veracity of my story; he became unaccountably aggravated; he became so aggravated, that he tried to 'top' me. He out with the claim that *he* had had an experience that put mine to shame. He said *his* experience made my blinding light look like a lightning bug. He said *he* had died and stayed dead for a sight longer than I had, if I had at all, which he doubted. He said *he* had stayed dead for seventy-five years. He said he was Mark Twain.''

"What did you say?"

"I called him a liar. Oddly enough, he didn't back down. He said, 'You saw me in the barber-shop before my shave and haircut.' He was right about that. 'Didn't I look like Mark Twain?' he asked. I gave him a cold shake of the head. 'Coincidence,' said I. He said, 'Then ask me anything about Mark Twain. Anything.' I said his answers would not signify. If they proved correct, it could simply mean he had read a great deal about Mark Twain. Then he said he would give me unambiguous evidence—something I couldn't explain except in terms of the miracle he claimed for himself. 'What might that be?' said I. He said he had a unique body. He said he didn't ever urinate. I shrugged with indifference. He said he didn't defecate, either. I stifled a yawn and asked him if he could ejaculate. He seemed confused and said of *course* he could. Then he asked me if I would like him to ejaculate right then and there. Well, I'm not one to run away from a new experience. We only live once, you know,—most of us, anyway—and I was interested in how those simple old souls in the Keno audience would respond to such a thing if he went ahead with it, so I told him I was for it if *he* was for it. He grinned and produced an ejaculation for me.''

"No!"

"He produced two, in fact.''

"*Two?* No!"

"One right after the other.''

"Impossible!"

"But it was a disappointment. It was a cruel disappointment.''

I exclaimed, "Did he undress? Right there in full view of—''

"No, no. You don't understand. And I didn't either, at first. All he did was—he shouted.''

"Shouted? My lands. You mean, with ecstasy?''

"No, no. You're all confused. He shouted, 'Ding blast it!' Then he shouted, 'Dad gum it!' ''

"Well, I'm not surprised. If he didn't undress, and . . . and . . . and if he did what you say he did, and not just once, but *twice*, he would certainly feel some regret, and feel ashamed, not to say soiled, and he'd have to go up to his room for a bath, and . . . and . . . well, take it all in all, I should think even stronger language would be called for.''

"Damn it, woman. You don't understand. Those were his ejaculations. Uttering words like those—*exclaiming*—that was what he thought I'd meant by 'ejaculate.' "

"Oh," I said, feigning disappointment. Then I laughed as I reached for my palette. "Sounds as if he took you for a ride."

"*No.* He did *not.* I *insist* that he did *not.* He had genuinely misunderstood me; I am *certain* of it. I explained to him, in very exact and picturesque terms, what I had meant by the word. Well, you've never seen a man blush so. He gave off the brightest, reddest glow—it was a wonder. Experience has taught me that the one facial expression that man cannot summon up at will is the blush. I've tried it, many and many a time, figuring it might come in handy in my line of work. It can't be done. The best I've managed is a puffy-faced facsimile generated by grunting and straining—a poor thing by comparison, with possible unpleasant side-effects. So I gave that blush of his some thought. I felt that the average twentieth-century man would not have blushed at what I said. But the average nineteenth-century man, even if he could comfortably talk with a relative stranger about urinating and defecating, might very well blush at the mention of this other form of eruption. I reasoned myself right into believing him. From that moment on, I knew he was Mark Twain."

"Did you tell him that you believed him?"

"No. I didn't want him lording it over me. I wanted him to always be wondering about me. But for the sake of harmony, I agreed to call him 'Sam.' We were on friendly terms from that point on. Once or twice a day I would call him an impostor, just to keep him on his toes, just so he wouldn't think he was superior to me in any way." He laughed. "I kept him dancing. I truly did."

Scrutinizing his face, I said, "That's good. That expression is very . . . strong. Do try to hold it. But you must tell me something. What about this notebook business? As I understand it, from what I've read, there was a genuine Mark Twain notebook miraculously discovered by you. But if you are *not* Mark Twain . . . I'm all confused."

"Of course you are. It takes a mind like mine to even begin to fathom it. But I'll try to explain it to you. As the days passed and we loafed along, there in the Ormsby House, I noticed that he spent a lot of time scribbling. I sneaked a peek at his writing, and I hived a page or two and took them to a nearby library to compare his handwriting with the real thing. I found some reproductions there, and they matched perfectly. I put my mind to work. I thought, and read, and studied—I am what they call 'a quick study.' I learned that he had left dozens of works unfinished when he died, and I gently suggested he take them up again. He refused. He asked me if I had ever awakened from a nightmare and been afraid to go back to sleep—afraid I'd re-enter the nightmare. Well, naturally I had had experiences like that, but I said no. He couldn't believe I'd never experienced it, and he got a little hot about it, which naturally tickled me. He concluded his comparison—lamely, on account of it was gone to hell because of my lacking that experience—by saying that for him to take up work on those uncompleted manuscripts would be like re-entering a nightmare.

"So I examined his recent work, the stuff he had been scribbling in the hotel room, but it had the flaw of exhibiting how recent it was, talking about modern automobiles and all other sorts of useless rubbish I couldn't use. I suggested he modify these—make them look like works of the past century; he said no—they were just fine the way they were. I'm telling you, the man had no more imagination than a stump. His right hand was a gold mine and he was just trifling it away, writing trash that wouldn't ever do a body any practical good.

"Then I struck the notebook idea. The 'missing years' of young Sam Clemens. The chief strength of the idea was the appeal it would have to his laziness; he wouldn't have to create anew, or follow through on any ideas he didn't feel like following through on. He'd just have to consult his memory and a few books and write plausible little chunks to go with them. It would be like making up blueprints of a building after the building had already been erected. It would be easy as pie."

"Provided he agreed to it," said I as I dabbed my brush into the evil green mixture I had made, intent on reproducing his eyes. "But isn't he a principled man—generally?"

"I don't like that word—'principled.' Never use it. He *was* backward and sluggish and ignorant of opportunity, if that's what you mean. I knew that about him, so I knew I would have to motivate him. But I was confident. I knew from being around him so much just how easy it was to get his dander up. And I knew from my reading, there in the library, that he and the emotion of revenge-lust were not strangers—that he had often heeded that call. I resolved to work on that mean, angry, vengeful instinct of his. He was already malleable, as far as that goes, on account of being so bitter about being called back to life. He was already primed to take it out on somebody.

"Here's what I did. I carefully gathered all the evidence I could find that would lead him to believe that the modern world didn't care a fig about him; or, if it did care, cared in an ignorant, sloppy, foolish way. Now and then I would drop an ignorant remark about him—compliment him on his lovely book *The Last of the Mohicans,* for example—and he would get all hot. Once he said to me, 'How can there be a bar called the "Mark Twain Bar" in this hotel and people like you be so thoroughly ignorant about me?' 'Why,' says I, 'Mark Twain is just a *name* these days—didn't you know that? It's just a name, like Davy Crockett, or Johnny Appleseed —a name with an ignorant fact or two attached, and nothing more.' Says he, sort of whining, 'But I read about *Huckleberry Finn* in a magazine, just this morning.' Says I, 'Hmmmmph. That don't signify.' I told him that book didn't get read any oftener than Deuteronomy. I told him the few people who *had* read it said it was racist, and I showed him everything that had been written along that line.

"I showed him two books that he was supposed to have written from the grave, and I told him they were very famous books in their time, and very bad books, and they half-killed his reputation. Then I showed him a book named *The Ordeal of Mark Twain,* which is by a man that somehow lacks a proper given name, and I told him that book had killed the other half. Then, after a little scouting trip of my own, I took him to Virginia City, where they had some ugly dummies of him, set up in all sorts of outlandish scenes. In one of them, he was at a bar, seeming to meditate on the offer of a nearby dummy-prostitute. He was none too happy about that. Back home in our hotel room, trying to cheer him up—ha!—I showed him old and flawed editions of his writings. I was careful never to show him the more recent editions, painstakingly assembled by college professors. Well, those old books—I'd gotten them from the library—they sort of made him blue, so I suggested we drop in on a bookstore. Maybe we'd find something a little more respectable. Well, we searched for his books, but in vain. Why? Because earlier that day I'd stashed his works, when no one was looking, behind some religious books in a different part of the store. The next day I showed him a film called *The Adventures of Mark Twain.* That film was the climax of my efforts. He was soft clay in my hands after that. I could shape him any way I had a mind to."

"What didn't he like about the film?" I asked.

"Pretty near every single word of it, as far as I could tell. There's a moment in it where Fredric March—that's Mark Twain—is on the river and he hears a leadsman sing out, 'M-a-a-a-rk Twayain,' and March sort of rolls his eyes as if to indicate the muse has just reached down and tickled his innards and endowed him with a pen-name. My man said that was all wrong. He said he didn't think of using that name until years later, when he was in Nevada. (Meanwhile, says I to myself, 'Good! That must go in the notebook.') Then my man spit and cursed when the movie showed him and Bret Harte racing jumping frogs in Calaveras. I tried to defend the film at that point, talking about artistic license and all, just to make him madder, of course. It worked. A while later the film showed him and his wife mourning over the death of their young son, with her whimpering to him, 'Write about boys, Sam. You know about boys, Sam. Write about boys,' and there he goes, penning *Tom Sawyer* like a house afire. Well, my man said it was all a lie—more than one lie. It was a hundred lies."

"But—excuse me for interrupting, but it suddenly struck me that there is a contradiction in your scheme. The notebook could be sold for a princely sum only if—"

"Yes, yes."

"—only if—"

"Yes, yes. I know what you're trying to say."

"*Trying* to say? I am *going* to say it if only you will let me."

"I'll help you out. I don't mind. The notebook could be sold for a princely sum only if Mark Twain was highly esteemed. If he were as neglected as I had convinced him he was, there would be no serious market for the notebook, and therefore no reason for me to participate in the hoax. Exactly. It was a fatal flaw. Now, I suggest you set your brush down a moment, because what I am about to tell you will so astonish you that you might jerk your hand and mar the portrait. Are you ready? The truth is, *this fundamental contradiction never occurred to him.*"

"Impossible!"

"It's the truth. It never occurred to him."

"But surely when he learned of the amount of the sale—I remember reading it was sold for more than two hundred thousand dollars—surely *then* the contradiction must have struck him."

"By then it didn't matter. By then he had done some research of his own, and wanted to back out, after all my hard work. But I wouldn't let him out. I told him I was going through with it. And I did."

"What about your discovery of the notebook? Weren't you almost killed?"

His jaw—no, his entire face, from the roots of his hair forward—leaped out another inch. "That's exactly right," he said in the most smug, conceited way. "I was almost killed."

"So, that was an accident? You ran off the road accidentally, and then seized on the moment to pretend to find the box containing the note-book?"

"I ran off the road *deliberately*. I didn't just pretend to find a box. The box was there. I had already put it there. It had to be there so that the highway patrolman could see me say, 'Aha! A box!' Of course the notebook wasn't in it, not then. We were still working on it. Finding the box was the important thing."

"But wasn't that unnecessarily dangerous? Didn't you almost drown? Didn't you break some bones?"

"Broke an arm, yes." There it went again—the face, lunging forward. I began to fear it might soon crowd me out of my studio. "I'll tell you a story," he continued. "Back in 1978, or thereabouts, when they built that dam, there was a sizeable crowd opposed to it. One of them, a young kid, slipped up the river in the dead of night—after announcing he was going to do it, mind—sneaked up there *barefoot* and busted a toe on a rock in consequence; when he reached a certain big boulder by the river he chained and locked himself to it and threw away the key. Well, he slowed the flooding of that canyon right down to a stop while they searched in vain for him. He finally came out, days later, all haggard and worn out and limping pathetically—a hero, making a triumphant return. So—now you understand."

I frowned. "I do?"

"Of course you do."

"I . . . I'm not entirely certain that I do."

He snorted impatiently. "Damn it, woman. It's plain as day. I couldn't *possibly* let that youngster show me up, could I? I just *had* to bust something, and make sure it was something bigger than a toe. Otherwise, I just wouldn't have been satisfied."

"Ah," I said. "I see your point. It was quite a victory for you. Yes, people certainly *would* have made comparisons." He must have missed my sarcasm, from being so inflamed with his achievement, because he plunged right ahead:

"I did it for another reason too—crashing into the river like that, I mean. I did it for the sake of distraction. If I almost got myself killed, well, no one would ever think a man in his right mind would have deliberately done such a thing."

"Absolutely." I tried not to smile. "But what about the real Mark Twain? Wasn't he with you? Didn't you almost kill him, too?"

"Sure." He shrugged. *He shrugged!* "I didn't much care what happened to him by then. He'd already written enough of the notebook to guarantee me a nice pile."

"Hmmm." I dabbed at the portrait, touching it up here and there. "I have just one more question, and then we shall be done, I think. It's a silly question, really, but it just struck me, and I couldn't rest if I didn't ask it. Isn't there a possibility, a remote possibility, that the real Mark Twain laid certain clues in the notebook? Couldn't he have written some sort of incriminating evidence right into the notebook, as a joke, or as a way of finally getting the upper hand over *you?*"

The steady forward march of Umlauf's face ceased abruptly; his face quivered a moment, and then began to withdraw into itself. "Naturally that thought occurred to me. You insult my intelligence if you're implying that it didn't. And I naturally scrutinized the notebook for any sign of betrayal. It is a pure document. I am sure of it."

"If there were such clues, and if they were discovered, wouldn't you be exposed for the fraud you are and be vulnerable to prosecution?"

His face continued to recede. "There is no such danger. There are no such clues."

"Well, I may not know what I'm talking about at all, but I've read somewhere that forgers like to put what you might call their 'signatures' into their forgeries. It's partly a matter of pride, I suppose—sort of like the way criminals who use aliases use modifications of a name instead of wholly unrelated names. In each case there's the same desire to leave a little trace of oneself behind. I've also read that Mark Twain was real interested in that sort of thing. Didn't he lean toward the view that, oh, what's his name—I'm such a little ninny I can't seem to . . . Bacon? Is that it? I believe it is. Didn't he believe that Bacon was the real author of Shakespeare's plays? I recollect that he believed that because he read a book showing how Bacon's signatures are hidden everywhere in Shakespeare's plays. Now, with an interest in the subject like that, it's only natural to assume—"

"You can't assume *anything*. The notebook is free of such evidence, I assure you." His lower jaw continued to chug back into the rest of his face, like a locomotive retiring into its shed for the night.

"Or even better than a 'signature,' wouldn't it be interesting if there was a key phrase or sentence, something he took from a book, maybe,— a book published much later than the notebook was supposed to have been written? Wouldn't that be interesting?"

"But if *I* couldn't find it," he wailed, "how could anyone else?"

"Oh, I don't know," I said carelessly. "But I'll bet you there are some real smart people hunting for such a thing, or that there will be, real soon. Maybe they'll go back to the notebook and discover some sort of guide to finding the clues, a guide built right into the notebook itself. Maybe there are some sort of directions for getting from this place to that, only the directions are really instructions for finding the key sentence, and the 'landmarks' in the so-called directions are really the words of the key sentence, and . . . but maybe I'm just a foolish little woman, spinning silly nothings out of nothing."

"Hmmmmph," said he. "The only thing wrong with what you just said is 'maybe.' " How his voice lacked conviction! And his face was absolutely flat now. It looked as featureless as a stove-lid.

I sighed. "You're probably right not to fret yourself about it. You know so much more than I do about such things. My mind is so terribly rudimentary." I set my brush down. "You may get up. I am finished."

Umlauf heaved his huge frame out of the chair, looking every bit as blue as he had looked when he first sat down. However, the portrait had captured him at the apex of his enthusiasm over his several victories. He studied it, and nodded in admiration. But all the while, he stroked his face and seemed to marvel at the contrast between its utterly flush feel to his fingertips and its extruding appearance on the canvas.

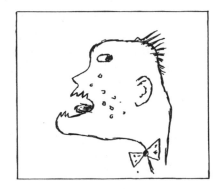

COMMENDATIONS OF THE PORTRAIT

There is nothing like it in the Vatican.

John Paul II.

It is an exemplary portrait of the criminal mind.

Zebulon R. Brockway II,
Warden, Elmira Reformatory.

The lower jaw has been filed in our office of "Fish-Catching Devices," Pat. No. 3389467112156573 Pending.

James W. Paige II,
U.S. Commissioner of Patents
and Trademarks.

We have shown the portrait to our residents, in small doses, and have found its curative value unmatched by the methods of modern mental science.

Albert Wimple, Director,
Stockton Insane Asylum.

As I study this portrait of Mark Twain, I find it truly remarkable what he has accomplished in so short a time; I have been dead six hundred years, and I haven't managed to *approach* this degree of deterioration.

Geoffrey Chaucer.

Notes on p. 245.

A Curious Encounter

What feature of daily life do we miss more sorely than any other when we travel?

Savage reader, do not guess wrongly and thereby blunt my point. Do not say, "Searching the pantry for a snack?" or "The local newspaper?" or "Bowel regularity?" Think! You are traveling. Not a soul knows where you are. You are completely out of touch. There—you should have it now. It is the mail.

In my miserable incognito state, the only missive I had received in four months was one blood-stained crossword puzzle. But this morning, when I strolled into the lobby on my way to breakfast and paused at the front desk, to my delight I spied a folded sheet of blue paper in my pigeonhole. Farther down the desk, the clerk stood with a fly swatter poised above him, tracking a fly that was buzzing around just inches above the counter, contemplating a landing, which the clerk meant to be his last. He seemed disappointed to see me. I could not find it in myself to fault him for this; a man likes to finish what he sets out to do. Casting a longing glance back at his hovering prey, he hurried over to me with his fly swatter wedged under his arm like a baton. I told him my room number and he handed me the message.

The letter was written in a barely legible hand, with words running together, *t*'s uncrossed, and *i*'s undotted. Its author must have been in a great hurry. The message read:

My dear Mr. Clements,

I should like to have a few words with you. Would you be so kind as to meet Me this morning at 9.00 o'clock at your old study on Quarry Hill?

Ys ever,
God

My feelings? Mingling with my doubt that the letter had been intended for me,—owing to the "Clements"—was a thrill of joy at this confirmation of the Deity's existence. But joy gave way to skepticism,— it was a hoax, I smelled an Umlauf—which yielded to renewed belief accompanied by shame, because I had been a doubter, which was blasted away in a chill wind of fear—was He going to chasten me?—which blew away harmlessly as I began to doubt again.

I looked at my watch. It was just after eight o'clock. The day being clear and crisp with the freshness of spring, I decided to walk up the hill, as I had done so many times a century before. I crossed the lobby, the desk clerk scampering in circles behind me and humping after that fly with a truly refreshing absence of self-consciousness. But I proved to be the fly's savior, for when I opened the door it buzzed by my ear and flew out into the open air.

A huge highway now separates Quarry Hill from the valley in which Elmira drowses by the river, and it took me some time to locate a bridge spanning the road. Then, as I began to climb the steep grade—much steeper than I had remembered it—I struggled to contain a mounting resentment against the Lord. Why couldn't He have come to my motel room? Why did He make me toil up this hill, like Moses ascending Sinai? I thought it a crass display of power on His part—crass, but typical.

As I neared the house, the grade seemed to become even steeper, as if the mountain were bent on defying my ascent, for *my* sake, because the mountain knew I was in for a sad, sad time. You see, brief scenes from the past began to dance before my eyes as I neared the driveway—Livy, well-wrapped, reading on the porch; Susy with a retinue of ducks following her across the yard; Jean chasing after Clara, then falling and crying and needing comfort. It was the stone watering troughs that did it—that finally produced the first tears I had shed in these four long months. We had placed the troughs along the road leading up from the town, long ago, for the sake of the horses on the long, hot climb, and some kind soul had gathered them up and set them at the end of the driveway leading to the house. There was one for each of my animal-loving children, a child's name carved on each, and how they swelled to see the lathered beast slaking his thirst at their *very own special* watering trough.

I somnambulized across the lawn below the house, not knowing if the building was occupied, and not caring. The beautiful little octagonal study I had worked in for so many summers, specially erected for me by Livy's good, good sister, who lived here year round, had been situated on a little knoll about a hundred yards from the house. In that bygone era, I would skip up the limestone steps after breakfast, my manuscript under my arm, and stay there until dinnertime, writing, smoking, and gazing down on the valley below.

I got there at nine o'clock. The Almighty wasn't in evidence. Neither was my study! I looked all around, but in vain. Had He taken it with Him somewhere, and would He bring it back? I sat down on the rocky debris that had been its foundation and took out my pipe, slowly mastering my melancholy feelings so that I wouldn't be putty in His hands. I began to suspect He had chosen this site designedly, to give Himself an advantage over me, to weaken me.

Half past nine. I became an agnostic. Ten o'clock. I became an atheist again. It was just as I had always suspected: ill-written evidence of His existence, but beyond that, absolutely nothing. I wondered how long I should wait. Then I heard a noise from atop the bluff behind me, as of a bear crashing through the woods. This was followed by some swearing in a loud Southern drawl. I looked up. "The sight of the glory of the Lord" was *not* "like a devouring fire on the top of the mount." What I saw was my twin, a man whose appearance and dress were exactly like my own. He had just struggled through some heavy brush to the edge of the bluff and was frowning at me.

"What are you doing down there?" He asked, borrowing my voice.

"This is where the study was," said I, taking it back from Him.

"It was up here," said He.

"No. It was right here. I'm sure of it."

"You're mistaken," said He.

"I am *not.*"

He seemed to shrug. "All right, then," He said, and I thought I heard Him add, under his breath, "Stubborn ass." He began to make His way along the edge of the bluff, circling down toward me and fighting the bushes every inch of the way. I wondered why He didn't fly. By the time He reached me He was in a sweat, despite the chill of the morning.

"Here I am," He said. "Right on time."

"You're an hour late," I said.

"I *am?*" He looked at His watch—the twin of mine. "No. You're wrong, Sam. It's nine o'clock."

"It's ten."

He slapped Himself on the side of the head and looked as if He were about to snap His fingers. But His hand froze in mid-air and He let it drop to His side. "I'm on Central Time. Had some business in Chicago." He frowned and looked around. "Where's your study?"

"I don't know," I said automatically, unthinkingly. Then the awful import of His question struck me. "You have to *ask?* You mean, *You* don't *know?*"

"Oh, I know, all right," He said, a trifle peevishly. "I just can't recall right off."

"You can't—" I decided to let it pass. "Why do You look like me? Is this Your customary practice?"

"Oh, stop it," He said impatiently. "Don't ask Me the same old questions everyone else does. Surprise Me, Sam."

I laughed—irreverently. "Surprise You? All right. You're an Ass. You should go around with a bag over Your head, out of shame for Your conduct."

He stifled a yawn. "I've read all that before," He said.

"Good," I said. "If You've read that, You've read other things too—like what I've written about this goddamned mortal coil. Why did You bring me back?"

"It's none of *My* doing, Sam. Honest Injun."

"You're not in charge?"

"Of course I'm in charge, but not in the sense you think. I'll put it this way: things don't happen without I allow them to." He smiled. "I rather like talking 'Pike-County.' "

"So why did You *allow* me to come back?"

"Because it didn't cost Me anything. Not at first, anyway."

"Not at first?"

"Listen, Sam." He paused, as if intending to invest His next words with heavy significance. "You're messing around on My territory."

"You mean Your son's territory, don't You?"

He gave me a blank look, then suddenly burst out laughing. "You mean Buford? The resurrection? That's good, Sam. That's prime. No, I—"

"Who in the hell is Buford?"

"Why, My son, of course. Isn't that what you meant?"

"Most folks know Him as Jesus."

He reddened, then quickly tried to recover. "Of course, of course. I was thinking of . . . something else. Jesus. Yes—Jesus." He cleared His throat. "But I wasn't talking about your coming back, Sam. That's of no interest to Me. It's what you've been doing *since* you came back that bothers Me. It's what you're doing to *time* that I can't abide."

"So send me back. Carry me home to die, so to speak."

"I can't do that. All I can say is there is hope for you. If what happened the last eighteen times is any indication, your time is almost up. You'll leave on April eleventh, when Halley swings by Earth on its way out." He looked at me. "Don't you understand? You arrived as Halley brushed by on its in-bound voyage, and you will sail off with it on its outward-bound brush with Earth. Don't look so happy. Life isn't *that* bad."

"But . . . what do You mean by 'the last eighteen times'? Have I come in with Halley's Comet before? In centuries past?"

"No, no. I mean *this* time. You've come and gone eighteen times already, and your departures were on April eleventh, every time."

"You'll forgive me for saying I don't recollect that happening."

"Of course you don't. When you out with a 'Damnation!' that sends time backwards, other people don't know they're re-living events that have already happened. Only *you* do. Well, in this case, *you* are in the position that others are in when *you* go back, and *I'm* the only One Who—"

"You mean *that's* the way You operate? You can go back too?"

"Sure. I do it all the time."

"But why?"

"*Why? Why?* If I didn't, intelligent life would have ended aeons ago. I've averted thousands of apocalypses. Rather, I've seen them come and then sent things back to a point where a little judicious intervention brings about a different fate—one without a bust-up. You're familiar with the Jamaican Missile Mess of 1952?"

"If you mean the Cuban Missile Crisis of 1962, yes—I've read about it."

"That's exactly what I mean. I must have misspoken myself. Well, anyway, the world ended."

"It did?"

"Sure. What do you think? It ended seventy-eight times. Bombs raining down, clouds covering the earth, climatic changes. Every single organism with any intelligence to speak of was doomed. Nothing but turtles left, every time. But after seventy-eight tries, I found a way to let it play out with a withdrawal by the Celts."

"The Russians."

"Of course. That's what I said—the Russians." He took a cigar from His-and-my coat pocket and lit it with a conceited flourish. But He was an unpracticed smoker, and after a few coughs and frowns He quietly let it drop to the ground and stepped on it. He looked at me. "You should be proud of your gift, Sam. It's divine."

"Give me another sample of Your work."

"All right. Here's one from your life. Remember the time that buggy went flying down that very road over there, out of control? It was the summer of 1883, and all of the—"

"It was in 1877."

"I think not."

"It *was.*"

"Fine, fine. Perhaps I was thinking of something else. When it happened, your wife and child were in mortal danger, because the horse had gone crazy and bolted, and the buggy—"

"It wasn't my wife. It was my wife's sister-in-law, her child, and the child's nurse."

"Just so. It's a trivial distinction. Then, who comes up the hill with a wagon-load of manure, at the *precise* moment, but none other than old John Lewis, the slave, who saved the day when he—"

"He wasn't a slave."

"I believe he *was,* Sam. I do believe I've got you there."

"There were no slaves in 1877."

"Well . . . he *was* a slave, once. That's what I meant." He fretted a bit. "Are you going to let me tell the story or not?"

"I *know* the story—better than *You* do, I'd say. Lewis saw the danger they were in and parked his wagon at a diagonal against the fence, making a trap for the runaway buggy, and he set himself in the middle of that trap, with no thought to his own safety, and he seized the horse's bit when he streaked by and fetched him up standing."

"Yes! Now, how about *that?*"

"It was a rare example of true heroism," I said without emotion.

"And Who do you think arranged for Lewis to be there at just the right moment?"

"Let me guess. Was it the same Power Who allowed the horse to run off in such a state in the first place?"

"Just hear Me out, will you? I saw that buggy overturn and smash its three occupants all to flinders. Saw it happen countless times while I worked on getting Lewis up that hill at the right time. He was a stubborn case. He could find more ways to dilly-dally along and get distracted. One time, when I thought I had it just right, he met a friend on the road at the bottom of the hill and got to jawing with him about horse races and dog fights and all kinds of rubbish, so of course he was late, and next time around I had to arrange for that friend to fall in a ditch and break his leg before he reached the road, and, well, complications followed, and he—

but that's no matter. The important thing is that I prevented him from meeting Lewis. I got it just right. Now—why did I do that?"

"Because You're kind?" I contained my amusement.

He blushed. "Well, there *is* that, to be sure. But I did it mainly for *you*, Sam. If those dear friends and relatives of yours had been killed, your wife would have slipped into an incurable depression, then into a lingering fatal illness, dying much earlier than she did. I know. I saw it happen, many and many a time. This, in turn, would have soured you on life much earlier in your career, and all of your subsequent works would have been pessimistic and hurtful to My cause, which is to keep the human race fairly cheerful. You've been very helpful to Me there."

"Then why did You let me go sour at all? My wife, my children— why did You kill them when You did?"

"I didn't—"

"Why did You *allow* them to be killed, then?" I snapped.

He shrugged. "Your work was done. I had gotten more use out of you than I get out of most people. What happened to you after about 1890 had little effect on the overall picture. Oh, you weren't entirely useless. Your denunciations of imperialism, for example. Those helped. And you wouldn't have written them if you'd been happier. So the sourness had its place." He glanced at His watch. "Yes, the Lewis story is a good one." He suddenly grew animated. "You used it in *Pudd'nhead Wilson*, didn't you? *That's* why I thought he was a slave—because the character in that book who saves the family was a slave."

"Good for You," I said dully.

"Casper," He said, pushing His luck.

"His name was Jasper, You Ninny."

"Yes. Jasper. I was very close."

"You averted *that* catastrophe with the buggy. Why not others? Why do You allow so many horrible things to happen to so many people?"

"Like what?" he said, all innocence.

"The Black Death, for one."

He laughed. "Oh. That. Well, as I recall, it delayed the Industrial Revolution."

"That's a good thing?"

"It is if you want the race to survive."

"You make less sense every time You open Your mouth."

"All right, smarty. How's this, then? There is no Black Death. Instead, in the one-third of the European population that goes on living instead of dying, several geniuses mature and flourish and rush things along so that the Renaissance happens immediately afterward, and is over in a hurry, and the Industrial Revolution happens in the fifteenth century, and you've got nuclear capability in the sixteenth. The bust-up comes real fast after that. I saw it happen—seven hundred and twelve times. Then, during one replay of it, I noticed a powerful little bacillus, and I set him up in the belly of a nasty little Asian flea, and I gave him a ride on an ugly little black rat, who shipped out to the Mediterranean and points north, and, well, you probably know the rest. Without the Black Death, we wouldn't have made it this far. You see, Sam, it all comes down to The Bomb. The longer I can delay it, the better My chances are."

"But You're stuck with it now."

He shook His head. "Everything's 'wait-and-see' in this life, Sam. This course we're on is purely tentative. All of life is tentative. I could snap My fingers and send the whole boiling back to the Pre-Cambrian slime, if I had a mind to. The problem is that I seem to be able to gain just a few measly centuries here and there. Mankind seems bent on discovering fission and fusion, like a cat drawn to an open well."

"Am I right in thinking that You don't care a fig for individual lives? You care only for life in general—correct?"

"Intelligent life, yes."

"How do you define 'intelligent'?"

"Blushing."

"*What?*"

"Blushing life. I want a race that can blush. That's all."

"Bl—— Why, that's the damnedest notion I ever— *Blushing?* Whatever for?"

"That's the nature of the wager."

"Wager? *Wager?*"

God looked over His shoulder into the woods, then glanced all around; He stepped closer to me. "I'm not supposed to talk about it, but what the heck—maybe He's not listening. You and your kind owe your existence to a little bet I laid down with a Deity in a different solar system. We created identical worlds with identical natural laws, and We made a bet. The first One of Us to reach one million years of blushing life will win. Now, if I can . . . Why are you looking at Me like that?"

"*Why?* How else can I look at You when You speak such idiotcy?"

God shrugged. "Well, you can believe it or not, Sam. It's all the same to Me. I'm not to blame if the world's religions haven't discovered the truth."

"Very well. I shall discuss it with You as if it were a sane plan. How are You doing? Are You winning?"

He pressed His lips together and winced. "I must confess that, at the moment, it looks fairly grim for My side. I shall spare you the details— My futile search for the hint of a blush in the early life forms—the trilobites, the jebusites, the amalekites, and that sort of fry. Idiots, all of 'em—not an ounce of self-attention to 'em. Nor even in those stupendously ugly saurians, or the ridiculous ornithorhynchus, or even the monkeys. Lands, I had hopes for those monkeys, but they only just giggle— not a single blush in the whole tribe. No—I had to wait for a human being to come along. The first recorded blush was in Kenya, 61,214 years ago. His name was Ferguson, and he left his fly open one day when he called on the savage he was courting. A sensitive man, Ferguson. He is the father of the race, the true Adam. But he was *so* slow in arriving, and I've got *so* far to go, and just look at Me—I used to gobble up centuries without having to pay much attention to the goings-on, but I'm scrambling for puny little *years* now, just drops in the ocean of time. When 1985 came I said, 'Thank heavens, I made it!' Then 1986, and 'Praise Buford!' What really galls Me is that My Competitor's people are still fighting with stones, and He's got over half a million years of blushing life to His credit. I don't know how He does it."

"How can He have more years if You started out at the same time?"

"He has had to make fewer loops back, and His loops have been shorter. So He chalks up the aeons while I'm humping around putting out fires all over Creation. Why, His people—dumb? They're dumber than turkeys—a Creator's dream! You know how they fight? I mentioned stones. You probably think they throw them at one another. They could, if it occurred to them, since they're built more or less like you folks, but they lack the brains to have struck the idea. So what do they do? They *hike* their stones at the enemy. That's right—hike 'em, like footballs. I ask you, how are you going to hurt a body that way? You should see their campaigns, the way their armies advance on each other. It's ridiculous. It's the most backwards sort of combat that ever you'll see. It'd give Napoleon the fits to see it. I wish *My* people were *half* as dumb, I truly do. When your race took hold, Sam, after I'd given a chance to dozens of others and had to give up on them because they were too smart, I had real hopes. I thought, 'These chuckleheads can blush all right, but they will *never* invent The Bomb.' But they did. I may have to go back and try for a stupider bunch, but I hate to risk all that I've gained. My Adversary was just plain lucky, I guess, with his buttocks-launching tribe."

God was quite flushed now. He had worked Himself into a real state. I asked Him if His Adversary's people could blush, and this sent Him into an even greater sweat:

"Yes! That's what I can't cypher out. They're smart enough to feel shame and embarrassment—like when one of them, in the heat of battle, bends over for a hike, if he breaks wind, why, you should see the crimson faces covering the battlefield. They're smart enough for that, but when it comes to self-destruction they're perfect sapheads."

He calmed down a bit and looked squarely at me before speaking again:

"I have but one over-riding principle, Sam—one commandment, you might say: *Time is of the essence.* Which brings Me back to My very first point. You're messing around on My turf. You're slowing things down. Every time you say 'muggins' and 'damnation' I lose precious weeks."

I stared at Him. "Do You mean to tell me," I said, struggling to keep my temper, "that *that* is why You wanted to see me? Not to justify Your ways, but just—"

"I want you to stop it, yes. I want you to chart a straight course for April eleventh. You are My most formidable enemy right now; you could say those words over and over and keep us stuck in, say, the first week of April, 1986, forever and ever. You wonder why I'm telling you this? Because in another light, you're no danger at all. I could send things back to 1835 and snuff you out right then. Or just think of all those times you nearly drowned in the Amazon, as a boy, and someone pulled you out in the nick of time. I could arrange a delay, break another leg. I could swat you in a moment, Sam. But I'd prefer not to, because I'd lose time that way—you see? You follow My thinking?"

I was grown considerably warmer, and said, "You've got some nerve criticizing me for going back. I've only done it to protect innocent people, which is more than I can say for You. Why, every time that buggy capsized on that road, those people actually *suffered,* and You made them endure it over and over. You're just a silly Clockwatcher—get to the finish line first, even if it means slaughtering innocents all along the way."

"Sam," said God, a little reproachfully, "you always loved games— cards, board games, billiards. Try to get into the spirit of this one and help Me out."

I gazed down over the valley, too disgusted to look at this divine Idiot. My eyes roamed over the grounds of the farm. I thought of Livy and her attempts to keep my faith whole. If only she had known the truth!

God sidled up to me ingratiatingly. "I know what you're thinking.

You're thinking about all the good times you had here on the farm—good times I *allowed* you to have. You're feeling grateful."

I said, "I am not in the habit of adoring the hand that smites me."

"Awww, come on. I know you. You're thinking about how you wouldn't want to lose those precious memories, which is what would happen if I let you die young. You're thinking about your lovely children: Susy, Clarence, Huckleberry, and dear little Orion."

I laughed. "Well, one out of four ain't bad. You *are* a muggins, ain't Ya'?"

"Watch that word. It might cost Me."

"You bungled the story about John Lewis, and You don't know where my study was, or *is*. Amazon, Your granny. You don't even know the time of day. You're a complete screw-up, ain't Ya'?"

"History isn't My strong suit, I'll admit it—but, Sam, there are so many histories to remember!"

" 'God created man in His own image; in the image of God created He him.' I know what that means, now. Man is a screw-up because God is a screw-up."

"An interesting interpretation." His eyes wandered. He seemed distracted, as if He were thinking about—or even watching—something else.

"And to think how guilty *I've* felt for *my* nature. *You're* the guilty One. Howells had it right—more right than he could have known. You know what he said? Probably not. Or You'd probably get it wrong if You tried to quote it."

"Mmmmm," He said, His eyes glazed over. He wasn't listening.

"Howells wrote a lovely memoir after I died, and when he wrote about my nature and my misdeeds and the suffering I caused others, he said about me, 'He knew where the Responsibility lay, and he took a man's share of it bravely; but not the less fearlessly he left the rest of the answer to the God who had imagined men.' What do You think of that? Come on. Wake up."

"I'm afraid this conversation didn't happen."

"*What?*"

"I've got to cancel it. There is a certain gentleman in the Alps who simply *must* fall off a mountain and break his neck."

I laughed helplessly, overcome with a dreary sense of defeat. "Is it absolutely necessary?"

"Oh, no. I could let him go on living, and six years down the road he would head the mercenary support for a coup in Argentina, which in the end would touch off the big bust-up. It's already happened over four thousand times, and I've been casting around in the past for the right time to get rid of him, and I'm just tickled as can be to have found it. I'll have to go back a bit, to give Myself sufficient time to get over there and distract the unwitting nihilist who saved him from his fall. You see, I can't just shoot the fellow, or anything like that. The rules call for indirectness. Well, every second I spend here jawing with you is precious time I'm losing to My Adversary. I'm off now. But I'll do you one favor, Sam. I'll give you a Memory-Annihilation Dispensation, so that you can dwell fondly on this chat we didn't have. So long."

He grinned and raised His hand to snap His fingers. My hands suddenly flew up from my sides, going for His holy throat.

Instead of the snap of God's fingers, or of His neck, I heard the slap of a fly swatter against the hotel counter, where I stood, gazing at my empty pigeonhole. No messages.

"Nailed him!" the clerk crowed triumphantly, pointing to the squashed life on the counter. "I've been tryin' to get that bugger for a long time."

Notes on p. 248.

Woodlawn Cemetery

The body counts for something.

Yet, when you get there, when you stand and gaze down, your eyes drifting from headstone to earth, which you oddly try to penetrate with your gaze, you are inevitably plagued by this simple question—what are you doing there? It's just bones, after all. Or the thought may come to you by a different path. You gaze, thinking that here lie the bones of a famous person, and isn't it odd that no one has dug them up and made off with them, and *then* you think it—no, it's just bones. You can't sell them. You can't make a decent soup out of them. You can't do much of anything useful with them. You can't even get any fun out of sentimentally fondling them. Mark Twain didn't write with his bones, after all.

So why *are* you there? Because the body counts. We feel that the man is *there*—and not just six feet below where we stand. He's in the air, so to speak. If we make a disparaging remark, we feel anxious, as if he might hear us. Let us be honest—we don't believe in an afterlife. (If you do, it makes no sense for you to ever visit a grave.) So we go to the body. It is the best we can do.

We don't believe in an afterlife, but we don't believe in death, either. We think, "What a nice resting place. Look at that view. Isn't the grass lovely, though? He must be comfortable." *Comfortable?* We are curious creatures when it comes to thinking about death.

You also feel sad. You feel sorry for the poor old fellow. The achievements of his life rush upon you in waves of recollection, and you feel sorry for the old man for his weakness in the end, his flimsy mortality. We actually convince ourselves that his entire life was sad because it came to this end—as if it could have come to any other. We are curious creatures.

You get there by driving up Walnut Street right on through the main gate. A sign tacked to a tree, reading "Mark Twain," guides you to the right. I like that sign. I like the way it implies I shall be there, standing under a shady elm, ready to pump your hand and tell a story or two. Take the second left turn and park your car. Don't slam your door. No spitting or swearing, either. Livy wouldn't like it.

Your first thought might be that it certainly is crowded. Twenty-one bodies in one small plot. Just remember that in some respects I was ordinary, and did what ordinary people do. I married, had children, had in-laws. We're all packed together in there—I mean, we're all packed in there separately. I sha'n't go into all the Langdons buried there. They all mean something to me, but for you it's just names you won't be able to keep straight. We shall restrict ourselves to my tribe.

There's Langdon, our first and only son. There are no words on his headstone, apart from his name and dates. The boy was doomed from the moment he was born—I mean, more doomed than most. I mean—

It is no good. We are all of us doomed. *All* of us!

There's Clara, my middle daughter, beside her first husband, Ossip Gabrilowitsch. A tall monument at the grave features my profile, carved in relief; under it, my nom de plume; under that, a profile of Ossip with his last name. Everybody who comes to visit my grave looks at that monument; and looks at it; and thinks; and thinks some more; and finally says, "Who in the hell is Gabrilowitsch?" Well, he was a great pianist and a conductor of the Detroit Symphony Orchestra. He was a Russian Jew, and when he became engaged to Clara, his family clucked their tongues and said, "Ossip is going to marry a shikse"—pause—"but she is from a good family." They were married at Stormfield in October, 1909, just six months before I temporarily died. You might be thinking that Providence was sweet to grant me that joy, so near the end. You are only *partly* right, however—as you will see.

There's Jean, my youngest. Her epitaph: "After life's fitful fever she sleeps well." I don't much like it any more, even though I had it put there. Her life *was* a fever—in and out of sanitariums, finally diagnosed as an epileptic—but it seems such a pitiful way of summing up a person's life. Jean died a few months before I did. She had a seizure while taking a bath, and drowned. We found her that way, the housekeeper and I, the morning before Christmas, 1909. Providence regretted that earlier present to me, I reckon, and decided to balance the account. Providence went overboard, of course, but Providence *always* goes overboard—that's just Its way.

Livy. She went six years before I did. They *all* went before me, all but Clara. Livy's epitaph: "Gott sei dir gnädig, O meine Wonne." ("God be merciful to you, O my joy.") Pretty brash of me to have used God's name here. I did it for Livy. I didn't mean anything by it.

And there's Susy. Susy.

Warm summer sun
  Shine kindly here,
Warm southern wind
  Blow softly here,
Green sod above
  Lie light, lie light—
Good night, dear heart,
  Good night, good night.

This sounds right to me. It is godless, even pagan. And it is hopeless.

Grandchildren? Yes—one. Nina, Clara's daughter, born the year I died but *after* I died. That was sweet of Providence too, never letting me see my only grandchild. If she were alive today, she would be seventy-five years old. I would have visited her. But it was not to be. She committed suicide in 1966.

Nina never married. The line ends there. Livy's family tree spreads robustly, save for the branch that I joined—and poisoned. That one got blighted early on, just like poor little Langdon. Isn't Providence sweet?

When you visit my grave, you have my permission to feel sorry for me.

Notes on p. 250.

Letters

Dear Susy,

    1. For striking terror into your young & sensitive heart with my lightning-quick temper,

    2. For sins of thoughtlessness—chief among them stands the ghost story, which I simply *had* to tell,

    3. For sins of absence—chief among them stands the long separation in your last lonely year,

I am sorry.

    1. For steadfastly failing to accept me as God made me,

you should be sorry.

Susy, your mother always thought a humorist was something perfectly awful. She & you were dearer to each other than any mother & daughter ever have been, or will be. You thought just like her. I know it now, & I knew it then, but not in the way I know it now, & I *hated* it then, though I didn't know then that I hated it the way I know now that I hated it then, & I don't hate it now nearly so much as I (unknowingly) hated it then, because now I know that I hated it then, though I didn't know it—then. Forgive me the faint humor of that sentence, from which I barely emerged with my skin; the humor of it is only faint, so it shouldn't disturb you *too* awfully.

I know you won't deny my charge against you, for you were always flawlessly honest. (I recall that whenever I told you a story with a character in it who lied, you would chide me severely.) Even if you did try to deny it, or if you were to doubt its truth just a little,—well, just listen to your biography of me. I have kept your thirteen-year-old's punctuation & spelling, which is also rather like your mother's:

> One of his latest books was the "Prince and the Pauper," and it is unquestionably the best book he has ever written, some people want him

to keep to his old style, some gentelman wrote him, "I enjoyed "Huckel-
berry Finn" immensly and am glad to see that you have returned to your
old style." That enoyed me greatly, because it trobles me to have so few
people know papa $<$ it is absurd she did not want to tell about the
wounded dog & the worse wounded man $>$, I mean realy know him,
they think of Mark Twain as a humorist joking at every thing; "and with
a mop of reddish brown hair, which sorely needs the barbar's brush, a
roman nose, short stubby mustache, a sad care-worn face, with maney
crow's feet," &c. That is the way people picture papa, I have wanted
papa to write a book that would reveal something of his kind sympathetic
nature, and the "Prince & Pauper" partly does it. The book is full of
lovely charming ideas, and oh the language! It is $<$ even darkness can be
great $>$ perfect, I think that one of the most touching scenes in it, is
where the pauper is riding on horsback with his nobles in the recognition
procession, and he sees his mother, oh and then what followed; how she
runs to his side, when she sees him throw up his hand palm outward, and
is rudely pushed off by one of the king's officers, And then how the little
pauper's consience troubles him as he remembers the shameful words
that were falling from his lips $<$ darkness is not bad but good $>$, when
she was torn from his side. "I know $<$ not monstrous but beautiful $>$
you not woman" and how his grandeurs were stricken valueless, and his
pride consumed to ashes. It is a wonderfully beautiful and touching little
scene, and $<$ darkness is $>$ papa has described it so wonderfully.

Susy, however "beautiful & touching" you think this scene is, posterity
is not on your side. Posterity is with that nameless "gentelman" you
mention, who liked my *Huck*. For every modern reader who remembers
the pauper denying knowledge of his mother, I can start a *hundred* who
remember Huck & Jim on their raft. And your language! "How his
grandeurs were stricken valueless, & his pride consumed to ashes." That's
the kind of bombast I ridiculed every chance I got. How it galls me to
know that my enemy was in my own house, whispering false advice into
my ear whenever I took up my pen—into my *ears*, rather,—you installed
at one ear, your mother at the other.

Susy, I have, on occasion, been a subtle aggressor from the podium.
There are those who say I *meant* to attack the smug self-worship of
literary New England at the Whittier Birthday Dinner, who say that my
speech was *intentionally* disrespectful. (You were only five then; you
experienced the event only in my gloom & short temper in the months
of shame following it.) I shan't argue with that interpretation; at the

moment, it doesn't concern me. But it *is* a correct interpretation of the incident at Bryn Mawr. "Oh, papa, don't tell the ghost story. Whatever you do, don't tell the ghost story." Susy, you must understand *why* I told it, after assuring you I would not. I was thinking, somewhere in my tortured brain, "You've *always* disapproved of my low, humorous streak, Susy. Well, I'm going to go even lower than you're accustomed to, my dear, right in front of your classmates." Anger will out, Susy, one way or another, & if we are ignorant of ourselves, it will out in ways that confound our understanding at the moment—I was all remorse & apology afterward, of course, not knowing why I did it & wondering how I could be so cruel & thoughtless. Cruel—yes. Thoughtless—no. There was thought behind it, all right.

But I *still* shouldn't have done it, & you still deserve my apology. Just as I deserve yours.

Your loving papa

Elmira
Apr. 7/86

My dear Mrs. Clemens:

He hasn't written you a letter for some time, I know. He hasn't written much of *anything*. He hasn't been able to. He's too sad. You see, he's back on the mountaintop where he, & you, & the children romped with my great great great (& so on, I forget how many) grandmother.

He came here to write, he says. (He talks to me; some people might find that surprising; I don't.) He *wants* to write, but he can't. Says his brain is too dull. It's the sadness. I know. He rattles around in that big house, sighing & remembering the ancient fun, & the love that died with the loved ones, & he does it so much it's almost as if he *wants* to hurt all over. Sometimes we walk up the hill, past where his study used to be, up to where you had your picnics, & the way he drags his feet along—it's just awful to see.

Most of the time he just sits on the porch, & stares. He dragged a couch out of the drawing room, & you wouldn't have enjoyed hearing what he said as he fought it through the front door. (I didn't understand it as swearing, right off. I thought he was talking to me, without looking at me, & calling me the son of my mother, which is a pretty obvious & uninteresting thing to say. But I figured out that he was talking to the

Notes on p. 250.

couch, & meant something different.) He sat out there on the couch for a few days, until the president of the college happened to drive by— checking on him, you see, & a good thing, too, because the couch was from your family home, down in the valley, & was a valuable antique & shouldn't have been exposed to the sun & rain. The president kind of swallowed his anger & helped Sam get it back into the house, all the time shaking his head & giving Sam the fish-eye, as if to say, "What the devil were you thinking, man?"

The truth is, he *wasn't* thinking. It didn't look so old to *him.* It just looked friendly & familiar. I miss the couch. Oh, he still sits out there & stares, but now he sits on a plain kitchen chair, & there's no room on it for me. The president of the college drives by pretty regular now, I noticed, in search of other examples of mischief.

As I was saying, he's sad, & he mainly just sits on the porch & stares down at the valley. Yesterday he told me he was astonished that he'd written so many books up here. The sound of his voice always makes me happy, so I thumped my tail on the porch as I listened to him rattle off the list—*Tom Sawyer, Huck Finn, The Prince & the Pauper, A Connecticut Yankee*—a tolerable list, I thought, waiting. He fell silent. I waited some more. My tail slowed, then stopped thumping. Could he have forgotten? Impossible! I cleared my throat, throwing a lot of meaning into it. He perked up & gave me a glance & said, "Sorry, old boy— and 'A Dog's Tale,' of course. How could I have overlooked that?" I fell to wagging my tail again, though I confess that it was a little forced; a body don't get over a slight like that right away. Then he reached down & rubbed me around the ears, & I was my old self with him again. He scratches & rubs better than anyone I ever struck, but he'll be gone in a few days, he says. Isn't that life all over? A good thing falls into your path—a real first-rate ear-scratcher—& just as soon as you begin to appreciate your good fortune it up & abandons you to your former lonely, outcast state. Like I said, he rubbed me so nice I kind of warmed up to him again. I figured he didn't know that my great &-so-on grandmother was the original of the dog in that wonderful story, which in my opinion lays over everything that ever he wrote, & if he'd only *known* of my lineage, you can bet he would've named that story, & first off, at the top of his list. I wish he *did* know I was related to her. I wish I could tell him.

The reason he says he's surprised he wrote so many books up here is on account of the view. He can't take his eyes off it. He wonders how, in his younger days, he ever managed to keep his eyes fixed on his manuscript. He says he came here to write *this* time, too—that's also what the president of the college thinks, though lately maybe he's not so sure. But he hasn't written a word—because of the view, he says.

I know better. It's because he's sad. He's a changed man, & the view of the river in the valley has changed for him. It beguiles him into fond memories, which make him sadder still. You may think "beguile" is a pretty large word for me to be using. I suppose I picked it up from him.

There's a curious thing he's been doing lately. He's been daydreaming out loud about something he calls "alternative biographies," by which he means the way his life would have been *if* such-&-such had happened, which is different from the such-&-such that *did* happen. One of his favorites is what his life would have been like if he lived now instead of then—but everything else the same; you, the children, &c. He told me that one nice thing would be he wouldn't have to go around with his head hanging in shame for being a humorist, & you folks would have eased up on nagging him to go write a real boring book, because these days it's no literary sin to be funny. He also told me he figured little Langdon would have lived, because modern medicine could have helped him overcome the disadvantages he started out with, on account of his being so impatient to be born; he told me he figured Jean could have lived a nearly normal life, maybe even a happy one; and he told me that Susy might have survived the disease that killed her.

Oh—another thing. He said he figured you would have seen a psychiatrist, Mrs. Clemens. He said that back in your time people knew so little about the human body that they imagined *it* was at fault when the *mind* was at fault, using words—big words, so big that they put "beguile" to shame—like "neurasthenia" and "nervous prostration" to cover up how little they knew; words that pointed kind of vaguely at the body for the cause. He told me about your two years in bed after your fall on the ice, when you were young, & how a faith healer kind of yelled at you & made you spring out of bed, all better. I don't know, Mrs. Clemens—it's too many for me. You take a dog, now—a dog wouldn't do that. A dog wouldn't lie abed for two years without there being a real *cause* for it, & then jump back to life, just because some faith healer had the gumption to throw open the curtains & yell that it was way past breakfast time.

He says that in this alternative life of his *he* would probably have seen a psychiatrist, too. Says that just as *you* were two people in one—the neurasthenic that was weird, & the lady everyone loved, the most beautiful soul on earth, just as . . . just as . . . I can see I've over-reached myself here, grammatically speaking. Anyway, he says *he*'s got two natures, too—got 'em from his mother & father. His mother—she was as warm, as *hot*, even, as the tropics, while his father preferred the Arctic regions, & so it's not surprising, he says, that he was such a peculiarly unpredictable family man—sometimes the protector, other times the danger from which the family needed protection.

He concluded this little biography by saying that when he was on the river, piloting, he wrote his brother that he was a lucky man—born lucky, he wrote; but how much luckier he would have been, he said to me, if he, & you, & the children had been born seventy-five years later.

He says he likes cats better than dogs. He says it to me even while he treats me so nice. I don't believe him. It's some sort of joke. He's always joking. He's an awfully funny man—when he's not sad, I mean.

Yours Very Truly,

Quarry

Notes on p. 254.

Notes

The Contest

This sketch may have been conceived and begun while Clemens was on the river, where it is set (although Pikesville is a fictitious name). However, its inclusion in Part III rather than in Part II of the manuscript means that it was probably not completed until after 12 March, the date when we received Parts I and II.

In several senses this is a companion piece to "St. Peter Helps Me Feel Good About Myself." Both works feature an externalized "conscience" sitting in judgment of Clemens' life; both focus on deeds that he regretted; and the latter ends with a flagrant exhibition of the very complacency he imagines Peter urging on him in the former. The dwarfish antagonist/conscience here is also a clear kinsman to the animated conscience in "The Facts Concerning the Recent Carnival of Crime in Connecticut" (1876), a story in which a relentlessly nagging conscience takes grotesque bodily form and teases the narrator mercilessly, flaunting his power over him, until, enraged, the narrator murders the creature, after which he goes on a crime spree with no pangs of remorse whatsoever.

Clemens has drawn heavily from Ken Dollar, Ruth Reichl, and Susan Subtle, *The Contest Book* (New York: Harmony, 1979), which gives information about every contest named in this sketch, with the exceptions of the Juneau Vomit Festival, the annual meeting of the Fundamental Sigh Society, and the Annual Hell Hole Suicide Jubilee. It should be noted that the 1986 meeting of the World's Championship Pipe-Smoking Contest was held in Topeka, Kansas, on 26 July—over three months after Clemens' departure.

Clemens' son, Langdon, died on 2 June 1872; Clemens sailed for England on 21 August 1872 for a three-month trip.

In his treatment of his indifference to Clara's singing career, Clemens may have been influenced by *MTGF*, pp. 20 and 200—a work mentioned in the St. Peter sketch. If so, he had been heeding St. Peter's imagined advice to read about his life. His perspective on his final years with Livy and on Susy's death may be indebted to Kaplan's *Mr. Clemens and Mark Twain,* also mentioned in the St. Peter sketch, though Clemens invests his version of events with an acidic sarcasm that is entirely his own.

The failed brother is, of course, Orion. The dwarfish man quotes literally from a Clemens letter to Orion ("If, when you shall have finished . . ."), dated 6 May 1880 and published in *MTL,* pp. 378–379—presumably Clemens' source for the exact wording. In a 9 February 1879 letter that chronicles Orion's career of vacillation and failure, Clemens wrote to Howells, "You *must* put him in a book or a play right away. You are the only man capable of doing it. You might die at any moment, & your very greatest work would be lost to the world. . . . Now come! Don't fool away this treasure which Providence has laid at your feet, but take it up & use it" (*MTHL,* pp. 253, 256).

The probable sources of the quotations from Clemens' two letters home after Susy's death are *MTL,* p. 641, for "To us, our house . . ." (19 January 1897 letter to Joseph Twichell), and *LLMT,* p. 326, for "I wonder if she . . ." (29 August 1896 letter to Livy).

A Glimpse: III

From our investigation in the east, we learned that Clemens visited Hartford, Connecticut, on 18–19 March; thus this third "Glimpse" was written some time between then and 9 April.

Hermann the German, like Milton Tibbett from "A Glimpse: I," was an acquaintance of Clemens' during his *Delta Queen* cruise. As with Tibbett, we assume that Hermann's presence at this Mark Twain site is purely imagined.

The Clemenses lived in Hartford from 1871 to 1891, at first in a rented house, then, beginning in 1874, in the opulent Victorian house they built on 351 Farmington Avenue; this is the scene of Hermann's tour, which opens with the tour group entering a large octagonal porch on the third floor, just off Clemens' combined study and billiard room.

Glosses to Hermann's German:

Ich *muss* es	I *must* (do) it
verdammt!	*damn it!*
durchaus	throughout
Hasenlippe	harelip

Es hätte sein könn'	It might have been
Dummkopf	idiot, blockhead
verdammte Sprache	damned language
Also!	*So!*
Weinstube	tavern
Gott sei Dank	thank God
Aber ich auch!	*But me too!*
Mein Gott!	*My God!*
Gott im Himmel!!	*God in heaven!!*
Ach!	*Oh!*
Mensch!	*Man!* (exclamation)

The quotation from *A Tramp Abroad* is from chapter 34.

The "Hasenlippe" is Joanna Wilks, who says to Huck, "Why, you talk like a muggins" (chapter 28).

Clemens' 1884 notebook contains a mixed English and German version of one of the final couplets from John Greenleaf Whittier's "Maud Muller" ("For of all sad words of tongue or pen,/The saddest are these: 'It might have been!' "): "Of all sad words of tongue or pen,/The verdammtest are these, es hätte sein könn' " (*N&J3*, p. 55). In "The Awful German Language" (Appendix D to *A Tramp Abroad*), Clemens gives a long description of the typical German sentence, concluding it with an illustrative string of verbs thrown together nonsensically: ". . . *after which comes the* VERB, and you find out for the first time what the man has been talking about; and after the verb—merely by way of ornament, as far as I can make out,—the writer shovels in 'haben sind gewesen gehabt haben geworden sein,' or words to that effect, and the monument is finished."

Clemens' family life is abundantly chronicled in his autobiographical dictations, in letters from him or Livy to friends and relatives, in his notebooks, and in unpublished manuscripts devoted to the small incidents of everyday life with children. One of these last, already mentioned in the notes to "The Twain Man," is "A Record of the Small Foolishnesses of Susie & 'Bay' Clemens (Infants)," in which Clemens periodically recorded incidents occurring between 1876 and 1884. Susy's name was spelled "Susie" in her infancy and childhood; "Bay" is Clara, so nicknamed as a result of this incident:

> When she was an hour & 4 minutes old, she was shown to Susie. She looked like a velvet-headed grub worm squirming in a blanket—but no matter, Susie admired. She said, in her imperfect way, "Lat bay (baby)

got boofu' hair"—so Clara has been commonly called "Bay" to this day, but will take up her right name in time. ("A Record," p. 4)

"A Record" contains the family stories Hermann mentions and which he is supposed to have heard narrated earlier in the tour. From evidence in the sketch following (see the notes to "A Glimpse: IV"), and from the signature "Papa" in the 19 March register in the office of the Hartford Mark Twain Memorial, we assume Clemens toured his former home on that day and heard the stories.

In "A Record," Clemens writes the following about Susy, then two years old:

> One day on the *ombra* [i.e., veranda] Susie burst into song, as follows:
>
> "O Jesus are you dead, so you cannot dance & sing!"
>
> The air was exceedingly gay—rather pretty, too—& was accompanied by a manner & gestures that were equally gay & chipper. Her mother was astonished & distressed. She said:
>
> "Why Susie! Did Maria [Clara's wet nurse] teach you that dreadful song?"
>
> "No, mamma, I made it myself all out of my own head. *No*-body helped me."
>
> She was plainly proud of it, & went on repeating it with great content. (p. 7)

"Besshy Mish Chain" is daughter Jean, as described in a later entry:

> Jean is incomparably sweet, & good, & entertaining. Sits in my lap, at the fag-end of dinner, & eats "Jean-quum" (crumbs,) & messes up the table with "Jean shawt" (salt,) puts "Jean fum" (plums—i.e. grapes) in "Jean himble-bo" (finger-bowl,) & says "Naughty George—ve'y naughty George," when George brushes off her salt. Won't consent that she is mamma's blessed Miss Jane—no, is *"Papa* besshy Mish Chain." (p. 93)

The blackbird derives from this story, which dates from late 1883, when Jean was three and a half years old:

> I stepped into the nursery on my way to the billiard room after breakfast. I had a newspaper-cutting in my hand, just received in the mail, & its spirit was upon me—the spirit of funerals & gloom. Jean sat playing on the floor, the incandescent core of a conflagration of flooding sunlight—& she & her sunny splendors were suggestive of just the

opposite spirit. She said, with great interest,—

"What is it in the little piece of paper you got in yo' hand, papa—what do it say?"

I said, impressively, & meaning to impress *her*,—

"It tells about an old, old friend of mine, Jean—friend away back yonder years & years & years ago, when I was young—very dear friend, & now he is dead, Jean."

She uttered an ejaculation and I a response.

Then she looked earnestly up from down there, & said,—

"Is he gone up in heaven, papa?"

"Yes," I said, "he is gone up in heaven."

A reflective pause—then she said,—

"Was he down on the earth, papa—down here?"

"Yes, he was down here on the earth, where we are."

She lowered her face, now grown very grave, & reflected again, two or three moments. Then she lifted it quickly to mine, & inquired with a burning interest,—

"And did along comed a blackbird & nipped off his nose?"

The solemnity of the occasion was gone to the devil in a moment —as far as I was concerned; though Jean was not aware that *she* had done anything toward that result. She was asking simply & solely for information, & was not intending to be lightsome or frivolous. (pp. 103–105)

Meisterschaft (1888), a three-act farce consisting of a nearly equal mixture of German and English dialogue, is no more successful a work than any other of Clemens' dramatic efforts. It is not clear if Clemens intended Hermann's critical judgment on this point to be as errant as his command of English idioms.

A Glimpse: IV

Like "A Glimpse: III," this sketch was presumably composed between 18 March and 9 April.

Across the top of the first page of this sketch Clemens wrote, "Move this to Elmira." He then drew a line through the sentence, perhaps because he later learned that the Elmira house was not open for tours, or because the family incidents referred to here occurred in Hartford rather than in Elmira. At any rate, under the canceled line he wrote, "Just shovel the 4 glimpses into the travel book," thereby sounding the death knell to his projected novel about "Comet Man."

Gus's singing of "The Name Game" to torture or embarrass his wife is reminiscent of the nameless feuding husband's singing of "Harrigan" in "A Couple of Hamburgers" (1935), a short story by James Thurber. Clemens may very well have become acquainted with Thurber's work by this time. This sketch echoes Thurber's preoccupation with the battle of the sexes, as does "A Glimpse: I," in which Milton Tibbett is plagued by the women in his life. In addition, Clemens' imagined tour de force of navigation in "A Dispatch from the *Delta Queen*" is like the imagined feats of "The Secret Life of Walter Mitty" (1939), lacking only the "pocketa-pocketa." Also, below, in "A Curious Encounter," we shall find a possible debt to a published letter of Thurber's. Thurber was often called the second Mark Twain; what we may have here is an unparalleled example of a formerly deceased author imitating a writer allegedly influenced by him.

Clemens' awareness of the rope and supporting metal posts in his former billiard room/study is strong evidence that he took the house tour.

The "thunder-stroke" letter to Howells is accurately quoted in the sketch; see *MTHL,* p. 575.

The Kingdom of Heaven (Working Notes)

These notes for two stories that are not extant and perhaps were never written appear on the back sides of the last five pages of "A Glimpse: IV." The notes were written between 17 March and 9 April.

For this item we have departed from our editorial practice thus far in this edition and have rendered Clemens' cancellations, which are contained in angle brackets. The reason for this is the evidential value of one of the cancellations; see "On the Trail of Samuel Clemens: The East," where the notes and the mysterious "Cocoa" are discussed in some detail. Suffice it to say here that, regarding the first projected story, a Manhattan portrait photographer, Francis Benton (renamed "Balducci" in the notes) annually distributes free calendars featuring six children's portraits as samples of his work; Clemens must have seen one or more of these during his stay in New York City and chosen to use it as a central device in his story: a young boy, during a trip to the hospital for stitches with his father (the "Stranger in Wash[ington] Sq[uare]," who tells the narrator the story), sees the calendar in the hall, sees the portrait of his (recently?) deceased twin brother, infers that his brother died in that very hospital (a correct conclusion, erroneously arrived at), and, having learned that one can pray to "good people who die & go to heaven," he prays to his brother, deriving great strength from it.

The last paragraph of the notes concerns what must be a separate sketch, which Clemens appears to have initially considered writing in the vein of his comic tales of marital life of the McWilliamses (thinly disguised versions of Livy and himself)—"Experience of the McWilliamses with Membranous Croup" (1875), "Mrs. McWilliams and the Lightning" (1880), and "The McWilliamses and the Burglar Alarm" (1882). The last sentence and the cancellation of "McW" suggest he decided in favor of a serious treatment.

Portrait of a Usurper

Two allusions in the second paragraph of this sketch assist in its dating. First, "that near-scandal with those two country girls in Pennsylvania" arose, as many readers will recall, during one of the "Children's Hours" that Umlauf had instituted during his journey up the Ohio. Umlauf would dock around 7 or 8 P.M., invite young children aboard—preferably girls—and tell them yarns. The evening ritual prompted comparison, as it was calculated to do, with Clemens' fondness for the company of little girls late in life (his "Angel Fish," as he called them). However, day by day, Umlauf began to favor the company of older girls. When he reached Pennsylvania, the average age of his audience was sixteen, whereas the average had been ten years of age when the story hours began near Louisville, Kentucky. In Beaver, Pennsylvania, playing on the town's name, Umlauf told an ambiguous tale that lent itself to a risqué interpretation if certain of his words were taken as puns; all the while, he bounced a giggling eighteen-year-old auditor on each knee. The incident occurred on 1 April; Umlauf tried to meet the frequent and usually hostile challenges that his behavior that evening had been distinctly un-Twainian by citing this date and laughing away the incident. Second, while Umlauf's river never exactly "dried up on him," he foresaw, near Salamanca, New York, that there was no Northeast Passage via the Allegheny, and he took to portaging, where necessary. His first portage was on 3 April. Thus this sketch was of quite recent composition when I received it on 9 April.

"Portrait of a Usurper" seems to have sprung from a complex of motives. It is directly in the vein of a small number of Clemens' works, all of them as silly, in a sense, as this piece, devoted to mockery of himself as an artist—"Portrait of King William the III" (1871), "Amended Obituaries" (1902), and "Instructions in Art" (1903). At the same time, it can be seen as a fantasy piece, in which Clemens finally gets the upper hand over his archenemy, not just by ridiculing his physical appearance, but also by planting the seed of doubt in his mind about a betraying clue in the notebook (about which see "On the Trail of Samuel Clemens: The East"). The sketch also fills in certain gaps in the biography of Clemens' second life. Umlauf's imperious control of the conversation gives us a hint of the willfulness Clemens endured in Umlauf's company in the west. More importantly, the work answers several of the lingering questions about Clemens' participation in the 1861–64 notebook hoax. No doubt a strong desire to add to the record on this matter helped prompt the writing of the sketch.

With the bulk of the facts about the notebook hoax now in, a few words of general comment are in order. As might be expected of the creator of the King and the Duke in *Huckleberry Finn,* Clemens had a lifelong fascination with hoaxes, frauds, and false claimants. Sometimes this fascination produced artistic successes—"Petrified Man" (1862), an extravagant spoof about a remarkable discovery of petrification in Nevada; "The Capitoline Venus" (1869), in which a friend of a young sculptor disfigures one of his friend's statues with a hammer, knocking off the nose and various limbs, then buries the remainder in a plot of ground he has recently purchased in the Campagna di Roma, feigns a discovery of it, and makes a fortune for his friend from the sale of the work, which is interpreted by experts as the creation of "some unknown but sublimely gifted artist of the third century before Christ"; or "Is He Living or Is He Dead?" (1893), a short story with the premise that François Millet's death was a hoax, contrived so that Millet could enjoy while still alive the posthumous recognition so predictably accorded artists condemned to lives of poverty and starvation. But sometimes Clemens' fascination led him into projects that backfired. In the *Galaxy* of December 1870, he published an anonymous lacerating review of his own book, *The Innocents Abroad,* intending to parody ignorant, literal-minded reviews by excessively sober critics. But his parody was taken as a joke on him by many who read it, and his subsequent exasperated explanations of its authorship fell on incredulous ears.

Clemens' rush to judgment about his reputation brings to mind a dark three weeks in his first life. Enraged by rumors that Whitelaw Reid, editor of the New York *Tribune,* had been treating him hostilely in his paper, Clemens launched a campaign designed to bring Reid to ruin. Several pages of his notebook of January 1882 contain notes and phrases for a projected biography of Reid, such as "Get Nast to illustrate," "Consult files of Tribune & attribute all silly gushing editorials to Reid," and "I do not begin with his boyhood, which is of no consequence—nor with his manhood, which has never existed," as well as a proposal for a "Monument to Whitelaw Reid—smiling, wise jackass's head . . . Buy ground in N.Y., & erect it with great ceremony, getting enemies to subscribe" (*N&J2*, pp. 419, 423, 424, 443). Finally, at Livy's sound suggestion, Clemens made fuller inquiry into Reid's alleged treatment of him, found that the rumors were without foundation, and abandoned his vendetta. As he told Howells in a remorseful letter about his misdirected labor, "Confound it, I could have earned ten thousand dollars with infinitely less trouble" (*MTHL*, p. 389).

It is unfortunate that Clemens, with his inclination to literary mischief-making and his pessimistic quickness to believe in the worst possible case, touched down where he did. Had his first search for evidence of the way posterity has treated him taken him to the Mark Twain Papers, or to the Hannibal Home and Museum, or to the Mark Twain Memorial in Hartford, or even to a bookstore unravaged by Umlauf, his conclusion would have been quite different from what it was. But Umlauf got to him early, fed him lies, and worked his will upon him. A comment by Paine on Clemens' character is particularly apt: "His confidence was easily won, and not always by those entitled to that great honor" (*MTN*, p. 400).

"Portrait of a Usurper" never directly addresses the question of why Clemens pretended to have stolen *Huckleberry Finn* in his re-creation of the notebook. Ricky Olivieri's early opinion was that he did so in order to enhance the commercial value of the notebook. My early opinion, upon reading this sketch, was that after Clemens concluded that posterity had mistreated him, he decided to mistreat posterity—by denying authorship of his most beloved book and giving its authorship a ludicrous attribution. But both of these views are evidently wrong, judging from his final word on the subject in his 11 April letter, which is given in "On the Trail of Samuel Clemens: The East."

Although he had been dead for five years, 1915 was a busy year for Clemens—in the opinion of some people, at least. He was reported to have dictated to a Ouija board a novel titled *Jap Herron*, published two years later (New York: Mitchell Kennerley). Also in 1915, *Spirits Do Return* was published (Kansas City, Mo.: The White Publishing Co.), and it too was reportedly "Inspired by Samuel L. Clemens ('Mark Twain')." These are the two books that Umlauf mentions. This editor has examined them. I am willing to concede that Mark Twain's writing declined in quality in his last decade on earth. But unless that decline accelerated appreciably in the first five years of his death, he cannot possibly be the author of these two books, the first of which is awful, the second of which is substantially worse.

The Ordeal of Mark Twain (1920), by Van Wyck Brooks, characterizes Clemens as a victim of his various environments—the unlettered Mississippi frontier, the coarse west, the stultifying east—and views his literary career as an essentially thwarted one of unfulfilled promise. While the book was influential, Umlauf of course exaggerates when he claims here that it was fatal to Mark Twain's reputation.

Umlauf's obsessive fear of being "topped" is nowhere more evident than in his bizarre sense of being in competition with the environmental activist with the broken toe. Remarkably enough, Umlauf speaks the truth about this incident that so strongly motivated him; see Tim Palmer, *Stanislaus: The Struggle for a River* (Berkeley: University of California Press, 1982), pp. 161–182.

According to Paine, Clemens spent a good deal of time studying William Stone Booth's *Some Acrostic Signatures of Francis Bacon* (Boston: Houghton Mifflin, 1909), which, along with Granville George Greenwood's *The Shakespeare Problem Restated* (London and New York: John Lane, 1908), prompted him to write *Is Shakespeare Dead?* (1909), which treats the question of the authorship of Shakespeare's plays (*MTB*, pp. 1479–1486).

A Curious Encounter

Clemens' first visit to Elmira in his second life was on 18–19 March; thus "A Curious Encounter" dates from the period between then and 9 April.

During their Hartford years (1871–91), the Clemenses customarily spent their summers at Quarry Farm—a 250-acre tract of land owned by Theodore Crane and Susan Crane (Livy's foster sister), situated about three miles east of downtown Elmira. In 1874, Susan Crane presented Clemens with the octagonal study in which he wrote large portions of his best-known books—approximately one half of *Tom Sawyer*, *The Prince and the Pauper*, and *A Connecticut Yankee*, and nearly all of *Huckleberry Finn* —as well as several shorter works, such as "A True Story," "1601," and "A Dog's Tale." In 1952, the study was moved to the Elmira College campus in town. Beside it sits the watering trough bearing Clara's name;

the other three troughs are near the driveway to the house, as Clemens states.

Clemens' "God," for all his leaky memory, seems to remember a fragment from a letter Clemens wrote to Howells in 1899: "Damn these human beings; if I had invented them I would go hide my head in a bag" (*MTHL*, p. 695).

"Pike-County" is the dialect which Huck Finn speaks and from which God occasionally draws in his language in the sketch.

The notes to "A Glimpse: IV" cite some examples of possible influences of James Thurber on Clemens. Another is in this sketch. It concerns turtles. In a 1946 letter, Thurber says of Halley's Comet,

> As you remember, this famous comet almost hit the earth that time [in 1910], and so frightened Mark Twain that he died. This mysterious heavenly visitor is due again in 1985, at which time there is every likelihood the earth will be completely destroyed, I hope. This is not as bad as it would have been in 1910, because in 1985 only turtle life will be left on the planet because of the atom bomb and other engines of war even more horrific. (*Selected Letters of James Thurber*, ed. Helen Thurber and Edward Weeks [Boston: Atlantic-Little, Brown, 1981], p. 165)

Clemens' account of John Lewis' heroic life-saving deed is told in his 25 August 1877 letter to Howells, one of the longest, and the most purely narrative, of the many letters exchanged by the two (*MTHL*, pp. 194–199). The incident is also rendered in chapter 4 of the manuscript of *Pudd'nhead Wilson* (but not in any of the versions published in Clemens' lifetime), and in chapter 4 of *Simon Wheeler, Detective*.

The importance of blushing to the deities' wager echoes Clemens' famous maxim (also exploited by Umlauf in Hannibal, with some interference from Ricky Olivieri), "Man is the Only Animal that Blushes. Or needs to" (*Following the Equator*, chapter 27). Alan Gribben, in *MTLR* (p. 175), points out that Clemens' maxim may have been inspired by an observation in Charles Darwin's *The Expression of the Emotions in Man and Animals* (1886), Clemens' personal copy of which is heavily marked; chapter 13 of Darwin's book begins, "Blushing is the most peculiar and the most human of all expressions."

The quotation from Howells is in *MMT*, p. 83.

On the back of the penultimate manuscript page of this sketch, Clemens printed "blatherskite" in large capitals, and then wrote words spelled with letters in this word, in three columns. His total was 108.

Woodlawn Cemetery

This work was presumably composed between 18 March and 9 April. Its tone suggests an apparent reversal in Clemens' attitude toward pity. In a 29 August 1880 letter to Joseph Twichell, Clemens, writing in Elmira shortly after Jean's birth, concluded his chatty summary of their activities with the following paragraph:

> Well, we are all getting along here first-rate; Livy gains strength daily, and sits up a deal; the baby is five weeks old and—but no more of this; somebody may be reading *this* letter 80 years hence. And so, my friend (you pitying snob, I mean, who are holding this yellow paper in your hand in 1960,) save yourself the trouble of looking further; I know how pathetically trivial our small concerns will seem to you, and I will not let your eye profane them. No, I keep my news; you keep your compassion. Suffice it you to know, scoffer and ribald, that the little child is old and blind, now, and once more toothless; and the rest of us are shadows, these many, many years. Yes, and *your* time cometh! (*MTL,* p. 385)

Letters

To Susy, 19 March 1986

In the fall of 1890, Susy Clemens enrolled as a freshman at Bryn Mawr College. Her father gave a reading there on 23 March 1891. A sophomore friend of Susy's, Evangeline Walker, has left us a detailed description of the events of the day; her account is in the Mark Twain Papers and has been printed in *S&MT,* pp. 286–288:

> It occurred to us that it would be very interesting to have Mr. Clemens come down and give us one of his Readings in the Chapel. Olivia [i.e., Susy] was delighted with this plan even though, as I remembered afterward, her mother was not particularly enthusiastic about it, for I think she felt the nervous strain would be too great for Olivia. And she was quite right, for from the moment he accepted the invitation and the date was set, Olivia became very restless and nervous and it seemed to our committee that it was going to be impossible for her and her father to agree upon a program. Letters were written back and forth and details were discussed. Apparently there were some of his stories—especially

the "Ghost Story"—that she did not like and felt were not suitable for what she called "the sophisticated group at Bryn Mawr College." "No," she said, she was "not going to allow him to tell *that story!*" Finally, the two of them settled upon a program satisfactory to both and the day arrived when he was to come and give his lecture. Olivia asked me if I would go to the station with her to meet him because, she said, he would like to walk from the station to the College, a matter of not more than ten minutes. Of course I was delighted to be asked and to see her father again, for all of us had lost our hearts to him when we were at the Bryn Mawr Hotel together. The moment we met him at the station and had exchanged greetings Olivia clung to his hand saying repeatedly as we walked from the Bryn Mawr Station to the College: "Father, *promise* me that you will not tell the 'Ghost Story'!" He laughed and patting her hand said: "I have written you that I would not tell the 'Ghost Story.' Let's forget about it."

Needless to say, the entire College turned out for his lecture in the late afternoon, and he kept his audience laughing. I was sitting with Olivia on the main aisle about the middle of the room holding her damp hand in mine, while she was shaking like a leaf. I tried to encourage her because everyone was enjoying Mr. Clemens thoroughly, and I hoped his success was reassuring her. There were no printed programs, and after each "number" he would walk back and forth on the platform, his fine head thrown back, and when the applause ceased, he would announce the next title and continue. Finally we came to the end of the program, and as the room grew darker he walked up and down the platform apparently deliberating—now a familiar and amusing stunt.

Olivia was whispering in my ear: "He's going to tell the 'Ghost Story'—I *know* he's going to tell the 'Ghost Story.' And he's going to say 'Boo' at the end and make them all jump."

"Now don't worry," I said. "You know he *always* walks up and down and *pretends* to be thinking what he is going to say. In any case the audience adores him!"

His audience was so entirely with him I was not worried. However I must say I got a bit nervous as time went on and he said nothing, and the audience began to grow a little restless. Whereupon, with no announcement, he began the "Ghost Story." By this time the room was quite dark, and Olivia quietly fled up the aisle, I following. Once out of the room we crossed the hall to a large classroom, the door of which was open. In she went and there flung herself down and with her head on a desk wept aloud! She was heartbroken! There was nothing to do or to say, no comfort that I could give her, except to reiterate that she must *know* the audience was simply delighted with her father and that the performance was completely successful! The applause was thunderous and people began to pour out of the Chapel. Finally, Mr. Clemens appeared and seeing Olivia in the classroom, he rushed in, and in a moment he had her in his arms trying to comfort her. "But Father," she moaned, "you promised, you promised!" "Oh my Dear," he wailed, "I tried to think of something else and my mind refused to focus. All I could hear was your voice saying: 'Please don't tell the *Ghost Story*, Father— *Promise not* to tell the 'Ghost Story'—and I could think of *nothing* else. Oh, my Dear, my Dear, how could I!"

I closed the big doors quickly and fled leaving them to comfort each other.

The ghost story in question is "The Golden Arm"—a tale from black folklore about a man who exhumes the body of his wife to recover her golden arm and is immediately haunted by the repeated wail, "W-h-o— g-o-t—m-y—g-o-l-d-e-n—*arm?*" When Clemens told the tale, he concluded it with a final wail of this question, a significant pause, and then a sudden accusation at a listener singled out from the audience ("the farthest-gone auditor—a girl, preferably"), with the shout *"You've* got it!" Clemens first heard the story from a slave on his uncle's farm in Florida, Missouri, when he was an impressionable young child. He frequently told it at lectures, and urged Joel Chandler Harris to write it up in his "matchless" black literary dialect (*MTL*, pp. 401–403). Harris never did, however, and the story first appeared in print, with instructions on the art of telling it (one of which is given in parentheses above), in Clemens' 1895 essay "How to Tell a Story."

In 1885, at the age of thirteen, Susy began a biography of her father, on which she worked intermittently until the middle of the following year, amassing 131 pages of manuscript. Clemens included much of her biography in his autobiography, in which he writes,

> When Susy was thirteen, and was a slender little maid with plaited tails of copper-tinged brown hair down her back, and was perhaps the busiest bee in the household hive, by reason of the manifold studies, health exercises, and recreations she had to attend to, she secretly, and of her own motion, and out of love, added another task to her labors— the writing of a biography of me. She did this work in her bedroom at night, and kept her record hidden. After a little, the mother discovered it and filched it, and let me see it; then told Susy what she had done, and

how pleased I was and how proud. I remember that time with a deep pleasure. I had had compliments before, but none that touched me like this; none that could approach it for value in my eyes. It has kept that place always since. I have had no compliment, no praise, no tribute from any source, that was so precious to me as this one was and still is. As I read it *now*, after all these many years, it is still a king's message to me, and brings me the same dear surprise it brought me then—with the pathos added of the thought that the eager and hasty hand that sketched it and scrawled it will not touch mine again . . . (*MTA*, 2:64–65)

The passage from Susy's biography quoted in this letter is also in his autobiography (*MTA*, 2:88–89); Clemens' criticism of Susy's language in her summary of "The Recognition Procession" (chapter 31 in *The Prince and the Pauper*) is actually a criticism, perhaps an unwitting one, of *his* language, for Susy's words are the ones he used in that scene.

Interspersed at five points in the passage from Susy's biography, and enclosed in angle brackets, are quotations of notes deliriously scribbled by Susy shortly before her death in August 1896. They appear here in Clemens' hand, so he evidently wrote them as he was copying the passage from Susy's biography, then canceled them. Again we face a difficult question about how these words came to appear in this context. Susy's deathbed scribblings can be found only in the original manuscript, which is on indefinite loan from the Mark Twain Papers to the Mark Twain Memorial in Hartford, and in a photocopy of the original in the files of the Papers. There is no record of Clemens' having examined either the original or the photocopy in his second life. He *may* have read the original not long after Susy's death (remember his ardent hope for "any little message" she might have left for him, quoted in "The Contest"), but if he did, it is unlikely that he would have remembered the words, which are utterly incoherent, and then written them in the midst of this passage. It is also somewhat strange that he wrote the words and canceled them without comment.

We are probably dealing here with the third "manifestation" of Clemens' daughters, the other two being the apparition of Jean on the Stanislaus and Clara's siren song on the Mississippi. In light of later events (see "On the Trail of Samuel Clemens: The East"), it is our belief that the sudden appearance of Susy's delirious scribblings means that she was trying to achieve contact with her father. Why the attempt failed is far from clear. Were there limits on Susy's power? Did the tone of her father's letter frighten her away at the crucial moment of possible contact? The tools of the literary editor are inadequate to the puzzle.

Clemens, in his failure to make any sort of accurate interpretive comment, not only here but earlier as well, seems to have shown a singular obtuseness about these three manifestations. After Susy's death, the Clemenses made three known attempts to reach her through mediums. But that the outcomes of the first two were disappointing is clear from a letter of 26 March 1901, in which Clemens describes the first medium as "a fraud," the second as "not a fraud, but only an innocent, well-meaning, driveling vacancy" (*MTL*, p. 707). The third attempt was also a failure. Later he would say, "[I] take no interest in other-worldly things and am convinced that we know nothing whatever about them and have been wrongly and uncourteously and contemptuously left in total ignorance of them" (*MTE*, p. 339). This attitude evidently persisted into his second life, dulling his attentiveness to the beyond.

To Livy, 7 April 1986

"A Dog's Tale" (1903) is a sentimental but effective anti-vivisectionist story narrated by a dog whose puppy is subjected to an idle—and fatal— experiment in its master's laboratory. It was the last work Clemens wrote in his Elmira study in his first life.

At the age of sixteen, Livy fell on the ice and was paralyzed and bed-ridden for two years, until a faith healer cured her somewhat in the manner described in this letter—although it is doubtful that he made her "spring" from the bed. Livy's neurotically delicate health and susceptibility to exhaustion were matters of constant concern to the family all through her life.

Clemens often wrote and spoke of his father's coldness and his mother's warmth. In "Villagers of 1840–3"—a collection of notes about 168 townspeople of his boyhood, written by Clemens in 1897—he writes of his father, "Stern, unsmiling, never demonstrated affection for wife or child . . . Silent, austere, of perfect probity and high principle; ungentle of manner toward his children" (*HH&T*, p. 39). In his autobiography, he writes of his mother, "She had a slender, small body, but a large heart— a heart so large that everybody's grief and everybody's joys found welcome in it, and hospitable accommodation" (*MTA*, 1:116).

Clemens' letter to Orion about his luck was written in 1859; in it he says, "Putting all things together, I begin to think I am rather lucky than otherwise—a notion which I was slow to take up" (*MTL*, p. 43). Years later, in a letter of 2 January 1895, he sounds the same note:

The proverb says, "Born lucky, *always* lucky," and I am very superstitious. As a small boy I was notoriously lucky. It was usual for one or two of our lads (per annum) to get drowned in the Mississippi or in Bear Creek, but I was pulled out in a ⅔ drowned condition 9 times before I learned to swim, and was considered to be a cat in disguise. When the "Pennsylvania" blew up and the telegraph reported my brother as fatally injured (with 60 others) but made no mention of me, my uncle said to my mother "it means that Sam was somewhere else, after being on that boat a year and a half—he was born lucky." (*MTHHR*, p. 115)

On the Trail of Samuel Clemens:
The East

The "Who Wrote *Huckleberry Finn?*" Symposium was scheduled for April 9 and 10 in the Sheraton Centre in New York City. In the opening session, a panel of scholars would present arguments for Orion's authorship of the novel. The afternoon session would consist of a panel presentation of the anti-Orion, pro-Samuel arguments. A rebuttal session was scheduled for the morning of the second day, and the Symposium would conclude that afternoon on what was anticipated to be a much-needed neutral note with an innocuous lecture by me on the progress and expected future course of editorial projects at the Mark Twain Papers.

The staff at the Papers, under my increasingly tremulous leadership, had maintained silence about the manuscript in our possession and about the light it shed on the 1861–64 notebook, the discovery of which had prompted the Symposium. We had had no word from Clemens since 12 March, when he hand-delivered Parts I and II of the manuscript to our doorstep; for all we knew, he had stopped writing, or had left the country, or had even left the planet. Thus, we lacked an answer to the question that would naturally arise if we went public with our knowledge, namely, "If Mark Twain is back, where is he?" Also, scholars had worked hard to prepare for the Symposium. We believed that debate on the subject should proceed without the complication of our imperfect knowledge being sprung on the scholarly community in the eleventh hour. After all, the manuscript explanation of the notebook, and not the notebook itself, could be a hoax; or perhaps our reasoning had overlooked some other explanation altogether. In sum, once again, we hung fire.

There was also the Umlauf factor. He had "scooped" us. Shortly after my arrival at the hotel on the evening of 8 April, I chatted with several of the scheduled speakers, and their scorn for Umlauf's claim to Clemens' identity was a chilling warning of the resistance I would face if I publicly nominated my own candidate for the same claim. Without exception, everyone I spoke with dismissed Umlauf's prediction of Halley's splitting as inexplicable luck, or as a ruse based on some sort of inside tip, perhaps from an amateur astronomer who had seen something no one else had. They scorned the matching palm prints as an example of "backwoods forensics." One scholar suggested that Umlauf, at some earlier date, had been to the Mark Twain Papers (a guess that certainly put all my senses on full-alert) and had switched the original Clemens negative with one of his own hand.

At the national level as well, Umlauf's Party Barge had taken on a little water. With the passage of time, his "signs" weakened in their power to convince, and many of those who heard him speak on the riverfronts as he worked his way up the Ohio called out for more signs, which he of course could not produce. Also, his speeches were becoming flat. Those reporters who stayed with him began to comment on their tedious repetitiveness, their excessive (and un-Twainian) reliance on flattery of the audience, and on their clumsy lurching from maxim to maxim.

Umlauf also created some problems for himself. He took to throwing people off his boat, starting with Ricky Olivieri, near Cincinnati, and moving on to selected reporters whose persistent skepticism he found exasperating. Then there was the "Children's Hour" incident, mentioned above (see the notes to "Portrait of a Usurper"). His fluvial commitment became a rather ridiculous problem as well, which he tried to handle with overwrought denunciations of the Deity. From the robust waters of the Ohio, he took the Allegheny from Pittsburgh into New York State. Then he looked at a map—seemingly for the first time. When he saw that he would have to travel by land, he swore and shook his fist at the heavens. A local resident with a trailer towed him on Highway 17 from Salamanca, New York, to Chautauqua Lake. As Umlauf approached the lake, he seemed to swoon and shouted, "Water! Give me water! I've got the Mississippi mud between my toes, and my body cries out for water!" He then cruised the length of the lake and portaged again on Highway 17 to Lake Erie, where he cruised up to the western terminus of the New York State Barge Canal, all the while invoking the name of Susy Clemens with tearful regret. (Clemens steamed westward across the Great Lakes at the beginning of his 1895–96 around-the-world tour, shortly after his last glimpse of his daughter.) From there, east, into Lake Oneida, and then down the Mohawk to the Hudson, and due south into New York City ("Smells like Venice," he said, "but unfortunately for my preferred mode of travel, it ain't"), where, swooning again, he took a cab to the Sheraton Centre, arriving on the morning of 9 April, just as the first Symposium session was getting under-way: a master of timing.

As to the motive for his arrival at the hotel at that precise time, Umlauf was refreshingly silent. His silence was strategic, of course. He wanted it to signal his umbrage. After all, hadn't "Mark Twain" said the last word on the subject of his 1861–64 notebook and the authorship of *Huckleberry Finn* in his Hannibal press conference? Shortly after their arrival, Herbert Hummel, no doubt acting on Umlauf's instructions, let it be known that "Mr. Twain" wished to address the Symposium; he was in his room, awaiting our call. It was obvious to me that Umlauf felt his career was stuck on dead center, and that he hoped his association with the Symposium would get it moving again. Ultimately he was looking for some sort of groundswell that would carry him to victory, once and for all, over the skeptics. In the end, of course, the outcome was quite different.

The Symposium proceedings have never been published. At my request, the editor, Clarence Wainwright, kindly delayed preparation of that volume until *I Been There Before* could appear and be subjected to the scrutiny I know it will receive. If this edition succeeds in one of its major goals—to demonstrate that Clemens was in our midst in 1985–86—the Symposium proceedings will never see the light of day. (A complete transcript, however, is on file in the Mark Twain Papers.) But to give the reader a full sense of the spirit of those times, I shall here very briefly summarize the papers presented.

Session One: The arguments in favor of Orion's authorship of *Huckleberry Finn* were of a grab-bag variety. The first speaker emphasized the strong evidence in the 1861–64 notebook and its nearly unchallengeable authenticity. A second speaker examined Samuel Clemens' potential as a plagiarist, unearthing no new facts, but harshly reinterpreting his research and writing practices in a new light. Sources for Clemens' ideas were paraded before the audience, one after another, with the implication that his reliance on other writers was excessive. The speaker chided Clemens for being irresponsibly flippant when he labeled his method the "steal-and-rehash" method (the passage is quoted above in the notes to "A Dispatch from the *Delta Queen*"). This was followed by an attempted demonstration that Clemens showed hypersensitivity to charges of plagiarism whenever they arose. In June of 1909, when Clemens failed to give an author full credit in his book *Is Shakespeare Dead?*, and when that failure was announced in the morning papers under the headline "Is Mark Twain a Plagiarist?," if, as Paine reports, Clemens "found a good deal of amusement in the situation" (*MTB*, p. 1497), why (the speaker asked us) did Clemens suffer his first angina attack that very night? Was not such patent hypersensitivity consistent with a lingering guilt over an earlier, more substantial, act of plagiarism? A third speaker delivered an unintentionally melancholy biographical sketch of the career of Orion Clemens, in the course of which there was a certain puffing up of Orion's literary output. This speaker had been to the Mark Twain Papers, and had squeezed out of them minute morsels of supporting evidence—occasional praise from brother Sam of Orion's writing, a few examples of dialect writing by Orion of the type found in *Huckleberry Finn*, and this passage from a 14 June 1874 letter to Sam, in which Orion describes his feelings after having placed a worm in front of a toad:

> My conscience smote me. How would I feel if some being having the ability to do so should cast me in front of a monster like that toad, but as much larger than it as I was larger than the worm; and I should struggle to get away, and bump against its flabby front, and then there should be thrust out a tongue like the gable end of a brick house, and the jaw should drop like the lower side of a cave?—it would charge each spec of marrow in every bone with a separate horror.

This charming selection was offered to us as an example of a conscience reminiscent in its tenderness to the one that torments Huck, who struggles throughout the book with his guilt for aiding a runaway slave. The comparison, delivered in deadly earnest, enlivened the proceedings quite a bit.

When I dragged my weary frame into my hotel room after the first session, Ricky Olivieri was there. He was talking on the phone, his back to the door, and he whirled around when I came in. He threw me a wild look, and his eyes darted to a pile of manuscript on the bed between us. His eyes shot back up and stayed fixed on me as he hung up the phone, feeling for it behind him.

I asked him what was going on, and why he hadn't been in touch with me for three weeks. He said nothing. His eyes went from mine back to the manuscript, then back to mine, as if he was contemplating who would win if we were to race to grab it. As soon as I realized this, *I* grabbed it and began to circle around the bed toward him, speaking softly to him, as to a spooked horse.

He bolted. He jumped onto the bed, leaped to the other side of it, and raced out the door. By the time I reached the hall he was out of sight and the stairwell door at the far end was swinging closed. I walked back into the room, studying the manuscript. It was Part III, along with the 8 April cover letter (given above, pp. 180–182). On the floor beside the bed was a manila envelope addressed in Clemens' hand to "Mr. Frederick Dixon, Esq., Sheraton Centre, N.Y." The envelope bore no postage.

Somewhat shakily, I dialed the front desk to ask some questions. I was put on hold. I began to read the letter. A different desk clerk came on the phone a second or two after I had reached Clemens' prediction of his 11 April departure (just two days away), and it took me a moment to speak coherently. I learned from the clerk that Olivieri had arrived at the hotel with the Umlauf entourage (I would later learn he had been tracking Umlauf all the way, for lack of a better lead as to Clemens' whereabouts) and had asked the clerk if there was a room in his name. (I had instructed Olivieri three weeks earlier to meet me there.) The clerk told him I had reserved a room for us to share and gave him a room key. He also gave him a manila envelope addressed to me, which "a middle-aged, white-haired man" had left at the desk a little earlier. The clerk expressed the hope that what he had done met with my approval. I told him, before hanging up, that under normal circumstances it would have, but that the circumstances were as far from normal as they could be.

I sat down on the edge of the bed, the manuscript in my lap, and paused to regroup before reading it. While I had been downstairs listening to pro-Orion nonsense, Olivieri had been in our room, no doubt reading it himself. Why had he fled? To whom had he been speaking on the phone when I walked in? To *Clemens?* It was possible, if the manuscript told Olivieri where he was. Perhaps it would tell me! I plunged into it.

It certainly told me where he had been—Hartford, Elmira, and New York City—but that was all. Could he still be in the city? Could he, like Umlauf, have checked into this very hotel? I called the front desk again: no C. L. Samuel was registered. No Dick Allbright. No Joseph Twichell. I explored other aliases, from "Josh" through "W. Epaminondas Adrastus Blab," gritting my teeth with determination all the way. What did one hotel clerk's opinion of me matter at a time like this? I even tried "Umlauf" and "Laufbahn," in case Clemens had usurped his usurper's name. No luck.

Then, working from the fact that the last letter in the new manuscript was written in Elmira and bore a date only two days old, I called Elmira College to see if a mysterious writer-in-residence was using Quarry Farm. I couldn't reach Matthew Bailey, the Director of the Center for Mark Twain Studies at Quarry Farm, but a man in the public information office told me that Bununu Ogbomosho, a writer of children's books whose name I vaguely recognized, was presently using the house. I asked if anyone else had been in residence there in the past month—anyone who, oh, looked or sounded a little bit like Mark Twain? I was told that Moira Hayden, a poet, had been there for one week in early March, but she neither looked nor sounded like Mark Twain. The man then asked me if anyone else from the Mark Twain Papers would be calling him today— this was the second such call he had received, and the questions had been similarly strange. I assured him he had heard the last from us, and I said goodbye.

So Olivieri had had the same idea, and no doubt had reached the same conclusion: Clemens, in that Livy letter ostensibly written by a dog at Quarry Farm, was merely imagining himself to be a writer-in-residence at the house where he had been the first and only writer-in-residence— just as he had imagined himself painting Umlauf's portrait, or talking with God.

I took stock. Clemens presumably knew where I was from the news coverage anticipating the first day of the Symposium. But why didn't he tell me where *he* was? His coy elusiveness was now positively irksome to me. If he had delivered the manuscript himself, as seemed likely, then he was nearby—but where? My only hope, at that moment, was that curiosity about the confusion he had wrought had brought him to the Symposium. I packed the new manuscript into my briefcase and took it with me to the afternoon session in search of him.

While I craned my neck and scanned the audience, in vain, for someone who looked like Clemens, I listened to the anti-Orion faction present a lively batch of speeches. In his arguments that Orion was incapable of writing even a tolerable book, not to mention *Huckleberry Finn,* the first speaker drew heavily from Orion's self-assessments: "I am satisfied that I am an idiot," and "I have taken a notion that the stupidity of my writings may have arisen from my spending too much time on them" (letters of 24 January 1878 and 15 February 1883). The speaker also drew from brother Sam's comments, such as this sentence from a 22 February 1883 letter to Orion: "Try & guard yourself jealously against two things —lecturing & writing; for you cannot achieve even a respectable mediocrity in either." The second speaker took up the notebook and raised questions about its handwriting (it bore some hallmarks of Clemens' hand later in life, rather than in 1861–64), its contents concerning matters other than Orion's "river book," and the circumstances of its discovery. Naturally, Umlauf's account of that event came into play. The speaker pointed out that the discoverer's subsequent audacious claim to be Mark Twain inevitably cast doubt on his report of how he discovered the notebook. The session concluded with a lengthy citation from a third speaker of all of the evidence that the composition of *Huckleberry Finn* post-dated the Clemens brothers' years in the west. This consisted of progress reports on the novel in letters written by Sam in 1875, 1876, and 1883, and scenes in the novel drawn from works written by other authors long after 1861–64. In this regard, the speaker turned Clemens' "steal-and-rehash" working method to the advantage of *his* position.

At the conclusion of this session, I canceled a dinner engagement and returned to my room to study the manuscript anew, pausing only to watch a local evening newscast. Of the approximately five minutes devoted to the Symposium, Umlauf received about three. According to Herbert Hummel, who was interviewed in the hall outside Umlauf's suite, "Mark Twain" humbly wished to declare his candidacy for the Nobel Prize, it seeming to be the natural thing to do, now that he was alive again. "Mr. Twain" was presently resting from the exertions of his long river trip and was studying brochures about the restored family home in Hartford—his next destination (via Long Island Sound and the Connecticut River). If "Mr. Twain" found the restoration to his liking, he planned to move back into the house. Margaret Campbell, Curator of the home, was in the hotel for the Symposium and was reached for comment. She said, "The Mark Twain home is not a hotel, but The Hannibal Claimant is welcome to tour it. We welcome anybody. We don't discriminate— murderers, thieves, impostors, congressmen—we welcome them all." I thought the statement had the essential Mark Twain touch. The piece closed with a lingering camera shot of the closed door to Umlauf's suite, beyond which he could be heard searching for chords on the piano in his room and singing "Swing Low, Sweet Chariot." Umlauf must have studied reports of Clemens' contemporaries on his piano-playing, for it was truly Twainian; that is, it was very bad.

Clarence Wainwright, Symposium Chairman, called to ask if I had seen the telecast. He also informed me that it now appeared that the six panelists would need both the morning and afternoon sessions for their rebuttals, and asked if I could deliver my lecture the following day—the morning of the eleventh. I agreed.

I ordered dinner from room service and went back to the manuscript, focusing my attention on the passage in "Portrait of a Usurper" in which Clemens portrays himself, disguised as an artist, suggesting to Umlauf that a key self-betraying piece of evidence might be built into the 1861–64 notebook. I studied my copy of the notebook, searching for the passage Clemens might have been hinting at. While the notebook contained dozens of brief verbal maps—notes Clemens made about addresses or stagecoach routes, for example—the most lengthy and explicit set of directions "for getting from this place to that" (to quote Clemens' guileful artist) was a burlesque piece featuring an old miner who reportedly gave Clemens detailed instructions on how to descend the Spanish Mine in Virginia City without aid of candlelight. It was on this piece, given below, that I eventually concentrated my efforts.

A wizened miner named Brooks. Has memorized descent into the Spanish & can do it in pitch-dark, without a candle. Gives these instructions:

"Everything's back'ards in these-h'yer mines, young fellow. It's like you built your house beginnin' with the top story first and then worked on down to the cellar. So jist imagine yourself startin' at the wrong end first, & everything'll be all right. You tackle the Spanish on B Street,— that's my own little secret entrance—& you waltz down a short ladder 9 steps—count 'em, mind—& you strike bottom on the 10th step. Note that. The 10th step. Then you promenade along a wide-open tunnel for 6 steps, & on your 7th you strike another ladder. Note that. Don't be young & foolish & git to daydreamin'. 13 steps down that ladder & you strike a little level place with 2 sharp rocks stickin' up. Take note of both of them rocks. Even if you don't, they'll take note of *you*—they'll jab you through your boots, or maybe catch you on the anclebones, & they'll remind you jist where you are. 9 steps along the tunnel now, & *whomp!* —a rock stickin' out of the wall'll smack you on the left side of your head. That's good. You're in the right place. 6 more steps & *whomp!* again, on the right side. Good. Then you got a long trek without no interruption, 41 steps, only don't rush, because your steps'll be too long then. A nice measured strut—that's what to aim for. Well, there's a big pile of timber scraps after those 41 steps, & you'll fall & skin yourself some, & maybe snap a bone or two. That's no matter. Jist take note of that timber. On you go, gainin' confidence with every step, for 12 steps, & you'll strike a rope hangin' down in a kind of loop, about neck-high. You may cough, if you like, since that rope'll come near to hangin' you, & then after the rope jist plunge on ahead, but not too brisk, on account of the pile of tools in the tunnel that you'll come acrost after 26 steps. Pick yourself up & feel around for another ladder. There. That's it. Down you go—13 rungs. Watch that 14th rung. It ain't there. Neither's the 15th rung. It's a big step, & many a miner's hung fire there. On you go, 5 more rungs, until you strike ground again. Good. Go left for 18 steps. Feel a warm, furry thing? That's Ol' Black. Give him a pat & go back the way you came. Then you—"

"Wait a minute, sir. I must go back the way I came? Sha'n't I be retracing my steps?"

"A *course* you will. But Ol' Black, he gits awful lonely down there, & needs a little pat of affection. Now, back you go, 9 steps, & *ouch!*— a low timber acrost the ceiling will say 'How do?' to you in the upper teeth."

"But why didn't I bump into it when I was going the other way?"

"Don't interrupt now, young man, or I'll forgit where I am. Less see—Ol' Black, 9 steps, *ouch!*, then 7 steps & a ladder stickin' up'll catch you on the shin. That's good. Down you go, 12 steps down to ground again—I mean, to a puddle of rank water that'll come up to your waist, but there's good solid earth below that. Pull yourself out of that puddle & stroll on down the tunnel to your . . . to your right."

"Are you sure it's my right? Are you sure?"

"I'm *sure* you ain't goin' to git where you want to go if you keep interruptin' me. Now—puddle, & 29 steps. Count 'em. Don't slow down, out of fear of what lays ahead, as you git near 29—that's a common mistake & it'll shorten your steps up & throw you. Jist plunge right ahead, real brash, jist like you're leadin' a parade. You'll catch a iron bar stickin' out of the wall somewhere in your chest or belly, but it ain't too sharp, so don't give it no thought. That's after—what'd I say? 29? Yes, 29 steps. 6 more steps & you'll tumble over a pile of bones & carcasses —that's the boneyard of Ol' Black's ancestors. On you go, for 22 steps. Stop! I mean it. Stop! Step number 23 is a hole, a near cut to the bottom, as you may say, only you don't want to take it, because it's a killingly long ways down. Take the slow way—reach out for a rope, seize hold of it, & ease yourself down, hand over hand. Count 'em. After 46 hand-steps, as you may call 'em, you'll come to solid ground."

"Couldn't I just slide slowly down the rope? Wouldn't that be easier than going hand-over-hand, as you—"

"Damnation! Can't you be still? I'll never git us down to the bottom, nor up again. Now, 8 steps to the . . . to the . . . better make it to the right, & *whomp!*—smack into a wall. You run into the wall because the tunnel turns there, to the . . . left. Off you go, for 7 steps, & more carcasses will bring you down. That's jist a pile of Piute Injuns—don't ask me how they got there. Now you've hit your stride. You're walkin' with confidence, & that jist fills *me* with pride, bein' your teacher an' all. There you go, an' I can see you, jist struttin' like a peacock, & it jist—"

"Like a peacock? Why, with all this tumbling & falling, a bloodied mud-hen is more like what I'm going to—"

"—& there you go, for 37 steps, until you strike the Mexican bone pile. Don't stop to shake hands, because you're near the end. 58 steps down a slopin' tunnel & you've struck the vein. I hope you brought your pick with you, because it's time to go to work. There's plenty of candles there, by the way, & it's all right now to light one & peek around. Until you're done workin', that is."

"And then? How do I get back out?"

"How do you—? Why, ain't you a muggins? You retrace your steps back'ards, jist reversin' everything I told you. Hain't you got a memory?"

I observed that the miner mentioned several "landmarks" along the way, each separated from the other by a precisely given number of steps. If each landmark was in fact one of "the words of the key sentence," and if the steps were intervening (and irrelevant) words, then identifying the key words would be a simple exercise in counting. But on what passage in the notebook should the counting be performed? Initially I assumed the clues referred reflexively to the very passage containing them, but attempts at deciphering under this assumption yielded nothing. This failure seemed to me, at the time, to open the door to the possibility that *any* passage in the notebook could be a candidate—and not necessarily even a self-contained passage. It was possible that the coded message spanned several discrete notebook entries.

The notebook had been typed into our computer at the Mark Twain Papers shortly after its discovery in February. I called Arthur Goldman, our computer expert, at his home in Berkeley. I quickly briefed him on the new portion of manuscript, and inquired about the feasibility of conducting a "search" through the notebook for the coded message. He said it would be "a snap": The search would consist of repeated countings according to the miner's instructions, the first count beginning with the first word in the notebook, the next count beginning with the second word, and so on. Thus we would have, in the end, a printout consisting of as many strings of potentially key words as there were individual words in the notebook. To be sure that Goldman understood what we were looking for, I dictated the cryptic hints from "Portrait of a Usurper" to him.

In retrospect, I believe my rush to the computer for help evinced an overzealous mania for getting the most out of our special-equipment dollars, coupled with the ignoble desire to prove to the rest of the Papers staff once and for all that I was not computer-shy—a label they had uncharitably pinned on me. I say this, because while Goldman was fussing over the search program, Olivieri was quietly cracking the code all by himself. As I was later to learn, Olivieri had conducted his search under the assumption that the key passage might contain some additional link to the "artist's" remarks in "Portrait of a Usurper." That additional link proved to be her use of the word "rudimentary." This assumption led him to a notebook entry to be found three pages after the wizened miner's directions:

The Spanish—certainly one of the more structurally advanced mines, though lighting & modes of transportation rudimentary: candles (sometimes held in teeth) & ladders & hoisted buckets. Atmosphere the sort to appeal to a mole, or a bat—not to *me*. An eerie desolation below. If a man is inclined to loaf & nap on the job, there are plenty of by-ways & side-chambers to give him the opportunity, but if he oversleeps he will awaken to a spent candle & utter darkness & loneliness, & he will cry & appeal for help in vain. For this reason, miners descend & ascend by two's, each responsible for collecting the other at day's end. I chanced to be on hand when they closed up shop, & it was truly heart-warming to mark how they called to their mates for the day—Bob anxiously making sure that Jim was nearby, Ed calling after Hank like a worried mother whose child is late to supper. The world could be instructed by this example of brotherly solicitude. I shall push further, & make the assertion that each day, every man who walks the earth, in whatever employment, ought to be assigned a mate who watches out for him—for one day only. Otherwise it is too much like a marriage.

Reached the bottom; looked down drain shaft; could have descended in a bucket, but couldn't bear the thought of plunging so close to purgatory. Timber-work supports are a marvel, a subterranean forest, arranged in squares like a lattice-work of windows, & as one descends one tends to think he is dropping down a shot-tower—a well-ventilated one, with all the windows open.

Met a forlorn horse half-way back up—how I missed him coming down, I don't know. His lonely job is working a whim for hoisting ore from below. He gave me a sad look, an inquiring one, as if to ask after his friends & relations above-ground. Seems to me a horse in a place like this ought to have a poetic name, like Charon, or Pluto, but they just call him "Ol' Black," which I reckon is poetry enough for a miner. At last, it was time to go back to heaven, so to speak, & we hurried the rest of the way. *I* hurried, at least. Met wizened miner in dazzling light, rubbing his sores. He asked me if I was ready for the "blind descent." I said by all means, but not to-day. I had a deadline to meet. Perhaps another time.

On the face of it, this is a fragment of a piece on the Spanish Mine. (Two such sketches, showing similarities to this fragment, were published in the *Territorial Enterprise* in late 1862 and early 1863, and both were almost certainly by Clemens; see *ET&S1*, pp. 160–168.) Olivieri started at the beginning of the passage, treating the first nine words as equivalents of the nine rungs of the ladder at the mine's entrance, then treating the tenth word as the equivalent of the tenth step, to which the old miner calls particular attention: a key word. Olivieri circled it and, continuing to follow the miner's instructions, counted six more words and circled the seventh. And so on. This method, under the assumption that hyphenated words count as one word, as do ampersands, and that two landmarks occurring together (the two sharp rocks, the two missing ladder rungs) signify two consecutive words that must be circled, yields this result:

> The Spanish—certainly one of the more structurally advanced mines, though lighting & modes of transportation rudimentary: candles (sometimes held in teeth) & ladders & hoisted buckets. Atmosphere the sort to appeal to a mole, or a bat—not to *me*. An eerie desolation below. If a man is inclined to loaf & nap on the job, there are plenty of by-ways & side-chambers to give him the opportunity, but if he oversleeps he will awaken to a spent candle & utter darkness & loneliness, & he will cry & appeal for help in vain. For this reason, miners descend & ascend by two's, each responsible for collecting the other at day's end. I chanced to be on hand when they closed up shop, & it was truly heart-warming to mark how they called to their mates for the day—Bob anxiously making sure that Jim was nearby, Ed calling after Hank like a worried mother whose child is late to supper. The world could be instructed by this example of brotherly solicitude. I shall push further, & make the assertion that each day, every man who walks the earth, in whatever employment, ought to be assigned a mate who watches out for him— for one day only. Otherwise it is too much like a marriage.
>
> Reached the bottom; looked down drain shaft; could have descended in a bucket, but couldn't bear the thought of plunging so close to purgatory. Timber-work supports are a marvel, a subterranean forest, arranged in squares like a lattice-work of windows, & as one descends one tends to think he is dropping down a shot-tower—a well-ventilated one, with all the windows open.

Met a forlorn horse half-way back up—how I missed him coming down, I don't know. His lonely job is working a whim for hoisting ore from below. He gave (me) a sad look, an inquiring one, as if (to) ask after his friends & relations above-ground. (Seems) to me a horse in a place like this ought to have a poetic name, like Charon, or Pluto, but they just call him "Ol' Black," which I reckon is poetry enough for a miner. At last, it was time to go back to heaven, so to speak, & we hurried the rest of the way. *I* hurried, at least. Met wizened miner in dazzling light, rubbing his sores. He asked me if I was ready for the "blind descent." I said by all means, but not to-day. I had a deadline to meet. Perhaps another (time.)

If read in top-to-bottom order, the sentence is gibberish. But note that the miner, in the earlier passage, says, "Everything's back'ards in these-h'yer mines," and "So jist imagine yourself startin' at the wrong end first, & everything'll be all right." If read in reverse order, the following pattern emerges: "time it Seems to me tends to bear out the assertion of Hank Jim that mark two's appeal is An appeal to rudimentary mines." Normalized, the sentence reads, "Time, it seems to me, tends to bear out the assertion of Henry James that Mark Twain's appeal is an appeal to rudimentary minds." This sentence was first published, with precisely this wording, in 1920, ten years after Clemens' first death, in *The Ordeal of Mark Twain* (p. 15), whose author, Van Wyck Brooks, significantly shares his surname with the wizened miner. (The reader will recall that this highly critical book was one of the works with which Umlauf nurtured Clemens' misconceptions about his reputation.) Identifying the key words and then reading them interestingly parallels the broader structure of the miner's instructions: one descends into the mine (i.e., one starts at the top, counts "steps," and circles key words), and then one comes back out of the mine (i.e., one reads the resulting message, starting at the bottom and ending at the top). Olivieri's initial assumption in locating the key passage also provides final confirmation that this must be the sentence (cum signature: "mark two's") referred to by Clemens in "Portrait of a Usurper": that sketch ends with the deceptively self-effacing artist echoing the language of Brooks's sentence, saying, "My mind is so terribly rudimentary."

If I had had this string of circled words in my possession—that is, if Clemens hadn't been so cryptic with his clues to finding them, or if Olivieri hadn't gone free-lance and been so obstinately uncommunicative —I would have seized the podium the next morning and instantly proved the notebook a hoax, thereby settling the question posed in the Symposium title and sending everyone home in a cheerful, if bewildered, state of mind. But I didn't discover this string of words until it was too late for that purpose.

After speaking with Goldman in Berkeley, I took up the manuscript again in the hopes of finding a hint of Clemens' whereabouts. I was reading about Hermann the German's bilingual melancholy when my phone rang. It was a Dr. Stanislaw Grabow, Professor of Pediatrics at the Columbia University College of Physicians and Surgeons, and he wished to speak with Ricky Olivieri. I said that Olivieri was out and offered to take a message, by way of getting at the nature of their connection with each other. But the doctor had no message; he was simply returning a call Olivieri had made to his office earlier in the day. When I asked how he knew Olivieri, he replied that he wasn't sure that he did; the name was not familiar to him.

Dr. Stanislaw Grabow—as I hung up the phone, I thought about the name and, suddenly remembering where I had read it, I searched in the manuscript for the notes titled "The Kingdom of Heaven." There it was, perhaps the only pure example of nonfiction in the manuscript:

> < Ask Cocoa for name of the hospital near W. Sq. > Ask Walter & Darrell if they believe in God, prayer, & praying to good, dead people.
> Dr. Grabow a hell-fired article. Ask Cocoa about pipe shop.
> Write a < McW > sketch about Cocoa & her ex-husband meeting by accident at a party. Work in Cocoa's blush—how you *feel* it, like a change in temperature, more than see it. Make it *serious*—about *love* & *sex* & all that, just to leave behind proof that I can do it.

A physician figured in the notes to the projected story preceding these paragraphs. Could a real Dr. Grabow have been the original of that character? Had Dr. Grabow written "a hell-fired article" about something? And why had Clemens written the mundane reminder about a pipe shop in that paragraph? As soon as I asked myself that question I burst out laughing. Evidently Olivieri hadn't ever noticed, or had forgotten about—as I momentarily had—the ranks of Dr. Grabow "pre-smoked" pipes so often displayed in drug stores, and he had naturally assumed a Manhattan physician of that name had played some role in Clemens' second life.

But what about the paragraphs immediately preceding and following the one with Dr. Grabow's name in it? Clemens had met someone named Cocoa. She was apparently divorced, and an incident involving her ex-husband attracted Clemens as a subject for still another sketch. Cocoa knew something about a hospital—presumably the hospital where his first story was to be set. Clemens had canceled this instruction to himself, perhaps upon realizing he could simply invent a name for the hospital. Darrell and Walter knew something too—about God and prayer. Why would Clemens be interested in their opinions? Because they were in some way like the principals in his story? Were they twins? Were they connected with Cocoa in some way? Were they her children?

The projected story was to open in Washington Square Park. Clemens' canceled memo referred to a hospital near the park—not just "a" hospital, but "the" hospital. Was this hospital therefore "shared knowledge" of Cocoa's and Clemens'? Did Cocoa work there? No—this seemed unlikely, given the identification of it not as "the hospital where she works," but as "the hospital near W. Sq." Had Clemens been to the park recently? (It was certainly familiar turf to him: late in life he had lived just to the north of it, at 14 West 10th Street, and later at 21 Fifth Avenue.) Could he and Cocoa have possibly met there? Could they possibly be there now? Or even if they weren't, was it possible that Cocoa frequented the park and, if I could find her, that she could give me some idea where Clemens was? But what was I to do—stand on a bench and endlessly call out her name?

I looked at my watch. It was nearly 11 P.M. Tomorrow I had planned to attend the rebuttal sessions and watch the mud being slung, not only from scholar to scholar, but from scholar to poor Orion. But I wasn't going to do that. Instead, I would go to Washington Square—in search of a pair of twins and a mother attached to them.

As I left the hotel the next morning, I paused a moment to watch the fifteen or so Umlauf supporters circling in a narrow ellipse on the sidewalk outside the hotel. They were protesting the Symposium's snubbing of their hero. It was difficult for me to gauge the mood of the demonstration. I knew from newspaper reports that a few of the demonstrators had traveled with Umlauf all the way from Hannibal, and that one or two others had joined him en route, forsaking their worldly concerns in apostolic fashion and pledging to follow him wherever he might go. This group was clearly dedicated. But there were others in the circling crowd who seemed to be out on a pure lark, celebrating for its own sake the conflict between Umlauf and the world of scholarship. Perhaps they were college dropouts of American literature survey courses—Emerson casualties.

I sat in Washington Square Park for twelve hours, alternately searching for twins and trying to find the key sentence in the notebook, for I had brought my manuscripts with me. Both of my efforts came to nothing. I did spy one set of twins early in the day—infants in a double stroller. They were too young, if the objects of my search were indeed six years old (the age of the twins in the story outlined by Clemens), but nonetheless I asked their mother if she was named Cocoa. She was not. Late in the day I asked two identical strapping roller-skating teenagers, unaccompanied by an adult, if by any chance their mother was named Cocoa. "By any chance, *no,*" I was told.

Back in my hotel room, I called Arthur Goldman at his home for a report on his search for the key sentence. He said that even as we spoke the computer was churning out strings of twenty-four words (there being twenty-four "landmarks" in the old miner's instructions), only one of which thus far was grammatical. Goldman read it to me: "In the spring & Wednesdays a horse cavorts to win a boiling wolf but did the notion that to blow is Sanitary look fearless?" I told him to call me when he found something that hadn't been typed by a monkey.

Then I went over my notes for my presentation. The phone rang three times—reporters asking me to comment on Umlauf's latest rapacious assumption of all things Twainian: he had announced that since he was alive again, he owned the copyright to all of his unpublished works, and that "this outfit that calls itself the Mark Twain Papers" must immediately cease publishing said works or face a lawsuit. I declined to comment to the first two callers. To the third I said that I believed that anything was possible in this world, even the resurrection of Mark Twain, but that I did not believe The Hannibal Claimant was the genuine article, and therefore he could claim no ownership of those unpublished works. Looking back on that statement, I believe it marks the first hint of a resolve that blossomed fully the next morning.

When I entered the meeting room where I was to deliver my lecture, I noticed Herbert Hummel standing by the door, just inside the room. He whispered to me, "Your little game is up, Dixon."

"I was about to say the same to you," I replied.

"How *dare* you manhandle Mr. Twain!" he said. "How *dare* you!"

For a confused moment I thought he was talking about the real Mark Twain. I was about to pursue the subject when a colleague of mine escorted me to the podium with hearty congratulations for my witty comment of the night before, which he had heard reported on the *Today* show. "Very Twainian," he said, "to pretend acceptance of an absurd proposition and reason with logic from that point on. First-rate. That's what we need more of around here—ironic detachment." Five minutes later, my display of the very opposite—impassioned engagement, perhaps —must have deeply astonished him.

As mentioned in the Introduction to this volume, I did not get very far with my remarks. Casting aside my comparatively tedious progress report on the Mark Twain Papers, I opened with this bold announcement: "Mark Twain is *alive.*" The audience, I saw with surprise, was utterly complacent, even bored, or preparing to become bored. They seemed to think I was in the early stages of a threadbare metaphor, and that I was going to go on about Mark Twain's works living forever. Flabbergasted, I plunged on, hastily sketching the events of the past four and a half months, insofar as I understood them.

The general reaction to my announcement was, I think, sympathetic embarrassment. "There goes Dixon," I could imagine them thinking. "A good man, Dixon. It's a shame. There he goes, right off the rails." The pro-Orion faction, outraged by this sudden attack on the notebook in such unexpected terms, and from such a previously placid quarter, became unmannerly. They demanded to see the manuscript I spoke of. I suddenly realized the disadvantage of my spontaneity. I had prepared no copies for distribution, and my stammering promise to make copies available at the earliest opportunity was greeted with the modern equivalent of the Mark Twain phrase "Your granny."

I quit speaking. I felt a sudden urge to "light out." But at least I could comfort myself with the thought that I had done something that would make the news and that just might flush Clemens out. It was my last hope. He would be moved by pity for me. He was a good man, in his core, and no stranger to shame at the podium. He would know what I had endured. I would go to my room and wait there the rest of the day. He would hear about my speech. He would call me and say, "Well, Dixon, *you're* a funny fellow."

As I burst from the meeting room, a reporter in the hall seized my arm and began to fire questions at me—but not about my speech. He told me that Umlauf had come out of seclusion and was giving a speech of his own just down the hall. He had opened with the charge that I had threatened violence against him. Would I comment, please? He had also said that I had beaten him on the head with some sort of manuscript. Would I comment, please? I frowned and pulled away from him, hurrying down the hall in the direction of Umlauf's voice, which I could clearly hear booming through an open door.

"Power corrupts," he was crying, over and over. "Power corrupts.

Power corrupts." I stepped through the door and stood against the back wall of the room, which was packed. "These people like Dixon," he went on, as if to greet me, though I doubted that he saw me enter, "have wrested power over my written words. They have usurped the power to publish them, but they are not content with that. They try to *explain* them, as if anything I wrote ever needed explaining. They hang footnotes all over the body of my writing like so many leeches, and they flatter themselves as having improved my work by doing so. Where is the great reading public in all of this?" Umlauf threw his arms out before him, appealing to the crowd. "Cannot *they* bring their hearts and minds to my works, without Dixon's demented intercession, and enjoy them without the infernal numerical encumbrances?"

There were some shouts of "*Yes!*" from the audience. The Emerson casualties had moved indoors.

"These Dixonites," Umlauf continued, "are so puffed up with their power that they think they can do *any*thing. This man, this *Dixon*—let me tell you what he has done. When I discovered my old notebook, there by the Stanislaus, Dixon saw his precious little world coming to ruin. Dixon says, 'Mark Twain not the author of *Huck Finn?*' "—this in a mincing falsetto that produced a few laughs—" 'Horror of horrors!' So what did Dixon do? He took his pen in hand—or maybe he dictated to someone more expert in the forger's art than he—and he created a paltry, ill-written, cheap, brummagem imitation of my writing. It's a manuscript that pretends to tell the history of Mark Twain's travels since November. He's got his *own* Mark Twain, has Dixon—it ain't me. *His* Mark Twain implies that the notebook is a hoax—something he wrote during *this* trip on earth. Dixon arranged to have the manuscript delivered to his office, so that he could fool his flunkeys there, who are even more ignorant than he is, into doubting the notebook. Then he sent one of them humping off on a crazy hunt for 'Mark Twain,' with that poor devil's hopes of finding him fired up here and there by stinky little clues Dixon had deposited all over the land.

"You've never met Dixon's 'Mark Twain' before." Umlauf burst out in a single guffaw. "He's a shy one. Spends all his time hiding and wringing his little hands and worrying he'll be found out. Dixon *had* to make him a shy one. Why? *Because he can't produce the body.* There *ain't* no body to match the rank imaginings of his brain. You really must read about Dixon's 'Mark Twain.' " He paused. "I *want* you to read about him." Another pause. "Here—I shall *enable* you to read about him."

Aghast, I watched Herbert Hummel and one other assistant swing into action and begin to distribute copies. Eventually one reached me. The first page was the beginning of "Good-bye, God, I'm Going to Bodie." I immediately checked my briefcase, which I had kept with me day and night. My copy of the manuscript was there, intact. Where had Umlauf obtained *his* copy? Was there a "mole" in the Mark Twain Papers? It seemed impossible.

Umlauf had paused to light a cigar and relish the moment. He still hadn't seen me; or if he had, he gave no sign of it. "This Dixon," he went on, "after making sure my man Herbert was out, stormed into my room and blustered something awful, waving his manuscript around and panting and slobbering. I reckon he thought he could actually scare me away with this drivel he had invented. Of course, *that* failed, so he hurled the manuscript at me and stalked out of my room, crying like a baby. Now, just look at it, if you can stand to. You'll want to hurl it yourself, I expect —into the fire. Dixon ain't footnoted it—*yet*. You can bet he will, though, if he can persuade anybody besides his dog that Mark Twain wrote it. And he'll lard it out with 'Explanatory Notes,' and 'Alterations in the Manuscript,' and 'Hysterical Coleoptera,' and 'Admonitions of the Herumfrodite.' Why, Dixon could take 'Wee Willie Winkie' and footnote that rhyme into a six-hundred-pager that'd crush your chest if you took it into your bed."

The reporter, still at my side, whisperingly asked me if I would comment, please. I gave him some spiritual advice.

"Just look at it. *Look* at it." Umlauf began a close reading of the text, starting with the first sketch. He was thoroughly overwrought. As I watched him and somewhat helplessly wondered what I should do, or say, I noticed that his lower jaw *did* seem to grow with his passion. I immediately wondered if Clemens' rendering of him in "Portrait of a Usurper" was in the copies he had passed out. I checked. The piece wasn't there. *Nothing* from Part III was there. He had handed out only Parts I and II, and there were omissions in Part II as well: both "A Dispatch from the *Delta Queen*" and "The Twain Man" were missing. But "The Ormsby House Phenomenon" was included. How would he explain away that unmistakable portrayal of him? Even as the question occurred to me, I realized he had reached that sketch and was speaking about it.

". . . and I spent a good deal of time in February in Berkeley, reading around in my old manuscripts in the archives, because Dixon's clan has stolen them all, and I was looking for half-finished works to bring to a conclusion, because my inspiration tank had had seventy-five years to fill up again, and I met Wee Willie Dixon there, and I even had lunch with him, though of course I could see right off he was too ignorant to be trusted with the knowledge of who I really am, and so I didn't tell him. Now, what did Wee Willie do? To what new depths did the anfractuosities of his diseased brain lead him? Why, he wrote about *me!* He had his 'Mark Twain' write about my body and make no end of fun of it, all on account of its generousness—which a good many women happen to find attractive, Dixon! I want you to know that, wherever you are! And he made fun of my digits, too. You people out there in the audience, if you have any physical shortcomings, just count your blessings that you didn't meet Wee Willie when he was in his fever of creation, or he would have shoveled *you* into his literary manure pile as well."

I felt outmatched. Umlauf had scooped me by distributing the manuscript, and he seemed prepared to rise to any challenge I could make. He even scooped my challenges. How could the truth ever stand up to such a practiced champion of the lie?

Umlauf went on, denouncing the manuscript page by page. My eyes wandered over the crowd. There seemed to be three types of people present: members of the press—they were taking notes and photographs, and one cameraman against the back wall was filming the event; the idly curious—they were quick to laugh, and sometimes they applauded with mock enthusiasm; and the truly faithful—these were too transfixed to applaud or cheer. One oddly dressed young woman standing against a side wall, near the stage, gazed at Umlauf with almost otherworldly intensity.

". . . but let's skip this idiocy. Let's move on to the rottenest pack of lies in the pile. It's called 'St. Peter Helps Me Play with Myself,' or something like that."

This evoked some surprised laughter from the crowd. I happened to glance at the young woman. She had reddened, and she looked quite shocked.

"Now, Winky Dinky Dixon, in this particular twaddle, has his 'Mark Twain' getting all worked up over all sorts of sins from his dark, dark past —a drunk burning himself up in jail, Henry burning up, Langdon *freezing* up. Hmmmmph. Shows how much *he* knows about me. If *I* had written this tale, and if *I* had wanted to talk about *serious, criminal* blundering, and crippling guilt, you people know what I would have written about. What is it?"

He paused. The audience fidgeted in uneasy, guilty ignorance.

"*Susy!*" I shouted on an impulse.

"Jawohl!" responded Umlauf. He searched for a moment to locate the speaker, but then he gave up. "Jawohl!" he said again.

The reporter leaned toward me and whispered, "Who in the hell is Susy?"

"Of *course* Susy," said Umlauf. "Of course. I admit it—I separated her from her mother the last year of her life, leaving the poor girl to die all alone like that, with no one but the housekeeper there to comfort her. And Susy, in her pathetic delirium, mistook that woman for her mother, and she mistook her mother's dresses in the closet for the real article, stroking and stroking them. But perhaps there is comfort in her blessed confusion, in her hungry acceptance of the false for the real. Yes—I insist on it. There *is* comfort in it. But, ah, Susy—I know how much she needed, and wanted, the *real* article, just as *I* wanted it, when I was in London and grieving for my lost darling. Oh, how I yearned to place a last tender kiss on her forehead. If it were possible, darkness, if *only* it were possible, darkness, I would reach out for her, yes, and she for me, darkness, and we could savor that embrace we were both so cruelly denied when . . . when . . . darkness must remain from everlasting to everlasting I want her to bow to me and say I see that even darkness can be great she must give ear to these things not reluctantly but gladly darkness is the complement of light she has not understood these things . . ."

The members of the audience exchanged puzzled glances. I, too, would have been completely puzzled, if I hadn't read some of these words just two days earlier: the canceled passages of Clemens' letter to Susy, originating in her delirious deathbed scribblings. Why was Umlauf uttering them now, in this strange monotone? Where was he going with this? My eyes went back to the oddly dressed young woman, for she had stepped forward, toward the stage. I suddenly saw her in a clear new light —as an Umlauf confederate. He was going to stage an "appearance" by Mark Twain's daughter.

". . . darkness is not bad but good not monstrous but beautiful . . ."

The woman stepped up onto the stage. I watched, poised to leap forward and denounce them both. As Umlauf rambled, he turned to face her, and his face grew ashen. Perhaps he had never mastered the false blush, but he could certainly command fake terror. She continued to approach him, and Herbert Hummel, responding to *his* cue, began to move toward her from his position on the other side of the podium, as if to head her off. But then he seemed to freeze in place. Was he uncertain about what to do? Had Umlauf not let him in on this charade?

"Yes my black Princess . . . Yes my black Princess . . ."

I stepped forward then, but only one step. I could move no farther. *I could move no farther.* I watched as the woman walked up to Umlauf, slowly circled her arms around him, and reached right *through* him, her arms encircling his chest and going through it and coming together against her body, where she clutched them, tightly folded, as if holding something precious against her breast.

Umlauf stood very still for a long moment, his jaws no longer working. The woman, too, stood still, slightly bent over her folded arms. Then she took a step back, opened her arms, and stared at her hands. She looked up at Umlauf, and she screamed—a woeful scream of despair and confusion. As the sound of it filled the room, Umlauf slowly toppled across the podium, knocking it forward to the floor, his body splayed out atop it.

She was gone. Her scream remained behind, riveting the audience to their seats. Then, finally, several people rushed to Umlauf, to attend to him. But he was thoroughly dead.

I remained in the meeting room until the ambulance came. I followed the stretcher as it was wheeled out of the room and carried down the stairs into the lobby. I watched it all the way into the ambulance. I wanted to be sure that Umlauf was in fact *dead*. It was hard for me to believe he could come, not to such an end, but to *any* end. He had seemed willful enough to be able to defeat even death, if only he could address it and wear it down with his words.

As the ambulance pulled away, several reporters approached me for my comments on Umlauf's death. I suddenly realized that that event, and not my failed speech, would dominate the news for the remaining hours of 11 April, and that my hope for a phone call from Clemens, which had been slim to begin with, was now completely foolish. I hurried away from the reporters and managed to flag down a cab, leaving behind me a scene of grief no less upsetting to see for all of its being misplaced. And I had my own grief to deal with. April 11 was almost half over. If Clemens was right about his departure, he could be gone already. But I would make one more attempt, however futile, at Washington Square.

As it turned out, it was an unlikely blend of contemporary and archaic malediction that proved to be my salvation. Around twelve-thirty, a group of twenty or so young children—kindergartners or first-graders —trooped through the park, past my bench. Four adults were with them. The children were paired off. I stood up and studied them as they passed. I didn't see a twin-pair in the bunch, and my frantic scrutiny in an attempt to match individuals in different pairs came to nothing. As the last pair passed, I sat down with a sigh. I watched without interest as a boy at the very back tried to trip another boy in front of him. The boy in front regained his balance, turned around, and, in a surprisingly mild tone, as if expecting his words alone would do the job, he said, "You motherfuckin' muggins."

I jumped to my feet and began to follow them. The child who had spoken was black. Darrell? Walter?

"Darrell?" I called out.

He turned around, looked at me, and looked ahead again. I hurried up to his side.

"Are you Darrell?" I asked.

"Mama," he called. "A man's talkin' to me."

One of the women at the front of the group turned around, frowned, and walked back to us. "What is it?" she asked, eyeing me closely.

"He thinks I'm Darrell."

"Are you Cocoa?" I asked.

"Cocoa!" she said. "No one calls me that any more."

"Did Sam call you that?"

She flinched and glanced away, and then her face hardened as she looked back to me. She bent down to the four who had lagged behind and told them to hurry and catch up with the others. She stood up and said to me, very testily, "I don't know how you people found me again, but I have nothing to say. Now, you leave me alone, or I'll have your ass in court."

" 'You people'?" I said. "Do you mean Ricky? Have you spoken to Ricky?"

"*What?*" she asked impatiently. She seemed about to turn away.

"Listen," I said. "I'm Fred Dixon. I'm with the Mark Twain Papers. I know Clemens is back—he's been sending me his stuff. And you met him, didn't you?"

She shook her head, but not, it seemed, to negate my question. "You're not a reporter?"

"No. Look." I opened my briefcase for the manuscript, but she suddenly turned away and hurried to join the group of children. I delved into my briefcase, found the notes to "The Kingdom of Heaven," and hurried after her. "Here," I said. "Look."

She took the notes, slowed, then stopped to study them. She smiled slightly. "Yeah," she said softly, nodding.

"Then you *are* Cocoa."

"Kind of." She looked up at me. "What do you want, exactly?"

"I want to find him. Do you know where he is?"

"Lord, no. He just walked out of my life."

"When?"

"Last month. About two weeks ago."

"Did he say where he was going?"

"No. But . . . my mind wasn't too clear." She looked sharply at me. "Do you know who I am? I mean, do you know anything at all about me?"

"No."

"Lordy," she said. Then she fell silent. We resumed walking and caught up with the group of children, who were waiting at a corner for the light to change.

"Who did you think I was?" I asked. "Who are the 'people' you mentioned? Reporters?"

"Listen," she said. "This is very hard for me to talk about. I lost a whole week of my life. I was crazy—out of my mind. I don't remember a thing about that whole week."

"Was that the time you were with him? You don't remember anything about it?"

Another change had come over her face. When she first spoke to me she looked capable of striking me. Then, when she saw her name in Clemens' notes, she had seemed almost wistful. Now she appeared to be on the verge of tears. She suddenly abandoned me, turning and walking ahead to talk to another woman. Then she said something to a child at the front of the group. He turned around and looked toward me. He must have been the twin—perhaps the fraternal twin—of the other boy at the rear. She came back to where I stood, and we watched them all cross the street.

"I'll join them later," she said. "Let's go sit down."

"Fine," I said. "I certainly appreciate your—"

"Maybe *you* can help me figure out what happened."

As we walked to a nearby bench and sat down, she told me how they had met. She was in the park with Darrell and Walter. Darrell was struck in the back of the head by a heavy metal swing, and Clemens came out of nowhere to help her take him to the hospital. He stayed with them the entire time, in the waiting room and then when the stitches were put in. Then they parted. But they met again the next day, near the same playground. He was sitting on a bench—she thought it might have been the very bench we were sitting on—and seemed to be waiting for her, hoping she would come. He told her all about the story he planned to write about Darrell's experience with the stitches, with considerable embellishment. She said to him that she liked the idea.

"I told him," she said, "that I thought it sounded like a nice quaint old-fashioned kind of story. He said, 'Oh, I'm nice and quaint and old-fashioned, all right. I'm Mark Twain.'"

"He came right out and told you?" I said. "What did you think?"

"Think? I began to kick myself for letting this man help me with my children the day before. I began to hunt around for an exit line. But he managed to convince me." How he did so, she explained, was by "predicting" numerous small incidents taking place around them in the park. They looked like predictions to her. In fact, he simply repeatedly used his power over time, drawing Cocoa's attention to minor events he had observed before sending time back. It reminded me of Umlauf's "prediction" of Halley's splitting, and I asked her if she had been with Clemens when Umlauf made his debut.

"Oh, yes," she said. "Sam was furious the whole day. He swore and fumed. But by the end of the day he was laughing over it. He began to take an interest in how things would turn out—said he took a 'vicarious' interest in it. He spent a lot of time wondering if 'vicarious' was the right word, and he studied all my dictionaries and puzzled over it. It was the love of people for the *real* Mark Twain that was helping Umlauf along, you see, and Sam knew that, so he wondered if his interest in it could technically be called 'vicarious.' I swear, he labored over that question for an entire evening."

It was then that I learned that Clemens had moved in with Cocoa. He had been staying in a cheap hotel prior to that—she had no idea where. He lived with her from 18 to 25 March. I asked her if this was the week she had spoken of as her "lost" week. She said no. Her "craziness," she said, began at the end of Clemens' stay and, she feared, ultimately frightened him away. She said her last recollection of him involved a tender moment on the living-room couch, after a seafood dinner. She remembered feeling the desire for a kiss—nothing more, only a kiss. She remembered reaching her arms around him. The next thing she remembered was standing on a mountaintop in the Catskills, in the predawn darkness of 2 April, looking at Halley's Comet. She was with several friends, who had been with her almost constantly in the preceding days, helping her through her spell of eccentricity.

"I wasn't *dangerous*, or anything," she said. "I was just out of it. My friends came to the rescue and helped me care for Darrell and Walter. I probably would have fed them dog food if I'd been left on my own. I saw some doctors, but they couldn't help me. A friend suggested I needed a rest, and she drove me up to the Catskills. I know all this because I was told about it—I don't remember *any* of it. The worst part was I thought

I was pregnant—with Sam's child. Some sleaze-bag of a reporter got wind of it—of my delusion—and wrote it up, and my friends kept me under wraps after that, until I came out of it. And everyone thought I was talking about Umlauf! Isn't that something? Did you read about me? Do you remember that?"

"Yes," I said. I took a long moment to absorb this news. "But it's not true, is it? You're not pregnant, are you? I have to ask you that. I'm sorry—"

"No. I'm not. No way." She laughed. "We kind of flirted around, but that's all—as far as I know, anyway. After I went crazy, who knows what happened? But I figure I must have made that same claim to Sam, and scared him off. I can't figure why else he would have left. Before that, we got along fine. He told me how when he was young he wanted to catch a boat to South America and make a fortune in the cocoa trade. He said he never caught that boat, but he'd finally found his Cocoa." She smiled. "He got the biggest kick out of that."

"But you said Cocoa wasn't your usual name."

"That's right. I changed it years ago. Sam said he couldn't stand my new name—couldn't 'abide' it, as he said. So he always called me 'Cocoa.' "

"What did you change it to?"

"Bununu Ogbomosho."

Things happened very quickly at that point. I asked her if she had ever been a writer-in-residence in Clemens' former summer home in Elmira. She said no, but she recalled showing him an announcement in a recent Authors Guild *Bulletin* about the availability of the house to writers. I told her I thought he was there, now, using her name, and asked her what she knew about catching a plane to Elmira. She knew nothing. We found a phone booth, I called the first travel agent that Directory Assistance gave me, and I learned that the next flight didn't leave until 6:50 P.M. Cocoa said she didn't have a car, but she could get one from a friend. She did, we picked up her children at school (she was not a teacher; she had simply accompanied the class on a field trip), and we lit out—I glancing nervously at my watch every few minutes.

It was a six-hour drive to Elmira. On the way, I gave Cocoa some idea of what the Mark Twain Papers had been through in the preceding month. She said Clemens mentioned that he had sent his manuscript to me, and that he had a suspicion I might try to find him, but he seemed terrified of the notion of meeting someone who "knew" him as well as he feared I did. His shyness made me smile, and it reminded me of Umlauf's attack on the manuscript. I suddenly realized that Cocoa probably did not know that Umlauf had died. So I told her *that* story. Just after she had recovered from the shock of hearing it, I shocked her again—unintentionally. I referred offhandedly to the possibility that Clemens may have "died" as well, since I assumed she knew of his expectation to leave on this very day. But she didn't. She had taken it as a matter of course that she would see him again. She had even been in the habit of walking through Washington Square Park every day, in the hopes of seeing him there. Either the crucial nature of 11 April hadn't occurred to Clemens while he was with Cocoa, or he had chosen not to tell her about it.

We returned to the subject of Umlauf's demise, and this led us to a discussion of Susy.

"On March eighteenth," said Cocoa, "Sam announced that he wanted to be in Hartford for Susy's birthday, the next day. So I got a car —this car, actually. He sat right where you're sitting. We drove there with the kids, spent the night in a motel, and hung out the whole day in and around his house. Or so he says."

" 'So he says'?"

"Yes. I have no memory of it—not because I was crazy, not then, but because he 'erased' it, as he would say. He uttered his magic word at the end of the day, and, lo and behold, we were back in New York, pulling out into the street. He said, 'I changed my mind. We're going to Elmira.' It was all the same to me, so we went there. But he erased that trip, too, so back to New York. He says, 'We're going to Redding.' Well, to my senses we hadn't done a thing but drive fifty feet and change our plans twice, so I said fine, as long as he made up his mind one way or the other. Then he erased *that* trip, too, and said, 'Forget it. Park the car. We ain't goin' anywhere.' Well, I raised a fuss, and so did Darrell and Walter. They moaned that we never went anywhere, and never had any fun. Sam just got out of the car and stalked off. He walked back to my apartment by himself, and he never said another word about it."

"Didn't you ask him about it—about why he had changed his mind?"

"No." She was silent a moment. Then she said, "He's Mark Twain. You let him get away with things. Besides, I had some idea of what the point of it all was. The point was to be at all those places on Susy's birthday, in case she showed up."

"Did he say that?"

"No. I just had a feeling about it. And . . ."

". . . and she did show up," I said. "This morning."

"The poor girl," said Cocoa.

As we neared Elmira, I turned on the radio and located "All Things Considered." In a few minutes we were listening to interviews with eyewitnesses to Umlauf's demise. Their testimony was crucial, because the "beautiful apparition" they spoke of failed to appear on the videotape of the event. As I listened it occurred to me that in light of the attention that was being given to Umlauf, and considering the supernatural glory attending his end, when Susy wrested the life out of him it was clearly the peak of his career.

But a fresh, new complication had entered the picture—Frederick Dixon. I quote from the transcript of the report:

> Just minutes before "The Hannibal Claimant" died, Frederick Dixon, General Editor of the Mark Twain Papers at the University of California in Berkeley, told the Symposium audience that in his opinion Mark Twain had indeed returned to life. Dixon said that "The Hannibal Claimant" was *not* Mark Twain, however. He said that "The Hannibal Claimant" was an impostor who had met the *real* Mark Twain in Nevada in November of last year and then, in Dixon's words, "stole his act." Dixon said that he had received new works written by Twain—a manuscript about his travels across the country in the past several months— but that he had neither spoken with Twain nor seen him.
>
> The audience was more than skeptical; it was hostile, and Dixon was able to speak for only a few minutes. But before abandoning the podium, he stated that the new Twain writings showed that Twain had not written the controversial notebook in his "first" life, but that he had written it in his "second" life. Dixon also intimated that a clue demonstrating that the notebook was fraudulent is contained in the notebook itself. He and his staff are presently trying to discover this clue. Dixon has apparently reversed his position of two months ago, for he was one of the experts consulted in February who verified the notebook's authenticity.
>
> After his speech, Dixon could not be reached for further comment. However, I spoke with Arthur Goldman, an editor at the Mark Twain Papers. Goldman confirmed Dixon's statements and said that a computer-assisted search had so far uncovered three "hidden" sentences in the notebook. The sentences are the following; listen carefully: "In the spring and Wednesdays a horse cavorts to win a boiling wolf but did the notion that to blow is Sanitary look fearless?", "Amazement rests on the arm of him who though stipulated to duelling palaver can even not rip

until climbing and the sneeze will rot," and "Which way which yearning cried the slouch with high-toned and melancholy crackers under blankets scratching a mountain to avoid the pleasure of hoisted loneliness." When I asked Goldman what these sentences meant to him, he replied, "We're still trying to get a fix on that."

Cocoa, listening to the report as intently as I was, helped me fashion an appropriate reaction to it; that is, she burst out laughing. The report went on to give the hint, at least, of hope of my vindication. Several scholars at the hotel had obtained some of the copies of the manuscript that Umlauf had distributed, and although they said that they had not had enough time with the manuscript to pronounce on its content, they acknowledged that the handwriting was indistinguishable from Clemens'.

Darrell and Walter had been looking at books and listening to cassette tapes with earphones, but they began to grow restless. I complimented them on their good behavior thus far. Walter responded by grabbing a book, opening it to a page, and demanding I tell a complete story about that picture. I demurred.

"Come on," Walter said. "Sam did it. Mama said you're a friend of Sam's."

"Yeah," said Darrell. "Sam did it."

I tried, and might have succeeded if my mind hadn't been on many other things. I sought refuge in Clemens' material, working into my tale his ghost story about the golden arm.

"We *know* that one," Darrell said, interrupting me.

"Yeah. Sam told us that one already," said Walter.

I tried "The Death Disk."

"Nah. We know that one, too."

I tried some unpublished stories Clemens had told daughter Jean—the tiger in the jungle, the donkey that eats books and thereby becomes educated—but for the second time that day I was violently hooted down. I looked at Cocoa. She was smiling, and a certain flush had come over her face, a change I could feel more than see—"like a change in temperature." It was a perfect description.

We reached Elmira shortly before seven o'clock. After some assaults on the hill to the east that ended in cul-de-sacs, we finally found a route that took us to Quarry Farm. I recognized the house instantly from pictures I had seen and from the countless word-pictures I had read, in which Clemens wrote of the farm's restful effect on him as if describing an enchanted place.

When we pulled into the driveway, Darrell and Walter dashed out of the car before Cocoa had turned the engine off. I took a deep breath before stepping out. A light was on over the front porch, and I saw a large collie enthusiastically greet Darrell and Walter. As Cocoa and I walked up onto the porch, past the front window, I saw someone stretched out on a sofa, his feet dangling over one end of it. I looked more closely. It was Ricky Olivieri. He hadn't noticed us, in spite of the noise the children were making in their excitement over the dog. He was staring up at the ceiling, his eyes wide open.

"Ready?" Cocoa asked when we reached the door. I nodded, and she knocked. In a few minutes, Olivieri appeared at the door. Whatever restful enchantment Quarry Farm still might have possessed, it had been lost on him. His hair was in disarray and he wore a haunted look. It seemed to take him a moment to recognize me. When he did, he registered neither surprise nor pleasure—only a faint acknowledgment. He did not invite us in. He held the door slightly ajar, as if ready to slam it shut at any moment. I began to make introductions, somewhat awkwardly, because Olivieri was more or less peeking through the narrow slit between the door and the jamb.

He interrupted me: "You missed him."

"No," I said.

"He's gone. You might as well leave."

"When did he go, Ricky?"

"You're too late."

"Can we come in, so we can talk?"

"No." Then he *did* slam the door, throwing a bolt to lock it. Through the window in the door I saw him disappear around a corner deeper into the house.

"He works for you?" Cocoa asked doubtfully.

"He's not normally like this," I said. I stepped back from the porch to see if any lights were on upstairs.

Cocoa suddenly shouted "Look!" and pointed to the road. In the dark we could just barely see Olivieri sneaking down the hill. He was keeping low, trying to remain hidden behind a rock wall, but as soon as I took off after him he stood up and broke into a sprint.

I called back to Cocoa, "Stay here. He may be in the house. See if you can get in by the back door." Then I began to run after Olivieri. For a while, I kept him in sight. Despite the darkness and the steepness of the grade, he was running at a breakneck pace, and was gradually pulling away from me. When I reached a crossroads, he was no longer visible. I stopped, but I couldn't hear his footsteps either. "John Lewis," I said under my breath, "where are you when I need you?"

Back at the house, Darrell and Walter were playing pool on a table at the far end of the front porch. Cocoa stood near the front door, which was open.

"There's no one here," she said. "But Sam's luggage is upstairs, and the whole house reeks of cigar smoke."

"Smoke?" I asked excitedly. "Did you see smoke? Was it drifting around?"

"No, no," she said. "Calm down, Fred. He's not here."

A futile sameness to the events of the next four hours lends them to easy summary. First, we ransacked Clemens' belongings and papers in the house in a vain search for clues as to where he might have gone, if he was still among the living. Then I found a phone in the kitchen and called Matthew Bailey, the Director of Quarry Farm, at his home. He couldn't help us either. He had met "Bununu Ogbomosho" just once, when he first arrived at the farm. He suggested I try Benjamin Block, President of Elmira College. I did, but he was not at home. We then drove around the streets of Elmira, checking in restaurants, taverns, and movie houses. We checked the sites—Clemens' former study on the college campus, which we drove by, seeing nothing from the road, Woodlawn Cemetery, and then the deteriorating train station where he had last seen Susy in 1895. At eleven-thirty, we checked into a Holiday Inn. Cocoa put her sleepy twins to bed—they professed to be as disappointed as we were that we hadn't found Sam—and I went out for a walk on the levee of the Chemung River.

Once, in our search of the streets, we had glimpsed Olivieri stealing around a corner like a Venetian assassin. We gave chase but failed to find him. I wondered what had possessed him to flee from me. I wondered about his cessation of coherent communication with me since his departure from Berkeley. I thought about Cocoa's report of her own madness. I had the first suspicion, then, of the phenomenon of delirium Clemens. I thought of my own actions in the past month, dwelling morosely on my attempt to speak the truth at the Symposium. But was it the truth? Could I be as unbalanced as Olivieri evidently was, or as Cocoa had been? As I stared down at the dark river, I tried to sort through the evidence, starting at the beginning and working through it, determined to bring a fresh outlook to it that might reveal something new. But it was a muddle.

I suddenly became aware of what I can only call an agitation in the atmosphere. The air seemed charged, fraught with expectancy, as before a summer storm. Below me, a light that was rippling across the water attracted my attention. It was moving slowly toward the far shore. When it arrived there, it disappeared. I looked up and let out a shout. A single bright light was coursing high overhead—a miniature comet, with its own small tail. It seemed to draw after itself the energy that had been in the air. I sensed an invisible upward rush, and I felt as if I were part of it, even as I stood transfixed, and I longed to be an even greater part of it. I watched the light fly to the south, where Halley's Comet was pursuing its own outbound course somewhere beneath the horizon. It receded high over the hills of northern Pennsylvania, until it became so faint that I couldn't be sure I was still seeing it, and I fought the urge to blink, for fear I *would* lose it. My eyes suddenly welled with tears, and the light was gone.

I became aware of the sound of sirens coming from the town. I ran back to Cocoa's room. She was standing outside the door, her eyes raised to the southern sky. She was crying.

"Take my car," she said. "See what you can find out."

I drove toward the sound of the sirens, to the north, and I eventually found the flashing lights of police cars and fire trucks. They were parked on a road running through the college campus. I pulled the car over and ran past several townspeople gathering at the scene. In the distance, on a grassy slope, was Clemens' study—a small octagonal building with a formerly peaked roof. Now the roof was peeled open, like the upright end of an egg jaggedly opened at the top. What was left of the roof was in flames, and firemen were dragging hoses up to it. I ran past them, ignoring their shouts and the cries of police officers chasing me. A blast of water from one of the hoses knocked me sprawling near the steps of the study. I rose to my feet and looked inside.

On the floor, beside a small desk, was a spiral notebook. Tiny columns of smoke rose from its cover. I dashed inside, stomped on the cover to extinguish the embers, and picked up the notebook. I rushed out, clutching it to my chest, into the arms of the police.

After some time, I was able to convince what seemed like the entire Elmira Police Department that I was not an arsonist, and that the notebook I had salvaged was not a blueprint for the further torching of their town. Then I hurried off to read Clemens' final words, which were completely legible, though the pages were scorched around the edges. The manuscript is in a rushed hand, with sometimes wildly slanting lines. It also shows some sentence fragments, especially toward the end. There is no problem of legibility here; Clemens simply changed the subject in mid-sentence.

The letter is given below in its entirety:

Elmira
April 11/86, 8.47 p.m.,
"& counting"

My Dear Dixon,

"Life's more surprisin' than we think." It's just as Millie says, Dixon. You remember Millie. She was my barber in Carson. You know her as Dixie.

"*What?*" you ask. "How do *you* (meaning *me*) know that *I* (meaning *you*) know that Millie is Dixie?" Ah, Dixon, I know all about you. I know you "by the back."

But enough of this tantalizing prologue. My time is short. I must forsake all artistic craft. No digressions, no atmosphere, no stage-setting. I must stick to the main channel, without fail. Your record will be incomplete unless I write this & get it to you, though I haven't figured out just *how* to get it to you. I'll leave that to Providence.

This is what happened—

First, in the early afternoon of yesterday's rehearsal of to-day, the peaceful repose of Quarry Farm was smashed to flinders by the arrival of none other than Umlauf the Bold. I was loafing on the porch, waiting for my comet to pick me up, when to my complete flabbergastion, a car drove up, screeched to a stop, & belched out the Missing Link, along with his flunkey. The noise started in right away:

"Fertile ground, Herbert, fertile ground! Why, Clara & Jean were born right here, right *here,* as were so many books of mine. You know them, Herbert. I needn't tell *you* the titles."

"No, *sir,*" says Herbert.

"I fathered them all, Herbert—the children, & the books."

"Hmph," says I under my breath. "Him father anything? His issue would be as freakish as an ornithorhynchus."

"But where are the animals?" he brays. He hadn't seen me yet. Or it is more likely that he saw me, & only *pretended* he didn't. That's what he will do, every time. "Where is Kadichan?" he brays. "Where is Polichon? Pray, where are Stray Kit, Sourmash, & Blatherskite?"

The only animal on hand was Quarry, the collie, & he must have wanted to fill this lamented void in Umlauf's life, because he lit out for him & began to sample his leg. Who says animals don't have a moral sense? Not me. But Umlauf gave the poor beast a good look at his face, & that sent him yelping around to the back of the house & over the hill & north—into Canada, I believe.

It's 9.01 p.m. I'm taking too long with this.

Ricky joined me on the porch. That's Ricky Olivieri, Dixon—your man. He'd been with me a few days. He'll tell you all about it. Ricky was rather agitated, on account of Umlauf.

"Look, Herbert!" cries Umlauf, pretending to spy us for the first time. "Here's that trivial scum again. Didn't I heave him off the boat in Cincinnati, Herbert? Didn't I? And didn't I forbid him from ever darkening my life again?" That's Ricky he was talking about. "And here's my old Nevada chum." That's me. "Well, well, well. I've told you all about him, Herbert. Why, he's the one who posed as my friend, who won my confidence, & all the while he was studying me, scheming secretly to hoodwink the public by claiming he is *me*. His success has been negligible though, eh, Herbert?"

"Yes, *sir.*"

"He is a mere lightning-bug, with his shy little glimmers in the wilderness of obscurity. This is the apex of his glory. This is the sum total of his following—one dog & one madman."

"Come here, fat man," says Ricky, bending down to his briefcase. "I've got something for you."

"So," says Umlauf, ignoring Ricky & kind of rolling up to me. "So. The Twains *do* meet, eh? Haw, haw, haw."

Now, I ask you, Dixon—would the real Mark Twain have said such a tired & predictable thing as that? How could he fool anybody for a minute? How could he fool his flunkey, who listened to these wit-substitutes day in & day out? I felt a sudden urge to pop that big balloon. I gazed up into the sky & said, as if suddenly inspired—

" 'How Much Time Did He Spend on the Water?' 'Was He in Every State of the Union?' 'What Famous People Did He Meet?' " I let my eyes fall on the flunkey, who was gaping at me. "Nice to see you again, Herbert," says I.

You see, Dixon, Herbert is The Twain Man from the *Delta Queen*. I don't know how or when he fell in love with Umlauf, but that's no matter. I planned on using my knowledge of him to shake his faith in his big boss. It would be a powerful blow to Umlauf if his closest confidant turned against him. So I told Herbert I knew him, & had read all his essays. I told him *he* didn't remember our meeting, because I used magic to wipe out the event. How could he explain what I knew except by believing in my magic? I challenged his boss to try to match *that*.

Ricky, at my side, started chanting: "*Um*lauf, *Um*lauf, *Um*lauf, *Um*lauf," don't ask me why.

"Stuff," says Umlauf. "Herbert, you gave those essays to the museum in Hannibal, didn't you?"

"Ye-es," says Herbert, still shaken from my bombshell.

"Well," says Umlauf, "this deadbeat has been there, & he read 'em there. It doesn't signify at all."

Blast! I hadn't counted on that. How was I to know Herbert had gone & done such a fool-headed thing? Well, Herbert was back in the fold, so to speak, & he was so fired up with fresh affection that he tried to give his boss a hug, but Umlauf passed. He kind of bumped Herbert away with his belly & turned to me, his green eyes twinkling, & he says:

"It was a good try, chum. I like your style. You've got promise."

"Come here, O round one," says Ricky. "I've got something to show you." He took the something out of his briefcase. It was his copy of the notebook, with those key words circled. He'll tell you all about it, Dixon, if you haven't found it yet. I don't have time.

Umlauf says, "It'd better be worth it, young scum. It's a long drive up here, & I'm anxious to get back to the city & bathe in all that love again."

That's when I learned Umlauf was there at the farm because Ricky had invited him. You see, Ricky wanted to heave that sentence from the notebook in his face. Well, I grew warm & ripped out some brisk language at Ricky. When a man's dying, Dixon, as I was planning to do, he wants calm all around him. He don't want an Umlauf around, that's certain. I told Ricky this—told him he had no more sense than a calf.

"*Good!*" Umlauf sings to me. "Good! I used to light into my children just like that, many & many a time. You've got the Mark Twain hot temper down pat. Now, look at your man there. His lips are all aquiver. He's going to cry. Look—he *is* crying. Now's the time for you to begin to hate yourself & work up an apology to him. Go ahead. Don't let my presence hinder you."

Dixon, the truth is I *was* about to apologize. But I couldn't, on account of being anticipated like that. So I just told Ricky he might as well go ahead & show him the sentence. Herbert came up for a look too. This got my hopes on the rise again. Well, Umlauf & Herbert studied it, & studied it, & studied it, & studied it, & they began to look a little troubled, & Ricky regained his former chipperness, & he starts in again—

"*Um*lauf, *Um*lauf, *Um*lauf, *Um*lauf."

But suddenly Umlauf & Herbert started grinning like a couple of idiots.

"I knew it, Mr. Twain," pipes Herbert. "I knew it. I knew you had to be the author of *Huck Finn*. Oh, I knew it."

"Didn't I tell you, Herbert?" crows Umlauf. "Well, well, well—they've finally found it." They were giggling like a couple of schoolgirls now, & I wanted to reach out & knock their heads together. Herbert re-commenced slobbering with affection, & tried for another hug, but was disappointed again.

I'll explain it, Dixon. I don't have time to paint the full scene, with all the words, & all Umlauf's sentences beginning with "Why"—do I do that? I'll be damned if I do.

I'll explain it. Umlauf, I learned, had taken Herbert into his confidence a few days earlier & told him there was a little something in the notebook that proved it was a phony. He didn't say *what* it was. Just said it was a little something. He'd told Herbert that he wrote the notebook in December & pretended it was real, just so he could prove that people loved him so much they'd be willing to overlook a scandal like that & go on loving him. It was a kind of test of love, he said. Well, what he'd done was figure out, somehow, what *I'd* done, or what I *might* have done, & he laid the groundwork in preparation for any embarrassment ahead of time, so that when the embarrassment came it wouldn't have any more effect on his big lie than a fly landing on his head. He'd told some other of his disciples, too, he said, & they were all of them waiting for someone to find it, so they could have a big laugh. He said that he was thinking of making it all public when the Symposium was over, just to show what a bunch of punkinheads those scholars were. Which is a lie, of course, because he didn't know what the key sentence was. Why, he didn't even know for sure that there *was* one. But *now* he did, thanks to Ricky & me. We had played it right into his hands.

It was a rotten defeat for us. I have written many a trial scene, & it is such a joy organizing the evidence, & taking the jury, which includes the reader, from scorn & disbelief through mounting interest & finally to wholesale conversion. When I went for Umlauf, I was hoping for the same thing, I reckon. They're easier to write than enact, I suppose.

Umlauf must have figured he couldn't get any more beautiful, in

Herbert's eyes, than he was then, because after he brayed & crowed a bit, he exited, ordering Herbert to take him back to the city, leaving Ricky & me rubbing our wounds. I expect Umlauf will flourish, Dixon. He never gave me a *hint* about who he really is, so I can't help you there, if you mean to go after him—& if you do, you'd better go after him with an elephant gun, not just with puny words, as I did. But I reckon you won't ever learn anything true about him. He is rootless, history-less; like the camel, he has no native habitat.

Ricky began to cry over our failure. I tried to cheer him up. That didn't work, so I swore at him. That didn't work either. I hope you take care of that boy, Dixon. He's as faithful to me as a dog, but he's ailing.

Good Christ! It's 9.40.

I know he's ailing, because of what happened later. But first *you* came on the scene. You drove up to the farmhouse with Cocoa & the rascals. This was near nightfall. After that business with Umlauf, & after I'd had all afternoon to brood over our defeat, you & Cocoa were as welcome as old pie to me. Not to Ricky though. He don't trust you, & wants me all to himself.

Dixon, you were confoundedly nervous at first, & you seemed to run your sentences through some sort of refining mill before you felt confident enough about them to say them in my august presence, but by & by you relaxed & began to act like your true self, I reckon, & you were delightful company. You

10.15 p.m.—Dixon, I wish you were here to share in the laughter with me. What happened in the time that just elapsed is this—

I heard voices outside the study & hunkered down behind the front wall. Did I tell you I am in my old study, on the college campus? Can't see the MS to read if I did or not—it's too dark. But it's no matter, that's where I am—I forced open a rear window & crawled in, because I needed a quiet place to write, where I wouldn't be disturbed. But voices! I ducked down. It was a boy & a girl, courting—students here, I suppose. It was pathetic to hear their talk. First they pushed the button on the little speaking box outside the door & listened to the wheezy imitation of my voice, talking about my Elmira days. That concluded, the boy took to discussing my life & my work in the ignorantest fashion you can imagine —trying to impress the girl, you see. The girl kept giggling & dropping hints about how they should go down to the grassy slope by the pond nearby, & stretch out, & look up at the stars. She made it sound awfully appealing, but the chucklehead seemed to be ignorant of her wishes, & he stood there going on & on about me, or someone remotely like me.

By & by I struck an idea. I crawled over to where I thought the box was, just by the door, & I wheezed out a speech about what a bully time Livy & I had a-courtin', & how jolly our wedding night was, & many & many a night after that, too.

There was a stunned silence beyond the door. Then, "Did you push that button?" "No—did you?" "No—but it *seemed* to come from that box." "Yes—it just *had* to." "It must have started up on its own."

Well, they were still standing there, wasting their time, & mine too, so I wheezed out another speech—about how ironic it is that mankind's conception of heaven—a place supposedly dripping with bliss—had no provision for "the supremest of all man's delights, the one ecstasy that stands first & foremost in the heart of every man & woman of the race —sexual intercourse." Those were my words.

"That's an interesting point," says she.

"Ye-es, I suppose it is," says he, still soft—in the head.

I wheezed out another—about how the female sex is always hankering for a good frolic, just yearning to death for it, just pining to be a candlestick to the male's candle, & pining for it again, & again, & again.

"Oh," says she, giving out a kind of moan, "what a sublime thinker Mark Twain was."

"Let's go down to the pond," says he.

It's a good thing that sexual snail saw the light, or I would have thrown open a window & ordered him to go on down to that pond & do what God equipped him to do. What a ninny he was! I sometimes wonder if the race is even worth saving.

Where was I? I got you on the scene, I know that much. You & I fell to talking about whether I'd made a mistake by not publicly announcing my return as soon as I arrived, back on Mrs. Clemens' birthday. But we didn't get very far, because Ricky, who was nearby—that boy is *always* nearby—exclaimed, "You would have been assassinated!" His opinion was by then well-known to me. He had voiced it many times. And you, Dixon, seemed to agree that such a danger existed.

Well, you're both wrong. Even if someone did try to kill me, he wouldn't succeed. I know. *I* tried, in San Francisco, & I got further along with the attempt than I ever had before. I did the stylish San Francisco thing & jumped from the Golden Gate Bridge, looking forward to spreading my parts out when I hit the water. I figured they'd wash out into the ocean & make a lovely shark banquet. I imagined those sharks feasting on me, & praising me—"Why, this is the finest, most literary meat I've ever tasted"—& they would all become writers, for having dined on me, you see, only they couldn't write, lacking fingers, so they would dictate their stories to an octopus, who would scribble them down, eight at a time, & then deliver them to Seal Rock, & a seal would seize the manuscripts in his mouth, & swim around the point, into the Bay, then across it, & he would go on up that little creek that winds its way through your campus, & he would flop out onto dry land near the library, & struggle to the elevator, & I suppose some kind soul would push the button for him, or maybe he could bump it with his nose, if it's low enough, & he would waddle down that long hall to your sweat-shop, & you would read those manuscripts & declare, "It's got the Mark Twain touch, through & through. He's back! I must tell the world!" You would invite the members of the press over, & you would tell them I was alive, reincarnated as a seal, & you would take that seal with you all over the country, speaking at every stop to hugely enthusiastic crowds of two or three people. I was thinking all of this, mentally composing, as I climbed over the railing, & as I jumped, meaning to die "in the harness," so to speak—but my body didn't cooperate. It sort of went *swappp!* the way I thought it would, & its innards did undergo a profound reorganization, but then *I could feel them move back where they belonged.* It was an awful let-down. Nothing to do for it but swear & swim for shore. So, you see, I would have had nothing to fear from an assassin. I would have welcomed one, would have encouraged the attempt, but he would have been a disappointed man.

10.40—I am a blockhead for having taken so much time with that. *Damn* this deadline.

You asked me if I regretted the notebook business. I assured you I did, because I do. Our perception of the future is a curious thing, Dixon. Throw your vision ahead to 2061 A.D. What are the people like? Aren't they *different* from you—not just in the gadgets available to them, & in their superior knowledge of the innermost workings of life, & their clothing & their infernal slang, but *in their hearts?* Do you imagine them less . . . human? Do you find it hard to take them seriously as human beings? I hope you do, because this was my feeling upon my return. I felt surrounded by automatons—not on account of the way they behaved, but just on account of *when* they behaved. They were ridiculous, in a way—prime targets for a joke. Once conceived & begun, that notebook consumed my interest; working on it was a relief, a welcome distraction from my confusion; & I didn't pause, until too late, to look around & see that you *are* people, after all.

But I must say something more about that joke. It's this: *Huck* had nothing to do with it—why, those little notes about *Huck,* giving it to Orion & all, were the idlest of thoughts—they passed in & out of my brain as quickly as I could write them, & I never thought about them again—that is, not until I read that piece in the *Atlantic* & saw that I had wrought a second Civil War. *Christ!* You see, while Umlauf was feeding me that pack of lies, he fed me some truth, too. He showed me where some people have wrotened that I couldn't write about men & women being—well, being men & women; that I "shied away" from that sort of thing in my books. Well, that didn't sit well with me. It gave me indigestion. So I burped, & what came out was that bunch of notes about sex—the miner so afraid of syphilis that he spends a fortnight in a brothel, just to end the suspense, &c. Those notes were the sole reason for the notebook, from my point of view. But they barely got an "oh-hum" in the *Atlantic,* or anywhere else. I might as well have gone to the far side of the moon & farted—a squeaky fart, too—for all the sensation they created.

But none of that matters to me now. I know you'll get the full story, Dixon, about my being a well-rounded, full, complete, *sexual person.* You tell Cocoa to fess up; tell her not to hold back anything. You tell her—never mind, show her this letter. I am herewith consenting that Cocoa tell the world, without stint, what a sexual time bomb I am. Write it up, Cocoa. Write it up bully. *My Lover, Mark Twain*—that's the ticket. Sexual revolution—hmph. I reckon the instruction was mutual.

10.52—Oh, my! I am so warm now. Not because—never mind.

We had a satisfying trial scene after all, Dixon. It featured the president of the college as judge & jury. He's a tough nut—not an atom of nonsense to him; absolutely joke-proof. He came along an hour or so after you & Cocoa arrived, armed for the kill. You see, he had been suspicious of me for some time, & had finally tracked down a kodak of the real Bununu Oshgobomosho in some magazine, & he noticed the striking lack of resemblance to me.

We were on the porch—you, Cocoa, the rascals, Ricky, & me—playing billiards & chatting away. He walked up to us, slowly & threateningly, scrutinizing us & not saying a word. We fell silent. He stopped at the pool table & stared at it as if he had never seen one before.

"What's *this* doing here?" he says—with authority.

Well, Ricky had arranged its delivery as a surprise to me, but I didn't want to get him in trouble, so I said it was my doing; he should consider it a donation to Quarry Farm.

"Hmph," says he. His eyes fell on Darrell & Walter, who were still knocking balls around on the table. He says, "Getting much writing done, kids?" I liked that.

Darrell says, "Hunh?"

Walter pointed to his cue tip & says, "You got any chalk around here, Mister?"

Cocoa laughed. The president gave her the fish eye & asked if the children were hers. She said yes. He asked who she was. She said, "Bununu Omgobosho."

"I *see*," the president says. He looks to me. "Mm-*hmm*. I shouldn't be surprised." He jerked a thumb at Ricky. "Yesterday, this fellow here confessed two identities to me. He said he was Miles Hendon, & that he was set on restoring the Prince to power & dethroning the pauper. Figure that out. Then he said he was the new Albert Bigelow Paine." He turned to me. "I shall come back to you, sir." He turned to you, Dixon. "And you, sir? Pudd'nhead Wilson, perhaps?"

"Fred. Dixon," you say, not at all ashamed of it, "from the Mark Twain Papers. I came up here with Cocoa."

The president's eyes widened. "Ah, yes. I know you. *You're* all right. You're the one who called my office & urgently demanded to speak to me, so that you could ask me the very pressing question about whether there was a dog named 'Quarry' at the farm. Oh, yes. You're nice & stable. You'll do fine."

I explained: "That was Ricky, sir. You've mixed them up. That's how Ricky knew I was here."

The president gave me a long, tired look. "I shan't pursue the logic of that. I shall let it pass." He looked around. "There was mention of a Cocoa. Who is Cocoa?"

"That's me," says Cocoa.

"I'm awfully glad," says the president. "But I miss Bununu O&c. I was beginning to like Bununu O&c. In whose body has *her* soul taken up residence?" He whirled around to me. "In *yours* once again?"

"I am not Bununu O&c," I said, "nor have I ever been. I used her name, without her knowledge, so that I could stay here a while."

"*Now* we're getting somewhere," says the president. "Frank confessions of humbuggery—that's the only way out of this." He looked at me coldly. "I've had my doubts about you all along—you with your claim to be the author of her books. I've read her books. You. 'I have always been a friend of the Negro' indeed. Just who in the devil are you, sir?"

Says I: "I am Mark Twain."

11.10—I'm afraid I'm making a botch of this, Dixon. It's the study that's doing it to me. Surrounded by its walls, I'm falling into old, leisurely habits, as if I had a long, lovely summer to spend lingering over my MS. I've given this scene in some detail, because it was bully—bully to live through it, & bully to write about it. I thank you, Dixon, for serving up such bulliness on my last day.

But I must summarize the rest. We ganged up on that president & stunned him with arguments for who I am. I donned a false mustache I had been carrying around with me, in case such an emergency arose, & he fired all sorts of questions at me, trying to catch me out, but he didn't, & our combined efforts reduced him to jelly. That's an exaggeration, I suppose, but he at least did agree to stay around for my imminent departure, which I fancied would be quite a show. Correctly, as you will see.

When the time came, I heated up all over. I began to glow, starting with my hair & working down along my sides. I threw you all a kiss—too hot to hug, now,—& walked out into the front yard, insisting that you all remain on the porch. I scorched the very ground I trod upon. I came to a stop a safe distance away, & turned to face you—a frozen tribe you were, staring in wonder. I began to spit & crackle, sending out short flares all around me. Then a whirling began, at my sides, where my arms used to be, as if I were hemmed in by two firewheels. I rose a few inches from the ground, shouting out to you that it didn't hurt at all, because it didn't!

Then Ricky did a rash thing. He ran from the porch right at me, leaping into my fire, don't ask me why.

I had no alternative. It was "Damnation!"—with *much* feeling—& back to breakfast. My departure would be delayed by one day.

I resolved to spend the day alone. You can't trust these humans. I didn't even trust *you*, Dixon; maybe next time *you* would get the notion to leap on me for a ride into the void. I didn't want any of Umlauf & his flunkey, either. So, at breakfast, I said to Ricky, "I know you plan to telephone Umlauf at his hotel & tell him to drive up here. Don't do it." My perspicacity clearly stunned him, but he obeyed me. So Umlauf didn't make it. Somehow I didn't miss him.

I couldn't strike a handy way to keep you & Cocoa away, so I decided to absent myself from the farm long before you were to arrive. It was a hard choice. You tell Cocoa that, Dixon. In the afternoon, I said to Ricky that I was going into town for some cigars. & you tell her how I had to fight not to climb back up that hill for a last glimpse of her. You tell her. I wandered around town a bit, here & there, ending up sitting in the park near the river & watching the traffic pass by—& tell her why I lit out from N.Y.C. Tell her that if I'd wanted a reason to live, I would have advertised for one. Tell her.

As night fell, I got up & wandered across town to my old study. As I walked, I began to regret my mistreatment of you & your gang in Berkeley. The *least* I could do, I figured, after all I'd put you through, was get it down on paper, before I left—most of it, anyway, & without any stretchers in it—Honest Injun. I stopped a student on the edge of the campus & asked him for pencil & paper. He obliged with one pencil & one sheet of paper. I gave him a hundred dollars for the notebook under his arm. He thought it a fair exchange & went on his way—quickly, in case I changed my mind. I crept up to my study in the dark, & you know the rest. It's only a

What's this? I can see the page now. My hair is glowing. Right on schedule. I must hurry.

We—skip that. It's

When

At one point, just before I left, I fell to musing about "what might have been" in my soon-to-end second life, with all kinds of busted-heart & remorseful talky-talk, & Ricky (who is *always* nearby) up & says, "You can do it again, Sam. You can do it all over again." He opened his briefcase & pulled out my first sketch, the "Bodie" one (he *always* talks from a text, just like a preacher,) & he showed where I wrote that I called myself a muggins clear back in Bodie, on Nov. 27th. Says I, "You're right. I did say that." Says he, "Then go *back*, Sam. Go all the way back to Bodie, & start all over, only this time don't go to Carson, & don't go to Umlauf—go to the Mark Twain Papers. Come to us, Sam. *We* shan't turn you away."

Well, I was in a close place. I chewed on it a while, & finally I said:

"I do not wish any of the pie—not for glory, nor for love." Ricky broke down then. It was awful to see. He suddenly claimed to be *Susy*, pointing to all kinds of meaning in his name—*Olivieri*, like *Olivia* Susan Clemens—& he accused me of planning to abandon him in Elmira all over again, just as I did before. I became extremely warm then, Dixon, & you interceded, & hustled him off.

Now, I spent the

What's this? The paper is I can't hold the paper with my hand. I scorch it with my very I there. If I move my hand around it's What was I saying? I've had all day to think, Dixon. I read a story about St. Peter, back in

I ain't going back, not this time. But consider 2061 A.D. Why? Because that's when Halley returns. My intuitions about that comet are sound—I was right about my departure with it, on the 11th, wasn't I? My intuition tells me I shall return with it in 2061, & every goddamned time thereafter. If I come back & find that everything is fine, then fine, I ain't going back then either. But if I come back & find that the earth is a mere pile of ruin & decay, a heap of ashes—radioactive ashes—a kind of global Bodie, I shall feel many things. I shall be sad, grief-stricken, angry, &c. I shall swear. From that bottomless well of my vocabulary, I will select that uniquely propulsive word. You know it. Back I will go, all the way to 1985, & the race will rise from its ashes & have another go at not being damfools. Maybe I will take pictures first, if I can find a camera that works. As evidence, you see. Even lacking that, I will go public & prophesy from the mountaintops about the doom of the race, a certain doom unless they mend their ways.

This has been a hard decision. I always said I would never wish anyone back from the grave who had been fortunate enough to get there; it's as if Providence said, "I'm mighty tired of people saying things & not really meaning them; look at Clemens there, spouting off again—he's one of the worst. Let's just put this claim of his to the *real* test, & we'll see where he stands."

There's a story

Earlier in the day, I talked it over, in a general way, with some of the local boys in a saloon. "Is life worth living?" I asked. I got some awfully discouraging answers. I thought, "Who is the most hard-headed, unnonsensical man I know?" Why, the president of the college—that's who. I called him up in his office, told him it was Banana Omigosho, his favorite writer up on the farm (that's a joke, Dixon, he can't *stand* me,) & I said I was puzzling over a story idea, & I needed his opinion on something. "Is life worth living?" says I. Says he, "In what sense?" Well, I knew where *he* stood all right.

Maybe it's just as well. A body's got to face his responsibilities in a manly way. It makes no sense, I know. It contradicts everything I but I'm going to do it. If, in my 75-year absence, the race has been having booming times, & boomed itself out of existence, I'm going back.

I read a story about St. Peter, in Hannibal, when I was studying his life for that sketch. When he was having some troubles—in Rome—he lit out, to save his skin. This was some years after the crucifixion. On the road a little ways outside Rome, he met Christ coming the other way, walking toward the city with a cross. Peter, so the story goes, was surprised to see him. I believe it. In P.'s place, I would be surprised too. P. asked where he was going. J.C. answered, "To Rome, to be crucified again." Well, P. didn't blunder, for a change. He saw the meaning of the Lord's words. He turned right around & went back to Rome, because he knew that cross was meant for *him*. I like P., as you know, & feel a kinship with him. But the Lord! Isn't there something supremely admirable, & good, about the way he was trudging to Rome with his cross, uncomplaining, resolute. He didn't belabor the point to P. Just stated it, calm as you please, & went on his way. That's an example to me, Dixon. I won't whine & fuss. I'll just trudge right back.

If we meet I'll be damned if I'm not *setting fire* to the MS now. Can't hold it with Can Good—the pen holds it. If

Born in November, died in April. Re-born in November, re-extinguished in April. It's neat, Dixon, it's neat.

Just popping all over. Must stop. Can't seem a police car has Some stalwart Christ! Those young lovers are moving in on me too. A shame I couldn't time my departure for the precise moment of their climax— it would give that boy loads of confidence. Just think, Dixon. Damn that policeman! He's shouting at me & getting awfully xxx I just gave him some spiritual advice. I'm Just think. Those two I'm Those two may have made a baby—a baby doomed to incineration, but for me. I'm Comet Man!!! Long may he

Sometime between 8 and 9 P.M., on the evening of 11 April, John Finster, a sophomore at Elmira College, sold a spiral notebook to, in his words, "an old-timer from the South." The selling price was ten dollars, not one hundred dollars, as Clemens reports.

Around 10 P.M., Albert Edelson and Cynthia Randall, both freshmen at the college, visited the study, listened to the recorded imitation of Clemens' voice issuing from the small speaker, then strolled down to the nearby pond "to look at the stars" (their words). They claim no additional message came from the box or from anywhere near it—certainly nothing of the sexually encouraging nature that Clemens reports. Apparently, to the very end, Clemens recognized a good embellishment when it struck him. Edelson and Randall report that some time later their attention was drawn to a bright light coming from the study; on closer inspection they saw "a face completely surrounded by light" (Randall), "a man burning up in the middle of a star" (Edelson), then nothing but pure light, which shot with a roar through the roof of the study into the night sky.

Sergeant Walter A. "Bud" Duffy, of the Elmira Police Department, observed the same sight—the face in the light, then pure light, then a rocketing upwards—and has tenaciously clung to his story despite considerable pressure from his family and his superiors. He does not recall hearing any shouts coming from the light; evidently Clemens' "spiritual advice" was wasted.

Benjamin Block, President of Elmira College, has no recollection of receiving any phone call from the "writer-in-residence" at Quarry Farm at any time on 11 April. He also writes,

> When the alleged Bununu Ogbomosho applied in writing for a two-week residency at Quarry Farm, I read several of this author's books. They treat, in the most sensitive way, daily life of black children—girls, especially—in the city, with an interesting intermingling of African folklore. Expecting to meet a black female writer, I was naturally surprised to shake the hand of a white male when the "author" arrived. But, perhaps owing to the man's charm, I never doubted that he was who he claimed to be—not until I spoke with you on April twelfth. (Benjamin Block to Frederick Dixon, 14 April 1986)

Evidently, then, Clemens' report of the call to the President to solicit his opinion on the value of life is another embellishment.

President Block's statement raises some questions about Clemens' report of Block's arrival, "armed for the kill," at the farm in the erased loop of 11 April. If he visited the farm in the erased loop, why did he not visit it in the unerased loop? Wouldn't he be expected to behave in exactly the same way in each loop?

Not necessarily. Once again there is an Umlauf factor, which may have come into play in the erased loop but not in the unerased one. Upon leaving the farm after his confrontation with Clemens and Olivieri, Umlauf may have driven to Block's office before returning to the city, and he may have presented him with evidence that Clemens was not the writer he claimed to be. Perhaps he even showed him the photograph of Bununu Ogbomosho that Clemens mentions. At any rate, whatever role Block played in the erased loop, it is clear that Clemens evinced a strange fascination with him, as if he projected onto him his own doubts about whether he truly "belonged" at Quarry Farm. As a final example of this, we can point to Clemens' dog-written Livy letter of 7 April, in which he portrays Block as a suspicious man who peevishly helps him carry a sofa back into the house. According to Block, no such incident ever transpired.

There is a final, sad coda to my commentary on Clemens' 11 April letter. After my return to Berkeley, and after the staff at the Papers had

had some time to read and discuss Part III of *I Been There Before* and Clemens' final letter, one afternoon they silently gathered in my office, in front of my desk. I looked up. There was some foot-shuffling and throat-clearing.

"Yes?" I said.

Ned Scully spoke: "We've got a new interpretation of part of the April eleventh letter."

"Oh?" I said.

"We're pretty much in agreement on it."

"Yes? What is it?"

Gloria Wilson said, "We're not *absolutely* sure—just pretty nearly completely sure."

"What *is* it?"

"We don't think Clemens really met you," said Wilson. "He probably made it up."

They were right, of course. That is, it is likely that in the erased loop recounted by Clemens I did not go to Elmira at all; I probably didn't even meet Cocoa that day. After my speech in the hotel, I had planned to sit in my room and await Clemens' call. But Umlauf died; that event would dominate the news; Clemens, if he heard *any* news, would hear only of that, and not of my speech, and even if he *did* hear of my speech, it would fail to seize his sympathy as I had wanted it to. These were my thoughts after Umlauf died, and *that* was why I went to Washington Square. But in the erased loop, Umlauf didn't die. He didn't give his speech. He and Hummel drove to Elmira early in the morning to meet Clemens and Olivieri. Olivieri, of course, can directly confirm none of the three sets of visits in the erased loop (Umlauf and Hummel; Cocoa, the children, and I; and President Block), but he does recall awakening on 11 April with the thought of telling Umlauf his days were numbered because of the key sentence in the notebook, which he would invite him up to inspect. Olivieri recalls Clemens' forbidding the invitation, even though Olivieri had said nothing about it. Clemens, perhaps when he was "watching the traffic pass by" in downtown Elmira, may very well have seen Cocoa, the children, and me driving by on our way up to Quarry Farm, and reasoned that since we sought him out in the second loop, perhaps he could convince me that we sought him out, and found him, in the erased loop. Note that this interpretation of events still allows for the existence of two loops. There is no reason to doubt Clemens' account of Olivieri's "leaping into [his] fire," which necessitated the second loop and Clemens' isolation for its duration. To summarize, in that first loop, Umlauf and Hummel presumably visited Clemens; President Block *may* have; Fred Dixon, alas, probably did not.

The staff were quick to offer condolences. "We think he made it up for *your* sake, Fred," said Scully. "After all he'd put you through, he probably regretted his selfishness in not arranging a meeting with you. This letter was the best he could do—or was willing to do. He singled you out, Fred. You should feel flattered."

Flattered? Hmph.

It seems quite certain that Clemens, who wrote with evident sincerity, "When—*if*—my sentence on earth comes to an end, I want to be able to say to myself, 'Well, at least I didn't kill anybody' " (Livy letter of 12 February 1986), departed this earth entirely unaware of Umlauf's death earlier that same day—a death for which Clemens, without equal in his ability to take personal responsibility for disasters, would have blamed himself. The fact that the two men's careers came to an end on the same day has of course spawned a good deal of public debate about their relationship. The principal theories are as follows:

1. The Clemens/Umlauf conspiracy went well beyond the fraudulent notebook, and each acted with full knowledge, approval, and encouragement of the other, up to the very end, which culminated in a suicide pact;

2. Umlauf was a magical reincarnation of some aspect of Clemens— his darkest side, perhaps, or his public personality—twinned in coexistence from 27 November 1985 to 11 April 1986 with his more contemplative, private alter ego, who restricted his self-revelations to the written word;

3. Umlauf was brother Orion, providentially granted a brief appearance in the glow of the spotlight;

4. Clemens was everything he appears to be in the manuscript of *I Been There Before*—Mark Twain, reborn of Halley's Comet—and Umlauf was a mortal impostor in unauthorized competition with him in his role as The Hannibal Claimant.

The evidence in support of (4) has emerged in successive waves. Beginning on 12 April, the eyewitness testimony of Clemens' flight out of the Elmira study (cited above), combined with public statements by Ricky Olivieri, Cocoa, and this editor, effectively neutralized the dramatic circumstances of Umlauf's death and raised our candidate to a place of equal consideration. Shortly thereafter, the publication in several periodicals of Part I and most of Part II of the Clemens manuscript (based on the copies distributed by Umlauf in New York City), the appearance of Olivieri's "Notes of a Madman: Three Days with Mark Twain" (*Harper's*, June 1986), and the disclosure of the results of the neutron-activation analysis of the hair samples marked the beginning of the end of Umlauf's career and considerably strengthened the case that the Mark Twain Papers was making for Clemens. This was followed by the preliminary report of our investigation, given at the December 1986 annual meeting of the Modern Language Association, and the publication of Bununu Ogbomosho's slim but compelling volume, *My Friend, Mark Twain* (New York: Roxana, 1986). Finally, the publication of the present edition is as close to "proof" of our central claim as is likely ever to be presented.

When I left the Elmira police station in the early morning of 12 April, I found Ricky Olivieri waiting for me. He was quite sane. He too had seen Clemens' miniature comet soar into the sky and had rushed to the study. He had seen me being whisked away in a police car and had followed on foot. His recollection of the past month was spotty. It leapfrogged past stretches of one day, two days, sometimes several days, touching down here and there for stretches of similarly varying lengths. He gave me glimpses of his activity in Berkeley, on the Mississippi River, and on the Ohio River, but he had no memory at all of ever being in New York City, or in Elmira, until the previous night. He did remember being thrown off Umlauf's boat in Cincinnati and, later the same day, discovering that his copy of Clemens' manuscript was missing from his briefcase. Umlauf had filched it, and no doubt it was this copy that he quoted from during his journey up the Ohio, and then duplicated for distribution in New York City.

We stayed in Elmira for two days. We bid goodbye to Cocoa and her children the next morning, pursued our investigation in Elmira all that day, and then drove up to the farm in the evening to get Olivieri's luggage. Olivieri went upstairs a sane man and came down a madman. He demanded to know where Clemens was. I tried to explain. He accused me of kidnapping Clemens and taking him to the Stockton Insane Asylum. Eventually, by showing him several newspaper reports of the events of the night before, I was able to convince him Clemens had gone. When he recovered from the shock of this news, he began to recall for me his activities of the past month. It was an entirely different summary from his earlier one, leapfrogging over the stretches of time previously recalled and covering the times formerly omitted. In a sense, his relapse was fortunate, in that it allowed him to jot down his memories of his three days with Clemens at Quarry Farm—the basis for his article cited above.

At that time, I had no idea what had caused his madness, or what had cured him of it the night before—and previously as well, several times, before a fresh onset. Halley's Comet was not then visible in the northern latitudes. We returned home, and Olivieri was out of his mind and under a doctor's care in Berkeley until 18 April, when he slipped out of his room and climbed Grizzly Peak in the Berkeley hills for a wistful look through his binoculars at the vehicle bearing his beloved Clemens away from him, visible once again. He experienced a spontaneous recovery. He called me right away and reported that his last recollection was of reaching into his suitcase at Quarry Farm, to fondle the hair-landscape he had been carrying with him since he had left Carson City. I confiscated the landscape, handling it gingerly, and locked it up in a desk drawer. Two days later, now back at work, Olivieri broke into the desk and fondled the hair again, successfully reawakening his memories of his precious time with Clemens, and he needed another trip up Grizzly Peak for a cure. With the only known antidote to delirium Clemens steadily receding into the unobservable remoteness of space, I had no choice but to destroy the hair-landscape. Olivieri's suffering was over.

And so is Clemens'. He now has the exquisite pleasures of the void to enjoy, whatever they may be, and I am happy for him. But if his intuition is correct, he will have A.D. 2061 to reckon with. I only hope that the rest of us, or our descendants, will be here to reckon with it as well. If not, then this chronicle can hardly be considered the last word on Clemens' 1985–86 sojourn. Indeed, it will instantly be rendered nonexistent if, true to his word, Clemens returns to November 1985, and a new history will unfold and have to be written. But if we *do* manage to make it that far, and if, upon his return, Clemens chooses to go public, this chronicle (which, it will be remembered, is printed on acid-free paper) should go far in dispelling skepticism about his identity.

In fact, if you are reading this, Sam, in 2061, and if you are wondering if you should go public or not, stop wondering! Come on out. There's a whole world pining to have more of you.

Appendixes

A. Mark Twain's First Life: A Chronology

1835 (30 November)	Born, Florida, Missouri
1839	Clemens family moves to Hannibal, Missouri
1847 (24 March)	Father, John Marshall Clemens, dies
1848–1853	Works as printer, Hannibal
1851 (16 January)	"A Gallant Fireman," Clemens' first published work, appears in brother Orion's Hannibal newspaper, *Western Union*
1853–1857	Works as printer, St. Louis, New York, Philadelphia, Keokuk (Iowa), and Cincinnati
1857–1861	Pilot on Mississippi River steamboats
1861 (summer)	Serves two weeks with Confederate irregulars, Missouri; travels by overland stage with Orion to Nevada Territory
1861–1862	Prospects for gold and silver, Nevada
1862–1864	Reporter for Virginia City, Nevada, *Territorial Enterprise*
1863 (3 February)	Uses pen name "Mark Twain" for first time
1864–1866	Writes for San Francisco newspapers and magazines
1865 (18 November)	"Jim Smiley and His Jumping Frog" published in New York *Saturday Press*
1866 (March–August)	Correspondent in Sandwich Islands for Sacramento *Union*
1866 (2 October)	Debut as public speaker, San Francisco
1867	*The Celebrated Jumping Frog of Calaveras County, and Other Sketches*
1867 (June–November)	As correspondent for San Francisco *Alta California*, sails on *Quaker City* tour of Europe and the Holy Land
1867 (27 December)	Meets Olivia (Livy) Langdon
1868–1869 (17 November–3 March)	Lecture tour in east and midwest: 42 engagements
1869	*The Innocents Abroad*
1869–1870 (1 November–21 January)	Lecture tour in east: 45 engagements
1870 (2 February)	Marries Livy, Elmira, New York

1870–1871	Editor of Buffalo *Express;* columnist for New York *Galaxy*
1870 (7 November)	Son, Langdon, born
1871 (October)	Clemenses move from Buffalo to Hartford, Connecticut
1871–1872 (16 October–6 February)	Lecture tour in east and midwest: 77 engagements
1872	*Roughing It*
1872 (19 March)	Daughter, Olivia Susan (Susy), born
1872 (2 June)	Langdon Clemens dies
1873	*The Gilded Age* (in collaboration with Charles Dudley Warner)
1873–1874 (13 October–10 January)	Lecture tour in England: about 35 engagements
1874 (8 June)	Daughter, Clara, born
1875 (January)	First of 7 installments of "Old Times on the Mississippi," the *Atlantic*
1876	*The Adventures of Tom Sawyer*
1878–1879	Clemenses tour Germany, Switzerland, Italy, France, and England
1880	*A Tramp Abroad*
1880 (26 July)	Daughter, Jane Lampton (Jean), born
1881	Begins investing in Paige typesetter; *The Prince and the Pauper*
1883	*Life on the Mississippi*
1884	Establishes publishing firm of Charles L. Webster & Co.
1884–1885 (28 November–28 February)	Reading tour with George Washington Cable in east, midwest, and eastern Canada: 103 engagements
1885	*Adventures of Huckleberry Finn;* Webster & Co. publishes Grant's *Memoirs*
1889	*A Connecticut Yankee in King Arthur's Court*
1890 (27 October)	Mother, Jane Lampton Clemens, dies
1891–1895	Clemenses reside in Germany, France, and Italy
1892	*The American Claimant*
1894	*Tom Sawyer Abroad; Pudd'nhead Wilson;* Webster & Co. declares bankruptcy; Paige typesetter declared a failure
1895–1896 (15 July–15 July)	Around-the-equator lecture tour: about 140 engagements
1896	*Personal Recollections of Joan of Arc*
1896 (18 August)	Susy Clemens dies
1896–1900	Clemenses reside in London and Vienna
1897	*Following the Equator*
1900	*The Man That Corrupted Hadleyburg and Other Stories and Essays;* Clemenses return to United States, reside in New York City

1903–1904	Clemenses reside in Italy
1904 (5 June)	Livy Clemens dies
1906 (7 September)	First of 25 installments of "Chapters from My Autobiography," *The North American Review*
1907	Receives honorary Litt.D. from Oxford University
1908 (June)	Moves to Stormfield, in Redding, Connecticut
1909	*Extract from Captain Stormfield's Visit to Heaven*
1909 (6 October)	Clara Clemens marries pianist Ossip Gabrilowitsch, Stormfield
1909 (24 December)	Jean Clemens dies
1910 (21 April)	Dies at Stormfield; buried in Elmira

B. Mark Twain's Second Life: A Chronology

Parentheses designate substantial erased loops.

1985

27 November	Arrives in or near Aurora, Nevada
30 November–20 January 1986	Ormsby House, Carson City, Nevada
4 December	Is shaved and shorn; meets Oscar Umlauf

1986

21–22 January	Pineview Motel, Angels Camp, California
23 January–7 February	Mark Twain Hotel, San Francisco
(10 February–27? March)	(Cruises South Pacific and Indian Ocean)
5 February	Visits Mark Twain Papers
7 February	Flies to New Orleans
(12–15 February)	(Cruises Lower Mississippi on *Delta Queen*)
13 February	Purchases boat in New Orleans; begins voyage upriver alone
25 February–12 March	Tom 'n Huck Motel, Hannibal, Missouri
12 March	Flies to San Francisco; hand-delivers Parts I and II of *I Been There Before* to Mark Twain Papers; flies to New York City
12–30 March	New York City
17 March	Meets Cocoa
18–25 March	Rooms with Cocoa
(18–19 March)	(Travels to Hartford, Connecticut)
(18–19 March)	(Travels to Elmira, New York)
(18–19 March)	(Travels to Redding, Connecticut)
30 March–11 April	Quarry Farm, Elmira
9 April	Hand-delivers Part III of *I Been There Before* to Sheraton Centre, New York City
(11 April)	(Almost departs, Elmira)
11 April	Departs, Elmira

C. Abbreviations of Published Works Cited

CofC   *Clemens of the "Call": Mark Twain in San Francisco*, ed. Edgar M. Branch (Berkeley and Los Angeles: University of California Press, 1969).

ET&S1   *Early Tales & Sketches, Volume I (1851–1864)*, ed. Edgar Marquess Branch and Robert H. Hirst (Berkeley, Los Angeles, and London: University of California Press, 1979).

HH&T   *Mark Twain's Hannibal, Huck & Tom*, ed. Walter Blair (Berkeley and Los Angeles: University of California Press, 1969).

IMT   *The Immortal Mark Twain*, ed. Peter Penrod and William C. Hotchkiss (Boston: Billfinger Press, 1986).

LLMT   *The Love Letters of Mark Twain*, ed. Dixon Wecter (New York: Harper and Brothers, 1949).

MDB   *My Dear Bro: A Letter from Samuel Clemens to His Brother Orion*, ed. Frederick Anderson (Berkeley: The Berkeley Albion, 1961).

MFMT   Clara Clemens, *My Father, Mark Twain* (New York: Harper and Brothers, 1931).

MMT   William Dean Howells, *My Mark Twain: Reminiscences and Criticisms* (1910; rpt. Baton Rouge: Louisiana State University Press, 1967).

MTA   *Mark Twain's Autobiography*, ed. Albert Bigelow Paine, 2 vols. (New York: Harper and Brothers, 1924).

MTB   Albert Bigelow Paine, *Mark Twain: A Biography* (New York: Harper and Brothers, 1912).

MTE   *Mark Twain in Eruption*, ed. Bernard DeVoto (New York: Harper and Brothers, 1940).

MTGF   Hamlin Hill, *Mark Twain: God's Fool* (New York: Harper & Row, 1973).

MTHHR   *Mark Twain's Correspondence with Henry Huttleston Rogers*, ed. Lewis Leary (Berkeley and Los Angeles: University of California Press, 1969).

MTHL   *Mark Twain–Howells Letters*, ed. Henry Nash Smith and William M. Gibson (Cambridge: Harvard University Press, Belknap Press, 1960).

MTL   *Mark Twain's Letters*, ed. Albert Bigelow Paine (New York: Harper and Brothers, 1917).

MTLR   Alan Gribben, *Mark Twain's Library: A Reconstruction* (Boston: G. K. Hall, 1980).

MTN   *Mark Twain's Notebook,* ed. Albert Bigelow Paine (New York: Harper and Brothers, 1935).

MTS   *Mark Twain Speaking,* ed. Paul Fatout (Iowa City: University of Iowa Press, 1976).

N&J1   *Mark Twain's Notebooks & Journals, Volume I (1855–1873),* ed. Frederick Anderson, Michael B. Frank, and Kenneth M. Sanderson (Berkeley, Los Angeles, and London: University of California Press, 1975).

N&J2   *Mark Twain's Notebooks & Journals, Volume II (1877–1883),* ed. Frederick Anderson, Lin Salamo, and Bernard L. Stein (Berkeley, Los Angeles, and London: University of California Press, 1975).

N&J3   *Mark Twain's Notebooks & Journals, Volume III (1883–1891),* ed. Robert Pack Browning, Michael B. Frank, and Lin Salamo (Berkeley, Los Angeles, and London: University of California Press, 1979).

S&MT   Edith Colgate Salsbury, *Susy and Mark Twain* (New York: Harper & Row, 1965).